JENNIFER LAMONT LEO
NAOMI MUSCH
CANDICE SUE PATTERSON
PEGG THOMAS

LUMBERJACKS & Ladies

FOUR STORIES OF ROMANCE AMONG THE PINES

All That Glitters ©2022 by Candice Sue Patterson
Winter Roses ©2022 by Pegg Thomas
Not for Love ©2022 by Naomi Musch
Undercover Logger ©2022 by Jennifer Lamont Leo

Print ISBN 978-1-63609-140-2

eBook Editions:
Adobe Digital Edition (.epub) 978-1-64352-142-6

All scripture quotations, unless otherwise noted, are taken from the King James Version of the Bible.

Cover Photo: Magdalena Russocka/Trevillion Images

Published by Barbour Publishing, Inc., 1810 Barbour Drive, Uhrichsville, Ohio 44683, www.barbourbooks.com

Our mission is to inspire the world with the life-changing message of the Bible.

Printed in Canada.

BY CANDICE SUE PATTERSON

Dedication

To my elementary librarian, Mrs. Fox. Your enthusiasm for the written word reached inside of me and took root. Thank you for your dedication to books and spreading the joy of reading to children. I endeavor to inspire half the minds you did as I follow in your footsteps.

Silver and gold have I none;
but such as I have give I thee...
Acts 3:6

Chapter One

North Lubec, Maine
June 25, 1851

If her father ever returned from California, she'd kill him.

Wini Hayes tucked in her shirtwaist while her eight-month-old nephew screamed on her bedroom rug, fingers shoved in his mouth, drool dripping onto his chubby bare chest.

"Patience, little one. The sooner you learn that virtue, the further in life you'll go." And it was a hard virtue to learn.

She made quick work of braiding her hair and securing the ends with a leather tie, then bent and picked up the damp baby, wincing at the drool that now coated her fingers. The aroma of pancakes and sausage seeped through the space at the bottom of her closed door, making her stomach growl. She adjusted Milton on her hip, and the next smell she got ahold of spoiled her fervor for the previous one.

"Time for you to see your momma."

The narrow hallway led to the kitchen where Wini's mother stood at the stove, cast-iron pans sizzling with food. Sweat beaded her mother's graying hairline as she stirred gravy in one pan and eggs in the other. Carrie must still be abed.

Wini swallowed her frustration. "Where's Carrie? Milton is soiled, and I have a trap to repair before setting out today."

Her mother pointed to the sitting room with a wooden spoon then went back to stirring. Wini strode that direction.

Her sister-in-law Carrie sat in a rocking chair facing the window that looked out to sea. No one spoke of the woman's melancholy, though Wini didn't understand why. It had gone on so long the weight of it burdened the entire household, and Wini tired of carrying the extra weight.

It began shortly after the birth of Carrie's daughter, Isabelle, nearly three years ago, and had progressed since delivering Milton. Then when Wini's father and brothers, Jethro and Crosley, had announced they were leaving to seek riches in California, Carrie had curled in on herself and taken up post by the window. Now all she could do every day was stare out to sea, cry, and await her husband's return.

When Jethro and Crosley returned with their father, they'd better be hauling a wagon full of gold, or Wini might kill them too.

If they returned.

While the Hayes family had never been wealthy, they'd lived comfortably and happily—until newspapers carried articles on Sutter's Mill and all the riches gained in the state formerly known as Mexico. Men across the country had drained their savings for passage and supplies, leaving their women behind to survive on their own. Tomorrow would mark a year since the Hayes men had left, with nary a word from them the entire time.

Okay, maybe she wouldn't kill them when they returned. A strong, swift beating might do.

Wini padded across the cold floor toward the rocking chair.

Tears ran down Milton's cheeks, but his sobbing had lessened to quick intakes of breath now and again. "You have a hungry, soiled son."

She lowered the baby onto Carrie's lap and smiled to soften her words. "He wants his mother."

Carrie looked at Wini from beneath heavy eyelids and put her arms around her son, as if the action took every ounce of energy she possessed. Wini hated being unsympathetic, but they'd realized that forcing Carrie to do minor tasks kept her from escaping to a dark place they couldn't follow.

Before Carrie, Wini had seen nothing like it, but she'd heard stories of women falling into melancholy after childbirth. Most were never the same again. As if the Hayes women didn't have enough responsibility taking over the men's jobs, they also had to keep constant vigilance over Carrie and encourage a will to survive.

Milton gripped his mother's nightdress in his chubby fists, pressed his nose to the fabric, and shook his head. Oblivious to her son, Carrie had already turned back toward the window. Wini guided her sister-in-law by the chin, forcing Carrie to look into her eyes. "You have a beautiful daughter and a sturdy son. They both need you. Jethro needs you. The men will be back any day now. And when they return, Jethro will be proud of how you've carried on without him."

Wini didn't believe a word she said, but if it gave Carrie enough hope to make it through one more day, the lies served a purpose.

Carrie's arms tightened around her whimpering son. With a sigh, she stood, gazed at Milton's face, swallowed, and then shuffled to the nursery.

Wiping her hands on her hips, Wini gazed out the window to the water glimmering with the rising sun. She could do this. Just as she'd done for the past three hundred and sixty-four days. All she had to do was conquer her fear.

She went back to the kitchen and enjoyed the large spread of pancakes, sausage, and biscuits and gravy. It had been so long since they'd been able to afford sausage. She savored it, unsure when they'd have the privilege of meat again.

After thanking her mother, Wini went to the barn to repair the broken lobster trap while Eden, her other sister-in-law, swollen with child, helped her mother clean the kitchen. Crosley had been late in joining the other Hayes men in Philadelphia to buy supplies until he'd shown Wini how to pilot the boat, set the traps, and haul them in. His anticipated parting had led to another mouth to feed. Wini hated to view the baby that way, but since the bulk of the burden to keep them all from starvation had fallen on her, it was hard to be excited.

Her mind wandered to Jeremiah, the way it tended to when insecurity crept into her bones. No doubt he was eating sausage and beef for every meal at his gilded table in his large house on the hill. He'd never have to worry about his Connecticut bride returning home from a day of work reeking of fish. How different Wini's life would be right now if Jeremiah had kept his promise.

Shaking off what could never be, she loaded seven traps into the skiff and gripped the edge of the stern. A wave of dizziness crashed over her. Her limbs quaked. The breakfast she'd just eaten threatened to make its way back up her throat. She could do this. She *had* to do this.

"Lord, give me strength. Bring me home again." She breathed deeply. "Alive."

Hand pressed to her stomach, she did what she'd done every day for the past year and thought of all that would happen if she didn't uphold the contract her father had signed to provide lobster for the prisoners. She lifted her skirt, climbed into the skiff, and reached for the oars with shaky hands.

If only Jeremiah had kept his word.

If only she wasn't terrified of the water.

If only she knew how to swim.

Jess Lee settled onto a boulder with a steaming mug of coffee and watched the sunrise push its way through the blanket of sea fog. Though he'd never traveled out of state, he'd bet his entire savings this was the best place to see a sunrise in all its glory, the way the Creator intended. Popes Folly might not be the Garden of Eden, but Jess guessed it was pretty darn close.

He breathed in damp, pine-scented air and thought of his father. Grief had lessened to a dull ache now but remained constant. Quiet moments like these brought his hero to memory, and the deep-throated laugh of his father nearly echoed through the surrounding trees. Jess removed the pocket watch he'd inherited and stroked his thumb along his father's engraved initials on the back. The action brought him comfort, but he needed to break the habit before he rubbed the initials away.

Turning the watch over in his palm, he flipped it open and checked the time. Any moment now, the little fisherman would row past the island, the boat and pilot a shadow in the veil of sunlight and fog. The trawler was punctual, if nothing else. As were the threats from New Brunswick over logging what they considered their territory.

Though the Treaty of Washington in 1842 declared the island owned by the States, the profit in lumber and potash had New Brunswick battling for the territory. In his six months on the island, Jess had seen fishermen cut each other's ropes, threaten a passing boat, and even come ashore looking for trouble.

For the moment, all was peaceful. Soon, the sounds of his crew rousing within the camp would carry to the shoreline and signal Jess to his duties. Halfway into his bitter coffee, the dip and splash of oars slicing through water caught his attention.

Though Jess had never seen the man up close, he guessed him to be elderly, with his slight frame and the way he sometimes struggled to lift equipment. Something about the scene struck him hard every morning, but Jess couldn't decide why.

Perhaps it was the dedication the man had to his occupation. The same dedication that had driven Jess's father. That drove Jess. Logging was shifting west to places like Indiana and Michigan, which were mostly forest, but he had no desire to move west. He was just as dedicated to the rocky coastline of his ancestors. Even if that kept him clearing small patches of land and selling logs to local folks like Reverend Jernegan for his mining company that extracted gold from seawater.

Jess raised the mug to his lips, trying to understand how a Baptist minister discovered the secret to mining gold. The fisherman's skiff paused through a break in the fog. It was hard to see at this distance, but the fisherman appeared to reach for a buoy and tug at the rope. Jess squinted. The man's motions were stiff and strained, as if the water resisted him. Jess would offer assistance, but he had no way to reach the fisherman other than swimming. A dip in the cool Atlantic was not how Jess preferred to start this day.

The fisherman yanked on the rope several times, rocking the boat. Stuck. The skiff swayed and dipped with the force. The little man stood and jerked the rope so hard the momentum of the action yanked him overboard. A yelp rent the air before splashing water silenced it.

Jess stood. Arms flailing, the fisherman's head bobbed above water as he attempted to grip the side of the boat. Did the man not know how to swim? Surely, he did.

Seconds passed, and the fisherman's movements grew weaker. Like it or not, Jess was getting wet. He threw down his mug, tore off his jacket and boots, and waded into the frigid water. He bit back a yelp of his own as cold water doused his torso.

"Hang on!" he yelled, hoping the man could hear him. Jess pumped his arms and legs as fast as he could, hoping to reach the fisherman in time.

Six feet away, the fisherman's head went under and didn't come back up. Jess dove beneath the surface and groped for something to grab onto. Something grazed his fingers, and he closed his fist around it, yanking it and himself to the surface. He prayed it was the fisherman and not a piece of equipment.

His head broke the surface, and he gulped air, teeth chattering. Arms burning and breath clouding, he continued hauling up his find. Fistfuls of brown and white fabric pooled atop the water. A skirt? He finally caught sight of a body emerging. Long, wet hair floated like tentacles around a pale, feminine face.

Shock nearly had him losing hold of the woman. Was she the fisherman or had he gotten hold of a dead body in his quest?

Before Jess could decide what to do, her eyelids fluttered. Thank God she wasn't dead.

He pressed her against him and felt for a pulse, kicking his legs to stay afloat. Her eyes opened in terror and water spewed from her mouth and nose. She turned her head to the side and coughed. Jess held her tight against him with one arm while he gripped the side of the skiff with the other. My lands, wet skirts were heavy. His energy was almost spent just holding her. How would he ever swim her back to shore?

A blast of water escaped her mouth before her arms and legs

thrashed in a panic. If she didn't calm down, she'd drown them both.

She shoved at his shoulders, dunking him beneath the water and breaking his hold on the boat as she attempted to climb up him to escape the water. Crazy woman, didn't she realize he was trying to save her? He broke the surface. "Stop it before you drown us both!"

Fear had taken her too far to listen. He couldn't even lift her into the boat, she was so hysterical. Doing the only thing he could think of to shock her into submission, he clasped the back of her neck and angled his lips on hers. It wasn't his preferred method to woo a woman, but at least their heads were above water.

She squirmed for only a moment, and then her stiff muscles relaxed against him. He continued kissing her, partly because he enjoyed the feel of her soft lips on his and partly because he was afraid if he stopped, she'd lose control of her faculties again.

Once he was sure she'd had enough time to gather her wits, he pulled away, secured his hold on the skiff again, and braced for the repercussions.

She blinked.

"You're safe," he said in the same low tone he'd use to speak to a wounded animal. "I'm going to lift you into the boat and then get in myself. All right?"

She looked around, assessing her predicament, and then nodded, chin quivering. He dropped his hold from her waist to her legs and grunted as he hoisted her into the skiff. She fell in with a *thunk*. Breathing heavily, he gripped the boat and pushed upward, swinging a leg over the side. He rolled to avoid landing directly on top of her.

Exhausted, they both sat and stared at each other. When she began shaking, he knew he had to get her warm and fast before she went into shock. He picked up the only oar he could find—the other must've gone overboard—and with all the effort he could muster, rowed them to shore.

The boat scraped against rocks and held them steady. He lowered the little sail and searched for the rope to moor to a nearby tree. Rope in hand, he started to jump out when the woman whimpered. Poor thing. He knelt in front of her, and for the first time noticed the vivid hue of her green eyes, the soft, young skin plastered with wet hair that had escaped its pins and stuck to her wet blouse.

His chest burned. She was a beautiful woman, even if her appearance resembled that of a baptized cat. "Are you all right, miss?"

Her lips trembled. She looked down at herself, assessing her condition. "Y–y–yes." Black, spiky lashes lifted, and her gaze latched onto his. He blew out a slow breath to steady his racing heart. "You gave me quite a scare."

Her mouth opened, but instead of speaking, her face crumpled, and an agonizing sob escaped. She buried her face in her hands, and her crying escalated to the point he was afraid she'd faint. At least they were out of the water. Legs weak, he sat again on the boat's bottom. "Hey, everything's all right. You're alive, I'm alive. It's—"

She flew at him, arms locking around his neck. Her wails deafened his left ear, but the rest of her felt pleasant. She was practically on his lap, which in any other scenario would be entirely inappropriate, but he knew her action was born from fear and a thankfulness to be alive. The mind caused a body to do things it might not do otherwise when it came that close to death. He reciprocated the embrace and pretended she was his sister, but since he didn't have any sisters and the woman on his lap was attractive in ten different ways, it didn't work.

Jess patted her back and spoke soft words of encouragement until her sobs turned to sniffles. His right leg was going numb, but he didn't dare complain. "Are you the little fisherman I see come through here every morning?"

She pulled back, but kept her arms hooked around his neck. The whites of her eyes were red, the skin beneath swollen, the tip of her nose pink. Fresh tears spilled down her cheeks. "I'm not a fisherman. My father is, but he's gone, and they all need to eat and..."

Another round of wailing began. He should've waited to ask. Releasing her with one hand, he shifted to the side and reached into his pocket. "Here."

He pulled out a handkerchief, only to realize it was a foolish gesture. The soaked fabric hung from his fingertips. He balled it in his palm and wrung out the water. "Never mind."

She laughed. And laughed. At first, he did too, but then he realized she wasn't going to stop. He wasn't familiar with or trained in women's emotions. As much as he hated—and didn't hate—to do what he was about to do, he needed to get her under control before she completely cracked.

With a prayer of forgiveness in his heart, he kissed her again.

Chapter Two

Wini was kissing a man. And it was glorious.

Euphoria floated above her like the fog then descended around her in the lightest of touches. He smelled like seaweed and pine. His warm salty lips tasted like life and youth and…coffee. Then reality trampled her like a runaway horse.

She was kissing a man.

A stranger.

On his lap.

Her eyes flew open, and she pushed away from him, the side of the boat jabbing into her back. "I—I…"

She didn't know what to say. One minute she was drowning and the next she was kissing a stranger. How had that happened?

Where was she?

Warm brown eyes studied her beneath knotted brows. He held up big hands. "Your virtue is safe with me. I promise. I had to end your hysterics somehow."

She shivered, noting the sopping state of her hair and clothing. "So you kissed me?"

Rivulets of water dripped from his hair and down his face. He brushed them away, sending little drops into the scratchy hair on his cheeks. "To be fair, you kissed me back."

Embarrassment heated her body. No argument there. She wanted to lash at him for taking such liberties with her, but he had saved her life. And she *had* been acting hysterical, now that she thought about it. She was torn between screaming for help and hoping he'd kiss her again.

He placed a hand on his knee and pushed to standing. "You're welcome." What an arrogant buffoon.

"I saved you and your boat, but whatever equipment you had inside is now at the bottom of the ocean."

He hopped out and tied the mooring rope to a nearby tree.

Oh. He hadn't meant she was welcome for the kiss, but for rescuing her. She pressed her fingertips to her throbbing temple. What was wrong with her? She'd never had trouble keeping her wits about her in the presence of a handsome man. Of course, she'd never come close to dying either.

Bracing herself on the side of the boat, she stood. He offered his hand, and she accepted it before jumping onto the rocks. Good thing she'd already set her other traps. She swiped wet hair away from her cheek and stumbled forward. Who was this man that appeared out of this patch of island woods?

"Thank you for saving me, Mister. . ."

"Lee. Jess Lee."

"Thank you, Mr. Lee."

"My pleasure. Since we've shared our lips, how 'bout you just call me Jess."

She cleared her throat. "Uh. . .very well. Winifred Hayes. Everyone calls me Wini."

A passing blanket of fog lifted, and sunlight poured onto her face, causing her to squint. Rays bounced off his hair and broad shoulders, making her heart do a funny leap.

"Nice to meet you, Wini." He tugged on his boots. "I will

admit, I wish the circumstances had been different though."

She echoed his wish.

"Where're you from?"

"North Lubec."

He tucked in the tail of his shirt and adjusted his suspenders. "May I ask why you were fishing way out here by yourself?"

Something in his tone made her bristle. As if she weren't embarrassed enough, she didn't want to explain her family's circumstances. "May I ask why it matters?"

He pointed at himself and ran a finger up and down his soaked form.

Fair enough.

"My father isn't able to fulfill his contractual obligations at the moment, so I've taken it upon myself."

He perched on the edge of a boulder. "Contractual obligations for what?"

She crossed her arms. "Lobster. It feeds the prisoners."

"Do you not have brothers?"

"I do."

"Then why aren't they taking over your father's duties?"

"They aren't able to do so."

He rubbed his jaw. "So multiple men in your family are fine with sending a woman who doesn't know how to swim out into the ocean to fulfill contractual obligations?"

It wasn't the first time since the Hayes men had left for California she'd received ridicule, but coming from this man, it hurt. She lifted her chin. "I'm certain they would not approve, if they knew I don't know how to swim."

"They don't know?" He blew out a frustrated breath. "You're wearing me out." He bent and picked up a tin cup lying in the moss. "I run Lee's Logging and Mill. Camp isn't too far north.

Mrs. Jennings is our cook. She can provide you with a hot meal, dry clothes, and act as chaperone on an island full of men. Once you're set to rights, we'll see you home."

He walked into the forest without a backwards glance. One soggy step at a time, Wini followed, peeved that he was irritated with her. Why should she care what this man thought of her?

Wet skirt gripped in her fists, she caught up to him and tugged him to a stop. "I have five people at home counting on me to keep them fed and another one to arrive by summer's end. I'm terrified of the water, and I don't know how to swim, but my mother is in no condition to take over the business, one sister-in-law is in her last days of confinement, and the other carries a sadness so heavy she can hardly get out of bed. It has to be me."

Why exactly had she revealed all that? Why did she crave his approval so badly? And why had she stomped her foot like a petulant child? Good thing her skirt covered her feet.

His features softened, giving her a glimpse of the boy who'd once existed beneath the layers of wet flannel and mounds of sinew. "Where are your father and brothers?"

She realized she still had a hold of his sleeve and let go. "They believed the lies in the newspaper about riches in California waiting for men to come along and snatch like daisies. They left a year ago. Haven't heard a word. We don't even know if they made it."

He looked at the ground. "That's a heavy cross to bear."

His statement hit the bulls-eye of her heart. Tears stung her eyes. "If I haven't properly shown my appreciation for your help, I apologize. The entire situation has me out of sorts."

Jess swiped her tear with his thumb. "You did a fine job showing your appreciation."

Her mouth fell open.

He gave her an impish grin and chuckled. "I'm teasing. Come on."

He held out his hand.

To her surprise, she took it.

Her soft skin against his rough palm nearly did him in. "We're almost to camp. I have a crew of good men, but they're probably rougher around the edges than you're used to."

"I'll be fine."

Her voice was husky for a woman's, but Jess found it appealing. Whether it stemmed from the near drowning or was natural, he wasn't sure, but he'd love to find out. "I'm going to let go of your hand now, but stick close until I pass you off to Mrs. Jennings."

She nodded, and he released her, leading her the rest of the way into camp. Raucous laughter, the jingle of harnesses being strapped to horses, and the bang of pots and pans echoed through the trees.

"Where you been, Jess?" Kent called from the stump he occupied by the fire.

Wini emerged from behind him, and the entire camp went silent, save for the birds. She stepped close to his side. He looked at the burly group through her eyes and understood her worry. Jess placed his palm on her back to let her know she had nothing to fear. "I thought it was a perfect morning to go fishing. Look what I caught."

Someone whistled low.

Kent scratched his beard. "A woman way out here is a mighty strange thing to catch. Being wet and all, I'd say she was one of those mermaid sirens I've heard tell about. Seeing as she's walking on land though, I'm doubtful."

A siren might not be too far from the truth. Wini Hayes already had a strange hold on him. "She fell overboard. I was in the right place at the right time."

"You poor dear." Mrs. Jennings broke through the crowd of men with her arms held out.

Jess let his hand fall from her back and reluctantly let the cook take over Wini's care. The older woman soothed and fussed and, within moments, Wini had disappeared into the cook's tent. Jess stood, dumbfounded by the events of the morning and by the bewitching, soaking wet woman herself.

McGrady slapped him on the back, jarring him. "Congratulations, boss. I do believe you're in love."

Jess shook off her spell. "Ridiculous. I just met her."

He stepped toward his tent.

"And what of it?" McGrady's Irish brogue rumbled behind Jess. "The good Lord doesn't drop a woman in the water next to a logging camp every day, ya know. And you, the best swimmer of us all, bein' the one there to rescue her. That's what I'd call a divine appointment."

Jess stepped over a bucket someone had left in his path. McGrady had a point. Jess's mother had always told him to be patient in finding a wife, that the right woman would come along in God's time.

McGrady blocked the flap of Jess's tent. "You've been restless for a while now, boss. Some might even say unhappy. We've all noticed. Maybe it's time to marry and make yourself some wee bairns, is all I'm sayin'."

Wini's passionate kisses played in Jess's mind, causing heat to flame up his neck. He poked a finger at McGrady. "Don't talk about her like that."

McGrady lowered Jess's hand and softened his tone. "I mean no disrespect to the lass. I'm simply relaying some possibilities here. Jobs are movin' west, boss. I want to see you enjoy other things in life besides cuttin' down trees."

With a pat on Jess's shoulder, McGrady stepped away. Jess turned. "If I didn't respect you so much, I'd wallop you good."

"It never stopped you when we were kids." McGrady laughed. "Why should it now?"

Jess entered his tent and looked around. A trunk of clothes, a bed, a Bible, a worn copy of *David Copperfield*, a lamp, and an old pair of boots. All of his worldly possessions. He could admit to himself that moving from camp to camp got tiresome. That sometimes the nights got long and lonely. For a moment he allowed his mind to wander to a life with Wini at his side. But logging was all Jess knew, and women didn't fancy sharing their husbands with the forest. Mrs. Jennings was the exception.

There was no use giving it any more thought.

Jess peeled off his wet clothes, grabbed a towel, and sat on the edge of his bed. He was chilled and exhausted and still needed to put in a full day's work while figuring out how to get Wini and her skiff home. Shivering, he ran the towel over his hair and then the rest of his body. After donning a fresh pair of clothes, he looked down at his boots.

Nothing was more miserable than working in wet boots.

Though the soles were worn to pancakes and they pinched his toes, he put on the old pair he kept around in case of emergencies and made his way to the fire for a quick rest and another cup of coffee to warm his insides.

Clark Jennings, their blacksmith, had a steaming mug waiting on him when he arrived. "The missus said it'll be a while before Miss Hayes is ready to return home. She's working on warming her up and has convinced her to rest a spell."

"Thanks. I appreciate her help."

"She's from North Lubec. Kent's rafting some lumber ashore tomorrow, but he could go a day early. I suppose that's the best way to get her back home."

Jess thought for a minute and agreed. "She has a small skiff we'll need to take back as well."

Jennings nodded.

The crew was loading tools onto the wagons and leading horses to the work site. A late start to the day since they'd waited for him. Jess stretched the knots from his neck. "Tell McGrady to lead the crew today and leave the potash until tomorrow. I'll go with Kent and Mrs. Jennings to see Wini—uh, Miss Hayes home."

Jennings smirked. "I'll tell 'em."

A few hours later, with a stack of lumber loaded onto the giant raft made of chinked logs, the passengers were seated. Jess steered the raft toward Lubec while Kent manned the sails. Wini's boat traveled behind them, tethered by a rope.

Now that her hair was dry, Jess noted the blond hue, rich and golden like honey. Her braid snaked down her back but the strands closest to her face blew wildly in the salty breeze. Light purple marred the skin beneath her mossy green eyes. Eyebrows thicker and much darker than her hair gave her a serious countenance, while high cheekbones and a jawline tapering to a pointed little chin balanced it all out.

She was beautiful and strong. And, if he guessed correctly, had a bit of Passamaquoddy Indian in her bloodline. He wanted to ask if he could see her again but rafting all the way to Lubec took time he didn't have to spare. Since she didn't know how to swim, he wouldn't dare ask her to come to the island. In fact, when he dropped her off at home, he intended to beg her to never leave her house again.

After docking at the mouth of Johnson Bay, Jess helped the women disembark while Kent took care of the lumber and moored Wini's skiff. Mrs. Jennings walked silently behind Jess and Wini, close enough to chaperone yet far enough away to give them privacy.

"Where to?" Jess asked.

"I'm a few streets up that hill." She pointed to a knoll dotted with houses. "Thank you again, for everything you did today."

"I'm glad I was there. And glad I got to meet you."

She looked away.

"What is it?"

"I can't go back out there." Her husky voice filled with defeat. "Every day for the past year, I've nearly swooned forcing myself into that boat. Now that I've glimpsed what it's like to drown, I'll never be able to get back in it." She kept her eyes focused on the hill. "How are we to survive?"

"I'll teach you how to swim."

She swiveled toward him but remained walking. "That's. . . How? When? It's scandalous."

"And genius." He leaned close to her ear and whispered. "Besides, I think we've already crossed over into scandalous territory."

Her mouth opened, but her lips curled into a smile.

They remained silent all the way to her door. Mrs. Jennings pretended fascination with the neighbor's flowers. Jess took Wini's hand and kissed it. "Until tomorrow then."

How he'd find the time, he didn't know, but it was too late now.

Her cheeks turned rosy. "What's tomorrow?"

"Your swimming instruction."

"You're not serious. We can't!"

"Then let me teach your dog to swim. Please, Wini. Any excuse to come and see you."

She shook her head, smiling. "I don't have a dog."

"Your cat then."

"No cat. I have hens in the backyard though."

"Nope. I don't like you that much."

She laughed, low and rumbly. She studied him for a moment, and her mirth fled. "What?"

"Your voice."

"It's awful, I know. It's kept many suitors away."

"I like it. So much so, I want to hear it more often."

Wini chewed her bottom lip, but the sparkle in her eyes told him he'd hit gold. "I'd like that."

His chest swelled.

Hands behind her back, she turned the knob, opened the door, and stepped inside. "Thank you again, Jess."

McGrady was right. Jess was in love.

Chapter Three

Wini was minus seven traps, a net, and fifty lobsters. How was she supposed to fulfill her quota to the jail by the end of the week?

She rubbed her tired eyes and stepped onto the front stoop. The air was fresher. The smells stronger. Life—fragile. She didn't know how she was going to fulfill their contract, or what she would do in place of hauling lobster and herring, but one thing was certain. She was alive, and she would never endanger herself like that again.

"Winifred Rose, you are not going into that boat again."

Her mother's cheeks turned a mottled purple, and her hands fastened to her hips. A figure once plump that was shrinking beneath the folds of her dress.

"You have my word I'll do nothing like that again."

"Where're you heading off to then?"

"To find Mr. Kirkus and speak to him about our contract."

"You know very well that a man will not discuss business with a woman." Mother's hands slipped off her hips and into her apron pockets.

"Mr. Kirkus is a kind man. He hasn't objected to me hauling in lobster thus far. I don't see why he wouldn't speak to me about the contract."

"Because you're a woman." Mother's soft voice held a world of truth.

"Then why did Father leave us to fend for ourselves in a world we can't navigate without men?"

Mother bowed her head. "Your father did what he thought was best. He didn't know after he left that the new cannery would steal our business."

Life had stolen much from Wini over the past few years. The Lubec Packing Company had stolen part of her livelihood, while the owner had stolen part of her heart. At least Wini, her mother, and her sisters by marriage weren't standing over bubbling cauldrons behind the house all day anymore, canning sardines and lobster meat at four cents a can. She wondered now if Jeremiah's feelings had ever been real or if he'd just been interested in how the local industry worked so he could bring his Southern money in and improve upon the conditions.

Wini kissed her mother's cheek. "I promise to stick to land. I'll be home to help with the washing."

She lifted a basket of clean laundry that her mother and Eden had washed for the guests of the boardinghouses down the road. Wini always carried it home and returned it, as the washing alone took a toll on the other women's backs.

Basket balanced on her hip, she lifted her skirt and descended the stone steps that led to the road. The briny scent of saltwater wafted on the breeze. Wini breathed it in. She loved the smell of the water, just not the water itself. Jess and his offer to teach her to swim made her smile. How she wished she had the liberty to do so. He ran a logging business and didn't have time for such things. She'd likely never see him again, despite his eagerness to continue their friendship yesterday, but the memory of him would be one she'd always keep close.

She dropped off the laundry with Ruby at the boardinghouse, then walked the two miles to the edge of the peninsula to the jail. If a prisoner wanted to escape, the only option besides walking out the front door would be to jump into the water. With jagged boulders jutting skyward and the tide whirlpooling around them, they'd only jump to their deaths. Few in her lifetime had attempted it, and none had survived. That knowledge made her unafraid to approach the facility unaccompanied, though her visit was sure to incite gossip.

Guy Rollings stood—or rather, sat—sentinel by the entrance, his head tipped back in sleep against the brick building. A fly circled his head twice before landing on his nose. Without waking, Guy thrust his head to the side and scrunched his nose, sending the fly away with a snort. Soft snores ensued. When the fly came back for revenge, Wini stole the opportunity to rouse the guard.

"Fine morning, isn't it, Mr. Rollings?"

The man's eyes blinked open, and he sat at attention. "Yes, ma'am, it is."

Wini almost laughed at the way he tried to act as if he hadn't been napping. "I'm here to see Mr. Kirkus, if he's free."

"May I tell him what you's needin' to see him about?" Mr. Rollings braced his hands on his knees and stood, joints popping the entire way.

Wini clasped her hands in front of her. "The contract he has with my father."

Pity radiated from the man's dark eyes before he turned to go inside the jail. "Stay put, miss."

Her stomach knotted with each minute that passed. When she'd stood long enough for the sun to gain strength and make sweat roll down her back, Mr. Kirkus finally emerged. "Miss Hayes. How may I help you regarding your father's contract?"

Wini took a fortifying breath. "As you know, I've been fulfilling our obligation since my father left. However, circumstances out of my control are threatening my abilities to hold to the bargain. If you'll simply allow me more time, I'm sure I can—"

"Miss Hayes." He jerked his head to signal her to walk with him. He shoved his hands in his pockets, and his shoes crunched against the little pebbles sprinkled on the dirt path. "Let me set your mind at ease. My contract with your father expired last week."

All the nervous energy she'd been holding released in one long breath.

"Well," she stumbled, "then now is the perfect time to discuss a renewal of the contract. I—"

"Unfortunately, I will not be renewing a contract with the Hayes family."

"But—"

"I'm sorry, Miss Hayes. There are two reasons behind my decision. One, the governor has issued a law that prisoners are only to be fed lobster three times a week. Apparently, shellfish served for every meal is cruel, and local physicians feel it will help curb some of the sickness that sweeps through from time to time."

"Oh."

"My apologies, miss. I shouldn't have spoken about delicate things in front of you."

Her reaction had nothing to do with the subject and everything to do with how she was going to feed her family. "What's the second reason?"

"It isn't fitting for a woman to be on the water doing man's work. You did a fine job in place of your father. But now that the contract has expired, I won't be party to endangering you any longer."

Wini looked out to sea. "What will I do now?"

Everyone in town knew of their circumstances, so it did no

good to pretend this wouldn't cripple them.

Mr. Kirkus stopped and rocked back and forth on his heels. "My suggestion, if you're determined to continue lobstering, would be to sell to the cannery."

"They won't buy from a fisherwoman." She'd already inquired with the work supervisor months ago.

"Well then, I hear the cannery is hiring. Maybe you could get a job working the assembly line."

She wouldn't work beneath Jeremiah Farthington if it was the last job on earth.

"I hear he's open to hiring family women and children now." Mr. Kirkus spoke as though attempting to tread lightly on her feelings.

Until now, Jeremiah had only been willing to hire men and women who desired to escape occupations of a less modest nature. He didn't hire what he called "respectable women," because a respectable woman should be capable of finding a husband to provide for her and, therefore, have no need of employment. Or so the newspaper article had quoted.

When Wini didn't respond, Mr. Kirkus tried again. "The new sea mining facility is looking to hire a few secretaries. You could check there."

That suggestion tasted as bad as the first. How could she work for a company centered on gold and greed when she despised her father and brothers for doing the same?

Mr. Kirkus patted her shoulder and walked back toward the jail. Evidently, he'd placated her long enough. This was her family's problem.

"Thank you, Mr. Kirkus," she mumbled.

He glanced back and waved. "Best of luck to you, Miss Hayes."

She was sure going to need it.

Uncertain what to do next, she moseyed down the road that weaved along the shore, her anger building with each step. Gold on the ocean floor. Who ever heard of such nonsense? But men for miles around were flocking to the sea mining company in search of work. At the newspaper's last count, the Reverend Prescott Jernegan had a payroll of over one hundred men. And yet women could scarcely find a job anywhere.

She walked until the sun hit its peak and the air had warmed enough to inspire her to roll up her sleeves. Scandalous, perhaps, but she was the only one on the road at present and, at the moment, she didn't care about propriety. She was angry, restless, and as much as she didn't want to apply at the mining company, it appeared to be her only option.

When she reached the marine salts company she stopped beneath a shade tree, leaned against the trunk, closed her eyes, and released a yawn. Why couldn't the men in her family have stayed and kept their comfortable life? She blew out an exasperated breath. She couldn't allow herself to wallow in the what ifs. If she did, she might end up like Carrie.

Wini opened her eyes to the most glorious sight.

Jess Lee.

She thought to never see him again, but here he was, ambling toward her, wearing a handsome and devilish smile.

Her pulse raced. She pushed away from the tree and started toward him when her brain registered that he'd just emerged from the Electrolytic Marine Salts Company office. Halting, she stiffened and turned her back to him. She marched as fast as she could in the opposite direction. It didn't matter how wonderful or heroic the man was. If Jess Lee supported in any way this sea mining nonsense or Reverend Jernegan, she wanted nothing more to do with him.

If he didn't know better, he'd believe his mind had conjured the lovely Wini Hayes and planted her in front of him.

Nope.

If he'd possessed the power to make her materialize, she would be running toward him, not walking away as fast as she could.

Lucky for her, he wouldn't let her get away so easily.

His long legs ate the distance between them in a matter of seconds. Jess nodded to the approaching man passing on the other side of the road and then said, "Miss Hayes. I'd like to discuss in more detail our discovery yesterday."

She scowled at him. "And what discovery is that?"

He made sure the man wouldn't hear him and said, "The one that proved how attracted you are to me."

Wini halted and swung toward him. Hands balled into fists, her glare turned murderous.

Jess laughed. Goodness, she was cute when riled.

"What's so funny?"

"You. I believe you were more pleasant to be around yesterday after you'd nearly drowned."

Liquid pooled in her eyes. "That isn't funny."

He gripped her elbow before she could storm away. "Hey, I'm sorry." He gentled his tone. "I was just teasing. I thought. . . Well, it doesn't matter what I thought. I should've conducted myself like a gentleman. My apologies."

He bent in a slight bow.

A puff of resignation left her mouth, and she jerked her arm away. "Stop it. You were more pleasant yesterday when you weren't acting so stuffy."

She continued walking, but now at a much slower pace. He

joined her, shoving his hands deep into his pockets. "My apology was genuine. I just thought after yesterday—"

"Yesterday was a dream. And a nightmare. It wasn't real. The feelings that happened between us, I mean."

Her statement knocked the breath out of him. "Oh, I see."

"Our kiss, the second one anyway, was a celebration of life. An ode to my rescuer. A..."

He nodded as her words trailed off. "I'm grateful I could assist you, Miss Hayes. I won't trouble you any further. Please, take care of yourself."

Heart throbbing with disappointment, Jess veered to the right and off the road, through the lupines bursting with purple he'd normally stop to appreciate. It might be the long way back to the docks, but better than the shorter way filled with rejection.

Swishing sounded behind him. "Would you slow down?"

He stopped.

Wini crashed into his back.

He turned, and she shook her head, stunned by the impact. He steadied her by the elbow.

"Goodness, like slamming into a tree," she mumbled.

"How may I help you, Miss Hayes?" Since it was all he was good for.

"Oh, knock it off." She slapped his arm. The force hit him like a fly bumping him. "What I really want to know is why you were there." She pointed to the Electrolytic Marine Salts Company.

"Conducting business," he said.

"What kind of business?"

He shook his head. "Nope. Not until you tell me why you were there and why you changed your mind about me overnight."

Her lips parted, but she closed them again. Her cheeks bloomed a pretty pink. The sun bounced off the golden streaks threaded through her dark blond hair. A sheen of sweat coated her forehead. No wonder, with all that fabric she lugged around. Jess searched for shade but found none, so he gestured for them to keep walking.

She lifted a skirt that looked as heavy as one of his logs and moved beside him, trampling every lupine along the way. "For one weak moment, I was considering employment. I found out this morning our contract with the jail ended last week. Not only does this put me out of work, but it seems I almost drowned yesterday for nothing."

"And that makes you angry with me?"

"I'm an unmarried woman. I have no dowry, and I'm not free to work a job the way a man can. My mother and sisters-in-law are not widows—at least not that we know of—and, therefore, don't qualify for charity. Washing laundry for the boardinghouses' guests doesn't bring enough income to support a household. I don't have the luxury of swooning over a man who rescued me. A man who, once his work on Popes Folly is finished, will move on to the next wom—I mean, forest."

He frowned. "Did you almost say woman? I assure you, Wini, I'm not that kind of man."

More color entered her cheeks. "Your turn."

"Reverend Jernegan and Mr. Fisher have been purchasing my lumber for the last year to expand their operation. This plant is named Klondike One. I came to see about payment."

"It's true then, that they're building another plant?"

"It is."

The skin between her brows crinkled. "By selling them your lumber, you're supporting their operation."

"I have to earn a living, Wini. That would be like saying because you sell your lobsters to the jail to feed prisoners, you support criminal activity."

Wini pursed her lips. "I suppose." She wrapped her arms

around her middle. "But the owners are earning a profit based on the assurance that men will become greedy. And a minister at that!"

"You don't know for certain. Maybe he's in it for the science."

She rolled her eyes. "Look at how many men have already flooded this town from away. With another plant in progress, there'll be more."

"It's providing jobs and bringing prosperity to the town. Encouraging other merchants to start businesses. That might mean more opportunities for your family too."

Wini shrugged. "I suppose we'll never come to an agreement on this."

"Perhaps not. That doesn't mean we have to avoid each other."

She sighed and looped her hand around his arm. "I just feel that a man called of God to share the Gospel shouldn't have enough time to traipse around the country gaining investors and mining gold from the sea."

He chuckled at her stubbornness. "So, you believe a preacher shouldn't have any interests other than shepherding a flock?"

"I believe the whole thing is a sham." Wini slowed her pace as they approached town. "Gold is found in mountains and streams. Not the ocean."

"Water runs down those mountains into streams which eventually feed into the ocean. So, maybe there is."

She raised a brow at him in surprise. "How old are you?"

"Twenty-five."

"How long have you been logging?"

Jess looked at the sky and did the math. "Seventeen years."

"All in the east?"

"Yes."

"In all your seventeen years in logging camps, floating logs down rivers and streams, have you ever seen gold in them?"

"No. But I haven't been looking for gold."

"Gold is formed in places where the earth's pressure is compromised—around volcanos, where earthquakes are prevalent, etc. Like in the west. Over time, water washes away the soil, exposing the gold. If not picked by human hands upon exposure, the gold might wash away into nearby streams and rivers."

As they approached the dock, she released him and faced the ocean. "If, over time, the gold travels from the streams to the ocean, how would it be discovered?" She spread her arms wide.

"Look, Jess. The ocean is hundreds of thousands of miles wide and several miles deep. It's just not possible. And for the reverend to claim that millions of dollars of gold are flowing through the Lubec narrows every day and that God showed it to him in a vision. . ." She snorted. "Preposterous!"

A fisherman mooring his boat down the way turned to watch them.

Jess stood between her and the man, blocking the man's view. "I won't deny you have what sounds like a valid argument. How do you know so much about gold?"

Her shoulders relaxed. "When I don't know about something, I read about it. That way I don't feel so intimidated."

Pretty *and* smart.

"I'm angry, Jess. I don't know if my father and brothers are alive. I don't know if this sea mining operation will be the best thing for this town, or if dozens of families will get their hearts broken. I don't know if I'll be able to find another place to work." Her voice filled with emotion. "I'm so angry."

Jess wanted to help her.

He also wanted to court her.

He definitely wanted to kiss her again.

But the way things were, she'd refuse him on all accounts.

"Work there."

Her brows arched. "Did you not hear a word I just said?"

"I heard every word you said. Don't let this operation intimidate you. Apply for their secretarial position and learn everything you can about the business. You'll either find the idea is lucrative, or you'll discover it's a scheme. In the meantime, you'll draw an income and be able to help feed your family."

She stared at something in the distance.

"And if that's not convincing enough, you'll get to see me once a week when I deliver lumber and collect my pay." He bent his knees so she'd look him in the eyes.

"Will it get me out of swimming instructions?"

"As long as you promise to stay away from the water."

"I'll consider your suggestion then."

"While you're doing that, will you also consider allowing me to court you?"

She grinned. "If I don't, then our behavior yesterday was both wasted and improper."

"Is that a yes?"

She continued down the dock without him, her skirts swishing around her like a bell. She called over her shoulder, "That's a yes, Mr. Lee."

Chapter Four

One hundred million dollars in gold? Wini could scarcely imagine a hundred dollars. How on earth could Reverend Jernegan and Mr. Fisher claim there was that much gold flowing through the channel when only two thousand dollars' worth was being extracted from the accumulators each week?

Footsteps pounded the floor in the hallway. Wini closed the cabinet where they stored the records, picked up the papers she was supposed to be filing, and opened a different cabinet.

Mr. Wimpleton, who reminded Wini of a grumpy harbor seal, stepped into the room. "Miss Hayes?"

She was thankful for the aged floorboards of the former grist mill and the hollow thump they made under travelers. Especially her heavyset supervisor. "Yes, sir?"

"You've been here nearly a week. It shouldn't be taking you so long to file your paperwork."

The comment sent fire up her spine, but she bit her tongue and lowered her eyes in submissiveness. "I apologize, Mr. Wimpleton. I'm certain I'll have your system memorized soon."

The man frowned, bulging his upper lip and pluming his whiskers like a bird spreads its wings. This time, she sucked in her cheeks and bit down to keep from laughing. She could not lose this job. Not only because the pay was helping to keep her family financially afloat, but also because she was sure if she investigated long enough she'd discover the source of the deception.

"Hurry along now, Miss Hayes. They're christening the *Gold Bug* in ten minutes, and I don't want to miss it."

She gave a little curtsy and made a show of rushing to file her papers. Why the man couldn't leave her alone for a second, she didn't know. Training her was one thing, but he followed her everywhere she went, as if afraid she might stumble upon something she shouldn't. Which was exactly why she wished he'd attend the christening of the company's new steam-powered boat by himself and leave her a few minutes of unsupervised time to see what she could find.

After completing her task, she followed Mr. Wimpleton's rotund figure to the water where a group of employees had gathered to watch the christening. She didn't care two figs about a vessel that would carry supplies and help fatten the coffers of the two men who in this morning's newspaper were described as "earnest Christian gentlemen." Christian they may be, but earnest was yet to be proven.

From what little she'd seen so far, numbers weren't adding up, the managers acted far too suspicious of their wards, and the security fence with No Admittance signs that surrounded the facility were uncivil to the town's peaceful nature.

Mr. Fisher held up his palms to gain the attention of the crowd. Where was Reverend Jernegan? Wini clasped her hands in front of her, blocking out the mundane speech about gold and the town's profiteering. Six days in and she'd already grown tired of watching the arrogant man pat himself on the back.

A light breeze blew across the water, a blessed relief to the sun beating down on her uncovered head. Long sleeves were not conducive to the outdoors in July, but anything less in the presence of men in a business establishment wasn't appropriate. How she missed the wild and woolly summer days of childhood when freedom and security had reigned.

Amid her musing, her gaze landed on a man not dressed in a suit like the others but in a worn pair of trousers—probably the nicest he owned—a clean white shirt, suspenders, and hat.

Jess.

She hadn't seen him since the day he'd asked permission to court her, but he'd written her the sweetest letter. He wasn't polished like the other men lining the channel dock, but he was far more admirable and handsome. And his eyes latched on hers.

Jess touched the brim of his hat in acknowledgment, one side of his mouth angled in a grin. A throat cleared beside her. Mr. Wimpleton scowled his disapproval. She jerked her head back to the *Gold Bug* and pretended to listen while daydreaming of what a courtship with Jess might entail. He was so tall and broad, but instead of making her feel small, he made her feel safe.

The ceremony ended with a glass bottle smashing against the hull of the vessel. She clapped along with the rest of the crowd, wishing she didn't still have another three hours of work. Though she'd no desire to live in the darkness of her thoughts, she was jealous of Carrie for escaping the pressing responsibilities that had been thrust upon the rest of them.

The crowd dispersed, and Wini followed Mr. Wimpleton inside the office, aware of Jess's presence behind her. She'd written him back and told him about gaining the secretarial position. He wouldn't dare visit her at work, would he, knowing the gesture would surely end her employment?

"Miss Hayes, follow me, please." Her vision struggled to focus in the dim room, but she followed Mr. Wimpleton's voice, banging her hip on a desk. She wanted to cry out but caught herself. It would do her no good to show weakness in front of these men.

Discreetly rubbing the spot that was sure to leave a nasty bruise, she trailed Mr. Wimpleton to his personal office, where he thrust a book and more papers at her. "These are investors who have promised Reverend Jernegan their support. Make a list of each business, in alphabetical order and, beside each one, write the amount they've committed to pay. Once you're finished, tally the total. Do you think you can handle this?"

The question stung as if he'd slapped her face. In order to gain her position, she'd had to prove she was proficient in math and organizational skills. Five other women had applied the same day, but Wini's skills had ranked the highest.

"Yes, sir, I'm confident my work will meet your standards." With a smile she didn't feel, she went next door and sat behind the tiny desk they'd given her. She took out a sharpened pencil, set it aside, and flipped through the papers, arranging them in alphabetical order.

A familiar male voice in the proprietors' office caught her attention. Though she continued to appear busy, she leaned closer to the hallway and concentrated on listening to every word. It was difficult to distinguish everything over the hum of the office, but it sounded as if Jess was in a heated discussion with Mr. Fisher.

"I understand your concern, Mr. Lee. Rest assured, you will get paid."

"It's been two months," Jess said. Jenny, the other secretary, rolled a cart past Wini's door, drowning out his next words.

Wini wanted to shout at the woman that it was impossible to eavesdrop with all that racket.

"...payment isn't received soon, I can't supply the lumber for you to continue building Klondike Two."

Where would the location of the new facility be? She'd have to remember to ask Jess.

"Like I said already, Mr. Lee, Prescott will return shortly, and you will receive payment immediately, even if we have to boat to Popes Folly and hand it to you personally." Mr. Fisher's tone was cordial but contained a controlled edge. Though the man was smoother than melted butter, Wini suspected he was also dangerous. "I'll tell you what. Take this as a sign of good faith in the meantime."

Cabinets being opened and closed next door interrupted.

"...we've been pulling so much of it up, that little vial won't be missed."

"Our contract states my payment is to be made in cash or banknote."

"And it will be, my boy. Consider this a bonus, for your patience and hard work."

Mr. Fisher sounded less like a business owner and more like a deadly spider, coaxing its prey into the web.

"Two weeks. And not a day longer."

Two men walked past, conversing in loud tones, followed by laughter. Wini continued alphabetizing the papers when something landed at her feet. She looked down at a small crumpled paper. Leaning backward in her chair, she saw Jess retreating. He must've tossed it in on his way past.

Using her elbow, she knocked her pencil off the desk. She bent to retrieve it and snatched up the note as well. Angling her body, she turned her back to the doorway and untangled the note.

See you at five.

She smiled. He was serious about his courtship then. Finishing the job Mr. Wimpleton had given her proved challenging now that she knew Jess planned to pay her a call. She double-checked her work, willing her brain to stay focused. Less than an hour later, she handed the alphabetized and calculated list to Mr. Wimpleton.

He glanced it over, bulging his upper lip as he did. She looked away to hold her composure. "Well done, Miss Hayes. Here"—he lifted more papers off his desk and held them out to her—"file these according to the first letter of the investor's last name and, once you're finished, you may leave for the day."

Wini took the proffered papers. "Thank you, sir."

He dismissed her by going back to his own work splayed across his desk.

She went to the filing room where a gentleman was assembling a new cabinet. At this rate, they would soon fill every inch of the walls. She filed the papers in the appropriate drawers, taking care to glance over each one as quickly as possible before moving on to the next. In the section of L's, her finger grazed upon Lee's Logging and Mill.

Sneaking a glance behind her at the cabinet assembler to make sure he was occupied, she slipped her finger inside to examine what lay within the file. Two contracts, several purchase orders, and. . . Her breath caught. A record of payment to Jess from four weeks ago. Both Reverend Prescott Jernegan and Mr. Charles Fisher had signed the banknote copy. Beneath their signatures was Jess Lee's.

She pulled out the banknote, quickly folded it, and slipped it into her pocket, then finished her filing, heart racing the entire time. It wasn't until she returned to her desk for her belongings and was halfway home that her pulse slowed to normal.

Wini took Jess's note from her pocket and scanned the writing. The cursive strokes on the banknote and the ones on her personal note were entirely different. She'd either misunderstood Jess about not receiving any payment in the past two months, or the owners of the Electrolytic Marine Salts Company were falsifying documents.

Chapter Five

The hearty clam chowder and warm bread slathered in goat butter was the best meal Jess had eaten in a long time. Greatest part was, there were no beans. How he tired of eating beans at every meal. He pushed back his plate and wiped his mouth with a napkin, stomach satisfied.

Mrs. Hayes stood and gathered his plate with stiff movements, one side of her face drawn as if in pain. Wini had told him about the endless hours her mother washed laundry for the local boardinghouses ever since the cannery opened. The woman's neck and shoulders hunched. What kind of man leaves his wife and daughter to fend for themselves while he chases fortune?

"You both go on and take a walk down the lane." Mrs. Hayes reached for his cup.

Jess scooted it toward himself. "After Miss Hayes and I wash up. It's the least we can do after such a fine meal."

The woman's eyes bulged as if he'd suddenly grown a second nose.

"A man washing supper dishes?" Eden's hand rested atop her bulging belly. "Have I died and gone to heaven?"

He laughed. "When my father was first starting his business, my mother would help us in the woods when we were short a man.

Of course, she got the lightest work. In return, we'd help her in the house when she wasn't feeling well or just needed a rest. I'm a good dishwasher, ma'am. Hardly ever break anything."

He winked.

Mrs. Hayes smiled and wrung her hands. "I've never had a man offer to clean up. I. . .I don't know what I'd do with that extra time."

Jess stood. "Anything you want."

Mrs. Hayes's forehead wrinkled. Poor woman probably hadn't had free time in years.

With a radiant smile, Wini stacked the remaining dishes then went to her mother, who stood in the doorway, jittery and awkward. Jess walked past with his stack as Wini whispered something in her mother's ear. The words *relax* and *hot bath* were the only ones he understood from the hushed conversation, but they must've been the right words, because the older woman brightened.

"I can't thank you enough, young man." Mrs. Hayes untied her apron. "Don't work too hard, and make sure you get in a pleasant walk before you take your leave."

"Will do, ma'am. Thank you again for hosting me."

Mrs. Hayes left the room. Wini followed him into the kitchen, where she took a steaming kettle from the stove and filled the washtub for the dishes. Then she and Eden went outside to fetch more water, presumably for their mother's bath, while Jess started scrubbing a bowl.

"I'm going to retire early tonight," Eden said, hugging Wini. "Don't worry about Carrie. I'll make sure she's eaten and is settled for the night. You enjoy your walk."

She gave Wini a knowing look, a twinge of sadness in her downturned mouth, and left them alone in the kitchen. The only sounds during their labor were that of clinking glasses, swishing water, and the squeak of a towel drying wet glass. A comfortable silence. The Hayes family must have been wealthy at one time, because the quality of their dinnerware and utensils, though worn, were that of upper-crust society.

Wini put the last plate away and turned to him, drying her hands on her apron. "I think the owners of the marine salts company are falsifying documents regarding your pay."

That got his attention. "How so?" He crossed his arms and leaned against the washtub.

She inhaled a deep breath, hands wringing the apron.

He stilled her hands with his. "Whatever you have to tell me, it's all right."

"I've been vigilant in my duties and in learning how the company operates. I was in the next room when you were speaking with Mr. Fisher today, and I overheard your concern about your lumber payment."

He scratched his cheek. She probably heard a lot of conversations around there being that she was a woman and therefore wasn't seen as a threat. "Go on."

"Well, unless I misunderstood the conversation, it sounded as if you've been waiting on payment for over two months."

He nodded, uncomfortable with discussing the financial side of his business with someone he barely knew, even if he planned to rectify that situation.

"I was filing papers after you left, and I came across your file. And studied the documents related to your company."

Jess blinked. She what?

"There was a copy of a banknote from four weeks ago that showed they paid you in full. It contains your signature."

"Are you accusing me of falsehood?" Warmth flushed his neck.

"I'm not accusing *you* of anything." She curled her fingers around his arms for a moment before she pulled something from her pocket. "I'm accusing them. Your signature on the banknote doesn't match the penmanship on the note you wrote me."

She handed him the banknote copy.

"This isn't my signature." A hundred feelings blasted through him as he studied the fancy script. Who signed the paper pretending to be him, and why? Why had Wini taken this when they would arrest her if she were caught?

"I know." She pointed at the amount of the banknote. "I had to be quick in my calculations, but that amount wasn't deducted from the balance that day. I went back in the books and looked. Yesterday's newspaper quoted Reverend Jernegan saying the channel holds gold valued at one hundred million dollars. If that's true, why can't he afford to pay you? Numbers just aren't adding up around there, Jess. Why are they counterfeiting your signature and maybe the signatures of others as well?"

That was the one-hundred-million-dollar question.

His first impulse was to march down to the company, find Jernegan and Fisher, and demand answers. But all that would accomplish would be getting Wini fired and arrested and him tangled in a long legal battle he wasn't prepared to fight. As much as he wanted his money, maybe it was best to wait until they had more substantial evidence.

"What are you thinking?" There was a hint of terror in her voice.

Jess cleared his head and cupped her soft cheek with his palm. "I'm thinking you're brave—and a little crazy—to take such a risk for me. I'm thinking we need more evidence before we attempt to take these guys down. I'm thinking I don't want you involved."

Wini leaned into his touch. "I'm already involved. I don't want to see you or anyone else hurt by these deceptive men."

"I want you safe."

"I'll be fine." She placed her hand over his still holding the side of her face. "I'm limited to certain parts of the facility because I'm a woman. The records that I'm sure hold major evidence are locked in Reverend Jernegan and Mr. Fisher's office. And no one is allowed in the laboratory except them. Makes me wonder what's going on in there."

Jess released her, folded the false banknote, and handed it back to her. "Act like nothing is amiss. Put this back and take nothing else out of that office. Whatever you see, tell me about. I'll believe you."

"What are you going to do?"

He scratched his cheek and thought for a moment. "First, I'm going to kiss you."

Jess bent and tasted those sweet lips he'd been aching to touch all evening. She kissed him back, and he almost forgot her question. Reluctantly, he pulled away. "Second, I'm going to put my best man in charge of the logging crew for a while and apply for a position at the marine salts company. Under disguise."

The next morning, a throat cleared behind Wini and she jumped, causing the cabinet door to slam shut. She spun, hand to her chest. "Mr. Wimpleton! You frightened me."

His whiskers flared. "What, may I ask, are you doing in here?"

Putting away something she'd stolen. Well, borrowed. Fear pulsed from her core. "You told me to file the tide and weather reports."

Mr. Wimpleton sighed. "Those reports get filed in the cabinets in that room." He pointed across the hall. "How many times must we go over this?"

She refrained from saying that once was plenty. That she had known they filed those reports in that room and that she could do her own job and his. "I apologize, Mr. Wimpleton. I'm certain I'll learn my way around soon."

He huffed. She stared at the floor to hide the look of annoyance she was sure played on her face and followed him into the hallway. With a grand, sarcastic sweep of his hand, he gestured for her to enter the correct filing room ahead of him. "Once you've finished, you need to report to my office. We've hired an additional ten men this morning, and I'll need you to record their information."

"Yes, sir." Wini got to work filing under the scrutiny of the grumpy seal. Ten new hires. Would Jess be among them?

She could only hope.

Chapter Six

"Thank you, Miss…?" Jess raised a brow at Wini as she handed him a paper, telling him which supervisor to report to. My, she looked beautiful in blue. He, on the other hand, looked repulsive in his burly disguise.

"Hayes." Eyes downcast, her eyelashes swept across rosy cheeks. Cheeks he couldn't wait to get his hands on later. As much as he wanted to stay and test the limits of his flirtation, the man with the bulging mustache who'd hired him was watching.

"Move along, Mr. Sutherland."

Jess nodded at the man, glanced at Wini one last time, and left out the back door that led to the labor part of the facility. The day was overcast and the scent of seaweed, salt, and freshly cut lumber filled the air. Lumber he'd provided that he was still awaiting payment for. A surge of pride filled him as he inspected the boards, even now being nailed into place for an additional work area.

He'd get paid. Even if he had to take it out of Charles Fisher's hide. Arrogant snake.

The paper Wini had given him said to report to the construction area of the facility, but he used the opportunity to look around. Passing the crew, he strolled along the fence border, familiarizing himself with the layout of the property. On the south end, a row of tiny shacks lined the fence in front of a locked gate. Jess looked around before opening the door of the first shack.

It held shelves of cast-iron pots and wooden slats, presumably materials used to assemble the accumulators. Shack number two housed dozens of copper plates. The last shack, filled with bottles of mercury, baffled him. What were they using mercury for?

All of the men hired today had been warned to stay away from the laboratory. As Jess went to report for his work assignment, he determined to get to the bottom of three perplexing issues: why no one except the owners had access to the lab, why they needed such exorbitant amounts of mercury, and why they'd falsified his signature on that banknote.

As Wini walked along the town wharf to work, she was grateful for another morning with enough food on the table. For that, she couldn't complain. Sleep, on the other hand. . .

Dozens of men were arriving in town daily in search of a job at the Electrolytic Marine Salts Company and for a place to stay. Everyone wanted to be at the helm of this booming business. Men who weren't so foolish as to travel across the entire country in search of gold. But men who wanted a part of it just the same.

With the influx of men, the boardinghouses were full, which meant more mountains of laundry for her mother and Eden. Folks with extra bedrooms in their homes were renting them out to strangers, and the property owners were recommending they have their belongings laundered by the Hayes women. They had more laundry than they could handle, but they weren't about to turn anyone away. They'd come too close to poverty for that.

Wini leaned her neck from side to side to work out the tension knotting her shoulders. Sleeping with a flailing toddler was never easy. If only—

Her thoughts scattered as she saw the line of men snaking out the door of the marine salts office, around the side of the building, and down the hill. At first, she thought they were men in search of employment, but the closer she approached, she saw faces she recognized. Mr. Scott, supervisor at the cannery. The Baumgardner twins, who hauled in more herring than any other fishermen. Mr. Long, the schoolteacher. Mr. McCammon, the preacher.

What were these men doing here that would cause them to take time away from their responsibilities?

Sidling up to the preacher, she casually gripped her lunch basket in front of her. "I haven't seen this many gathered since the Williams's home caught fire."

The preacher adjusted his spectacles. "Now if I can just figure out how to get them all to fill my pews."

She chuckled. "What's going on?"

"Haven't you heard?" Mr. McCammon pulled a folded newspaper from his breast pocket. "They extracted five thousand dollars in gold last night. The company is offering shares for one dollar apiece. I plan to buy twenty."

"Twenty!" Wini swallowed to keep from saying anything further.

"I wanted to buy forty, but Heather said if I did, she wouldn't feed me for a week."

"I see your predicament. I wouldn't want to go without her blueberry pie either." She waved a farewell and continued to the office, squeezing through the door with a mumbled, "Excuse me."

"Miss Hayes." Mr. Wimpleton stood from behind the desk, sweat beading his forehead. He was jumpier than a grasshopper in a field of wild horses. "It's about time."

She glanced at her timepiece. Three minutes early.

"Here." Mr. Wimpleton waved her behind his desk. "Record

these gentlemen's names, residences, and how many shares they wish to purchase." He pointed his plump finger at each category, as if she couldn't look at his previous recordings and figure that out on her own. "I'll collect their money."

Of course. That task would be too hard for her.

For the next two hours she asked each man in line the same questions, writing until her fingers cramped. The office stayed stuffy on a normal basis, but the inpouring of extra bodies had her dripping. How she longed to find a pool of water somewhere private and sink into it. One where her feet would touch bottom, of course.

After the last man left the building, she pushed a fist into her lower back and stretched. Mr. Wimpleton closed the cashbox and secured the latch, his mustache twitching. "What a morning."

"I didn't realize the company was selling shares."

"Neither did I until I received a telegram from Mr. Fisher this morning. I'd say two thousand dollars for his first day isn't bad."

Bile burned her throat. These were good men, investing their life savings in a company that was counterfeiting documents. But the deception went much deeper than the documents. She was certain. She needed to talk to Jess. They had to sort this out, and fast.

If I were a dishonest man running a gold mining scheme, how would I do it?

The question bounced around as he sat along the channel, watching the water ripple past. Two days ago, five thousand dollars' worth of gold had been extracted from the sixty accumulators. That was approximately four and a half ounces of gold from each one. An ounce of gold was worth just under nineteen dollars.

He'd seen a gold bar once, in Boston, when he was a teenager.

He and his dad had paid passage on a ship to retrieve supplies and buy his mother a new dress for her birthday. A man dressed in the finest suit Jess had ever seen walked up to the counter at the department store and paid with a one-ounce gold bar. Jess had been in such awe, the man smiled and asked if he'd like to hold one. He reached into his pocket, pulled out another one, and handed it to Jess.

Jess had been both dumbstruck and disappointed. The gold bar wasn't as heavy as he'd imagined it would be, barely an inch long and only about an inch and a half wide. This was what men searched the ancient world to find? Seemed like a lot of trouble, sacrificing their lives for such a small thing. But to be rich enough to carry around gold bars in his pocket like candy? Jess couldn't imagine that either.

It took a lot of gold flakes to make an ounce. How had they separated the gold from the conducting materials, and how was gold attracted to them in the first place? According to the newspapers, it had something to do with mercury poured onto copper plates that were charged by a battery through wire. He wasn't scientifically minded and didn't understand the workings of a battery. Few existed, but Fisher and Jernegan had connections in Boston somehow.

"You ever gonna eat?" Troy Emberton asked beside him. "Break's almost over."

Jess yanked his thoughts to the task at hand and opened his lunch pail. He took out his cheese sandwich and sank his teeth into it.

Troy took a swig of water from his tin cup. "I've never seen a man sit and stare at nothing when there's food to be eaten. What's got you troubled?"

"Just trying to imagine putting a box into the water and bringing up five thousand dollars."

Troy chuckled. "Crazy, isn't it? Wish I'd thought of it first."

"You ever hear how they do it?" Jess took another bite.

"They claim the tides in these narrows do most of the work." Troy lay back on the grass and covered his eyes with his hat. "When the water rushes through the accumulators during the changing tides, the chemicals attract the gold. I heard it's especially successful during a storm, like the night before they surfaced the five thousand dollars in gold."

Jess considered this as he finished his sandwich and started on a piece of apple pie Mrs. Jennings had brought him—bless her—before she and her husband left to join the others setting up camp on Treat Island.

"How do they separate the gold from the mercury?" Jess asked. He didn't know much about the compound but knew sometimes folks died after tampering with it. "And how does the battery work?"

"Don't know on both counts."

The lunch bell sounded. Troy sat up, righted his hat, and tossed his utensils in his lunch pail. "No one can go inside the laboratory except Mr. Jernegan and Mr. Fisher."

Jess stood. "Folks don't find that odd?"

Troy shrugged. "Guess if they let us in on that part of things, any of us could go start our own sea mining business. Pretty smart, if you ask me."

Troy walked away. Jess stared at the water again, wishing he could see beneath its waves to the bottom. He believed the entire operation had less to do with smart and more to do with deception.

Chapter Seven

"You lookin' weary, Miss Wini." Ruby reached for the basket of clean and folded laundry Wini balanced on her hip. The relief of it not digging into her bones anymore almost made her sing.

"I'll come by on my way home and pick up the next load."

"I s'pect you workin' both jobs, huh?" Compassion filled her friend's dark eyes.

"Would you do any less?"

Ruby cackled. "No, miss, I wouldn't." She sobered. "Any word from yo' daddy or brothers?"

Wini's heart sank. "Still nothing."

"Then I's a keep on prayin'." Ruby's warm hand squeezed Wini's in the briefest of touches.

"Thank you, friend." Was there ever a more faithful prayer warrior than Ruby?

A wail caught Wini's attention. She turned to face Dr. Pressman's home, and a woman dressed in black exited the doctor's home, a handkerchief pressed to her nose.

"Poor dear soul," Ruby said behind Wini.

"What happened?" If anyone in this town knew, it was Ruby. Wini tried not to stare at the retreating woman, but her wails were full of such despair she couldn't resist.

"Husband died. They's just passin' through and he stopped to go fishin' while she napped b'neath a tree. Fo' too long, he was cookin' fish. The smell o' it made her sick 'cause she's with child. He ate it all. That night, he got bad sick. Started talkin' out his head. Next day, he was gone."

Wini's heart went out to the woman.

"We's all suspect he had some kind o' heart condition, but the missus say he was healthy as a stock horse. After his examination Doc said he ain't never seen nothin' like it. A heart condition wouldn't cause him to talk out his head. Don't know what happened. Guess that shows when the good Lord's ready to call us home, ain't nothin' gonna stop Him."

"I suppose so," Wini whispered. The woman was merely a speck in the distance now.

Ruby patted her back. "Now don't you go worryin' none. I'm sure yo' daddy and brothers are just fine and'll be home any day now with pockets full o' gold for ya."

"Thank you, Ruby." Wini stepped off the porch and walked the long road to work, her mind and heart heavy. As the business loomed before her and another line of men purchasing shares came into view, the burden she carried inside grew heavier.

Jess fought a yawn as he walked Wini to her door. He'd gladly give up sleep to spend more time with her, but he had her reputation to consider. Fireflies lit the darkness like beacons calling wandering souls home. Her skirt swished against the flowers that lined the path. A skirt that, when saturated with water, had almost taken her life. He thanked God every day he'd been there to help.

He assisted her onto the stoop. "Why so distracted tonight?"

The light from his lantern spilled over her face where trouble was brewing. She didn't answer him. His gut twisted. He prayed it wasn't that she'd decided they didn't make a suitable match.

"Wini?" He stroked her cheek with his thumb.

She sighed. "We sold another fifteen hundred dollars in shares today. Almost all locally. A few prospectors came over from New Brunswick."

"That's what's bothering you?"

"These are good men, Jess. Some with businesses and families. Some who are already struggling to provide, and now they're offering every spare penny to a dream that doesn't exist. I know what it feels like to be on the other side of that. It's awful. The only difference is these men will have to go home every day and look at their loved ones and watch them waste away. Unlike my father who—"

Emotion choked her words.

Jess tugged her to him and tucked her beneath his chin. He held her, rocking her, until she relaxed against him. "What if we're wrong?" he said in a low, cautious tone. He'd been working at the company for three weeks now and hadn't stumbled across anything incriminating. "What if what seems suspicious to us is just a lack of knowledge in the realm of science?"

She leaned back to look at him. "That scenario doesn't explain the forged banknote."

"True. That could result from something else entirely. Or someone else in the company being dishonest. Like that grumpy seal guy."

She shook her head and pulled away from him. "Mr. Wimpleton's a grouch, but I believe he's harmless. Something isn't right with this gold mining, Jess. I feel it." She touched her heart. "The way they talk and present their case to potential investors—it's too smooth. Reverend Jernegan acts more like a high society peddler than a preacher. He never even talks about God. And what about his wife and child? Why are they still in Boston? What reverend do you know would leave his church, his family, and his profession to pursue other business?"

Jess lifted a shoulder. "I'm not saying they're innocent. I'm simply trying to see it from all angles. We won't give up though. If this matters that much to you, and you truly believe something is amiss, I'll keep digging."

"I do."

"Then we're in this together." He leaned over and gave her the lightest of kisses. He wanted to kiss her properly but constrained his desire. All in good time.

He waited for her to enter the house and then walked down the path toward the wharf. Ships of all sizes dotted the water. Moonlight glimmered on the waves between masts and bound sails. He was ready to retreat to the boardinghouse and sleep, but his responsibilities during the day kept him from investigating, so he walked by the light of his lamp to the outskirts of the mill.

The tall grass rustled beneath his steps. He lowered the lantern's wick and walked toward the marine salts company, guided mostly by the light of the waxing gibbous. His father had taught him all about the moon phases and the stars, and in this moment, he could sure use his father's wisdom.

He walked along the channel for nearly an hour, looking for a breach in the privacy fence or anything that stood out as odd. At the sound of splashing, he doused his lamp and crouched in the grass. The noise seemed to be fifty yards away. It grew louder as a shadow emerged from the water and crawled onto the shore.

The moon cast a silvery glow on the figure.

A human.

Big awkward steps *thunked* as they stepped onto the grass. The figure seemed statuesque in its form and movement. After minutes of struggling in seeming desperation, the person removed something from their head and sucked in loud gulps of air.

A diving suit? Jess had heard of them and seen drawings in books but had never observed one in person.

One heavy footfall at a time, the diver moved to the fence, opened a gate, and disappeared inside the perimeter.

Jess had just walked past that section of fence, and the gate had been locked. Whoever this was had a key. The only individuals that would likely have a key were the owners. What would Jernegan or Fisher be doing in a diving suit in the water with the accumulators at night?

Jess sank onto the grass. Whatever they were doing out there wasn't honest. He could feel it in his core, as tangible as the grass beneath him.

Chapter Eight

August heat permeated the old mill, making Mr. Wimpleton extra grumpy. Wini had completed every task he'd given her in good time, and yet he still barked orders. At least he had the liberty to remove his suit coat and roll up his sleeves. She did not. Sweat rolled down her back and legs in uncomfortable rivulets beneath the layers of corset and petticoats. While she didn't miss almost drowning, she missed the cool fresh air on the water and the freedom to answer only to herself.

She rounded the corner of the file room into the hallway and slammed into a body. She stumbled backward a few steps, and a flush of embarrassment sent her body temperature rising a few more degrees. "I apologize, Mr. Fisher. I promise to be more vigilant of where I'm walking."

The man tweaked the side of his nose in annoyance but pasted on a smile. "Quite all right, Miss Hayes. Accidents happen." He smoothed a palm over his slick hair. "Like the one currently in the laboratory. Have you seen Mr. Wimpleton? I'm in need of his help."

"Yes, he's getting ready to go mail your letter at the post office."

Mr. Fisher ran his thumb and forefinger down the sides of his mustache. He led her by the elbow into the main office. "Wimpleton."

Mr. Wimpleton looked up, a stack of letters in his hand.

"Miss Hayes can run the errand at the post office. I knocked a shelf of mercury over in the laboratory, and I need your help cleaning up."

Mr. Wimpleton's mustache twitched. "My help, sir?"

"The building crew left a few hours ago to work on Klondike Two. I believe you and I can handle the task ourselves." Mr. Fisher released Wini's elbow and beckoned Mr. Wimpleton with his finger.

Clearing his throat, Mr. Wimpleton handed Wini the letters as he passed. "Ask the postmaster if we've any mail."

Wini bobbed a small curtsy. "Anything he gives me I'll set on your desk, sir."

Mr. Wimpleton nodded, adjusted his spectacles, and followed Mr. Fisher from the room.

Wini sighed in relief as she stepped outside. The day was still hot, but at least now she caught a breeze dancing off the water. It brought Jess to mind and their walk along the dock last evening. She loved his easy manner, the way he made her laugh, the solidity of his presence. Where nearly drowning was a low spot in her life, Jess's presence in her world gave her hope to keep going each day.

She took her time walking the mile to the post office and enjoyed the afternoon. Mrs. Espisito, who owned one of the boardinghouses in town, greeted Wini from her front porch. "I'm glad to see they let you out for a while." The woman's teeth gleamed against her tan skin. "Many around my supper table have complained about the heat. Imagine, boarding up all the windows. And for what purpose? Do they think so poorly of our citizens that they fear we'll break in to steal their gold?"

Wini agreed that boarding up most of the windows was strange, especially since the facility was surrounded by a fence. "It has been rather miserable this week."

They talked about the weather and Catherine Marsh's recent engagement announcement. Her betrothed hailed from Portland and was captain of a shipping crew. Catherine also had a dowry at her disposal, even if a small one. Wini had nothing to offer a man except her heart.

When her time came, would it be enough?

Wini tightened her grip on the letters. "I agree. The new church will be lovely for a Christmas wedding. I must continue my errand. It was wonderful to speak to you. Tell Mr. Espisito to take it easy on his injured leg."

"Will do, Miss Wini."

The post office smelled of paper, wooden crates, and ink. The town's newspaper office shared its space, and the crank and release of the printing press sounded in the background. Mr. Dillard, the postmaster, stepped up to the counter and asked how he could assist her.

"They sent me in Mr. Wimpleton's stead. I'm to post these and retrieve anything you might have for the marine salts company."

"Of course." Mr. Dillard took her stack of letters and marked them accordingly. She paid, and he gave her change in return. "I'll be right back."

He left to retrieve the company's mail while she watched the two men in the back working the printing press. Ink the stamps, lay the paper, crank, press, crank, peel the paper. It amazed her that an entire page of news was created in a few simple steps.

Mr. Dillard blocked her view, breaking her musing. He passed her several letters and a package wrapped in brown paper with string tied around all sides. A corner of the paper had ripped, exposing a sliver of the box. "Send my regards to Reverend Jernegan and Mr. Fisher. The entire crate of mail fell off the wagon during transport. It's a little banged up but still intact." He pointed at the damaged corner. "Be glad it wasn't the looking glass Mr. King ordered for his new bride."

The man's gaze shifted to the side, and his eyebrows shot upward. Mr. King was a force to be reckoned with on a good day. She couldn't imagine having to tell him about the mirror. "I'm sure it'll be fine. I'll relay the message." She smiled. "Anything for the Hayes residence while I'm here?"

She hated the tinge of hope in her voice.

His expression fell. "Nothing today, Miss Hayes."

The same line he'd said to her nearly every day for the past year. Even when they received a missive, it was never from Father or her brothers. "Thank you for looking, Mr. Dillard."

"Good day."

Wini checked her timepiece as she stepped beneath the shade of a tree. As much as she wanted to dawdle, she'd already been gone for close to thirty minutes. She didn't know how long it took to clean up a mercury spill, but she also didn't want to be lectured by Mr. Wimpleton on how incompetent women were in the world of business.

Again.

With a groan, she started down the path. Where was her father at this very moment? Her brothers? Were they still together? Alive? Dead? Rich or destitute? Why weren't they sending word about something, anything?

A small dog dashed across the road in front of her, followed by a boy. She came to a halt just before crashing into him. He was doing his best to catch the dog, but his little legs weren't fast enough. A moment later, he tripped on a rock jutting from the ground and rolled down the hill. Wini hurried to help, dropping her burden on the grass.

"Are you all right?"

She recognized the boy as the general store owner's son, David. The boy sat up, holding his leg below a nasty scrape on his knee. Blood marred the hem of his knickers. "Sorry, Miss Hayes. I was trying to catch my puppy."

David tried hard to be brave, but tears clogged his words.

The troublemaker with a wagging tail trotted up beside David and stuck its wet nose to his cheek.

"No need to apologize." She looked around. "You're a tough boy, so I'm sure it's your pride that hurts more than anything." At his nod, she continued. "Lucky for you, no one else saw. I promise to keep my lips sealed."

She pretended to lock her closed lips.

He sniffled and rubbed his eye, putting an arm around his dog. "What'd'ya got all over your hands, Miss Hayes?"

Wini inspected her golden fingers. "I. . .don't know."

She lifted her hand for closer inspection, baffled. A dusting of sparkling golden powder had collected on the tips of her fingers. How had it gotten there? Why, if she didn't know better, she'd think it was—

Her head whipped around to the box. Gold dust.

"Miss Hayes?" David whimpered.

"Here, let me help you up."

Once the boy was steady on his feet, she patted the top of the dog's head and sent them on their way. David scolded the puppy as they retreated.

She knelt to inspect the box Mr. Dillard said had been knocked around during transport. Sure enough, a fine layer of gold dust covered the corner where the paper was ripped. Some particles were larger than others, but all held the consistency of the precious metal. At least she thought they did. She'd never actually seen gold flakes.

It had to be gold. But why was it being shipped to the company, when the company was shipping the gold found in the accumulators to Boston to be made into gold bars and deposited at the bank?

More questions piled up with each passing day. Questions to which Wini was determined to find the answers.

Where was Wini?

Jess stepped farther into the empty office, grateful to have escaped his stuffy disguise, and bellowed a greeting to let someone know he was there. A petite young woman with dark hair and a pointed chin rushed from a room in the back. "May I help you, sir?"

"Indeed. I'm here to inquire about pay for Lee's Logging and Mill company."

She clasped her hands on the desk. "Our accountant, Mr. Wimpleton, is out of the office at the moment. If you could come back later today, I'm sure he can get you taken care of."

Jess smiled patiently at the lady, though his patience in the matter had fled weeks ago. "The issue, Miss. . . ?"

"Eversoll."

"The issue, Miss Eversoll, is that I've been attempting to collect payment for three months now. I've another shipment of lumber to deliver, and I will not deliver it until I receive payment for the last."

"Oh." Her mouth formed the perfect vowel shape. "I'm not sure why there's been such a delay, but Reverend Jernegan just arrived from Boston. He can help you. Please, follow me."

Finally, someone willing to help him. Jess followed Miss Eversoll through a hallway and to the third door on the left.

She knocked on the open door. "I apologize for interrupting you, Reverend Jernegan, but this gentleman needs to speak with you about his payment for Lee's Logging and Mill Company."

Jess stepped into the man's office. "Good day, sir."

The pale man blinked at Jess's forceful entry. "Uh, good day, Mister. . ."

"Jess Lee," he reminded the reverend. He offered his hand and Jernegan accepted. "I'm here to inquire about a lumber delivery you've requested, as well as my pay."

Jernegan gestured for Jess to take a seat. "Ah, yes. How may I help you?"

"Well, sir." Jess leaned against the chair's back and crossed an ankle over his opposite knee. "I'm unable to fulfill your order until I receive full payment for the last delivery."

The man's eyebrows folded over deep-set eyes. "That's rather strange. I remember handing you a banknote directly several months ago. Perhaps you've forgotten, or the accountant at Lee's Logging has made an oversight."

Jess swallowed his barely constrained ire. "My books are in perfect order. I guarantee you I have not received payment." He removed a paper from his pocket, unfolded it, and dropped it onto Jernegan's desk. "Here is a list of dates and the details behind each attempt to collect payment. January tenth, upon my delivery, you promised payment for the next week. April twentieth, you and Mr. Fisher were out of town seeking investors. May first—"

"I can read, Mr. Lee." Jernegan twisted the end of his curled mustache. "However, I remember meeting with you in May and settling our account in full."

Jess put both feet on the floor and leaned forward, ready to jog the man's memory to the truth, when Miss Eversoll knocked on the door once again. "Mr. Jernegan, sir, I found this in the files, if it helps you."

She walked in holding a paper she delivered to Jernegan. "It seems you paid Mr. Lee, just as you said."

She looked down at Jess with a hint of disdain, her shoulders squared, proud to assist her boss, who smiled at her. "Thank you, Miss Eversoll. As you can see, Mr. Lee, I have paid your account. In full."

He turned the paper in Jess's direction and pinned it to the edge of his desk with a finger. Jess studied his false signature for a moment then flicked his gaze to Jernegan's. "The problem is, that's not my signature."

Jess took a folded paper from his pocket and laid it on top of the banknote. "This is my signature. On the lumber contract we drew up that I've yet to be paid in full for."

Jernegan picked up both papers and held them side by side, comparing. His mouth opened and closed, but no sound escaped. Miss Eversoll's face turned crimson, and she shrank in stature.

Jess pointed to the banknote. "On top of wondering where my money is, now I'm wondering how a signature I didn't make ended up on this banknote. Maybe the judge can sort this out."

Jess started to stand, but Jernegan held up a palm. A soft, almost feminine-looking palm that had probably never seen a day of hard labor in its life. "I'm unsure how or why a signature that is not yours ended up on this banknote, but I assure you I will discover the answer. In the meantime, I will issue you a new banknote for the full amount with Miss Eversoll as witness."

"That'll do fine," Jess replied.

While Jernegan retrieved the book from his desk and Miss Eversoll fiddled with her nervous hands, Jess stood and looked around the room. An open window blew a pleasant breeze through the gaudy curtains. One of the few that hadn't been boarded. There wasn't much to the room other than a couple of chairs and a shelf containing a dried starfish, a few old coins, and a daguerreotype of two women standing on a porch beside an elderly woman in a rocking chair who was holding the arm of a mischievous-looking boy as if she'd been afraid he'd run.

Jernegan as a boy, most likely. Seemed he'd needed moral guidance even then.

A particular coin with three stars in the middle caught Jess's eye. "Your coin reminds me of the pirate's treasure my grandpa used to tell me stories about when I was a kid," he said. "Dixie Bull, my grandpa called him. Buried his treasure somewhere in Casco Bay a couple hundred years ago."

"It is from the same." Mr. Jernegan tore out a fresh banknote and held out the quill for Jess to sign.

"You're telling me those coins are from Dixie Bull's treasure?" He dipped the quill in ink, scraped it along the jar to remove any excess, then signed his name. "Bet you paid handsomely for that."

"I'm a capitalist, Mr. Lee. I don't invest in historical trinkets. I invest in businesses that turn a profit."

"You inherited the coin?"

Jernegan stood, no longer trying to hide his annoyance. "If you must know, it was discovered in a diving expedition three years ago."

"You dive, sir? Impressive."

"Absolutely not. I value my life too much to chance going under water in a weighted device that might betray me."

"A gift from a family member then?" Jess would pry until the man threw him out.

"From Mr. Fisher, actually. He trained in diving while overseas in the British Army. He's also skilled in artillery." The hardness in Jernegan's eyes and jaw were a warning to Jess. "Now, if you'll excuse me, I have more important matters to attend to than chatting about pirate treasure. Good day, Mr. Lee. See to my next shipment of lumber as soon as possible."

Jess left the room, satisfied. Not only had he gotten paid, but he'd also discovered the identity of the mysterious night diver.

Chapter Nine

Jess was hungry enough to eat a whale.

His supervisor held the gate open for the crew returning from Klondike Two. Jess followed the line. He'd skipped lunch in order to inquire about his pay. Now his stomach gnawed on his backbone, and if he didn't eat something soon, he might tear something apart.

Troy appeared at his side, a pickax on his shoulder. "Some of the crew are heading down to the saloon. Wanna come?"

"Nah, busy." Jess's gut released a mighty growl.

"You must be, skipping lunch and all. They serve food at the saloon, you know."

In his younger days, Jess might've accepted the offer. Time and wisdom were excellent teachers. "Nope. Try not to lose too badly. I hear Sims is a cheater."

"Suit yourself." Troy walked ahead.

Jess scratched his cheek, ready to wash out the mixture of ash and coal dust he rubbed into his beard and hair every morning to make it darker. A beard had always made him itchy, which is why he stayed clean shaven. Only in the bitterness of winter did he tolerate the change.

After putting his tools away and cleaning up, maybe he'd

find Wini and offer to take her to the café he'd spotted in town. He was used to eating three meals a day, meals large enough to fill a fox den. The small portions at the boardinghouse and bite-sized lunch the proprietor made for him for an extra fee didn't hold him for more than an hour. He'd lost weight since he'd started at the marine salts company. Could feel it in the looseness of his clothes.

As he approached the toolshed, the laboratory door opened. Mr. Wimpleton, the man Wini described as a grumpy seal emerged, running his fingers through his hair. His ruddy face, shifty eyes, and twitchy movements made Jess suspect the man wasn't comfortable with whatever he'd witnessed inside that room. The room only Jernegan, Fisher, and, now, this man had access to.

Was Mr. Wimpleton in on the scheme? Maybe Jess and Wini were overlooking other key players in their quest to expose the owners of fraud. He'd ask Wini to pay closer attention to Mister Grumpy Seal.

Tools returned, Jess snatched up his lunch pail and headed for the freedom outside the gates.

"Got plans for the evening, Jess?" Tucker, a young widower from Connecticut, slapped Jess on the shoulder as they filed out.

At that moment, Wini stepped from the office onto the knoll and raised her face to the sky, as if she too relished the freedom outside the tightly secured company. Before Tucker invited him to the saloon, Jess said, "I do. See you Monday."

Jess left the man and chased Wini down the road. At his footfalls, she turned. Her expression turned radiant when she saw him. "Something on fire, Mr. Sutherland?"

She winked.

He offered his elbow, despite being dirty from labor. She curled her hand around his arm. He leaned to her ear and whispered, "My heart."

His pride took great satisfaction in watching her eyes grow large and her face tinge pink. She bit her lower lip and grinned up at him, the sparkle in her eyes telling him everything he wanted to know. He laid his hand atop hers, cringing at his dirty fingers. "Hungry?"

"Famished."

"How about I walk you home and then go get cleaned up before I take you to the café for dinner?"

"The café will be closed but there's a dining room inside the Lubec Hotel."

"Fine dining it is then." Now that he'd gotten paid, he could afford to take her someplace nice.

"I accept your invitation." Wini nodded a greeting at a man walking the opposite direction. Jess's stomach chose that moment to howl again. She laughed. "I think I'd better see my own way home so you can wash and we can get to dinner faster."

He angled them down the next road. "Nonsense. What kind of suitor would I be if I didn't see you home first?"

She stopped. "A practical one. Please, Jess. We've a lot to discuss, and the later we arrive, the more crowded it will be."

"You've discovered something then?"

"I have."

"So have I."

"Then you'd best make it quick before anyone else hears your stomach and thinks there's a wild bear on a rampage."

"You're too sweet." He gave her a mock scowl as he took a step back, breaking their contact. "So sweet, I don't think we're gonna need to order any dessert. Wouldn't want a stomachache."

She looked around to see if they had an audience, then moved closer. "I guess I won't share my secrets with you then."

"Oh, yes, you will." He ran his knuckles down her velvety cheek. Her eyes closed in pleasure.

Before he made any more bold moves as Mr. Sutherland for the entire town to see, he walked toward the boardinghouse, whistling.

The Lubec Hotel's dining room was blessedly sparse. Jess scanned the area. Couples occupied two of the tables and a family of four another. He suspected many of the tables would be full within the hour.

"Follow me, sir." The host turned away, but Jess stopped him with a tug on the man's coat. The host turned, eyebrows raised.

"My apologies," Jess murmured. "I have something of great importance I'd like to speak with the lady about tonight, and we would appreciate privacy."

"Ah." The man's curiosity turned to delight, and his gaze bounced between Wini and Jess. "I have the perfect table. Follow me."

Jess knew what Wini must be thinking, with her mouth opening and closing like a fish ashore. Much like the day she'd almost drowned. As he had that day, he desired to still her lips with his, but when he asked her that particular question, it wouldn't be in the dining room of the Lubec Hotel.

After Wini was seated, Jess occupied the space across from her. The cozy table for two was nestled beside a window that offered a spectacular view of the ocean. A large sailing vessel moved slowly on the horizon, its giant sails billowing.

He abandoned the view to ask Wini what she'd like to drink and frowned at the look of terror on her face. "Breathe, my dear. I don't plan on proposing."

Her shoulders relaxed, but her eyes were a mix of relief and disappointment.

"Not tonight anyway."

She kicked his shin lightly beneath the table. "Scoundrel."

He smiled.

The server introduced himself and took their orders. "Unfortunately, sir, we're unable to provide you with the braised halibut this evening. May I suggest the chicken and gravy sauce?"

"That'll do." Jess couldn't wait for the man to leave.

"Very well. I'll be back with your tea and bread and butter." The server bowed.

Few times in his life had Jess ever been in a restaurant so fancy. He wasn't sure whether to be impressed or uncomfortable.

"So, it's true then?" Wini asked, looking away, almost as if speaking to herself.

"What's true?"

"Several in the community have gotten sick in the past couple of weeks. Dr. Pressman told my friend Ruby that they all had one thing in common—fish. The symptoms range in severity, but each one started feeling ill within a few hours of eating fish from the narrows." She lowered her voice. "One patient even died."

"You think that's why the hotel isn't serving fish?"

She nodded.

"Word's gotten out then," he said.

"What could be wrong with the fish?"

Jess hesitated to say anything at the moment, as the two situations may not have any bearing on one another. But then he decided not to keep anything from her. "Two nights ago, after our walk, I went to the marine salts company and walked the perimeter of the fence from the outside, looking for weaknesses or anything suspicious."

"What did you find?"

"A diver coming out of the water."

She blew out a breath.

The server returned with a pot of tea, two cups, and a basket of bread and butter. Once Jess was sure the man was out of hearing range, he continued. "I don't know if the diver is related to the fish sickness or not, but I'm certain it was Charles Fisher."

Jess relayed all the pertinent details, watching the surprise flitter across her face. "After he struggled to get the helmet off, he sucked in air as if the helmet had stolen his breath. Something must've gone wrong. Anyway, he unlocked the privacy gate and walked straight into the facility grounds. I learned from Jernegan earlier today that Fisher's skilled in diving."

Her brows crinkled in thought for a moment before she pulled a folded handkerchief from her pocket and pushed it across the table. "Open it carefully. I believe there's gold dust inside."

Stunned, he did as she asked. He studied the fabric in fascination as she relayed her trip to the post office and the little boy chasing his dog.

"This is gold," he said.

The question at the forefront of his mind was the same as she expressed—why would gold dust be shipped to the company when it should all be going to Boston?

They discussed plausible reasons and what areas they should investigate next as they savored their dinner. He'd just talked Wini into sharing a piece of chocolate cake with him when a commotion at the entrance caught his attention. A black woman gestured wildly to the host.

"Ruby," Wini whispered, and stood.

When the woman spotted Wini, she gave up on the host and weaved through the tables, her face in sheer panic. Jess stood too. "What's wrong?"

"Forgive me for interruptin,' but yo' mama asked me to fetch you." Ruby's eyes were wide and locked on Wini's. "It's your father. He just returned home. Alone."

Wini didn't wait for Jess to escort her from the restaurant. The moment Ruby finished speaking, she raced through the dining room, out the front door, and down the road, heavy skirts lifted in her fists. At the base of the hill that led to their home, she stopped to catch her breath, hand pressed against the stitch in her side. A hank of hair had come loose from the pins and tumbled down her back.

Jess yelled her name. She hadn't meant to abandon him, but Ruby's declaration had punctured a bubble of emotions that had been fermenting under pressure for a year. Wini had to see her father. To ask him why some nuggets of gold were worth more than the health and safety of his family. To hear what had become of her brothers. Bracing herself, she continued up the hill to the house, hand nursing her aching side.

"Wini, wait." Jess reached her by the time she got to the door.

She turned to him, unsure what to say, unsure what to do with this tide of uncertainty looming over her. He grasped her hand and brought it to his lips, then pressed their tangled fingers to his chest. "I'll wait out here for you. Take all the time you need, just. . . I can't leave until I know you're all right."

A single tear escaped. She leaned her forehead against his cheek.

"You're a strong woman, Wini Hayes," he said. "You'll be all right."

Oh, how she'd needed to hear those words. Jeremiah, her father, her brothers, the four of them had always suppressed her growth. Jess encouraged it.

But there was no time to soak in what that meant for her

future. She put her hand to his face for only a moment, then went inside the house.

An old man was stretched out on the settee, head propped on her mother's prized pillow. Candles and a lantern lit the area, casting shadows across the room. Wini approached, stunned at how much her father had aged in the last year.

Mother walked in carrying a tray with a teapot and two cups. "I'm glad you're home. See to your father's tea."

With shaky hands, her mother rested the tray on a small table and went to her father's side. Wini concentrated on keeping her movements stiff, as to not spill the tea. Steam rose from the cups as her mother fussed over her father's condition. Eden walked in through the kitchen, declaring Dr. Pressman would come to examine Father as soon as he'd finished examining his growing line of patients. Carrie was absent. Upstairs with sleeping children, Wini presumed.

Wini paced the parlor as her mother helped her father sit up enough to drink. She rubbed his head and asked him how he fared, so casually, as if he'd never left. Wini wanted to scream.

Her mother's face grew sober. "How are our sons?"

"We. . ." Father cleared his throat, voice weak. "After four months of traveling, we purchased a small claim at the base of the Sierra Crest. A man told us he'd had all he wanted of prospecting but there was plenty left to get. By the time we paid him for the land and supplies, we barely had any money left."

He coughed. The deep rattle and longevity of it had Wini close to running from the house. What ailed him? How had he come home in this condition, and where were her brothers?

Fighting frustration, Wini dropped into a chair and gripped the arms.

Mother patted Father's back and encouraged him to drink

more. He obeyed, and a few minutes later, continued. "We soon discovered the man thought to swindle us. He believed he'd already found all the gold available at the site. Once we made a discovery, he came back, claiming we'd stolen his land. It took a good number of weeks to keep the man off our land. Time and energy wasted. After that, we struck it big."

"How big?" Mother fiddled with the handle of her teacup.

"We were the wealthiest prospectors in a ten-mile radius of our claim."

Yet here he was in ragged clothes and poor health with two absent sons. "What happened after that?" Wini asked.

"We were robbed on our way to San Francisco to deposit the gold in the bank."

Mother gasped.

Father held up a hand. "We were smart and divided the gold amongst our possessions. Some in our boots, some sewn into our clothes, some in our luggage, some secured on the underneath side of the wagon. They stole about half. May've had better luck had we just headed straight home east. We continued on to San Fran though, and that's when it really got bad."

"What do you mean, Jim?" Mother rubbed her chest.

Father adjusted his position on the settee, wincing. "The merchants there are overwhelmed, melting the gold into ingots and securing their businesses against theft. We had to wait. To pass the time, we had to live carefully. Not spend too much to avoid suspicion. That's when Jethro started frequenting the saloons. Picked up gambling."

He ran a hand down his face. "The boy won't be coming back. He took his share of the gold and his winnings from playing cards and purchased a general store. Plans to profit on all the men heading west or those too broke to leave and go home. Thinks many of them will decide to stay and work and will eventually send for their wives and children."

"Except for him." Carrie stepped from the shadows, barefoot and in her nightdress. Her dark stringy hair hung limp around her face. A letter dangled from her fingertips. "He won't be sending for me and the children. Says I'd never survive the journey. He's probably right."

The brokenness in her voice cracked Wini's heart wide open.

Carrie wiped her tears. "Says he'll send us money. That if, one day, I get stronger, he'll consider letting us join him."

Carrie broke on the last word, and she crumpled to the floor in sobs. Wini ran and dropped to her side, holding Carrie's head against her chest and rocking her.

Wini hated money. She hated gold. She hated the greed that poisoned a human heart and tore apart families.

Eden crept farther into the room, hands wrapped around her large belly. "And. . .my Crosley?"

Fear dangled in the air like a thick fog.

"He's on his way," Father said. Another long round of coughs ensued. "Stayed long enough to sell our claim. Should be about a month behind me. But he'll have to do the same as me. Use the rest of his share to get home."

Eden nodded, tears she'd been holding back escaping.

Wini looked around the room at the condition of her family. Once happy and prosperous, now full of regrets and broken dreams. Something deep within her snapped.

She stood, fists shaking, and buried them in the folds of her skirt. "And what of you, Father? Your health has declined to that of an invalid. One son lost. Another wandering. No occupation, no fortune. Was it worth it? What did you gain? What do you plan to do to make this right with your family? With your neighbors, who have supported us in your absence?"

Her bold and disrespectful actions surprised her. Had her outburst come a year earlier, her father would have put her in her place. Now, all of his retribution radiated in regretful eyes.

"I gained nothing but heartache. I'm not exactly sure how, but I'll spend the rest of my life making things right with my family. As for making it up to my neighbors, I brought him."

He lifted a bony finger to a shadow hovering in the corner. Wini's hand flew to her chest, and she stepped backward. How had she not noticed the man?

"Don't be alarmed, miss." The man walked into the center of the room, candlelight playing across his face. His wiry mutton-chops put Wini in mind of older men about town, but they belied his youth. Not a graying hair or wrinkle about him. "I am William Phelan, private investigator, Boston. I am here to expose the fraud of the Electrolytic Marine Salts Company."

Chapter Ten

Jess jerked awake at his shoulder being shaken.

The front porch chair creaked with his weight. Darkness had descended, illuminating a beautiful blanket of stars. Crickets sang in the distance. How many hours had passed while he'd waited for Wini?

He cleared the sleep from his throat. "How is he?"

"Not well." Her voice sounded small, defeated. He stood and reached for her hand. She came to him willingly. Now that her father was home, Jess planned to ask for her hand once the man was well enough to have the conversation.

"There's a man. Inside," she said. "Father met him on the coach and brought him home. He knows Fisher and Jernegan and claims he's here to expose their fraud."

Was he still dreaming?

"Did you say he knows them?" He grasped her upper arms and leaned close to see her face. "As in personally?"

"Yes. I told him we both worked there and suspected fraud. He wants to speak with you. We'll have to make it quick though. Mother is ready to get Father settled for the night."

Jess followed her inside to the parlor, lit by candles. A feeble man lay on the settee. Wini's father. Another man sat across the room, elbows perched on his knees, fingers steepled.

He introduced himself as William Phelan. "I understand you work for the marine salts company with Miss Hayes."

"I do," Jess answered. "How are you acquainted with the operation?"

"I met Charles Fisher at the A.I. Namm and Son dry goods store in Brooklyn, New York, a few years ago. He was a floorwalker."

Having never been to a large dry goods store like A.I. Namm, Jess asked, "What's a floorwalker?"

"Someone who walks the store, taking care of customer complaints and returns. Mr. Adolph Namm hired me to investigate Fisher's returns. I soon discovered that Fisher was approving returns for items that had never been purchased and the proceeds were finding their way back to Fisher through an accomplice who got a portion for his role in the scheme. After my report to Mr. Namm, he fired Fisher."

Mr. Phelan rotated his hat, brushing the brim against his fingertips. "Not long after, Mr. Namm called me again and said Mr. Fisher had returned, as a customer this time. He made a large purchase of household goods and paid for them to be shipped to Lubec, Maine."

Jess leaned closer. "So you followed him here."

Phelan lifted a shoulder. "Not exactly. Shortly after, I received a telegram from Fisher. He wanted to hire me this time."

"To investigate Namm?"

"To help him and Jernegan trick investors into believing gold can be extracted from sea water."

Wini sagged against Jess, and he slipped an arm around her waist. "It isn't possible then?"

Phelan placed the hat at his feet. "No."

"But then how are they doing it?" Jess asked.

"The accumulators. They're nothing more than cast-iron pots inside of buckets. They're lined with copper, and a thick layer of mercury is poured on top. To trick investors, Jernegan allowed them to pour mercury they'd purchased themselves into one of the accumulators. To give the illusion they were in control.

"From there they lowered it into the ocean where Fisher waited in a diving suit." Phelan paused for a breath. "I managed the line for Fisher to follow, while Fisher spilled the investors' mercury out and replaced it with new mercury already sprinkled with gold. The next day when the investors hauled the accumulator to the surface, they took it to the assayer of their choice to have it verified. Since the mercury contained gold, the investors gave up their money."

"Why did you do it?" Wini rubbed her eyes. Poor thing could hardly hold them open.

Phelan turned his face away. "Fisher knew I was desperate. My wife died of tuberculosis a year prior, and not long after, my nine-month-old son was diagnosed as well. I sent him to a sanatorium in hopes it would save his life. He was young, strong. With the right care, maybe he'd have a chance. I needed money, and fast."

Wini pressed a hand to her chest. "How is your son?"

Phelan swallowed. "He's with his mother."

A groan came from Eden's lips. Wini rested her head on Jess's shoulder.

Jess offered his condolences. "Why are you confessing now?" he asked.

"After my son died, I lost my mind for a good bit. Fisher and Jernegan cut me out because I was too distraught to continue my part. They paid me a sum to keep quiet. For nearly two years, I did. Now that I've come to my senses again, I want to be a man my wife and son can look down on from heaven and be proud of. They'll never be able to do that until I make this right."

"What do you plan to do?" Jess took a deep breath.

"Return the money I've received from this and encourage Fisher and Jernegan to turn themselves in."

Jess huffed. "Their coffers are fatter than a Thanksgiving turkey. You think they're just going to turn themselves in?"

"I'm going to offer them a chance to do it quietly. If they don't, I'll turn them and myself over to the authorities."

"How do we know you're actually going to do that?" Wini asked.

Phelan nodded. "Fair enough. For one, I escorted Mr. Hayes home. If I was planning to run, I wouldn't have revealed my identity. Two, I've told you everything you need to know about my part in the operation, so, again, if I planned to run, I wouldn't have done that."

Jess looked at Mrs. Hayes's pale face. "I believe him. All the same, I'd like to stay this evening as well, if you're agreeable, and offer you ladies my protection."

"That would be wonderful, Jess. I'll make you a pallet by the fireplace." Mrs. Hayes left the room to retrieve blankets.

Jess pointed at Phelan. "You have twenty-four hours to either convince the men to confess or turn them in. After that, you'll all three deal with me."

Was Wini's life reduced to mending and wet laundry?

She raised the sopping shirt in her fist and secured it to the line with a clothespin. Once word of the scheme got out, Wini was sure to lose her job. Mr. Phelan had left after breakfast that morning to find his accomplices. Jess had followed behind him to make sure he did so. Now, while they waited for what came next, Wini was taking over the boardinghouse laundry while her mother assisted Dr. Pressman with delivering Eden's baby. The pains had started at dawn, but Eden had said nothing until they'd grown more intense. By evening, there was sure to be another Hayes added to the family.

Would Father ever be well enough to continue fishing? How long would it take Crosley to return? Why had Jethro chosen to abandon his family for money? Yes, Carrie was difficult to care for, but Jethro had spoken promises to his wife before the entire town. Had made a covenant with God.

A dozen more questions ran through her mind as a shrill scream sounded from the open window upstairs. Wini began hanging clothes twice as fast. Any moment they might need her, and she didn't want to leave the task undone.

Three hours later, Eden was still laboring, her cries more frequent and much louder. Wini had finished the laundry and started loaves of bread rising on the windowsill. She paced the parlor while her father napped on the settee, waiting for news from either the doctor or from Jess.

She couldn't help wondering where their relationship would go from here. He'd received his pay, and once the scheme became public, he'd no longer need or want his job at the marine salts company. He'd return to logging, and where would that leave her? Alone, like she'd been after Jeremiah had alluded to marriage and then moved on to pursue business. She didn't want to go through that again. She didn't want to live a life like Carrie's, pining for a man she had no guarantee would return.

Of course, comparing Jess to Jeremiah or her brother, who'd never been satisfied sitting still, wasn't fair to Jess. Or herself. Maybe he'd ask for her hand in marriage. She'd have to leave her family to follow him wherever his logging took him. Could she leave her overworked mother with an ailing father who'd likely never work again with all those mouths to feed? Would that make her just like Jethro, wanting to escape to a better life?

Guilt clawed at her. Guilt she felt she shouldn't have to carry.

Wini stilled. The house had gone quiet.

She tiptoed across the rug, one ear angled toward the stairs. Seconds ticked by like an eternity, knotting Wini's insides. This was Eden's first child. What if something had gone wrong? What if Crosley returned to discover—

A tiny wail split the silence. Wini released the breath she'd been holding. A door opened and closed. Wini waited as her mother appeared at the top of the stairs.

Carrie appeared instead, Milton propped on her hip. Dressed in her best blue gingham, her hair brushed and pinned to perfection, Carrie descended the steps. Milton wore his finest knickers and socks, black shoes polished and hair combed to the side. He gnawed on his chubby fist, eyelids fighting to stay open. Isabelle peeked out from behind Carrie's skirts, thumb in her mouth. Wini commented on how nice they looked, then frowned at the suitcase in Carrie's other hand.

"Where are you going?" Wini pressed her hand to her throat.

"Home."

Wini hadn't heard Carrie speak with such conviction in months.

"I can't stay here any longer." Carrie looked up the stairs, a tear glistening in the corner of her eye. She sighed and turned back to Wini. "I'm going to live with my parents. When Jethro—" She looked down at her feet and swallowed. "If Jethro returns, tell him where I've gone."

Wini's heart sank. "Of course. Are you sure? How will you afford the coaches all the way to Portland?"

"I have some money saved aside. Enough to travel comfortably. Goodbye, Wini."

Wini blinked her tears away. She couldn't speak. Didn't know what to say. She was shocked that not only had Carrie rallied herself, but she'd hidden a secret stash of money this whole time that could've helped feed them on days when they had nothing but potatoes or beans.

Choosing forgiveness, Wini wrapped her arms around the pair she'd likely never see again and kissed Milton's salty cheek. "Goodbye, sweet one," she whispered. She hugged Isabelle next, asking her to promise to be a good girl.

Chin held high, Carrie walked to the front door and opened it, then looked at Wini one more time. The knob gave a small click behind them, stealing Wini's view. She stared at the doorknob, as if expecting it to perform some kind of miracle. Then she glanced into the parlor at her father, his chest still rising and falling in gentle breaths.

Footsteps sounded at the top of the stairs. "Wini?"

Mother.

"Oh, there you are."

Wini pivoted away from the door.

"Oh, don't look distressed. Eden is fine! You have a new niece. Her name is Alana Aurelian Hayes. She's simply beautiful." Mother dabbed at her eyes with a handkerchief. "Let me get her cleaned up and then you can see her."

Wini hadn't seen her mother smile in so long she wanted to bask in it for a while. She hated when Mother left to go back to Eden's room. Feeling small and weary, Wini sat on a step and buried her face in her hands.

Alana Aurelian—precious gold.

Chapter Eleven

Jess smoothed a hand over the back of his head as he walked toward the church. If only today were his wedding day and not just the day he planned to ask Wini's father for permission to marry her. True, they hadn't known each other long, but Jess wasn't wasting any more time. Not when he was certain that Wini was the woman for him.

He'd checked in with his crew. They were cleaning up the last of the stumps on Popes Folly, turning the remnants into ash for soap and potash. They'd soon set up camp between East and Sipp Bays for the winter. He wanted his bride secured and happy before the first snow.

He knew she'd worry about her family, especially with the new baby, her brother's refusal to return home, and Carrie leaving, but Jess planned to help them as much as possible until their financial situation improved.

The only thing left was for Wini to say yes.

A sizeable crowd gathered on the grass in front of the church. Jess checked his pocket watch. Strange. He'd have thought the congregation would be seated inside by now.

Mrs. Middling, the church pianist, was the first familiar face he saw. Something was definitely amiss if she wasn't already pounding the out-of-tune keys. Mr. Burke, who owned the general store, rushed away from his wife's side to a group several feet away. Was that Mr. Sager he was speaking to?

At the sound of his name, Jess spun, scanning the sea of faces. Wini hurried toward him, her skirts in one hand and her other hand bracing her hat. She looked lovely, even if the purple fabric was faded. "What's going on?" he asked as she neared.

"You haven't heard?"

Jess shook his head.

"Reverend Jernegan and Mr. Fisher refused to turn themselves in. Mr. Phelan revealed all while playing cards at the saloon last night. Word spread fast, and a group of men rallied together at the marine salts company to confront them, but they'd wiped their offices clean. Same for the small home they shared near the channel. They've taken everything—the money, the gold, most of the paperwork. Gone."

Jess was most furious that he hadn't seen this coming. Of course they'd run. Why had he given Phelan twenty-four hours?

"Has someone alerted the authorities?"

"Yes. Mr. Hearst at the bakery witnessed them leaving in their boat when he woke this morning. He lives near the pier. By the time the sheriff got to the docks, they'd vanished."

Jess looked around at the distraught and angry faces. An entire town and dozens of wealthy investors duped by a supposed minister and a sea merchant's son. Two soldiers of fortune who'd battled their fellow man's sensibilities and won.

Wini approached what was once the Electrolytic Marine Salts Company. Reporting to work after all that had happened over the weekend was silly, but she hadn't known what else to do. Her mind was heavy. Her heart confused. Her body exhausted. All this time, she'd thought when her father returned everything would go back to the happy times they'd once had. How naive she'd been.

How naive they'd all been. Over three hundred men were now unemployed. Almost every family in town had invested money they'd never see again. Wini had known from the first day she'd listened to Reverend Jernegan's speech on the town square that something wasn't right. She thought she'd help bring about justice, not watch the men of the town shrivel in regret.

If only they'd caught them sooner.

Wini stepped inside the office, and her breath caught. Papers were strewn about on the floor. Drawers had been dumped or left open. The door that led to the fenced area where the laboratory and work sheds were located swayed open in the breeze.

Jenny Eversoll entered from the hallway, clutching a stack of papers in her arms. She startled at the sight of Wini. "You frightened me."

"What happened?"

Jenny shivered and set down the papers. She crossed her arms and rubbed her palms up and down on them. "An angry mob of men busted in the door about an hour ago, hoping to get information out of Mr. Wimpleton. Seems he's disappeared too."

Guilty, or afraid it would all fall on him?

Wini looked around. "How can I help?"

Jenny shrugged. "The sheriff is dispersing the mob. He asked me to clean up in the meantime."

With no more words, they picked up items off the floor, righted the drawers, stacked the papers, and swept the remaining mess. All the while, Wini thought about Dr. Pressman's declaration that the sickness sweeping through the town was from the mercury Mr. Fisher had dumped into the sea. It affected the fish living in the channel, thus spreading to the people who ate it. Not only did Mr. Fisher and Mr. Jernegan owe a substantial amount of money to innocent people, they also had blood on their hands.

Wini walked from room to room to inspect the damage throughout the rest of the building, shaking her head at the open cabinet doors where all the important financial records had been kept. There'd be no proof of how much money was lost and to whom it was owed.

This town would never be the same.

Her boots clicked on the floor as she returned to the front. "Jenny?"

The back door creaked on open hinges. Where had Jenny gone so quickly? She wasn't in any of the rooms Wini had just passed. Had she gone home?

Wini grabbed the broom that was propped against a desk and swept a small pile they'd missed out the back door. The fenced property that was normally bustling with men was now deserted. Goose bumps skittered up her arms. Dark clouds jogged overhead. At that speed the rain was likely to pass over and hit Whiting instead.

As she turned away, her gaze snagged on the building marked LABORATORY and the sign underneath that read KEEP OUT. If the whole thing was a hoax, what had they been doing in there this whole time? Would there be any evidence that hadn't been taken in the men's escape to help the judge prosecute them?

Knowing she should leave the matter to the sheriff, she nevertheless rooted through the mess in Mr. Wimpleton's desk for the key and strode to the laboratory. Thunder rumbled above. She'd only stay a minute. Just long enough to see what was inside.

The stiff pins in the lock fought against Wini, but after a little wiggling, the key turned. A strong odor shocked her senses and made her take a step backward. She waved a hand in front of her face. Was that lingering from the mercury spill the other day? Unsure if she should tread farther, she thought of all the townspeople with lighter pocketbooks and made her choice.

She lifted a lantern that hung on the wall by the door and lit the wick. The flame flickered and a curl of black smoke swirled the glass. She adjusted the wick height and stepped into the lab.

Shelves lined with bottles surrounded the room. Two long tables in the middle nearly ran the entire length of the building. Wooden buckets took up space on one end. She held the lantern over them and peeked inside. A black pot rested in each with a thin layer of liquid silver covering the bottom. These must be the accumulators.

She sniffed. The strange odor wasn't coming from the mercury. Holding the lantern above her head, she walked around the room. Glass bottles and tubes were strewn about next to a large roll of copper wire. She tripped over something and tightened her grip on the lantern handle as she plowed into the corner of the table. Fighting back a howl, she rubbed her hip and looked down to find the culprit.

A pair of men's shoes.

The smell of smoke touched her nose, and she adjusted the wick again. Good thing she hadn't dropped the lantern, or the laboratory would be aflame. She toed the shoes out of her way and continued her inspection, rubbing her throbbing hip with each step.

The smell of smoke grew stronger. She held the lamp in front of her face and studied the wick. It couldn't be the lantern. A scuffle sounded behind her, and she turned, prepared to scream. Mr. Wimpleton appeared in the front doorway.

She released a breath.

"What are you doing in here?" he yelled.

Wini started to apologize but stopped. If this wasn't even a legitimate company, did he have the right to scold her?

His mustache bulged. That's when Wini noticed his disheveled hair, the dark circles under his eyes, and crooked tie. Poor thing must be as sick as everyone else.

"I'm sorry."

The burning smell grew stronger. She looked behind her in confusion before facing him again. "It's not your fault, Mr. Wimpleton. You didn't know it was a hoax."

He shook his head violently, then his gaze darted around and behind him. "I. . .I'm sorry."

Before she could blink, he grabbed the door handle, backed away, and slammed the door shut.

"Mr. Wimpleton!" She set the lantern on the table's edge, rushed to the door, and yanked the knob.

Locked.

"Mr. Wimpleton!" She screamed and banged her fists as the crackle of burning wood announced itself at the back of the building.

Tears streamed down her cheeks. No! This couldn't be happening. All she'd wanted to do was look inside the laboratory, not make it her grave. She screamed again and pounded her fists on the door until her hands buzzed with pain.

It was no use. The property was deserted.

God, help me.

She sank to the floor, her back against the door.

Why had she needed so badly to find answers? The answers to those questions that had run through her mind all morning no longer mattered now that she was going to die.

Chapter Twelve

"This may very well be proven the colossal swindle of the age."

Jess looked from the accumulator to the assayer's frown, then to the other employees gathered round the saloon. There was enough tension in the air to control the rise and fall of the tide. They had been told that sixty out of two hundred and sixty-four accumulators were pulled up every week, and each load contained around two thousand dollars' worth of gold. All two hundred and sixty-four accumulators had been pulled up in the last twenty-four hours, and not one held a speck of precious metal.

The other men in attendance grumbled.

Jackson Dillard pounded his fist on the table, making the assayer jump. "I say we threaten to string up this Phelan fellow until he talks some more. He's in on this. He's gotta know where Jernegan and Fisher took off to."

Someone whooped, and the crowd grew boisterous.

A whistle followed by a "hey" settled them to a dull roar. Sheriff Canon walked through the group like Moses parting the waters. He joined the assayer at the front, who had the green tinge of a seasick shipmate. The sheriff held up his hand.

"William Phelan will remain in custody until the judge in Machias can hear his case and decide his fate. Until then, you all better obey the law, so you don't end up on trial as well. As for Prescott Jernegan, I have on record that after emptying his bank account in Manhattan and purchasing several bonds, he sailed out yesterday morning with his wife and son on the steamship *Navarre* under a false name. We believe he's headed to France."

"What of Fisher?" someone yelled.

"We're not sure yet." Sheriff Canon raised his hand again as the noise in the room got louder. "However." He waited for silence. "Mr. Shanahan will see to your pay on Thursday next. The marine salts company's president, A.B. Ryan, has been exonerated of any wrongdoing and is transporting funds to the Lubec Bank & Trust as we speak."

Jackson Dillard stepped forward. "If he's the company's president, how can he be exonerated?"

"According to his bank records, he's also an investor. He's lost a lot of money that will probably never be recouped. Captain Tremaine of the Boston Police says Mr. Ryan is as ill about all this as everyone else."

"Somebody's gotta pay," an angry man Jess didn't recognize shouted. "What about this Wimpleton fella? He took care of the books. He had to have known."

Indeed. Jess suspected the man was behind his falsified banknote.

"Now, now." Sheriff Canon adjusted his hat. "I know you're all itching for a hanging, but that's not how we do things in my town. Andrew Wimpleton has fled his property as well, but as soon as we find him, he will be detained, questioned, and prosecuted if he's found guilty."

"Running away proves he's guilty."

"Sheriff!" A feminine voice broke through the room. "Sheriff Canon."

A hand waved behind the men's heads in the back.

"Yes, ma'am?" The sheriff moved forward, and so did the woman. The room went quiet. "Ah, yes, Miss Eversoll. How can I assist you?"

"Mr. Wimpleton is back. I saw him at Klondike One." She fiddled with the cameo at her throat. "He was pouring some kind of liquid around the base of the laboratory. I think he plans to burn it down. I came as soon as I saw him."

Men moved into action. Jess started for the door when he saw Miss Eversoll stop the sheriff. "Wini Hayes. She was there too. Helping me clean up. Make sure she's safe."

Jess broke into a sprint, shoving people aside so he could exit. He'd make sure she was safe or die trying.

Wini held a handkerchief to her nose and took slow, shallow breaths. Angry flames licked at the boards of the back wall. She crouched low with her back against the door, her fingernails torn and sore from trying to claw her way out. A hot tear ran down her cheek. Her father, her brothers, Jernegan and Fisher—disciples of greed that destroyed people's lives. The prestige, the comfort, the satisfaction of material wealth—none of it was worth it. It would all burn with a fervent heat one day, just as the Bible said.

Until then, she would.

It was getting harder to breathe. She rested her head on the dirt floor and closed her eyes. All the fruits of life she'd never get to enjoy played in her mind. Any moment, she'd feel the pain.

Something banged against the door. Wini would've thought she was dreaming, but the sensation jarred her back. And again. Someone was trying to break down the door. "Help me!" she screamed. Racking coughs choked her words.

The door's center split. She moved out of the way as best she could without moving too far into the smoke. Another bang and the door split further but didn't break. Wini sent a prayer heavenward. Another bang and the door splintered into pieces.

The heat of the fire intensified, making Wini's skin feel as if it were melting off her body. She leaped for the opening as smoke rolled out around her. Coughing and sputtering, she felt hands grab her and drag her away. She floated in and out of consciousness, unsure where they were taking her.

"Wini?" Someone smacked her gently and consistently on the cheek. "Wini, sweetheart, wake up."

Annoyed, Wini swatted the hand away, her eyes rolling open to see Jess's smiling face. "There's my girl."

He cradled her to his chest. Her weak arms circled his neck. She was alive. God had answered her prayer. Now if He would make her lungs stop burning.

"Here." Jenny Eversoll turned Wini's chin and held a cup of water to her lips. Cold droplets spilled all around and soaked Wini's dress, but it eased the pain in her throat. After she took the last sip, a round of coughs ensued.

Jess patted her back. "You all right?"

Wini nodded, and another tear rolled down her face.

"I'm here now." Jess held her face between his hands. "And I'm never letting you go."

"Never?" Wini rasped.

"Never." He kissed her forehead, muttering a prayer of thankfulness. "Marry me, Wini. As soon as we can arrange it. I know a logging camp isn't the gilded castle you deserve, but I'll make you happy. I swear it."

She didn't need a castle. Just being alive and in his arms made her happy. "I don't want a castle. You're all I need."

He kissed her. She started coughing, and he patted her back. "Sorry, I couldn't help myself."

Wini nodded through the discomfort, watching Sheriff Canon escort Mr. Wimpleton off the premises, his wrists bound by rope. Life was too short and too fragile to be enslaved by greed. The entire town of North Lubec now felt that truth to its core. Wini rested her head against Jess. Of all that happened, she was the one to strike it rich.

AUTHOR'S NOTE

I hope you enjoyed Jess's and Wini's story centered around the real hoax that rocked the town of Lubec, Maine. To fit my story's timeline, I had to change the decade in which it happened, along with a few minor details I hope readers will forgive me for.

The hoax actually started in 1887 around the time of the Alaskan gold rush. To make it fit within the boundaries of my timeline, I centered it around the California gold rush. Prescott Ford Jernegan really was a Baptist minister from Martha's Vineyard, and he and Charles Fisher were childhood friends. Both were sons of wealthy sea merchants and both are recorded as being mischievous since boyhood. William Phelan really was a private investigator hired by A. I. Namm to investigate Fisher's dealing at the dry goods store and was later brought in on the hoax. He didn't get too deep into the hoax before backing out. He later revealed publicly how Jernegan and Fisher pulled off the hoax; however, it was too late.

While Jess and Wini are entirely fictional, along with the rest of the secondary characters in the story, the details of the hoax are historically accurate to the best of my knowledge and research, except for the following.

Phelan's backstory about a wife and child with tuberculosis is entirely fictional. Research didn't turn up much on the man, and I needed to give him a reason for joining the hoax.

Mr. Wimpleton didn't really exist, nor did the burning of the laboratory. I added both to enrich the plot.

There is no record of anyone getting sick or dying from the mercury that was dumped into the ocean, but with the knowledge we have today, it's plausible some folks were affected without understanding the cause.

The Lubec Packing Company (the cannery that Jeremiah Farthington owned in the story) wasn't founded until 1880. It employed entire families in need of employment and served the community for many years. Jeremiah is a fictional character.

Before lobster became a delicacy, their prominent presence in Maine waters made it cheap and convenient to feed them to prisoners. Yes, at one time in history, prisoners were fed lobster for every meal, and later, a law was passed to limit the serving to prisoners to a few times a week.

Lubec, Maine is one of my favorite places to vacation, and it saddened me to learn of the "gold to sea water hoax" that rocked the town two centuries earlier. However, once I learned of the deception, I knew I had to write a story about it.

Lubec is as far east in the United States as one can travel and offers many delights from nature to history to lighthouses to amazing food. If you enjoyed the setting of coastal Maine, you can visit again in many of my other books with stories ranging from WWII to present day. See a complete list at www.candicesuepatterson.com.

If you'd like more about Lubec specifically, try *Saving Mrs. Roosevelt*, part of Barbour's Heroines of WWII series.

Thank you for taking time out of your busy life to spend it with my characters. Readers are the best!

Candice Sue Patterson studied at The Institute of Children's Literature. She lives in Indiana with her husband and three sons in a restored farmhouse overtaken by books. When she's not tending to her chickens, snuggling with her Great Pyrenees, or sharing her passion for reading with students as an elementary school librarian, she's working on a new story. Candice writes Modern-Vintage Romance—where the past and present collide with faith. Find out more at www.candicesuepatterson.com.

Winter Roses

BY PEGG THOMAS

Dedication

This book is dedicated to the flannel-clad workforce of the 1800s who transformed Michigan from a land covered in forest to a rich farmland that is still the United States' top producer of asparagus, tart cherries, chestnuts, pickling cucumbers, and potatoes for potato chips. At the same time, Michigan boasts twenty million acres of managed forests and is the fifth largest timberland in the nation, growing nearly twice what is harvested.

And to my granddad, Leonard Earl Lewis, who took me for long walks down the tote road behind the cabin near Pine Stump Junction in Michigan's beautiful Upper Peninsula. Granddad was the best of storytellers and filled my ears with countless hours of history about our state. Love you and miss you every day.

Chapter One

December 10, 1865

He wasn't about to let a narrow doorway and a duffel bag bulging with all his worldly possessions trap him aboard the *Atlantic*. Wesley Fisk was a man of solid ground and strong horses. He'd charged onto many a battlefield. But booming cannons and screaming Confederates were nothing compared to the vessel under his feet. The overgrown washtub had lurched, groaned, and smashed into floating hunks of ice that should have sunk it to the bottom of Lake Huron. He'd been warned the trip could be hazardous this late in the season, but he'd wanted to save time.

In the future, he'd stick to horses, slower or not.

In the passageway barely wider than the door, he braced his feet and heaved on the duffel bag until it popped through the entrance. It smacked into him mid-chest, and he staggered back a step—right into someone else.

"Umph!"

Out of the corner of his eye, he caught the glimpse of a dark blue cap even in height with his own.

He said, "Pardon me, sir—"

"Sir!"

That one word carried a caisson's weight of outrage. It also held distinctly female tones.

Uh-oh.

Wes twisted around as best he could in the cramped passageway. The *Atlantic* hadn't been built for men his size.

"My pardon, ma'am. I didn't see you."

In his defense, it was dark in the passageway, and she was covered in a plain dark blue coat that hung below her knees and matched the knitted cap. Besides, no woman had a right to be that tall. But one look in her stormy gray eyes, just inches from his own, convinced him to keep that observation to himself.

"Perhaps you could move along so I can disembark." The flinty voice matched her eyes.

"Yes, ma'am. I'm truly sorry to have—"

"It's miss, not ma'am."

Could he say nothing right? He touched the front of his cap in a half-salute, hugged his long duffel bag to his chest, and waddled down the passageway toward freedom. Freedom from the confines of the floating coffin, freedom from the war he'd left behind, and freedom from sticking his foot in his mouth regarding the woman on his heels.

Orange and purple sky greeted him as he stepped through the passageway opening and onto the deck. Breathing in the scents of sawdust, woodsmoke, and fish, he could hardly wait for his boots to strike solid ground again. But he stepped to the side and skidded on the icy planks of the boat.

"Be careful, miss, it's slippery." He extended his hand. "Can I assist you down?"

She took his measure from the top of his ratty wool cap to the toes of his brand-new boots. From the set of her lips, he'd not met her standards. She pulled her thick coat aside and breezed past him with a curt, "No, thank you."

Out in the open, he shouldered the duffel and followed her down the gangplank to the dock. Two steps and he floundered again, slipping and staggering to catch his balance even though the gangplank was free of ice. From ahead of him came a muffled snicker. He braced his legs, regained his balance, and then marched on, carefully watching where he put each foot. He stepped off the gangplank to the dock and had another moment of disorientation.

"It's called finding your land legs." The woman's voice held less flint and more humor this time. She glanced over her shoulder. "You obviously haven't sailed often."

"Not ever." The truth slipped out before he could think better of it.

A smile tugged at one corner of her mouth.

He pulled his attention away from her lips and to his new surroundings. It'd taken the better part of four days from Buffalo, New York, to reach this bustling port in Michigan. A sign at the end of the dock, hanging a little askew, read WELCOME TO ALPENA. At least he'd landed in the right place.

The tall woman waited at the foot of the dock, holding a large carpetbag in each hand, and ignored the ruckus of men rushing around unloading barrels and crates from the *Atlantic*. The boat was lashed down fast, and sailors poured from its decks. It appeared the captain was a man of his word. Captain Pratt had made sure Wes understood the boat would not be returning south. It'd stay the winter at port and not sail again until the ice cleared in the spring. Whenever that might be. Not that it mattered.

For Wesley Fisk, there was no going back.

Where was Louie? Eliza Beth Edmonds refrained from tapping her toe at the end of the dock. Refined women did not tap their toes in public. She'd spent too many months at Boyd's Young Ladies' Seminary to lose her poise over that oaf from the *Atlantic*.

The stranger was behind her, gawking as if he'd never seen a port before, and she'd rather not draw his attention again, so she turned her face away. Being mistaken for a man had put the crowning insult on two weeks of crushing disappointments. She didn't wish to rehash it.

"Miss?"

She closed her eyes and took a deep breath before facing the stranger again. After all, being rude was something refined women never were. When she opened her eyes, the wide red stripe down the sides of his trousers knocked the breath from her.

Union blue trousers. With sergeant's stripes.

She gritted her teeth for a moment before loosening them to issue a curt response. "Yes?"

He pulled the cap from his head, releasing a thick mat of sable waves that contrasted pleasantly with his hazel eyes. "I'm sorry for the misunderstanding."

She nodded, once more resisting the urge to tap her toes.

"You seem to know this place. I was wondering if you could point me in the direction of a hotel."

The tension eased a bit from her shoulders. After all, it wasn't like *this* veteran would be taking her job away. "I've been away for several months, but the new hotel on Chisholm Street should be finished by now. I heard they were to call it the Alpena House."

"Chisholm Street." He mashed the cap in his hands, his ridiculously large sack leaning against his hip. "And where might that be?"

She turned and pointed as a voice rang out.

"Eliza Beth!" Seated on a high-wheeled cart, Louie waved one hand above his head.

"Looks like you've got a ride," the man said.

"Yes. If you'll excuse me." She walked to where Louie was stopping the cart.

"Golly, am I glad you're here." Louie's words were quick and tense. "There's been an accident."

The blood drained from Eliza Beth's face, leaving her even colder than the December wind off Lake Huron.

"It's your ma." Louie's usually mischievous face was pulled into stressful lines.

Eliza Beth dropped her bags and clutched at her coat's collar. "What's happened?"

"Don't rightly know. Someone found her on the floor when they came in for supper. I went straight to Doc's house first—did you know we have a doctor now?—then here to fetch you. So let's get you aboard."

Eliza Beth fumbled with her coat and skirts to mount the cart.

"Let me help you." The man from the boat steadied her. She grasped his hand while his other came behind her and tugged her coat free of the wheel's hub. "There you go." Once she was seated, he handed her carpetbags to Louie. "I hope everything turns out all right."

She glanced down and murmured, "Thank you," as Louie slapped the reins, sending old Buster down the street at a fast trot.

"Can't you go any faster?"

"Not in town, it ain't safe." Louie shot her a look that said he understood. "And not much faster outside of town. Buster raced all the way here, and it's getting too dark." He shrugged his narrow shoulders. "I'm real sorry, Eliza Beth. Real sorry."

She gripped his shoulder. "I know. Thank you for getting the doctor first."

Last week's dismissal at the school had been the low point in her life. She'd been sure it couldn't get any worse. How wrong she'd been. Fumbling to remember a suitable prayer, she closed her eyes and mentally whispered, *Please Lord*, over and over as the cart left the town streets to bounce along the frozen ruts of an old tote road.

Ma was all she had left.

Chapter Two

Dawn had barely broken the horizon as Eliza Beth wiped the last plate and stacked it away. She stretched, pressing her fist against her lower back. Wrangling a classroom of wiggly students was its own exercise, but it didn't prepare a body for life in the lumber camp. Even so, she'd toughen to the work soon enough. Muscles she'd taken for granted a few years ago would return, and she'd be her old self.

Stuck in a lumber camp.

She shook the creases out of her towel and hung it on a rod over the massive black cookstove, then entered the room behind the stove. "Ma?"

"Everything all done?"

"Yes. All cleaned and put away. I'll start the midday meal soon. I'm soaking salt pork to fry. There's plenty of bread and cheese to go with it. They'll have to make do with a cold meal today."

"Don't forget the coffee."

Lumberjacks would work their fingers to the bone for a cup of Ma's black-as-midnight coffee boiled in the huge cauldron that took two hands to lift. "I won't forget. How are you feeling?"

"Embarrassed to be lying abed while my daughter does all the work."

"You gave everyone quite a scare."

Ma grimaced. "Gave myself a bit of one too. I've been a mite tired—"

"Exhaustion, the doctor said. That's something more than a mite tired."

"Well, at least you're here now to share the burden." Ma sighed, a heavy lifting and lowering of her shoulders. "I can't tell you how much I appreciate it."

"I only wish I'd come straight away and not wasted a week."

"You had things to put in order, and I doubt you'd have found a vessel coming north any sooner this time of year."

Ma was right. Eliza Beth had been very lucky to catch the *Atlantic*. Otherwise, she'd have had to piece together a route of railroad and hired horse, if not walking on her own two feet, to get here. That would've taken far longer.

"Do you need anything?"

Ma shook her head, eyelids drooping.

"I brought some books with me. I could read to you for a while."

"Why don't you take a walk to the river?" Ma's voice trailed off at the end.

Eliza Beth's favorite place had always been the river, but did she want to see it again?

"Go on. Get it over with." Understanding filled Ma's face, deepening the wrinkles that lined her cheeks. "You'll see it hasn't changed."

"It's just. . ."

Ma grasped her hand and squeezed. "I know. But you and he always loved the river. And he'd be the first to tell you not to resent it. He'd tell you to go there, make peace with it. Say a prayer and think of him."

Could she?

"Go on."

"You're sure you'll be fine while I'm gone?"

"You won't be long. Go."

Eliza Beth undid her apron and pulled on her thick coat. Not the neat blue wool she'd arrived in, but the old coat Ma had kept for her. One with almost as many patches as original fabric. Her camp coat. She traded her shoes for a pair of thick boots and headed out the door.

Snow had fallen during the night, and the sun made crystal sparkles everywhere. The camp still looked new, the logs of the buildings not yet grayed with age and retaining much of the bark in places. Bubbles of sap had hardened on their cut ends. It wasn't the camp she'd left. That camp had run out of forest last year. This one was much farther from town.

Much more isolated.

She pulled the coat closer around herself, paused to listen, and turned to her left. She followed the sound of the river to its banks. It was a short fall from where she stood to the deceptively calm water below. The land rose upstream where the *thwack* of axes cut through the crisp air. The men would line the banks there with huge logs, ready to roll them into the river come spring, then float them down to the mills at Alpena.

As much as it hurt, she let her mind drift to the previous spring when she'd been finishing her studies downstate and Pa was one of the men at the river by the old camp. He'd been a sawyer, one of the best, but in the spring they all helped to get the logs into the river. Nobody was sure just how it happened, whether his clothing had gotten caught, or maybe his foot, but in one swift and awful moment, Pa had tumbled with the logs.

The men had done their best to get to him, but with the logs clogging the surface, they'd been unable to find him in time. Quite likely, the logs had crushed him before he ever got to the river. It still hurt to look upon the smooth surface and think about Pa trapped underneath it, unable to get to air.

Sunshine hit the water, and it flashed, as if aimed right at her. Like a wink from Pa. Her throat closed, but no tears came. Ma was right. Pa wouldn't want her to blame the river.

Or the lumber camp.

"I'll try, Pa."

She'd returned to Alpena against her choosing but was now thankful to be there for Ma. She drew in a long breath and let it out in twin streams of white vapor. It was time to start the midday meal. The lumberjacks needed to eat, and it was up to Eliza Beth to feed them. She marched back to the cook shanty with determined steps.

Between cooking and cleaning and tending to Ma, she'd have little time to mope over losing her teaching position.

She hoped.

Wes tapped his pocket and barely heard the faint crinkle of an envelope through his thick coat. He was used to early cold weather, coming from upstate New York, but he hadn't planned on walking so far through the wilderness. In new boots. He was a teamster, a horseman, and all the walking had rubbed more than his heels the wrong way.

He'd been out since first light and had been tempted to turn around when a faint whiff of woodsmoke reached him. Had he found the place? His weary legs and sore heels discovered a new burst of energy as he rounded a thicket of brambles clogged with snow and last fall's stubborn leaves. Beyond it, a settlement of crude buildings came into view.

At last.

Smoke poured from one of the two long buildings—the cook shanty, no doubt. The other long low building would be the bunkhouse. There were four square shelters for livestock, with pole corrals around them, and another building that probably held the blacksmith and carpenter tools. In all, it looked much like the lumber camps he'd seen before the war when he and Pa had delivered horses.

He hitched his duffel bag higher against his back and made for the only building with any sign of life. He was halfway there when the sound of axes reached him. The crew would have been working since daybreak, as soon as there was enough light to see by, if they were like the crews in New York. He glanced at the sky. The sun was close to its zenith.

His stomach grumbled. He'd arrived at a good time.

The door to the cook shanty opened as he reached it. A huge black kettle filled the doorway. He dropped his duffel bag and grabbed the kettle's long, curved handle.

"Oh!" The woman from the boat stared back at him, her gray eyes wide.

"Miss? Here, let me." He took the rest of the weight of the kettle, freeing her hands.

She blinked. "Why are you here?"

"How is your Ma?" They spoke over each other.

"She's going to be fine. But what are you doing here?"

"If this is Stanley Rabeau's outfit, I'm hiring on."

Her mouth dropped open for a moment, then snapped shut. She tipped her chin toward a platform on skis that had been pulled up next to the door. "Might as well start. Put the coffee cauldron on the sled. You can help me get the midday meal to the men."

Wes did what she said. Might as well get used to taking orders, especially if she was the cook. She reappeared with crates of food she stacked on the sled.

"Come on. They'll be hungry."

He stowed his duffel bag in the shanty, then grabbed the sled's rope and dragged it after her retreating figure, trotting to catch up with her long-legged stride. She really was too tall for a woman.

"We didn't meet properly yesterday, miss. I'm Wesley Fisk. Friends call me Wes."

Her stride never lessened, but she shot him a glance. "Nice to meet you, Mr. Fisk. You may call me Miss Edmonds."

So much for friendly. The young man on the cart had called her Eliza Beth. Not Elizabeth, but Eliza Beth. Odd. It fit her though. Not common. Not exactly pretty but handsome enough. And a force to be reckoned with, unless he missed his guess.

"One good thing about having an early snow," she said, interrupting his study of her, "we can use the sled to take out the midday meal."

"Is the snow early here?"

She shot him another look. "Didn't think you sounded local."

"No, miss. I come from New York."

Her step faltered for a moment. "The city?"

He grinned. Seemed everyone asked him that. "No, miss. In the north, an area like this. At least, it used to be. Now most of the trees are gone." And with them the customers who had purchased Pa's hearty draft horses.

She gave a curt nod and strode on, ignoring him.

It wasn't as if he were there to make a good impression on a woman—any woman. No, sir. He had one goal for the winter, to make himself some serious money. He needed a good stake to set up a horse-raising operation of his own. Be his own businessman. He wanted to raise things instead of blasting them to pieces.

And everybody knew that business and women didn't mix.

Chapter Three

Eliza Beth parked the sled and carried the empty crates into the cook shanty. If the men had been unhappy with the cold meal, they hadn't let on. She'd make it up to them tonight by baking pies this afternoon, if Ma had apples on hand.

"Eliza Beth?" Ma called.

"Coming." She dumped the last armload on a table and stripped off her coat before entering their room at the end of the building. At least it had two beds and even a window cut through the thick logs to let in the natural light.

"Do you need anything?"

"Mostly just to see you." Ma pushed herself up in bed. "Sit and rest a while."

Eliza Beth's muscles almost audibly sighed as she sagged onto the surprisingly comfortable mattress of her narrow bed.

"How did it go?"

"Fine. The men didn't complain."

Ma snorted. "Not likely they would. Hungrier than spring bears, they are."

"They work hard for it though."

"We have a half hour or so before we need to start on supper."

"I'll do it. You need to—"

Ma held up her hand. "I can sit and peel potatoes or something else. I won't lie abed while you work yourself to death."

"Like you almost did?" When had Ma become so. . .old? The grooves in her face were deeper, her iron-gray hair thinner, and while she'd never been a hefty woman, now her shoulder bones almost poked through the robe she wore. If Eliza Beth hadn't returned. . .

But she had. Almost kicking and screaming the entire way, so caught up in her own miseries that she'd never once thought about Ma in the camp slaving away by herself. If her youngest brother, Leon, were still here, she'd boot him into next week for running off to join their two older brothers in Wisconsin.

Ma sighed. "I should have asked for help. Mr. Rabeau would have spared a man, I'm sure. I was too prideful, but I've learned my lesson."

"Leon shouldn't have left."

"Don't go blaming your brother. He's got the pine in his veins, just like Henry and Christopher." She sighed. "Just like your pa."

"He should have stayed until. . . Well, he should have stayed."

"It was hard for him here, being seen as the camp boy for so many years. Better he move to a new camp where he'll be seen as one of the men. Easier for him that way."

"Louie stayed."

"He's younger than Leon. Now that Mr. Rabeau has assigned him to the skidding crew, I expect he'll be moving on come spring."

"I'm just glad I'm here now."

"But this isn't where you want to be either." Ma's eyebrows rose just enough to let Eliza Beth know that she wouldn't settle for less than a fully honest response.

"Not because I don't want to be with you." That was true. She'd thought she'd be able to bring Ma to live with her by her third or fourth year of teaching. That she'd be able to afford a modest house and support them both. "But after all the studying, all the exams passed, all the preparation, setting up my very own classroom, and then to lose my position like that."

Ma's eyebrows rose. Eliza Beth sighed, not wanting to rehash all the circumstances that led her back to the woods.

"To a man who walked away from it, who'd been gone for years. And then he returned, and I was let go without a thought." Bitterness crept into her voice, but she couldn't stop it.

"Oh, honey." Ma patted her arm. "The men coming back home still have families to feed and clothe and house. They need their jobs back. And after all, don't we owe them for the risks they took and time they sacrificed for our country?"

"Of course we do!" Eliza Beth pushed to her feet and moved to the window, gazing out at the snowy camp. She waited until she had her emotions in check, then turned around. "But didn't they owe me something too? For stepping in and teaching their children?"

Ma rose and came to her side. "They paid you an honest wage for honest work, which you gave them. They don't owe you anything else, Eliza Beth. That's not how things are."

"Maybe it's how things should be."

"Most young women find a good man and settle down."

"I won't find one here." She wasn't going to marry a lumberjack. That much was certain. Living in town, seeing him on Sundays—if the camp was close enough—or hiring on as the camp cook and living in the middle of it all. Ma had done both while raising her and her three brothers. Lumbering was grueling work and dangerous. A poorly felled tree, a snapped chain, or a log slide could leave a woman a widow in moments. As it had Ma.

Eliza Beth didn't want any part of it.

"You never know. God has a way of putting people in our paths when we least expect it." She gave Eliza Beth a hug. "But the men won't be looking favorably on either of us if we don't get supper cooking."

"You can sit and peel apples, if there are any. I'll make pies this afternoon."

"There are plenty in the cold bins. The men will love you for it." Ma winked. "Who knows where that might lead? I'll get dressed and join you."

Eliza Beth tied on her apron and entered the main room of the shanty.

Ma and Pa had been happy with lumber camp life. She was sure of that. But the only man who'd come across her path whom she hadn't known since childhood was that oaf from the *Atlantic*. She snorted in a very unladylike way.

It would snow in July before she'd ever look at a man who mistook her for a *sir*.

A low groan escaped as Wes slipped from the back of the horse he'd ridden into camp. He was careful to not tangle in the harness. Alderic Aube, the older teamster he'd worked alongside, had walked beside his team, but Wes's raw heels appreciated the lift. After a long day of hauling sleighs piled with logs, the weary horse hadn't objected to a rider. Wes gave the mare a good scratching before he tied the team and began unharnessing.

The equipment was top notch, and he appreciated that. Nothing worse than working with inferior equipment. Accidents happened when harnesses or chains broke, and an accident while hauling tons of timber meant almost certain death, if not for the man at the reins, for the horses.

And horses were harder to replace than men.

He could almost feel the other man's eyes on him as he stripped off the harnesses and hung them in the shelter where Alderic had lit a lantern. He ran his hands as well as his eyes over the leather, chains, and buckles for any sign of undue wear or weakness.

The old man grunted and handed him a currycomb and a rag.

Wesley brushed and rubbed each animal. The smell of horses without the added whiff of gunpowder took him back years. Back to happier times. The muscles across his chest and shoulders relaxed with the rhythmic motions.

Alderic's rusty voice cut the evening air. "You done a good job handling Berry and Bright."

He grinned at the old man. It hadn't escaped Wes's notice that the team of young mares was a little rough around the edges. But he wasn't intimidated by that. The newest man on the crew wouldn't get the best team in camp. He patted them each on the rump before turning them out into the corral.

The best of horses had some fight in them. He liked that. Charging across the battlefield with a team pulling a limber and caisson loaded with powder and cannonballs required horses with grit in their bones and the bit in their teeth.

Wes gathered armfuls of hay and tossed them over the fence. He was dusting off his clothing when movement caught his attention. Across the corral, a figure was stroking the face of a horse. A womanly figure. A tall, womanly figure.

His stomach rumbled. Haulers and landing men were always the last to come in for supper, and then the haulers had to care for their horses before they could eat. It was full dark, and he wouldn't have seen Miss Edmonds if not for the light coming from the blacksmith's shack. He ought to apologize once more so they could get off on better footing. In camp, it was paramount to keep the cook—or cooks—happy. Army camp or lumber camp, those in it wanted their meals tasty, filling, and timely.

She was slipping something to the horse as he approached. The scents of cinnamon and baked goods clung to her.

"What are you feeding him?"

She startled, the snow having silenced his footsteps.

"Nothing bad."

"I didn't assume—"

"Didn't you?" She fairly bristled, like a poked porcupine.

"Miss Edmonds, I only came over to say once again how sorry I am for how we met." He pulled his cap off. It may be a lumber camp and cold to boot, but Ma had drilled manners into him. "I hope you can forgive me for my clumsiness." Best not to mention that other mistake. Wes didn't know much about women, growing up in a family of boys and stepping into the army as soon as he was old enough, but he wasn't a complete fool.

"Right. Of course." She glanced around him toward the bunkhouse. "Mr. Aube doesn't approve of me slipping the horses treats, but we baked apple pies today. Buster enjoys the cores." She smiled, the first he'd seen. Even in the dark, it transformed her. "Buster is my favorite. When I was young, he'd let me ride him around the corral."

In the dim light, Wes could just make out the smattering of white hairs in the old horse's face, the prominence of his hip bones and withers.

Eliza Beth Edmonds rose mightily in his estimation right then. Any woman who'd buck old Alderic to feed apple cores to an aging horse was his kind of—

"He bothering you, Eliza Beth?" Louie materialized beside her, squinting through the dark at Wes, fists tight at his sides.

"It's all right. He saw me feeding Buster."

The young man's stance relaxed a bit—but not too much. "I'll walk you back to the cook shanty if you're done."

With a nod in his direction, Miss Edmonds left with Louie.

So that was how things were.

Chapter Four

The scent of fried doughnuts lingered in the cook shanty as Eliza Beth swabbed off the tables one last time. Sundays were the only days the men didn't work. Most didn't come in for breakfast, preferring to sleep as long as possible. They needed it after a rowdy Saturday night of music and storytelling, dancing and laughter. The camp was too far from town for regular visits, but last night three wives and their children had arrived in a wagon. Possibly the last time they'd make it through before the snow got too deep.

Ma rested in one of the chairs the men used when they played music on Saturday nights. Eliza Beth joined her, plopping into another chair.

"All done."

"Until we start again."

Eliza Beth snorted. "It's not fair that we don't get at least one day a week off like the men do."

"Then who would feed them?" Ma shrugged. "And besides, we don't work nearly as hard as they do."

"Hard enough that you collapsed just a week ago. On a Sunday, no less." Why did Ma refuse to see the discrepancy in the expectations placed on men and women?

"Even so, it's not as if we're felling trees or skidding logs or handling the cant hooks."

Maybe Ma had a point, but the endless cycle of cooking, serving, and scrubbing never ended. Until summer. Come summer, maybe Eliza Beth could find a job in town, something that would pay enough for her and Ma to live together. If not teaching, maybe in a store. She was smart enough to keep books and good with numbers. They'd have an easier life. Ma especially.

Shouts erupted outside.

Eliza Beth went to the window. The lumberjacks stood in a group waving their arms and calling out a welcome.

Ma joined her. "What on earth?"

The jingle of bells reached them through the thick walls, and then a sled pulled by five dogs came into view.

"Who is that?" she asked Ma.

"I suppose a tinker. We haven't had one come by on a Sunday for weeks." She pressed closer to the window. "I don't recognize this one."

A tinker. A connection to the world outside of camp.

"What do you wish he's brought, Ma? What do you need?"

"I have no needs at present. How about you?"

Eliza Beth let her fingers trail down the cold glass. "I hope he's brought news."

"I've yet to meet a tinker who didn't." Ma chuckled. "How much of it is the gospel truth is another thing."

Gospel truth or not, Eliza Beth was starved for news of the outside world. The lumber camp was its own little world, removed from civilization by distance, weather, and the lack of hours in a day to pursue anything other than the lumber industry and all it took to bring the massive trees to market.

"Let's go see." Eliza Beth ran to their room and fetched their coats, her nice blue coat instead of her everyday patched one. They joined the men circling the narrow sled piled with trunks of different sizes.

The new tinker was a handsome man, fully as tall as Mr. Fisk, with a closely trimmed beard. He was all smiles as he talked and laughed with the men.

Mr. Rabeau stood beside the tinker and gestured to Ma and Eliza Beth.

"Here are our cooks. You'll find none better in the county, perhaps not in the state. This is Mrs. and Miss Edmonds."

The tinker swiped off his cap, exposing curling hair the color of seasoned red oak. "Ladies, it's good to meet you. I'm Barlow, Charles Barlow, new tinker in these parts."

"It's good to see a tinker again," Ma said.

"Allow me to show you my wares." He pointed to the trunks on his sled. "I'm sure these gentlemen will happily wait their turn."

Eliza Beth pulled her attention away from the man's blue eyes. He would do well in sales. He had that type of charisma about him. Pa would have said the man could sell spectacles to the blind. But she wouldn't fault someone for being good at their work. No, in fact, it was a trait to be admired. That it came in a handsome package on a tall frame was a pleasant bonus.

"Have you a newspaper?" she asked.

The tinker's face drew into a sorrowful mask. "I am fresh out. Sold the last one just minutes ago. But"—he held up one gloved finger—"I'll be sure to bring an extra, just for you, next week."

Disappointment hit harder than it should have. After all, she'd only been in camp a week, not for months on end. But how was she to face the entire winter if one single week had her missing the outside world this much?

Wes tucked the newspaper under his arm and headed for the cook shanty. It was dark, but light still shone through its windows. Louie had stared a hole through him when he'd seen Wes reading the paper in the bunkhouse, and eventually it came out that Miss Edmonds had wanted to buy one from the tinker. Wes had retreated with his purchase as the women had come out of the building, so he'd missed their exchange. But that wouldn't clear him in Louie's eyes. The young man was too smitten.

Still, now that he knew she'd wanted it, he felt it only right to take her the newspaper. He'd read most of it that afternoon, and there'd be no time for reading again until next Sunday. She might as well get the enjoyment from it.

He stepped into the room, and both women stopped what they were doing to stare at him.

"Hello." His voice sounded hollow in this room where the men rarely said a word. Meals were taken in silence, as he'd learned his first day. Eating took priority. He cleared his throat when neither spoke. "Louie mentioned that you wished for a newspaper, Miss Edmonds." He pulled out the carefully folded paper. "I've finished reading it."

She took a step toward him, then paused and looked at her ma. There was no mistaking they were mother and daughter, one being the older and mellower version of the other. Mrs. Edmonds gave her daughter a nod and then went back to whatever she'd been doing near the stove. Miss Edmonds joined him near the door.

"Thank you, Mr. Fisk. This is very generous of you." Her eyes gleamed when he handed it over, as if he'd given her some sort of treasure. "I'll be very careful with it and return it to you."

"Please, keep it. It would only get burned in the bunkhouse anyway."

She clutched it tightly, as if to protect it from the flames. "Thank you. Let me reimburse you for it then."

He held up his hand. "No need. I've read what I wanted."

Her cheeks flushed a rosy hue, adding to her charm—not that he needed to notice such things. He cleared his throat again. "I'd best be—"

"Did you read anything of importance? Anything that captured your interest?"

Mrs. Edmonds paused in the background, her attention on the pair of them.

On the third page was a story about the CSS *Shenandoah*, the last Confederate combat ship. It had finally surrendered on November sixth. Somehow it seemed fitting that his first glimpse of news in the wilderness marked the nail in the coffin of the war that had taken up so much of his life.

"Well, yes, but I'm not sure it's something that would interest you."

"Tell me anyway." She gestured toward the closest table. "Will you sit for a bit?"

Wes barely stopped himself from gaping at her. Where was the prickly miss he'd bumped into on the boat? Or the suspicious one he'd spoken to at the horse corral? She smiled, and he sank onto the bench.

She sat across the table from him, eyes expectant, and before he knew it, he'd poured out the whole story from the paper. Mrs. Edmonds joined them, sitting next to her daughter, and even asked him about the war.

Miss Edmonds was laughing at his story about trying to cook a catfish for the first time when Louie poked his head in the door. The young man frowned at them.

"You need anything done before I turn in, Mrs. Edmonds?"

"No, but thank you for asking." She stood, and Wes and Miss Edmonds followed suit. "I suppose it's time for bed already."

"That it is, ma'am." Louie's scowl was all for Wes now. "As long as we've done all our chores." The emphasis on *all* was unmistakable.

Wes forced himself to relax under the implication that he'd neglected Berry and Bright. "Right. Time for bed. I'll see you ladies at breakfast." He marched past the young man in the doorway and could almost feel the waves of resentment breaking over him. He waited until the cook shanty door was closed before he spoke.

"My team is cared for, my harnesses oiled, and I don't appreciate your implying otherwise."

"Stay away from Eliza Beth. She ain't for the likes of you." Louie turned his back and stalked to the bunkhouse.

The young man had it bad. But Wes couldn't blame him. The cordial and engaging woman in the cook shanty would turn any man's head.

Maybe even his.

Chapter Five

Every day since he had arrived seemed longer than the last.

After tossing the horses their hay for the night, Wes stifled a yawn and looked between the cook shanty and bunkhouse. He was starving, but almost too tired to eat. The noise from the shanty was an added draw to the food, and tomorrow being Sunday, he could sleep in a little. Not too much, as the horses still needed to be cared for, but an extra hour would be wonderful.

He opened the door, and the scent of something savory got his insides to grumbling. Only Bruce Kent was still eating. The landing man had come in with Wes, the two of them having off-loaded the final sled of the day. The rest of the men were gathered around old Alf Gougeon, who was spinning a tale of some lumberjack's exploits. Wes stamped the snow from his boots and then joined Bruce.

Miss Edmonds slid a bowl of something thick and meaty in front of him and dropped a handful of biscuits onto the plate between him and Bruce.

Wes shoveled in the first spoonful and didn't stop until he hit the bottom of the bowl. He grabbed a pair of biscuits and was chewing on them while listening to the storytelling at the far end of the building.

"Been a long week." Bruce leaned back and stretched.

Wes swallowed a mouthful of buttery biscuit. "Aren't they all?"

The older man rubbed a finger along the side of his nose. "I reckon they are. But the money's good and the food's better. At least, in this camp."

"It's a far cry better than what I ate during the war."

"Figured you for a soldier boy."

Wes looked down. "The trousers give me away, but I hated to spend the money on new clothes when these aren't worn out."

"Wasn't only that. It's the way you work, all precision-like." He raised his hand when Wes opened his mouth. "That's not criticism, no sir. It's good to work with a man who's dedicated to doing whatever he does well."

Wes didn't know what to say. Compliments weren't given in the army, at least, not often. Pa hadn't been too loose with them either. It made it all the sweeter when one came his way.

"You've done a fine job with that team." Bruce chuckled, a rusty sound. "The last fellow we had couldn't get them to pull in tandem half the time."

"I grew up with horses like them. My pa raised and trained them for the logging camps all over northern New York. I hope to do likewise when I get a little money in my purse."

"More stew? Or are you men finished?" Miss Edmonds paused beside them, smudges darkening under her eyes. Her work was as long and hard as his own. He could have eaten another bowl of stew, or even two, but she needed to clean up so she could retire. He handed her the empty bowl.

"I've had plenty. I believe I'll head to the bunkhouse."

"So soon? You won't stay for the entertainment?"

She seemed surprised, and he couldn't blame her. Most of the men lived for Saturday nights and Sunday mornings. But bone-weary fatigue had him by the suspenders, and he craved sleep more than entertainment.

"Maybe next week."

"You have two days off, you know." She smiled again, the expression that lightened her face only rarely. "Mr. Rabeau called Monday off on account of it being Christmas Day."

He hadn't heard. It was tempting to stay as long as she'd talk with him, but from the corner of his eye he caught Louie's glare.

"Even so, I believe I'll say good night." He hadn't even remembered it was Christmas. He should have penned Pa a note at least. Come to think of it, he hadn't let Pa know that he'd arrived safely. He best take care of that and soon. Maybe he could purchase paper and pencil from the tinker.

And another newspaper to share with Miss Edmonds.

The tinker pulled into camp midmorning to the same *hurrahs* that had greeted him the previous week. His team of dogs flopped down in the snow, panting with the dog equivalent of smiles on their faces.

Eliza Beth straightened her hair before stripping off her apron and reaching for her coat.

"Hoping for the newspaper he promised?"

She paused and faced Ma. "Aren't you? You read every word after me this past week."

"It is nice to have news of the world around us."

The world around them was nothing but trees and river and snow. That was the last thing Eliza Beth wanted to concentrate on. She pushed her arms into her coat and slipped her money purse into its deep pocket.

"Do you need anything this week?"

"I believe I'll stay inside and rest by the stove," Ma said. "He won't have anything worth me getting cold over."

She shot Ma a quick glance. Her color was good, but she looked tired. "Maybe you should lie down for a bit."

Ma waved her away. "Go on with you. I can take care of myself."

Eliza Beth wanted to argue the point considering just two weeks ago Ma had been unconscious on the roughly hewn floorboards. But the pull of a newspaper was too strong, and she slipped out into the biting wind.

Snow flurries, so small they were almost invisible, stung her face. She plunged her hands into her pockets and bent her head against the wind. Perhaps Ma was right to stay inside.

Eliza Beth joined the half-circle of men around the dogsled, all standing with their backs to the wind. A shadow moved over her and the wind hit her backside with less force.

"I plan to purchase another newspaper today." Mr. Fisk's voice rumbled close to her ear. "I'll share it with you, and you can save your pennies for something else."

Her heart did a little skip of surprise.

"That's very generous of you."

"That's what you said last week."

"So it was." What an odd conversation whispered between them. And yet it felt. . . She couldn't put a name to it, but she liked it.

"My dear Miss Edmonds!" The tinker's voice boomed above the wind. "I didn't see you join our ranks. Come closer. Men, allow the lady to the front, if you will."

He reminded Eliza Beth of a circus barker she'd seen once in Detroit, flamboyant and in control of the crowd.

The men parted like the Red Sea, and she moved forward.

"I remembered to bring an extra newspaper, just for you." He produced it with a flourish that would have made the circus barker proud. The tightly wrapped paper defied the wind.

"Mr. Fisk has laid claim to the newspaper already." She peeked back at him, and he smiled, causing that odd feeling to come over her again.

She turned back to the tinker. "What else do you have to read?"

His face shifted from irritation—directed toward Mr. Fisk—to smooth confidence when he met her eyes. "I have a new seed catalog if you enjoy gardening."

"Oh yes." She refrained from bouncing on her toes. "I would like that very much."

He dug into one of his trunks and brandished the catalog in front of her. "The latest and very best varieties in flowers and vegetables, all organized and with plenty of illustrations."

What a sales pitch. She pinched her lips together to avoid laughing at him while she dug her money out of her pocket and handed over the amount he'd quoted. Then she clutched the catalog and moved to the back, watching the others make their purchases.

Most bought tobacco, either chewing or pipe. Some bought soap or socks or other everyday necessities. Many bought hard candy. Some bought stamps and affixed them to letters the tinker would deliver to the post office. When Mr. Fisk's turn came, he bought his newspaper, some writing paper, and a pencil. Then he returned, once again blocking her from the worst of the wind. The men drifted away with their purchases as the tinker repacked his wares.

"It looks like you'll be writing a letter." She nodded toward the package in his hand. "Would you like to use a table in the cook shanty?"

His brows lifted a bit. "That would be helpful. My handwriting is sketchy on the best of days."

"Come on then." She led the way.

Ma had been dozing in a chair when they entered and the door banged shut. She shot a glance between the two of them as she straightened.

"Mr. Fisk needs a table to write a letter."

Ma waved toward the tables. "Please, sit." The cook ruled the shanty. It was her domain, one the lumberjacks didn't encroach on lightly.

He sat on the bench near the stove, and Eliza Beth took the bench across from him. He laid out his paper, and she spread out her catalog. While his pencil scratched across the paper, she got lost in the woodcut illustrations and vivid descriptions of roses.

Roses.

How long since she and Ma had planted flowers? She loved them all, their cheery colors and heavenly scents, but roses were her favorite. She traced one of the illustrations with her fingertip.

"Roses?"

She startled when his voice broke the silence.

"Yes." She shrugged. "They are my favorite."

"Is that the *latest and very best variety*?" He mimicked the tinker's booming voice.

Eliza Beth giggled. Then she slapped her hand over her mouth. She'd actually giggled. Like a silly schoolgirl.

He gave her his slightly crooked grin.

Ma's eyebrows were almost lost in her hairline.

"I c–couldn't say," Eliza Beth stammered, her face on fire. "I just think it's lovely." She stood. "I best start on supper. It'll be here before we know it, right, Ma?" She shot a desperate glance at Ma.

"As you say, daughter."

Mr. Fisk rose and collected his papers. "Thank you for letting me use the table. Pa'll be able to read this when he gets it." He pulled his ratty cap over his thick mane, touched the front of it, and ducked out the door.

"He's a fine-looking man, Eliza Beth," Ma said as she passed by, a note of mirth to her voice.

Yes. Yes, he was.

But he was also a lumberjack. She'd as soon fall for the fine-looking tinker.

Chapter Six

Even though they'd worked five days instead of six, Wes was tired. He was also cold, wet, and cranky. Sleet pelted him, finding every hole in his wool cap. It melted into icy rivulets inching down his scalp. But he couldn't finish his load until Louie got that last log skidded to the sled. He stamped his feet and tucked his gloved hands into his armpits.

Berry snorted and tossed her head, shifting in her harness.

"If he had a good team like you gals, he'd have been here half an hour ago." But Louie skidded with a pair of oxen. Steady and sure and slower than cold molasses. The clank of chains had reached them a few minutes ago, and finally Louie and his beasts crested the small hill blocking the sleds from the view of the cutting site. He pulled a huge log, its cut end coming halfway to the young man's hips. They'd never get that monster onto the top of Wes's sled. It'd have to go on the bottom of another.

Wes ground his teeth. He could have been at the river and unloaded, on his way to a hot meal and a warm bed.

Louie had raised his hand in greeting when a loud snap broke through the sleet and wind. A sound that stopped Wes's heart cold. The breaking of a chain. It had happened to him once on the battlefield, and he'd never forget that sound. Not as long as he lived.

The scream that followed was also reminiscent of the battlefield.

Helpless to do anything, Wes and the loaders watched as the huge pine log canted sideways on the icy hill and plowed into Louie and the oxen. Louie jumped and was thrown over the log as it crashed into the oxen.

The wreckage landed well clear of Bright and Berry, but Wes had his hands full keeping the horses under control. The bawling of the oxen and crashing of the log had them rolling their eyes and dancing on their toes.

The loading crew raced to Louie. "He's alive!" came the cry from the first man who reached him. Two men stayed with him, and the other two checked on the oxen. "One's dead and we'll have to put the other one down. Leg's broke. Anyone got a knife?"

Wes's stomach turned. They weren't horses, but the beasts worked hard side by side with the men. A quick cut would end the beast's misery, but it deserved better. They all deserved better.

"Fisk, hitch your team to an empty sled." Alf Gougeon took charge. "We'll load Louie on it. His leg is broke. And we'll haul the oxen in for Mrs. Edmonds."

The oxen would feed the camp for days to come. It didn't seem right, but leaving them for the wolves wouldn't serve them any better.

By the time Berry and Bright were in place, the loading crew had gutted the beasts and loaded them onto the sled with Louie at the front. All four men jumped aboard. Wes mounted last and clicked to the horses.

"How you doing, Louie?" he asked.

"Mighty glad I'm not an ox." The young man's face was white, but humor was a good sign.

"We'll get you back to camp as quick as we can on this ice."

"Much appreciated." For once, there was no animosity in the younger man's face.

"Hup, Bright. Hup, Berry. Let's go home, girls." Wes had to keep a firm hold on the lines, both horses eager for their shelter and hay, but the tote road was getting slipperier by the minute. They didn't need a second accident.

As they pulled into camp, Alf hollered for help. Men poured out of the bunkhouse and cook shanty, most tugging on coats as they ran. They knew minutes could make the difference if someone was injured.

Mr. Rabeau checked Louie over, talking to the young man. Then he started slinging orders, sending one man to town for the doctor with explicit orders to make it there and back in one piece. He ordered another trio to carry Louie into the cook shanty and designated six more to cut up and hang the ox carcasses in the cold storage shed tacked on the back of the cook shanty.

Wes unhitched his team and took them into their shelter, giving each a huge armload of hay after he brushed and rubbed them dry.

Mr. Rabeau joined him as he finished up. "Give me your version of what happened, Wes."

"A chain snapped. I heard it. He was hauling a monster log." Wes shrugged. "On the ice. . ."

"That's what Alf said too." The older man sighed. "We couldn't afford to lose those oxen."

"How's Louie?"

"Broken leg, no doubt, but not crushed, nothing through the skin. He's young. He'll be fine."

Especially under the tender care of the two women. Wes glanced toward the glow of the cook shanty's windows. He almost envied Louie.

Almost.

"Help me with the cot, Eliza Beth." Ma tugged a bundle of wood and ticking from the tall corner cupboard in their room. "We'll set it up behind the stove. He'll stay nice and warm there. Can't have him getting chilled and risking pneumonia."

Ma's voice was tight, her movements jerky.

Eliza Beth put her hands on Ma's shoulders. "I'll take care of this. You go watch over Louie."

"I can—"

"He needs you. I can handle this. Go." She gave Ma a gentle shove.

Louie had been all elbows and appetite when he'd arrived at the camp—the old camp several miles closer to town, where Eliza Beth had grown up. He'd claimed to be fifteen, but Ma had him pegged for not a day over twelve. She'd taken him under her wing and pretty much raised him along with Eliza Beth and her brothers. She loved the boy like one of her own.

Eliza Beth swallowed the lump that formed in her throat. If anything happened to Louie, so soon after Pa's accident, it'd go hard on Ma. It'd go hard on her too. She busied herself with setting up the cot, shaking out the tick, and fluffing its contents. She smoothed on a fresh sheet and then pulled the thick quilt from her own bed before approaching the table where they'd laid Louie, his wool coat draped over him.

"I've got the cot ready. You'll be more comfortable there."

"Reckon I'm not too eager to move just now, Eliza Beth." His face was pasty white, his lips drawn thin and tight to his teeth. Her heart twisted as she smoothed the hair away from his forehead.

"I'll fetch you a pillow, at least."

"That'd be much appreciated."

"I'll be right back." She gave his hair one last touch as the door banged shut behind a group of lumberjacks, Wes Fisk among them. His eyes traced from her to Louie and back again. It was nice of him to be concerned over Louie.

"I'll see to the men after I fetch the pillow," Eliza Beth said to Ma. "You stay with Louie."

Ma held the young man's hand, low on the table and sitting so the others couldn't see. She nodded to Eliza Beth.

Once plates and cups were filled and the only noise was the scrape of forks and knives, Eliza Beth started on the mountain of dishes. It'd be a wait for the doctor. The long distance, the icy road—it wasn't a good night for an injury. Not that any night was.

She'd have the men carry in another bed from the bunkhouse so the doctor could stay the night. Safer than traveling back to town. There'd be no entertainment, even though it was Saturday night, unless they kept it in the bunkhouse.

She was lost in thought when Mr. Fisk set a stack of dirty plates beside her on the worktable. He gave her one of his crooked grins.

"Figured you could use the help tonight." He nodded toward Louie and Ma.

"Thank you, Mr. Fisk."

"It's Wes." His voice was a low rumble that fit his rugged looks. His too-long hair hung in waves almost to his shoulders. The combination made it hard to draw a full breath.

"Then you should call me Eliza Beth." She cleared her throat and grabbed another stack of dirty plates, plunging them into the sudsy water. "Ma's plenty worried over Louie."

"We all are."

"That's kind of you." She cocked her head at him. "I suppose you've seen much worse. During the war."

His eyes clouded over, and he glanced away. "I have."

"I pray he'll be all right."

He looked back at her, measuring her in an unsettling way. A way that was becoming familiar. A way that made her heart beat a little erratically.

"He's special to you, isn't he?"

She nodded, her throat tightening again. Yes, Louie was special. But there was something special about the man in front of her as well.

Chapter Seven

Eliza Beth leafed through the garden seed catalog while sitting next to Louie's cot. Ma had finally retired to their room for a nap. She said she hadn't slept a wink through the night. Eliza Beth squelched a yawn. She hadn't gotten much sleep either. But Louie was sleeping like the dead, only groaning a bit when he tried to move his leg.

Doc had checked him over again before breakfast and left at first light. Only one of the lower leg bones had broken. Doc said it'd snapped back into place with no problem, even though Louie had passed out cold. No problem didn't equate to no pain. He'd have to stay abed for a week with the splint. Doc would be back to check him then.

Ma already had ox bones cooking for a restorative broth. Eliza Beth was sorry for the poor beasts, but Ma's broth would have Louie's bones knitting back together in no time.

She ran her fingers over the illustrations of roses. At the old camp, they'd had their own house, and Ma had planted roses by the front steps. This new camp didn't have any family houses yet, but no doubt some would be built come summer. It would be good to have other women close by.

She closed the catalog and stood. What was she thinking?

She had no desire to return next winter. None. She paced to the window. The icy world glittered in the morning light. Ice, snow, timber, and back-breaking work. It wasn't what she wanted out of life. She wanted to teach, to touch the minds of children so that they could do more than fell trees and ride logs down a river. Safe things. She wanted—

"Eliza Beth?"

"Coming, Louie." She'd wrestle with her discontent later.

He was resting against his elbows, giving her a sheepish grin. "Guess I slept through breakfast."

"I guess you did."

His stomached grumbled loudly enough that they laughed.

"Ma's got broth all ready for you."

"Oh, Eliza Beth." He groaned. "Can't I have a real breakfast?"

She wagged a finger at him. "Not until Ma says you can."

He grumped out a sigh but then looked at his splinted leg. "Before I eat, I...um..." He shifted on the cot. His face was turned away, but the tops of his ears glowed a bright pink.

Oh! "I'll call one of the men to help you." Eliza Beth kept her face averted so he didn't see the humor in her eyes. Of all the things to get embarrassed over. A body still needed to function, broken leg or no.

She opened the door, set to yell, but seated on a barrel outside of the bunkhouse was Mr. Fisk...Wes. In answer to her wave, he set aside whatever he was whittling and came to her.

"Louie needs help." She pointed at the outhouse.

He ducked through the doorway. Louie wouldn't cause a man his size any problem. She stayed by the door, then held it open while Wes carried Louie through, the younger man complaining he didn't need to be carried like a baby. But Doc had said no walking for a week, so Louie best get used to it.

Ma emerged from their room, her hair neatly pinned, and looking rested. She joined Eliza Beth at the window.

"Wes carried Louie to the outhouse."

"Wes?" Ma's eyebrows rose. "So that was the commotion I heard."

"Did they wake you?"

Ma waved her question off. "I wasn't asleep, just resting a mite longer. I'll get the broth ready for Louie. I imagine he's starving."

"And chaffing at the thought of just broth."

Ma chuckled. "Best start a pan of biscuits then."

Eliza Beth was elbow deep in flour and baking powder when Wes carried Louie back into the cook shanty.

"Can you hold him a moment?" Ma asked. "I'll fetch a crate to prop his leg on, and he can sit in one of the chairs."

Between the two of them, Ma and Wes had Louie comfortable and wrapped in a quilt before Eliza Beth got the biscuits cut. She met Wes at the door as he was leaving.

"Thank you. Ma and I will have to manage him between us tomorrow."

"I'll carry him over before I leave in the mornings and when I return. It should only be for a week. Then he'll be walking with a crutch."

"Well, until then, I appreciate you doing this for him."

He touched the front of his ratty cap, eyes unreadable, then smiled and left.

She knew what she would purchase from the tinker when he arrived.

Wes stared at the cook shanty, his whittling forgotten in his hands. Why did he care that Eliza Beth had admitted her feelings for

Louie last night? He seemed a good enough kid. In fairness, nobody doing the work Louie did could be considered a kid. It was a bit of a stretch to call him a man. Young man, then.

Then this morning, she'd asked Wes for help. Help with Louie, but still.

He shifted on the hard barrel. It was positioned out of the wind, and the sunshine was surprisingly warm, so he stayed outside. The bunkhouse smelled like it was full of dirty men and dirtier socks. Which it was.

It was good that Louie could stay in the cook shanty while he healed.

But what did it matter? Why was Wes sitting here on a barrel in the middle of nowhere thinking about it? Thinking about her?

Because she's something special. Like a lone flower in a plowed field. A flower. She liked roses. Well, it wasn't as if he could find her any in the wilderness in winter.

Thin clouds swirled overhead, and a ray of sunlight caught a string of icicles hanging from the bunkhouse eaves.

Or could he?

A recognizable shout and jingling bells came from down the tote road. Wes leaned over and banged his fist against the bunkhouse door.

Bruce pulled it open and stuck his head out. Another shout and a few barks. "Hey, fellas, the tinker's here." He disappeared back inside and shut the door.

Wes would buy another newspaper today. Sharing it with Eliza Beth on Sunday evenings had become a habit he looked forward to. Her ma hadn't objected, even though it was pretty obvious that the older woman favored Louie.

By the time the tinker got his dogs stopped, the women were out of the cook shanty, and the usual gathering began. Wes joined them, standing behind Eliza Beth. She tossed a smile over her shoulder. He leaned close to her ear.

"The newspaper's mine. Don't even think of purchasing it out from under me."

She laughed, a sound that drew more than just his attention. One man elbowed his neighbor and jerked his chin toward Wes. Well…let them notice. He stood tall and waited his turn.

"Ladies!" The tinker sketched a bow. "Come forward. Men, let the ladies pass. There you go." He beamed at them. "What can I get for you today?"

"Do you have any wool yarn?" Eliza Beth asked.

The tinker went on to extol the excellence of the yarn he carried, then presented her with three hanks of different colors. She made her choice, paid him, and stepped back. Ma picked out some spices. Then they returned to the cook shanty, but Eliza Beth glanced over her shoulder at Wes before she entered.

It warmed him to his heels.

He purchased his newspaper, and with it tucked under his arm, he walked past the bunkhouse, breaking off an icicle almost as thick as his wrist on his way. He headed for the horse shelter.

Inside, out of the wind and with the warmth and smell of the horses surrounding him, he laid aside the newspaper and pulled out his knife and the icicle. He hadn't done this in years. It was somewhat like whittling, but more delicate. It took him one, two, three tries before the knack came back to him. Until a perfectly formed ice rose nestled in the palm of his glove. He hid it on an overhead beam, picked up his newspaper, and returned to the bunkhouse to read as much as he could before supper.

Then he would share it with Eliza Beth. The highlight of his week had become Sunday evenings in the cook shanty. He took some mild ribbing from the other men over it, but he didn't mind.

He grimaced as he flopped onto his bunk.

This evening he'd sit with Eliza Beth under the watchful eyes of Mrs. Edmonds…and Louie.

Chapter Eight

New Year's Day came without fanfare in the logging camp as Eliza Beth finished scrubbing the bean pot. Breakfast was the same—salt pork and beans—every morning, and the first day of 1866 was no different. The enormous cast-iron pot was filled and lowered into the pit outside in the evenings, tucked in a bed of glowing wood embers, covered with a tin roof that was weighted down with cut logs, and left to cook until morning. It was filling and hot and gave the men a good start to their day. Eliza Beth had risen extra early to make cinnamon biscuits for a treat as the only nod to the New Year, glad Ma had thought to purchase more of the spice the day before.

Eliza Beth dried her hands. "Do you need me for anything else this morning?"

"Not for an hour or so." Ma stacked the cleaned and dried plates. "Are you itching to get into your knitting?"

"I am."

"What are you making?" Louie asked from the chair where he sat with his leg out straight and propped on a crate.

Eliza Beth stripped off her apron. "A cap."

He nodded, then returned to the newspaper she'd loaned him. She hadn't read much of it last night, just skimmed the headlines while Wes discussed with them what he'd read. She'd have the whole week to do it justice. After her other project was completed.

She slipped into their room, sunlight making it a cheery place to knit for an hour. Something glinted at the window and caught her attention. The glass was deeply set into the thick logs of the wall, so ice and snow rarely lay against it. Frost, on the other hand, often painted its delicate lacework there. But it wasn't frost. She stepped closer. In the bottom corner, up against the glass, was a rose. She pressed her forehead against the cold pane. A rose formed of…crystal? No. Ice. An ice rose.

Suppressing a little squeal, she shoved her arms into her coat sleeves and hurried out the door, through the main room of the shanty, past Ma's surprised expression, and outside. She carefully lifted the rose from the windowsill. It was perfect. She turned it one way and then another, letting the sun create prisms of color through it. She sniffed it, and then chuckled. If she took it inside, it would melt, a travesty for something so beautiful. She reluctantly replaced it.

The camp was empty. Even the blacksmith was in the woods working on-site, as he did much of the time. Only Buster remained behind, drowsing in a sunny spot in the corral. He was mostly retired unless someone needed to take the cart or cutter into town. And for sure he hadn't carved the ice rose.

So who? She hadn't retired until after dark last evening. It could have been anyone.

The handsome tinker maybe? He could have placed it there before he left. He always seemed happy to see her, but then, she suspected he'd be happy to see anyone clutching a coin. On the other hand, he knew of her affinity for roses, since she'd bought the seed catalog.

So did Wes.

Something fluttered inside her. Did she want it to be from Wes?

She enjoyed their talks on Sunday evenings. Ma often joined them. Last night, even Louie had entered their discussion. She couldn't remember Louie ever being interested in current events before, but he'd grown up while she'd been away.

Maybe he'd been more interested in Wes than the topics. He'd seemed to stare at the man, as if trying to read his mind. Or maybe he was thankful that Wes had stayed behind with his team on Saturday night. If he'd gotten impatient and left before the accident, things could have been much worse for Louie. Wes's dedication to the job may have saved Louie's life, or at least kept him from hypothermia. Wes and his team had brought Louie to camp far faster than men carrying him could have.

When she entered the cook shanty, Louie and Ma glanced at her but then resumed whatever they'd been talking about. Eliza Beth hurried back to their room and pulled out the dark red hank of yarn she'd purchased. The color would go well with Wes's hair. And heavens, the man needed a new cap. She draped the hank around the spindle back of the chair that sat in the corner, then rolled the yarn into a tidy ball.

Wes was a lumberjack. A handsome one, and tall, with nice manners, but still a lumberjack. He lived a life Eliza Beth didn't want to share.

She tossed the ball onto her bunk and fished a set of knitting pins from Ma's trunk. She'd make the man a cap. A kindness she'd extend to anyone. Nothing more than that.

It didn't mean she planned to marry him.

For once, Wes's sled wasn't the last one to be off-loaded at the river. After the landing men with their cant hooks emptied the sled, he'd unhitched the team and was heading back to camp in record time. Berry and Bright stepped lively, as if they knew it was Saturday night. The moon had risen, gleaming off the snow and lighting their way.

Wes had a little extra life in his step as well, striding behind them, hands loose on the reins. He'd been in camp almost a month and had hardened to the work. That was part of it. His new boots were no longer new and didn't hurt his feet. That was another part. But the best part was knowing that the doctor would have visited today and likely announced Louie fit to move back into the bunkhouse.

Then maybe Wes could find a moment to speak with Eliza Beth.

Had she found the rose?

Not a word had passed between them all week. Meals were still the silent business of shoveling fuel in a burner that needed to fire all day—or all night. But it was Saturday. The rules were relaxed. There'd be storytelling, loud and off-key singing, and maybe even some foot stomping that passed for dancing among the men.

He grinned into the night air.

Eliza Beth had captured his imagination from the moment he'd bumped into her on the *Atlantic*. Well, he'd noticed her anyway. How could he not, when she met him almost eye for eye. But a tall, sturdy woman would be handy around a farm. She'd be able to pull her weight as efficiently as the horses he planned to raise. That was the kind of wife he needed.

A wife who hadn't been in the plan at all until he'd met Eliza Beth.

Of course, there'd have to be some wooing done first. He was pretty sure women expected that. The rose was a fine start. He just needed to be sure she understood it'd come from him. He whistled a few notes, his breath frosting the air and blowing around his face.

Maybe he should shave before meeting with Eliza Beth tomorrow. Women appreciated a man who kept himself presentable, didn't they? He scratched at his month-old beard. It helped keep him warm in the woods. Maybe he'd keep it until spring.

Before he could decide, he arrived at camp and drove the horses to the hitching post outside their shelter. He'd gotten them unharnessed, curried, and fed when movement across the corral distracted him. Near Buster. A womanly figure.

Could he be so lucky?

He beat the front of his coat with his gloved hands to knock off the worst of the dirt, raked his fingers through his hair, and resettled his cap. That would have to do. Even with the moonlight, it was dark enough that he should pass muster.

"Eliza Beth."

She turned to him without a hitch, so she'd known he was there.

"Hello, Wes." Her voice was low and smooth, not high and squeaky as so many women's were. He liked that. In fact, he liked everything about her.

"Visiting Buster, I see." He leaned closer. "Need me to be your lookout for old Aube?"

Her laugh was quiet but graceful, not a silly twitter.

"I've already slipped Buster a crust of bread, and he's disposed of the evidence."

Silence stretched between them for a few moments as she stroked the old horse's face. It was a comfortable silence until his stomach rumbled long and loudly.

"You must be starved."

He clamped a hand to his waist. "I can't deny it after that."

"Then here." She pushed something into his hand. "Now go

and fill your stomach." She whisked away before he could say anything, trotting across the snowy ground to the cook shanty.

He held up the bundle she'd passed to him. A cap. A warm woolen cap the exact color of the yarn she'd bought from the tinker last Sunday.

So, she wasn't averse to him.

He removed his old cap and stuffed it into his coat pocket, then smoothed back his hair and settled the new one in place. He'd taken a few strides toward the cook shanty when a limping figure left the bunkhouse and made its halting approach to the cook shanty. On a crutch.

Uh-oh.

He'd forgotten about Louie and the obvious prior claim the young man had on Eliza Beth.

Chapter Nine

With a nod toward the day's last hauler and the landing men who entered the cook shanty, Wes stuffed the final piece of gingerbread into his mouth. His stomach had gone from growling to groaning, but he was finally full. More than full. He could just about lay his head on the hard plank table and fall asleep right then and there.

The men sat across from and beside him. Eliza Beth brought heaping plates of beef and potatoes and slid them in front of each man. She filled the bread basket and put it within reach of the men, but her eyes met Wes's.

He touched the front of his new red cap she'd given him earlier, since in camp a man wasn't required to remove it at the table. He flashed her his best smile, and her cheeks, already flushed from working over the cookstove, took on an even rosier hue, giving him a boost of new energy. After all, she'd made him a new cap. This whole wooing thing would have been easier than he'd hoped…if not for Louie. Wes genuinely liked the younger man, and it wasn't in him to poach someone else's girl. At least, it hadn't been.

A sound somewhere between a scalded cat and a slipping logging chain screeched across the room. Alderic Aube stood at the far end of the building with a fiddle tucked under his chin.

"The tinker brought me new strings last Sunday, boys. What

say we have ourselves a dance?"

Hollers and claps and foot stomping turned the solemn room into an uproar. Men shoved tables and benches against the walls. The late hauler and the landing men who were still eating grabbed their plates and finished standing up.

A handful of the older men made a circle in the middle of the cleared space.

Alderic drew his bow across the strings again, but instead of a screech, he played a jig. The older men stomped and clapped and cavorted like colts on fresh spring grass.

Wes clapped along with the others, his toe tapping, but his attention was caught by Eliza Beth and her mother. The dishes were stacked, many still not washed, and the ladies were clapping, watching the dancers. The song came to an end, and someone called out the name of another one.

Mr. Rabeau stepped up to Mrs. Edmonds, swept his cap from his head, and offered her an arm. She curtsied, as formal as could be, then took it. The two danced by themselves in the middle of a ring of men until Bruce Kent approached Eliza Beth. Those two followed suit, joining the older couple already dancing.

A slow burn gathered under Wes's collar.

"Show them how, Eliza Beth!" Louie called from the sidelines, leaning against his crutch and grinning from ear to ear.

She waved at the young man without losing a step.

Graceful and lovely, her dancing put the men's attempts to shame. Wes couldn't take his eyes off her. The fiddle wound down, and he moved to her side.

"May I have the next dance?"

Her gray eyes widened a bit, but her smile was welcoming. A few of the men hooted at him for moving in to claim her before they did. Then the fiddle started again with a slower song. Eliza

Beth moved into his arms as if she were made to be there. Did she feel it too? He'd never been a very good dancer, but with her, it was as natural as breathing. He swung the two of them around, and over her shoulder. . .

Louie's dark eyes came near to boring a hole through Wes.

It was one thing to dance with Mr. Kent, a happily married man and father of four. It was something else entirely to have Wes's arms come around her. Eliza Beth shot Ma a glance, long enough for a permissive nod before turning her attention back to the tall man in the red hat in front of her.

The music moved, and they did too. She'd danced with more polished partners at the seminary. Dancing was considered an essential part of a young woman's accomplishments there. But those partners had generally been older and shorter. Much shorter. She'd always felt like Hans Christian Andersen's ugly duckling during dance class.

Not anymore.

Wes moved and she moved, they came together, then drifted apart, only to be twirled back as a pair. Eliza Beth lost track of time, swaying through the motions, a touch here, a touch there. Too soon, it came to an end. His hands dropped to his sides, and he gave her a slight bow, his hazel eyes never leaving hers.

"I sure wish I could dance with you next." Louie's voice came from her elbow.

She blinked and turned to him. "As do I, but the doctor says you're healing fast, so we'll dance before the snow melts."

"Unless Mr. Aube saws through his strings again."

Eliza Beth laughed. The old man did have a tendency to do that.

"May I have the next dance?" came from her other side, and

before she knew it, Eliza Beth was dancing again. Every dance. By the time Mr. Rabeau called it a night, her feet ached and her throat was parched.

She almost groaned at the stack of dirty dishes still to be washed. Ma came alongside her, gripped her elbow, and steered her toward their room.

"Those can wait until morning. Let's get off our feet."

"Sounds heavenly."

"I enjoy a good dance as much as the next woman." Ma squeezed Eliza Beth's arm. "I just wish there were a few more women to lighten the load."

"Next winter there will be." The crews would have time to build some family cabins over the summer months. But Eliza Beth didn't want to be here to see them. She didn't.

And yet, the hazel eyes and crooked smile of a certain lumberjack wouldn't leave her alone. He'd danced with her only once—the same as every other man—but she'd caught his glance from across the room several times.

"That Wesley Fisk is some dancer, don't you think?"

Had Ma read her thoughts? "Yes, he is."

"And so tall." Ma shut the door to their room and scratched a match to light the lantern. "You make a handsome couple."

"He's a lumberjack, Ma." Eliza Beth sat on her bed, fully clothed. "I can't be interested in a lumberjack." Not even if he was the one who'd carved the beautiful ice rose, and she still wasn't sure it'd been him. "This life"—she spread her hands—"it's just not for me."

Ma took her hands and squeezed. "I'm not trying to marry you off, daughter, but I'd have you keep your eyes—and your options—open. Sometimes, God puts people in our paths for a reason."

Like keeping her locked away in the backwoods of nowhere? No thank you.

So much for being tired. Sleep was the furthest thing from Wes's mind as he checked on his horses one last time. The moon had found some thin clouds to hide behind, but enough light leaked through to see his way to the horse shelter. Berry bobbed her head at him, and he rubbed under her chin. Bright dozed with her nose almost to the ground. She was smart enough to know that a body needed sleep after a long six-day work week.

He knew it too, but thoughts of Eliza Beth filled him. Thoughts he didn't want to put to rest. His goal hadn't changed. He still wanted to start a horse farm and raise fine draft horses like the pair in front of him. But now he wanted a wife alongside him. A strong, capable woman.

Eliza Beth Edmonds.

Berry snorted and knocked his shoulder with her nose.

"Sorry, girl." He resumed rubbing. "I have a different filly on my mind."

If only she were a filly. He knew how to handle those. And while he was pretty sure Eliza Beth enjoyed his company—even his dancing—the look Louie had skewered him with and the look she'd given Louie after her dance with Wes. . . It was a hard knot to untie.

If the lad had a prior claim to her, what right had Wes to disturb that? He liked Louie. The young man was a hard worker. That he was protective of Eliza Beth spoke well of him. And she seemed to enjoy his company. But she didn't seem averse to Wes's attention either.

He gave Berry's face a final pat and headed for the bunkhouse.

Louie sat on the barrel outside the door, huddled in his coat with his crutch leaning against his leg. "She ain't for the likes of you."

Wes stopped short. "You said that before."

"She's a real lady. Real smart too. She graduated from that fancy school in Detroit. With high marks."

Wes opened his mouth, then snapped it shut.

"I'm obliged to you for what you did." The young man tapped his splinted leg. "This ain't personal."

It wasn't? Wes had no idea what to say, so he didn't say anything. He entered the bunkhouse and dropped onto his bunk, eyes wide open.

Chapter Ten

The newspaper crinkled in Eliza Beth's hands. She blinked and read the words again. "Teacher needed for the new township of Ossineke in southern Alpena County." Buried in the back of the newspaper, like a nugget of gold, was the answer to her dreams. She sank onto the nearest bench.

"Ma?"

"Hmm?" Ma yawned from the chair where she'd been dozing since Wes and Louie had left after their Sunday evening visit to share the newspaper. "What?"

"An advertisement." Eliza Beth shook the paper. "For a teacher."

Ma hurried to her side and squinted at the paper where Eliza Beth pointed.

"Well. I'll be."

"I'm going to send them a letter."

"I believe you should."

Eliza Beth left the paper on the table and took the lantern to their room. She held the light high as she entered, trying to remember where she'd stowed her writing tools and paper. Something glinted in the window. She shuttered the lantern and peered through the glass.

Two ice roses.

Beside the original was another rose. Not a copy, but a unique flower with its petals only partly unfurled. It was beautiful, even with only the moonlight to shine on it.

A second rose on a second Sunday. Why on Sunday? The day the tinker, Mr. Barlow, came with his trimmed beard and flashing blue eyes. Was he carving the roses?

Or was it Wes? He whittled wood most Sundays, sitting on that old barrel and waiting for the tinker. She'd never seen anything he'd finished, of course, but certainly if he could carve wood, he could carve ice.

Did she want it to be Wes?

She pushed the thought aside, opened the lantern, and searched for her writing tools. Finding the box under her bed, she stood and looked at the ice roses again, then shook her head and hurried to the main room to write her letter. After all, teaching was her dream.

This was her chance to make it happen.

The morning's gentle snowflakes had changed to blowing, stinging ice pellets by midmorning. Wes bent his head against the wind, keeping on the leeward side of his load of logs, but still unable to escape the onslaught. The icy mix caught in his beard, stiffened his gloves, and coated his horses.

"Ho there!" came a shout through the storm.

Wes pulled the team to a halt while a shadowy figure came toward him. "Boss says to unhitch at the landing and tell the men to get back to camp," Alderic said. "They can unload when the storm breaks."

"Gladly. It's not fit for man nor beast out here."

The older man clamped a hand on Wes's shoulder. "The horses

need out of the weather for sure." As always, the old horseman was more concerned for his beasts than the men working with them.

Wes chuckled, then flicked the reins. "Come on, girls."

The horses leaned into their harnesses and moved the small mountain of logs chained to the sled through the almost blinding snow. Wes trusted the team by now, young as they were, to keep their feet under them even on the slippery tote road. He kept a sharp lookout for anything in their way. Winds like this could bring down icy limbs and block their path.

It took longer than usual, but they made it to the landing, and men swarmed toward him, ready to unload.

"Boss says to leave it and unload after the storm," Wes hollered above the wind.

The men cheered with their cant hooks raised to the sky.

Bruce Kent joined Wes and helped unhitch the team while the rest of the men headed for camp. "We won't be back for a while, I don't think." He used the end of his cant hook to break ice from the harness chains to unhitch them.

Wes clicked to Berry and Bright, keeping a firm hold on the reins against the mares' eagerness to get out of the storm. "You don't think we'll be out tomorrow?"

Bruce raised his face to the sky, hand cupped above his eyes. "It'll be a gillen tomorrow."

A gillen, a free day, a day when the weather was too severe to work. There was little the lumbermen enjoyed more than a gillen. Although this would be Wes's first, he'd heard stories told of them. Relieved just to be getting out of the storm, he was mostly looking forward to some extra sleep.

Something to replace what thoughts of a certain well-educated lady had robbed him of the night before.

A gillen. Eliza Beth leaned her forehead against the window in their room. The ice roses were completely covered in the pellets of snow that had forced their way into the deep recess of the logs. The wind still howled, but the icy chatter of frozen branches swaying in the treetops could be heard above it. It wouldn't be safe to venture into the forest today.

She for sure wouldn't be going to town to post her letter regarding the teaching position.

In the past, a gillen had been a fun day. A time to relax and enjoy a break from their labors. Even she and Ma had a break of sorts. They'd not have to haul a midday meal out to the lumberjacks. And it was a day the men could linger over their meals, talking and laughing. It gave the camp a feeling of. . .family.

She pushed away from the window. The camp wasn't family. It was isolation, pure and simple. Eliza Beth picked up the letter, all sealed and ready to post.

"A few days won't matter," Ma said from her bed where she'd stretched out after breakfast. "Nobody will be posting or delivering letters in this storm."

"I know." She tapped the edge of the letter on her palm. "It's just that I want it so much."

Ma sat up and patted her hair into place. "I know, dear. I know."

The wealth of understanding in those words made Eliza Beth's eyes burn. Had Ma ever wished for a life outside of the logging camps? She'd seemed happy with Pa and her and the boys. There'd been sad times too, of course. Ma and Pa had buried two children, a girl before Eliza Beth and a boy after. Eliza Beth had been too young to remember, but surely Ma had struggled then. If she'd been in a larger town with a doctor, things might have been different.

The doctor in Alpena had only arrived while Eliza Beth had been at the seminary. Before that, people had relied on home remedies and God's grace in times of illness and injury. And injury was part of the logging camps.

"Why don't you find something to do to pass the time?"

Eliza Beth stopped pacing, only then realizing she had been. "I have enough yarn left to knit another cap. I'll do that. Louie could use a new one."

"He'll cherish it if it comes from you. The boy dotes on you."

He might not be her real brother, but those three had run off and left her and Ma to muddle along on their own. Louie deserved a new cap at the very least.

And it would keep her fingers busy while she was forced to wait out the storm.

They'd worked just a half day on Monday, and now it was Thursday. Wes only knew that by the big calendar Mrs. Edmonds kept tacked to the wall near the stove. The first couple of days off had been nice. He'd slept more than he'd thought possible. But going into the third full day of nothing to do was a bit much. At least the wind had died down at last.

The blacksmith's hammer rang out in the stillness after the storm. Mr. Rabeau had told him to make all the horses and oxen new shoes. The storm had alternated between ice and snow, leaving a dangerous mix at least a foot deep covering the ground. New shoes with iron cleats would help the animals keep their legs underneath them once they were back in the woods.

Hopefully tomorrow.

Wes needed to get away from camp. Away from Eliza Beth. His dreams of wooing her had amounted to nothing. Two and a half days in camp, and she'd stayed mostly in her room other than during meals.

Until last evening.

He swallowed down the disappointment that had hit him between the eyes when she'd handed Louie the cap. The young man had visibly choked up, then wrapped her in a bone-crunching hug. She'd laughed and kissed him on the cheek.

Kissed him. Right there in the cook shanty with half the camp watching.

It couldn't be any clearer than that.

She hadn't kissed Wes when she'd given him his cap. She'd just shoved it at him and fled.

He needed to concentrate on his job now, save every penny he earned—except for purchasing the weekly newspaper—and look for land come spring to start his horse farm.

Alone.

Chapter Eleven

"The tinker will be here tomorrow. Why don't you wait, Eliza Beth?"

Ma's forehead wrinkled, and Eliza Beth suppressed a twinge of guilt for causing her worry. "My letter will go out quicker if I post it today. I'll take Buster to town after the midday meal. I can be back before supper."

"I don't see that one day will make a difference."

"It might, Ma." Eliza Beth twisted her apron at her waist. "I just—"

Ma sighed. "I know. You go on. I can handle the midday meal. It's just cold beef, biscuits, and coffee today."

"I won't shirk my duties. I'll go after."

"I'd rather you go now, so you're there and back in the daylight."

Eliza Beth opened her mouth and then shut it again. Ma was right. Safer to travel the icy path with good light. "All right. If you're sure?"

"More than sure. Go on with you. And don't hurry. Go slow and careful."

She gave Ma a quick hug, stripped off her apron, and went into their room for her good boots and coat. Within minutes, she was on Buster, a pair of her brother's old britches keeping her legs warm underneath her layered skirts. She gave the blacksmith a cheery wave, he raised a set of tongs in reply, and then Buster was picking their way toward town.

"This is my chance, boy." She patted the old horse's neck. "My chance to get away from camp life for good." She glanced at the bunkhouse but shoved the mental image of Wes away. "Eventually I'll get a small house near the school. Ma can come and live with me so she won't wear herself out working from before sunup until after sundown."

It felt right. It felt good. And it felt bone-numbingly cold.

She'd forgotten how much colder it was on top of a horse than walking, but Buster's long legs and iron-shod hooves made better time through the snow than she could have. So she pulled her legs high, huddling under her skirts, and wrapped the muffler she'd donned tighter around her head and neck.

It would be worth it to get her letter posted.

More than an hour into the ride, Eliza Beth halted Buster in a small clearing to give him a breather. She clutched the saddle as the old horse lowered his head and shook, then blew twin streamers of mist.

"Just a bit more." It wasn't though. They were traveling slower than she'd thought. Each step broke through the layers of snow and ice. Buster had to pick his feet up and place them down with force. It was wearing the old horse out. Maybe she should have listened to Ma.

She twisted in the saddle, looking around for landmarks. As near as she could figure from the contour of the river they followed, they were closer to town than camp. It'd be a waste to turn around at this point. Once Buster was rested—

Buster's head jerked up, nearly smacking into Eliza Beth's shoulder, since she'd been off-balance in the saddle. She scrabbled for a hold, her feet dropping down the saddle's fenders, searching for the stirrups. Buster spun in a tight circle, or attempted to.

The saddle fell away under Eliza Beth. Her feet still free of the stirrups, she kicked away from Buster. He crashed into the icy snow with a sickening thud, and she landed an arm's reach away, one hand still clutching a rein. Her hip connected with the frozen earth, sending shards of pain lacing down her leg.

Then a deep-throated growl drove away all thoughts of pain.

Wes sniffed. The unmistakable scent of biscuits filled the air. If the blacksmith could replace Berry's shoe right away, he could help the women carry the midday meal back into the woods. At least something good would come out of the morning's debacle.

Or maybe he should hitch Buster with Bright and keep going. The old horse could handle a half-day in the woods. Although, it was always best to keep a team together. The horses worked best with a partner they were used to.

He stopped the team outside the blacksmith's shack. The burly man filled the doorway.

"Berry threw one of her new shoes already."

The blacksmith came forward and ran a hand down Berry's leg, lifting the hoof. He grunted. "She busted the nails. I'll have to knock out broken bits." He dropped the hoof and faced Wes. "You find the shoe?"

Wes pulled it free from his belt where he'd secured it, handing over the almost dinner-plate-sized horseshoe. "I did."

"Good man. That'll make the job faster."

"If you think it'll take some time, I'll harness Buster and finish the day."

"Can't do that." The blacksmith lifted his whiskery chin toward the corrals. "He ain't here."

"Someone already hitch him?"

"Nah. The girl rode him to town."

The girl? Eliza Beth? "Why'd she do that?"

The blacksmith leveled a stare at Wes. "How would I know? She saddled him and rode off."

Wes left the horses in the blacksmith's care and headed for the cook shanty, the warm air enveloping him as he entered. Mrs. Edmonds was sliding a huge sheet of the golden circles from the stove.

"Mr. Fisk." She set the pan down and dropped the towels she'd used to hold the hot metal. "What can I do for you?"

"The blacksmith says Eliza Beth rode into town. Is anything wrong?" Because why else would she go out on a day like this?

"No, nothing wrong. She had a letter to post."

"A letter?"

The older woman tucked an errant lock of gray hair into the knot at the back of her head. "Yes."

"Ma'am, did she realize how hard it is on the horses out there?" He pointed toward the closed door. "My Berry caught a rim of ice and wrenched off a shoe."

The woman's face paled.

Wes wanted to kick himself. When would he learn to think before he spoke to womenfolk? "But she's on Buster, and that old horse knows his way around." He rubbed the back of his neck. "I'm sure she'll be fine."

He wasn't. He wanted to go after her. But he couldn't. He had a job to do. Chasing after a woman wasn't part of it. A woman who'd kissed another man in full view of everyone in camp.

The clang of hammer against metal broke the silence.

Mrs. Edmonds wiped her hands on her apron nervously.

"I'd be happy to help you deliver the midday meal, ma'am. I'll unhitch Bright and fetch the sled." Within minutes, he'd rigged the large mare to the small sled and helped load it with the enormous coffeepot and two crates filled with biscuits and whatever else Mrs. Edmonds had stuffed in there. "Why don't you sit on the top of that crate, ma'am?" He pointed to the sled. "Bright won't even know you're there." Which was true. The cook's sled was tiny compared to the huge loads of logs the horse pulled daily.

She climbed aboard, and Wes walked beside. The sled wasn't large enough for the both of them, and he didn't mind walking. His feet had gotten used to it over the past weeks.

They arrived to the usual cheers, and Wes helped Mrs. Edmonds divvy out the food, making sure everyone else ate before helping himself to his portion. After all, he couldn't do his job until he had Berry back in harness.

"Thanks for pitching in." Mr. Rabeau clouted him on the shoulder as he brought back his empty mug and plate. "Was Smitty able to reset the shoe?"

"He's probably done by now. I'll take Mrs. Edmonds to camp and then get back to work."

"Good man." The foreman strode off.

But Wes wanted to go in search of Eliza Beth.

A wolf. In broad daylight. Staring at her from beneath the snow-laden branches at the forest's edge. Then another stepped to the side of the first.

Buster snorted and scrambled to his feet, showing no sign of injury. Eliza Beth gripped the rein with all her might. If she lost Buster now…

She tried to push herself up but bit back a scream of pain. Her arm wouldn't work.

Buster pawed at the icy snow, the whites around his eyes showing.

"Whoa, boy. Whoa. They won't come after a big guy like you." Would they? Two of them? Or were there more? Was it a full pack?

Fear and pain broke a sweat over her. She shifted off her throbbing hip and attempted to stand, but the pain was too much. She collapsed. Buster sidestepped, and she wound the rein tightly around her good hand. If he took off, he'd drag her, but if he left her behind. . .

Another growl, and she managed to climb to her feet and limp to Buster's side. He took a step away from her, still facing the wolves.

"Easy, boy." She stepped toward him again, and he sidestepped again, his attention never leaving the pair under the trees.

What if he wouldn't let her mount? And how could she with only one arm working and one hip threatening to buckle under her?

Why had she been so willful? Why hadn't she listened to Ma?

Because she wanted more out of life. She wanted to teach. She wanted to leave the forest and the lumberjacks and the wolves behind. A desperate sob worked its way up her throat. What would happen to Ma if the wolves attacked? There was no earthly way Eliza Beth could protect herself.

Oh, God. I need You now.

Chapter Twelve

Could anything else go wrong today? Wes ran his gloved hands over the harness, then glanced at the sky. Clouds hid the sun, but it must have been closer to evening than noon. Even if it wasn't, he was done for the day until the harness was repaired.

"Mr. Aube," he called to the senior hauler, whose sled came in behind his to the landing site. "That last load stressed the harness." He held up the leather.

The older man waved and pointed toward camp.

That was all the permission Wes needed. He finished unhitching Berry and Bright, then turned them toward home. The mares pranced on their toes, despite the icy surface, and he had his hands full calming them down.

"Easy there, girls. I swear you know it's Saturday, and you look forward to the day off as much as the men. Watch your feet on that ice." He chuckled, then sobered.

Had Eliza Beth returned from town yet? She'd had a long road to travel in those conditions. Foolish woman. What sort of letter was so important that the tinker couldn't have collected it tomorrow?

Not that it was any of his business. Even so, he chirped to the horses and let them pick up the pace a bit. He needed to know she was safe. Why he needed to know. . . He'd think about that later.

Women could sure tie a man's insides in knots.

He stopped the team in front of the blacksmith's, but the man wasn't there. Buster wasn't in his corral either. Wes tied the horses and strode to the cook shanty. The scent of roasting meat greeted him, but no women.

"Mrs. Edmonds?"

A scuffling sound came from behind the cookstove where the women's room was tucked away, followed by Mrs. Edmonds, a shawl wrapped around her shoulders and lines grooved into her forehead.

"Eliza Beth hasn't returned?"

"No, she hasn't." She looked out the window, then back at him. "I'm concerned something has happened."

Quite likely, but saying that wouldn't help the situation or calm Mrs. Edmonds. "I'll ride out and look for her."

"You aren't needed at the site?"

"Harness needs repair before I can work again. I won't have time to do that before dark."

Mrs. Edmonds cut two large squares from a pan of cornbread and a handful of what looked like jerked meat and shoved them into a bag with a long strap. She handed it to him with a steady look in her gray eyes. "In case you don't get back for supper."

He wasn't much good at reading a woman's thoughts, but hers were as clear as new ice. "I'll find her, ma'am, and bring her back." He slung the sack's strap over his head. "If she's closer to town, we'll go there and return tomorrow."

He probably broke a record for unhitching Berry. She'd seemed a little tender on the hoof that'd been re-shod earlier. Not lame, but best to ride Bright. He led Bright to the bunkhouse and tethered her to one of the low beams off the roof. She neighed for her partner, and Berry answered.

"Steady, girl."

Wes slipped into the bunkhouse and took Mr. Rabeau's rifle from its brackets on the back wall. He hated to think of it, but if the old horse had gone down on the ice... A bullet was kinder than letting him suffer. He slung the rifle over his shoulder by its strap and then stopped, one hand resting against the sturdy logs of the wall. *God, let her be fine. Let them both be fine.*

He hadn't done much praying since the war, hadn't seemed to need to like he had then, but it gave him an added sense of security as he strode out of the bunkhouse and swung onto the mare. She danced and jigged for a moment, crow-hopping across the yard and demanding all his attention just to stay on her back. Most draft animals weren't used to being ridden, but he finally got her straightened out and headed toward town.

Mrs. Edmonds raised her hand from the doorway of the cook shanty.

Between the sweat and the tears, Eliza Beth was in trouble. Another violent shiver shook her like a sapling in a windstorm. Buster tossed his head, snorting and shifting, keeping the two wolves in sight.

How long had it been? Two hours? Three? It didn't matter. She hadn't much strength left. The old horse had stayed with her, obeying her pull on the rein, but should he decide to make a run for camp, she'd be powerless to stop him. Her only hope would be if the wolves followed him and left her behind.

If Buster ran, with the poor footing, they'd likely bring him down. As big as they were, they weren't punching through the layers of ice and snow like the horse did. Their broad paws worked more like snowshoes, Buster's iron-clad hooves like hammers.

Another tear escaped, an icy burn down her already chapped cheeks.

Would anyone come looking for them in time?

One of the wolves got bold enough to enter the clearing again. Buster squealed and stamped his front hooves on the well-trampled circle of snow, head tossing, nearly pulling Eliza Beth off her feet. She hung on. When the other wolf slunk to the opposite side of the clearing, she faced that one and yelled. If her arm would work, she could at least find a stick to brandish. As it was, all she had was her voice.

And even that was giving out.

But the wolf backed off and disappeared into the trees. Where would it show up next? She dashed another tear from her eyes by rubbing against her shoulder as best she could. They formed as much from the cold wind as from her fear, but either way, they blurred her vision and froze to her face.

Buster squealed again, a higher-pitched alarm. The wolf he faced had advanced closer than ever before. It was halfway into the clearing, head down, yellow eyes assessing. Eliza Beth turned her head, watching for the second wolf, as Buster reared, pulling her off her feet.

The rein slipped from her nearly frozen hand. "Buster!"

Without it to help steady her, she collapsed into darkness.

Wes pulled Bright to a halt. Had he really heard a shout above the wind? The mare pranced, and tried to turn back. She didn't like leaving Berry behind. He'd steadied her again when the squeal of another horse cut through the forest.

It had to be Buster.

With a swift jab of his heels, Bright bolted forward. Ears

pinned, she headed for the sound of trouble like a trooper. She'd have made a good war horse. Wes had his hands full keeping her at a controlled charge through the ice and snow. At least she had iron cleats on her shoes.

They broke into a clearing, Buster in its center on his back feet, front hooves pawing the air. A gray body slunk toward the trees, and Wes grabbed the rifle's strap at his shoulder, but the wolf was gone. Buster came down to earth, nickering at Bright. The mare's sides quivered between his knees as she answered.

Where was Eliza Beth?

Buster moved, and she came into view. A crumpled form on the ground. Wes vaulted from Bright, who was side-stepping and snorting, catching the scent of the wolf.

"Easy, Bright. Whoa, girl."

He led the mare to the unmoving woman on the snow.

"Eliza Beth?"

Nothing.

He knelt beside her, ripped a glove off with his teeth, and touched her face. It wasn't warm, but her breath misted against his hand.

Alive.

"Eliza Beth? Can you hear me?"

Her eyelids trembled but didn't open.

"Eliza Beth? I need to get you out of here. It would be better if you woke up now." He tapped her cheek lightly.

She blinked and then moaned, eyes shutting again.

"Where are you hurt?" Nothing. "Eliza Beth?"

Fear crept to the center of his bones. Should he move her? On the battlefield, they waited for stretchers so as not to do more harm. But there were no stretcher bearers here. This wasn't the aftermath of a war. This was the wilderness with a wolf lurking somewhere beneath the trees. Wolves were almost never alone. And it was well below freezing.

Buster hadn't moved. The old horse seemed to sag on his hips, head hanging to his knees. He was close to used up. Wes would have to put Eliza Beth on Bright and hold her there, praying the mare would behave herself.

He lifted Eliza Beth's arm to gather her.

She screamed. A hoarse but terrible scream. He fell back on his haunches.

"Eliza Beth?"

She looked at him, recognition sparking the depths of her gray eyes. "Wes?"

"Where are you hurt?"

"My arm, it won't work. My hip is painful. And my fingers and toes may be frostbitten."

Bad news on top of worse. They couldn't stay here. Darkness wasn't far off. It was closer to town than camp, and she needed a doctor.

"I'm going to get you up on Bright."

"I can't."

"You'll have to. You can't stay here."

"There's no saddle."

"I'm sorry. You'll have to hold on to the harness as best you can."

"Take the saddle off Buster."

He shook his head and tried to ignore the moisture in her eyes. "Bright's never been saddled. Better to use the harness. I'll get you aboard and then mount behind you. You can lean into me. I won't let you fall."

Bright, you'd best cooperate. He took a moment to tie Buster's reins so the old horse wouldn't step on them, then led the mare closer to Eliza Beth.

It took a lot of grit for her to allow him to manhandle her onto the horse. Bright, for her part, had calmed down with Buster at her side. Wes led the mare to a nearby stump so he could mount behind Eliza Beth without dislodging her in the process. Bright took a couple of side steps but settled once she bumped into Buster. The old horse held his ground, as if understanding what Wes needed him to do. And when they stepped out toward town, he kept beside the mare as if they were harnessed together.

Eliza Beth groaned, then slumped against his chest, her head lolling to her shoulder. Passed out. From the pain or the cold, it was hard to say, but he wrapped his arms around her to keep her as still and warm as he could. Despite everything, he couldn't help but notice again that she fit against him as if she were made to be there.

Maybe he'd have to have a word with Louie when they got back to camp.

Chapter Thirteen

Needles picking at her cheeks, fingers, and toes roused Eliza Beth from sleep. Piles of blankets weighted her down on a soft mattress too large to be her own. She fought against the grit in her eyes to pry them open. Pain throbbed in her shoulder and hip when she shifted on the mattress.

"Eliza Beth?"

Wes hunched forward in a chair, elbows on his knees, brows drawn together. A flickering lantern lit the sable waves of his hair. He badly needed a haircut. And a shave. But she'd never been so glad to see anyone in her life.

"You found me."

"You can thank Buster for that."

"How is he?" She never should have asked the old horse to take her to town in such conditions. If he'd been seriously hurt in that fall, she'd never forgive herself.

"Warm and happy at the livery down the street."

She looked around at the dimly lit room. "Where are we?"

"Doc's house. He and the missus went to bed a couple of hours ago, after he said you were past danger."

"Danger?"

He rubbed his jaw, then met her eyes. "You were close to losing a few of your toes, and maybe a finger. But Doc says you warmed up in time."

She closed her eyes and shuddered.

"My arm?"

"Not broke, but the shoulder was dislocated. Doc popped it back into place. Good thing you weren't conscious for that."

"My hip?"

"Bruised, but nothing too bad according to Doc."

"Ma must be worried sick."

"I told her I'd bring you to town if it was closer. Now that you're going to be all right, I'll head back to camp and let her know. It's close to morning anyway."

Eliza Beth tried to shove the blankets off, but his hand stopped her.

"You have to stay here, Doc says. For at least a couple of days."

"Ma needs my help."

"You won't be a help until Doc says you can be up and around. You stay here, do what he says, and I'll fetch you back to camp as soon as I can." He rose.

She fumbled for his hand. His strong fingers wrapped around hers, and she ignored the pain from the frostbite, enjoying his warmth. But what warmed her more was the heat in his eyes. It did funny things to her lungs as well, and she had trouble drawing a full breath.

"Thank you."

"My pleasure, Miss Edmonds." He let go of her hand and touched her cheek. "Don't fret. I'll be back for you."

He closed the door softly behind him.

Her cheek still tingled from his touch—or maybe the frostbite—and she hadn't even thought of the letter in her coat pocket. The letter that had almost gotten her killed.

If not for a handsome lumberjack named Wesley Fisk.

Wes had paid the liveryman the night before, so he saddled Buster and harnessed Bright, deciding to ride the older horse and lead the younger. His thighs were chafed enough from the harness leathers and buckles. He led the horses from the stable as a line of pre-dawn orange outlined the blackness of Lake Huron.

He mounted, glanced once down the street toward the doctor's house, then reined Buster around and headed for camp.

There was something about sitting on a horse that let a man think. Deep thoughts, the kind that didn't occur to him on the ground when he had to pay attention to where he put his feet. Eliza Beth was a special woman, no doubt about it. She'd survived an ordeal that could have brought a man down, much less a woman.

He patted Buster on the neck. "You too, old fella." Then he tilted his head back and searched the brightening sky. "Thank you, Lord."

He'd seen enough of the Lord's work on the battlefield to know it was real. An old horse, an injured woman, dangerously cold temperatures, and a wolf—quite likely more than one. That was a recipe for disaster if ever he'd seen it. But Eliza Beth would be fine. Buster was fine. God was good.

He didn't have much to offer just yet, but if Eliza Beth would give him a year or two, he'd have a nice little horse farm. Somewhere nearby, on land the loggers had already cleared. A place to raise fine draft animals. . .and maybe a houseful of youngins, tall and strong like their folks. It painted a pretty picture in his mind.

If only he could erase the memory of that kiss she'd planted on Louie's cheek right in front of everyone.

As they neared the camp, both horses quickened their pace, eager for home and hay. A shout rose from the man sitting on

Wes's favorite barrel outside the bunkhouse. Louie eased off the barrel onto his crutch and yelled again. The cook shanty door flew open, and Mrs. Edmonds rushed out, her hands covering her mouth at the sight of him alone.

He let Buster charge the rest of the way into camp, dismounting even before the old horse stopped in front of the group of men who'd gathered outside of the cook shanty.

"She's all right, Mrs. Edmonds. Eliza Beth is at Doc's in town, but she'll be fine."

"You're sure?"

"Yes, ma'am. I didn't leave until she woke up this morning, and I talked to her. Doc worked on her most of the night, and he says she won't lose any toes or fingers. The frostbite wasn't too bad."

The woman's face blanched, and Louie put an arm around her.

"Frostbite?"

He'd done it again. "A mild case, ma'am. But we got to Doc's in time. She'll be fine, honest."

"What happened?" Louie asked.

"Near as I got it figured, a wolf spooked Buster." He pointed at the old horse, already being led away alongside Bright. "She must have come off. Doc had to pop her shoulder back into joint." He flinched when Mrs. Edmonds did. "Doc says she's got a mighty big bruise on her hip. She couldn't get back on the horse. Her and Buster were holding off the wolf when I arrived."

"A lone wolf?" Alf asked, disbelief in his voice.

"I only saw one, but it's likely there were more."

"Never seen a lone wolf in these parts," Bruce said around the stem of his pipe.

"But she's going to be all right?" Mrs. Edmonds lips trembled.

Wes stepped to her side and gripped her arm. "Right as rain, ma'am. Now let's get you back in where it's warm." She hadn't even pulled a shawl over her shoulders, much less a coat. "Before you get frostbite too."

Her smile shook some, but she patted his hand. Louie on her other side with his crutch, they walked her back to the cook shanty. The scent of bacon greeted him, and his stomach let loose with a terrible growl. He gave Mrs. Edmonds a sheepish grin.

"Guess I missed breakfast."

"I'll fix you a plate. Have a seat."

"I'll see to my horses first—"

"Mr. Aube was leading them into the corral. He'll take care of them." Louie pointed to the table with its long empty benches. "Sit."

Wes did, plopping both elbows on the table and resting his forehead on his palms. He was beat. He hadn't slept since night before last. If he weren't so hungry, he'd skip breakfast in favor of his bunk.

A hand came down on his shoulder. He looked up. Louie's face was pulled into solemn lines. "I can't thank you enough for riding after Eliza Beth."

"No thanks needed."

Louie cocked his head, studying Wes as if he were a bug in the soup. Maybe it was best to just spill it out on the table. Here and now.

"I know you don't think me fit for Eliza Beth, and I know you have feelings for her, but so do I." There. He'd said it plain.

Louie's mouth dropped open for a second, then he grinned. Not just a smile, but a big ear-to-ear grin. And then, of all the crazy things, he clouted Wes on the shoulder and laughed. Laughed! Then he shook his head and limped away. What in the world? The door shut behind him as Mrs. Edmonds slid a plate in front of Wes.

"Eat up, young man. And thank you."

But the wrinkles around her eyes looked a lot more like laughter now than concern over her daughter.

What was going on?

She'd never felt so useless in her life, but Eliza Beth kept her mittened hands buried in the thick wool blanket Louie had pulled over her lap once she'd gotten seated in the cutter. Her feet rested on a warm brick from Doc's hearth. She was wrapped in her coat, her muffler covering everything but her eyes. Moving would be difficult, but she needed to keep her sensitive fingers and toes out of the wind.

Louie plopped on the seat beside her and gave her his cheek-splitting grin. He looked twelve years old again. He slapped the reins on Buster's hips, and the cutter slid away on a fresh cushion of snow from the night before.

"What are you grinning about, Louie Dewey?"

"Was I grinnin'?"

She shot him her best big sister glare, although it probably lost effect with most of her face covered. "You know what I mean."

"Why, Eliza Beth, I'm just pleased as punch to be able to escort you home, that's all."

Horsefeathers. The boy was up to something. But he obviously wasn't going to tell her what. She huffed. "I was surprised to see you." Since Wes had promised to fetch her. She swallowed down a niggling feeling of disappointment.

"Oh?" He blinked at her, all owl-eyed innocence.

"That does it." Actually, it was too much. "What are you up to?"

"Could it be that you were hoping *someone else* would come to fetch you?"

Her cheeks burned hot enough to scorch the muffler hiding

them. "Of course not."

"Uh-huh." He drew out the syllables long enough to make her teeth hurt.

"Louie. . ."

He put his hands up, Buster stepping lively at the lifting of the reins. "I just thought maybe you'd had your heart set on Wes coming after you, him being the one who rescued you and all."

"I thanked him before he left."

"Uh-huh."

If he drawled that out one more time, she'd bash him with the hot brick. Better change the subject. "How is Ma?"

All humor drained from his voice. "She was worried something awful, I don't mind telling you. What was so all-fired important about that letter that you'd risk your life for it?"

"I didn't realize—"

"Well, you should have, Eliza Beth Edmonds. You was raised in the north woods. If you don't know the dangers by now—"

"I know the dangers. That's why I want out." In her anger, the words exploded before she could think.

"Out?"

"Why do you think I went to school in Detroit?" She straightened the blanket that didn't need straightening. "I don't want to live in a lumber camp all my life. I don't want to fret about loved ones every day of my life." And that—more than anything—lay at the heart of her determination to leave it all behind. Why hadn't she admitted as much to herself before? It had nothing to do with wanting the finer things in life. It had everything to do with *life*.

Louie took the reins in one hand and wrapped his other arm around her shoulders. "I know." He gave her a comforting squeeze. "But if you feel that strongly, you best decide what to do with a certain log hauler who was chomping at the bit this morning when

I was sent to town to fetch you back instead of him."

What would she do about Wes? She couldn't deny she had feelings for him, but the strong aversion to living in a lumber camp was still there too. And now she'd finally admitted to herself, and to Louie, what her discontent truly stemmed from. The fear of losing those she loved to the dangerous work. Like Pa.

She was glad she'd mailed the letter.

Wasn't she?

It was far better to take a teaching position than stay and fall for a lumberjack, only to have him taken from her in yet another accident.

Chapter Fourteen

Wes whittled from his barrel, awaiting the tinker and carving another ice rose. He wasn't sure why. Eliza Beth hadn't spoken to him since she'd returned three days ago. She'd been avoiding him.

Why?

Wasn't a woman supposed to be grateful when a man rode in and saved her life? Wasn't that what the fairy tales said?

Not that he'd done it for that reason. He'd have saved anyone in such a situation. But it seemed like a woman would be especially thankful. Maybe even show the man a special favor or two. An extra-wide slice of pie at dinner. A touch on the shoulder as she poured coffee. Or a special look across the room during Saturday night storytelling. Something.

She'd barely looked at him and had spoken not a word.

How was a man supposed to attract a woman if saving her life didn't cut it?

Perhaps she just wasn't interested.

And then there was Louie. That fool had walked around with a stupid grin on his face ever since Wes had ridden back with the news of Eliza Beth's safety and admitted his feelings for her.

Maybe the people around here were just strange.

The jingle of bells and familiar whoop reached him. He

pocketed the ice rose and slid off the barrel. He'd buy his newspaper, and hopefully Eliza Beth would sit with him in the evening to talk about it.

Unless she'd rather avoid him then too.

Trying to woo a woman shouldn't be this complicated.

Hovering near the window of the cook shanty, Eliza Beth almost jumped when the whoops of greeting started. Would Mr. Barlow bring a letter for her today? That was the question that had robbed her of sleep last night. She grabbed her coat from the table where she'd kept it handy, thrust her arms into it, and wrenched open the door.

"Wait for me."

She clenched her teeth and shut the door. Ma took her time settling a shawl over her head before donning her coat.

The dogs were yapping in the yard before she joined Eliza Beth and nodded toward the door.

Finally.

It was the same routine as every Sunday, but it sure seemed like everyone was moving at half speed. The tinker called her and Ma to the front. Ma purchased a spool of sewing thread and a packet of shiny new sewing needles.

"And what can I get for you today, Miss Edmonds?" Mr. Barlow's booming voice almost made her flinch, but she found a smile instead.

"Is there any mail for me?"

The tinker's brow wrinkled beneath his cap before he dug into one of his trunks and thumbed through a small stack of envelopes. He looked at her and shrugged. "Nothing today. Got one for a Wes Fisk though." He handed it over her head to Wes.

"Oh." The news deflated her. "Maybe next week."

"Can I interest you in. . .?"

But she'd already turned away, heading not for the cook shanty, but for Buster's corral. The old horse perked his ears and came to the fence. She had nothing in her pocket for him, but he enjoyed a good face rub as much as a treat.

When Wes appeared beside her, she wasn't surprised. Perhaps deep down she'd even hoped he'd join her.

"Have you fully recovered?"

"I suppose I have, but Doc said I'll have to be extra careful for several weeks, probably the rest of this winter, and not to allow my toes or fingers to get too chilled."

"You were lucky."

She tucked her chin and mumbled, "You mean I was foolish."

"That too."

She jerked her head up. His eyes crinkled at the corners, and his lips twitched. She looked away.

"Mr. Fisk, I do not appreciate being laughed at over this."

"My apologies, Miss Edmonds. Perhaps if you shared the nature of the mission you were on, I could better understand the urgency that put you in such a dangerous situation in the first place."

That rankled her. What right had he. . .? "I don't see that it is any of your business."

His hazel eyes drained of all hints of humor.

"My personal affairs are just that. Personal." She stepped around him and headed toward the cook shanty.

"Even though your actions put me and Buster, as well as you, in danger?" His voice was low and conversational, not condemning.

That stopped her in her tracks, and she turned to face him with her head down. "I don't mean to sound ungrateful, Wes. I appreciate all you did for me. More than you know. If anything had happened to me, what would've become of Ma?" She drew in a long breath before meeting his eyes. "It just confirms what I've known for a long time."

"What's that?"

"I don't belong here."

She left him standing in the snow, his face a study of confusion. But what else could she say? She couldn't very well tell him that she was attracted to him. That if they'd met in a different place, she'd have welcomed his attentions gladly. She couldn't come out and say that if he just weren't a lumberjack...

She could fall in love with him.

Wes brushed snow from the dark window sill and slid the new ice rose beside the two others. Would she notice? She'd never mentioned them. Not once. Women were supposed to love flowers, but maybe not icy ones. He snorted, dusted the snow from his gloves, and turned away from the building, almost bumping into Louie.

"I figured it was you and not the tinker."

"What was me?" Wes shouldered past the younger man, not really in a mood to talk to anyone since Eliza Beth had accepted the newspaper with stilted politeness and claimed she had no time to discuss it this evening.

"The roses."

He stopped and faced the other man. "You knew about them?"

"Eliza Beth mentioned them to me."

Wes snorted and then mumbled, "Of course she did." Proof that her affections lay far away from himself.

Louie pushed the heel of his palm into Wes's shoulder. "Is that all you're going to do about it?"

The younger man was strong, crutch or not. Wes caught his balance. "What are you talking about?"

"It's plain as the blaze on Bright's face that you're smitten with Eliza Beth."

"It is, is it?" Did he expect Wes to fight with him out here in the dark and cold? Fight with a broken-legged man? Madness. Not that Wes wasn't hot enough to throw a punch if there was someone deserving of one within reach.

"Yup." Louie's finger poked him in the chest this time. Hard. "You ought to go back into that cook shanty and talk with her."

"Why?"

Louie snorted and crossed his arms. Even in the dark his glare was a solid force. "Because she's half in love with you, you idiot."

Had someone snuck liquor into camp? Because the boy must be drunk. Half in love. . . She barely even looked at him. Hadn't since they'd talked over the newspaper two weeks ago.

"I don't know where you got that idea, but—"

"I got eyes, man, and I know Eliza Beth better than most."

Now Wes did want to punch him. The implication that he knew her in a very intimate way. . . His fists tightened until the heavy leather creaked.

But Louie chuckled. "Not that way."

"How many ways are there?"

Another snort. "Mrs. Edmonds took me in when I came to camp. I lied about my age, and I guess she knew it." He shrugged. "Treated me like one of her sons." He leaned closer. "Eliza Beth is the closest thing to a sister I have on this earth. If you treat her right, you and I are good. If you mistreat her in any way, I'll find you." With that, he left.

Wes closed his mouth. Louie wasn't in love with Eliza Beth? Eliza Beth wasn't in love with Louie?

Then why was she keeping Wes at arm's length?

There was only one way to find out.

Chapter Fifteen

"You're going to wear a path in the floor." Ma looked at Eliza Beth from her chair across the room, where she was darning an apron.

"I'm just waiting for the fire to settle before lowering the bean pot into the pit."

Ma let her hands rest on her mending. "Are you sure that's all?"

Eliza Beth shrugged. She couldn't remove from her mind the disappointed expression she'd seen on Wes's face when she'd all but turned him out of the cook shanty. She paced a few more steps and then whirled back to Ma.

"You know I don't belong here, don't you?"

Ma sighed, letting her head rest against the high back of the chair. "I know you're afraid."

She did? When Eliza Beth had only recently figured it out for herself? But still she asked, "Afraid of what?"

"Even before your pa died, you dreaded the injury or—God forbid—the death of anyone in camp. When Louie was hurt, I saw it in your eyes."

Eliza Beth pressed her fingertips to her forehead. "What am I going to do if the school doesn't hire me?"

Ma rose and came to her, wrapping her in a long, warm hug.

"Honey, listen to me. We can plot and plan and map out our futures all we want, but sooner or later, we have to acknowledge that only God is truly in control."

"I know that." Eliza Beth wiped moisture from under her eyes.

"Do you?" Ma tapped her chest. "Do you know it here?"

"I think I do."

"Then be open to what the Lord puts in front of you, even if it's not your choice for your future." Ma tipped Eliza Beth's chin, gazing at her with eyes full of motherly love. "Will you do that?"

"I'll try."

The shanty door burst open, and Wes marched into the room as if he had a full head of steam behind him.

"Eliza Beth, we need to talk."

Twin pairs of eyebrows—one set a generation older than the other—pulled together as matching gray eyes examined him from across the room. He might have been a minnow in the shallows under a pair of blue herons. He swallowed, clearing his throat.

Then he wished he'd thought of something—anything—to say before he'd opened the blasted door.

"I'll just get on with my mending." Mrs. Edmonds retreated to a chair at the far end of the shanty. Eliza Beth stood as if she'd taken root near the cookstove.

He moved to stand in front of her, then cleared his throat again.

"Yes?"

"Louie says you're half in love with me." As soon as the words had passed his lips, even before her strangled gasp, he wanted them back.

"I don't know why you'd listen to anything Louie says."

"Because he loves you too, but not in. . .that. . .way." Too. Had he actually said that? *Too*. As in, so did he. Heat crept from under his collar and threatened to set him on fire.

"I. . .I guess he does."

"And you love him like a brother, don't you." It wasn't a question, because he didn't want any answer other than yes. "That's why you knitted him the cap."

She nodded, her face a study in confusion and something else. Fear?

He took a step back. "That's fine, then." *Where to go from here?*

Her hands landed on her hips with enough force that he winced. "I'm happy to have your permission to love Louie like a brother, Mr. Fisk."

This wasn't going anything like he'd planned. Well, like he'd have planned it if he *had* planned it. Why couldn't women be more like a good mare? He'd know what to do then. He'd never had a sister of any kind, so Louie was ahead of him there. And it wasn't as if he'd mixed with women during the war. In fact, Eliza Beth was his first. . .sweetheart.

"I have work to do, Mr. Fisk." She marched to the door and swung it open, making it painfully obvious that he was to use it.

He touched his cap and nodded to Mrs. Edmonds. "Good night, ma'am."

She dipped her chin, but he had the feeling it was more to hide her mirth than to acknowledge his nod.

He touched it again as he passed Eliza Beth. "Good night, Miss Edmonds."

She sniffed as he walked past, the door slamming on his heels.

Well. . . He'd made a hash out of that.

Eliza Beth whirled around and faced Ma. "He's got a lot of nerve."

Ma coughed, not meeting Eliza Beth's eyes. "I'd say the poor man has it bad."

"Has what bad?"

But Ma only shook her head, keeping it bent over her sewing.

Eliza Beth huffed and marched to the room they shared. Moonlight glinted on the window, or on something outside the window. Her ice roses. She stepped closer and saw a third rose nestled in with the others.

It was Wes. It had to be Wes who'd carved them.

But he was a lumberjack!

She needed to think about this rationally. She needed to hear about the teaching position. She needed a way out of the lumber camp.

And she needed to set the bean pot in the pit before it got any later. She plucked the muffler off her bed and wound it around her head and neck before putting on her coat. She went to the cookstove and lugged the heavy pot, already filled with salt pork, beans, and water to the door. Ma said nothing but continued sewing in her chair.

Didn't even offer to help.

With a huff, Eliza Beth got through the door and plopped the bean pot in the snow while she shut the door.

"Here, let me." Wes took the pot as if it weighed no more than a mug of coffee and carried it to the pit. She wanted to grab it back from him. And then again, she didn't. Instead, she pulled the covering off the pit and used a stout stick to rake out the glowing coals. Wes settled the pot and they worked together to put the roof in place and weight it with logs.

Then, Eliza Beth straightened to her full height, met him eye to eye, and said, "I cannot marry a lumberjack, Wesley Fisk. I don't want this life forever."

He rubbed the back of his neck, one side of his mouth pulled down. "I'm not a lumberjack."

She flung one arm out, indicating the camp, and cocked her head at him.

"I am now, of course, but this"—he flung his arm in a similar motion—"is only temporary."

Oh.

"Only temporary?" Her voice came in a breathy rush, her heart seeming to have stopped.

He took a step closer. "Eliza Beth, I'm a horseman. That is, horses are what I know. I've been saving every penny—except for a weekly newspaper to share with you—to purchase some land nearby for a horse farm."

"A horse farm."

He grinned. "To raise strong draft horses and sell them to the lumber camps, or the farmers who will fill the land once the trees are gone."

Her heart kicked back into its regular rhythm. "You're not a lumberjack?"

"No. I'm not." He took another step closer, close enough that their coats brushed together. "And what about you, Eliza Beth? What are you?"

"A teacher. Or I was, and I hope to be again. That's why. . ."

He took her hands in his warm ones. She really should have put on her mittens. "Why what?"

"Why I had to get to town and post the letter. I applied for a teaching position in Ossineke."

His brow crinkled. "Where is this Ossineke?"

"In the southern part of the county. Not too far."

"Have they cleared land in that area yet?"

"I believe they have."

He dropped her hands and gripped her elbows, drawing her

closer still. "And do you suppose, once I purchase a nice plot of ground and get a cabin raised and a barn, that a certain horseman might be able to call on a certain schoolteacher?"

"Maybe."

"Maybe?" His forehead wrinkled rather adorably.

"Maybe, if there's a window in that cabin." She couldn't keep the smile out of her voice. "One deep enough to hold winter roses."

He growled deep in his throat, but unlike the wolves, this growl caused her breath to hitch in a perfectly delightful way.

"What if a certain horseman planted rosebushes in front of the cabin?"

"That would be more than acceptable."

He wasn't sure if he'd tilted his head or if she'd tilted hers, but once their lips met, it really didn't matter. She fit into his arms as if she'd been made especially for them. It gave him a funny sort of feeling, on top of the headiness of her lips. A feeling like he'd finally come home from the war.

The winter wouldn't last forever. Spring would bring the river up. The logs would float away. And he'd buy the best piece of land he could find.

Right next to the schoolhouse.

They'd raise stout horses and tall children and grow old together. He'd have to write Pa back and let him know. Maybe even bring him to Ossineke to live nearby. Pa'd get on well with Mrs. Edmonds. They'd have a circle of family around them.

But first, he lifted the woman who'd stolen his heart and gave her a twirl in the snow. And when she stopped laughing and her feet hit the ground, he kissed her again.

Just to be sure.

Maybe women weren't so different from a fine horse after all. But that was a thought he'd keep to himself. For a few years, at least.

AUTHOR'S NOTE

I loved setting this story in my own backyard of Northern Michigan. Growing up, I heard colorful stories about the lumberjacks and walked many a "tote road" they'd left behind. The area where I live was cleared following the Great Chicago Fire and used to rebuild the Windy City. Today, much of it has regrown, and we have hundreds of acres of both state and federal forests within a stone's throw of our farm.

This collection is special to me for being able to work alongside three other authors I adore. Naomi Musch and I go way back to the early days of writing forums on the internet and have more things in common than any two people should. Candice Patterson is one of my critique partners, a valued member of the Quid Pro Quills, who writes clean heat romance that will satisfy any romantic. Jenny Leo and I met while I was working as the managing editor of Smitten Historical Romance and is a proofreader of incredible talent as well as a wonderful author.

We owe a debt of thanks to agent Linda S. Glaz, who never gave up on this project, even though it took years—literally *YEARS*—to come to print.

Special thanks to Wes Oleszewski for his assistance finding a Great Lakes vessel—the *Atlantic*—which sailed from Buffalo to Detroit in December of 1865 and explaining the how and why it would have been feasible for it to reach Alpena even in the month of December. Wes has written many books about Great Lakes boats, available on his website: www.authorwes.com.

Pegg Thomas lives on a hobby farm in Northern Michigan with Michael, her husband of *mumble* years. A life-long history geek, she writes "History with a Touch of Humor." When not working on her latest novel, Pegg can be found in her garden, in her kitchen, with her sheep, at her spinning wheel, or on her trusty old horse, Trooper. See more at PeggThomas.com.

Not for Love

BY NAOMI MUSCH

Chapter One

CHIPPEWA COUNTY, WISCONSIN
1881

Maggie Duncan understood how the notion sounded to her big brother—the idea of a young widow writing a letter to find a new husband in the logging pineries up north—but that was no call for Charlie to be letting his Irish temper show. Her long brown braid swung around her shoulders like a whip as she pitched another forkful of manure out of the stall past her brother's head. If he didn't settle down, she might not miss him with the next one.

"Are you out of your pigheaded mind?" The blast of Charlie's words went up another decibel.

Maggie stuck the pitchfork into the manure pile with a force that belied her small stature. "I won't be listening to you, Charlie, if you keep on using that tone. I've made up my mind, and this is the way it's going to be. This farm needs a man."

"But Maggie!" Furrows consternated his bushy brow. "You aren't even out of mourning. Do you have any idea what sort of trouble you're asking for? I don't think you do! How can I go home and sleep nights wondering if you're safe or if some woman-starved maniac has come down out of the woods with notions in his head?"

She rolled her eyes and shoved past him to heft up the wheelbarrow of manure and rotting straw. "You just worry about your own place and your own wife. I haven't asked you for anything."

Charlie followed her. "Why don't you just move in with me and Nancy?" He seemed to rally with this new approach. "You know we'd love to have you. You'd be at home with us."

She pushed her load down the snow-packed lane toward the edge of the field, snow clinging to the hem of her heavy skirts.

"Here, let me get that." Charlie stepped beside her. Silently, she relinquished the cart and trudged behind him to the end of the path. "Well?" he asked as he emptied the load and scattered the dung.

"We've had this discussion before, Charlie. Put yourself in my shoes. Would you want to give up your place if Nancy died?"

"'Course not, but I'm a man. You can't run a farm by yourself."

"Exactly my point."

"But Mags. . ." His voice turned pleading.

She stiffened her shoulders. He always called her that when he was trying to soften her up.

"Aw, Maggie, why you got to be stubborner than an old mule anyway?" He jerked the wheelbarrow around.

"For the last time, Charlie, I'm not being stubborn. I'm being sensible."

Charlie's jaw worked. "What are people going to think? Where's your sense of decency?"

Maggie brushed her gloves on her old wool barn coat. "I can't afford to let it matter what they think. It's the only way I can keep this place. I haven't got the money for a hired man, and I'm not so stupid I don't realize that I can't take care of it on my own. But it's *my* farm, Charlie. Mine and Bobby's, and I don't want to lose it.

So if I get married again to somebody who wants a share in a farm and is willing to make mine a good one, then I can keep it. There's nothing indecent about it."

"But why would you want to? Do you think this idea of yours would make Bobby proud?"

She lowered her hands to her sides as tears she thought she'd finished shedding weeks ago threatened again. She blinked hard against their burning and against the pain of Bobby's loss searing her anew. "That's low, Charlie, bringing Bobby into it like that. I don't expect I'll ever love another man, and it's not that I'm *wanting* to marry. You must see that. It's clear why I have to do this." She stared hard at her brother a moment longer, then her voice softened as she repeated what she'd told herself many times before. "It's all I'll ever have of Bobby's and mine. Farming is what we both loved. And I'm good at it. Better than I am at cooking or washing or the other kinds of things I'd have to depend on to make a living."

Charlie sighed but he didn't apologize. "I ought to just drag you off and let Nancy try to talk some sense into you. Won't you please just reconsider staying with us?"

"And selling? No."

"All right, then. But this isn't over." Smacking his hat against his overalls, Charlie let her go back to mucking out the cow's stall, but she could hear him fuming to himself as he stalked away.

When Maggie was sure he was good and gone, she wheeled out her last load of manure. Charlie would never understand her need for the farm, her love for the earth, but mostly her tenuous hold on Bobby's memory. If they'd had children for her to remember him by, things would be different, but they hadn't. They'd only had this farm together, and they'd birthed it as much as any baby. She'd not let it go. She'd die holding on to it if she had to. "Don't you worry, Bobby," she muttered as she tipped the wheelbarrow. "I'm staying. I'm not going anywhere."

With a final heave she shook out the manure. She returned the wheelbarrow to the shed, exhausted as much from the emotional strain of her argument with Charlie as the physical work of the day's chores. Closing the shed door, she trudged down the mushy path to the pump beside the house and forced water into the bucket she used to fill the reservoir on the cookstove.

Her bones ached. Not from the weather or the farm work, but from rawness dredged up over Bobby and the awful predicament she was in. Hers was a soul rawness. An anguish from her and Bobby's love having ended too soon, leaving her with an open wound that only time, if anything, could heal. She supposed it really must seem crazy to Charlie and Nancy, her writing a letter to find another husband so soon, but she could see no other way. The very fact that she'd even dreamed up such an idea alarmed them. Truthfully, it alarmed her too. Still, it was the only solution she could think of. Time wasn't on her side.

Maggie had been a widow for only two months, but springtime was closing in, and there would soon be too much work to tackle alone. Usually, come spring, Bobby would come home from the logging camps where he'd worked away the winter, and the two of them could handle the farm until after the fall harvest. They'd market the spring calf, get the hay up, slaughter a hog, and pile up a mountain of firewood. He'd fix the place here and there, make sure the fences were sound, tighten up the roof or the window sashes, do a little more clearing of the woods to enlarge field and pasture, and whatever else needed to be done. Then, come the crisp days of autumn, he'd go back up the river to the logging camp, and she would cozy in for winter, taking solace in her daily tasks of milking the cow and feeding the chickens, knitting socks and mending britches, and trying to stay warm in the blasting Wisconsin winter. This had been the pattern for three out of their four years of marriage. Then Bobby died, killed by a falling dead limb aptly called a "widow-maker." No matter how much she wanted life to remain dormant since that day so she could grieve a while longer, it pushed her forward like spring sap flowing up a maple tree.

She did love their farm, and she still carried within her all the dreams they shared for it. She refused to let them die with Bobby. So when the circuit preacher came through and stopped to see how she was faring, she put her plan into motion. At first she wasn't sure she could go through with it, but she handed him the letter, reminding herself there really was no other way.

She'd written plainly, telling that she was looking for a husband to help her run her farm. She didn't want any slacker or drinker or gambler, just somebody who might have ambitions to farm and was willing to marry.

The preacher was more than a little hesitant. He turned the letter over in his hands. "I know you lost your folks before you and your brother came to Wisconsin, but what about Charlie? What does he say to this idea of yours?"

Maggie's skin flushed hot. "'Course Charlie doesn't think too highly of it. He worries about how things will work out. But you've known me for five years, Preacher. You married me and Bobby. You must understand. I have to keep the farm. That's why I'm asking for your help to do it right."

"I don't know if it's so much a matter of understanding as being awfully careful about knowing what the will of the Lord is. Have you considered that part of it?"

Maggie nodded. "'Course. That's why I'm asking you for help."

She trusted him to present her plan in the best light possible to the most likely candidates. He knew some of those fellows up in the woods, and she felt she could trust Preacher Branton to take care who heard the letter read. Still, he wavered. She explained again that she wouldn't accept just anyone. Why, that would be like prostituting herself for the sake of the farm. And she admitted to him that her heart still longed for Bobby. Yet she had to try this avenue. No other idea had come to light, and didn't God sometimes author the notions that came into our minds?

The preacher shook his head skeptically at her logic, then sighed. "I can't promise that everyone who hears your letter will have a soul of integrity, much as I might wish it otherwise, but I'll do my best. We'll just have to pray very hard that the Lord directs the right one along if it's in His will for you to do this." He pinched his lips together then sighed again as he looked at her. "I hope you've really thought this through, Mrs. Duncan."

Mrs. Duncan. Maggie gave him a solemn nod, already praying silently as she watched him tuck her letter inside his black coat.

"Lord, don't send me no fools," she whispered now again, as the cold water she poured hissed into the reservoir on the cookstove.

Chapter Two

Charlie still hadn't made good on his threats to send Nancy over to "talk sense into her." Nancy might try doing so given time, but Maggie was confident she could handle her soft-spoken sister-in-law. Meanwhile, Maggie went about her days as usual, wondering now and then if the preacher had read her letter to anyone, but mostly trying not to think or worry too hard about it.

There was still a sharp nip in the air one late morning when the dog barking outside alerted Maggie to someone coming up the drive. The dog never barked at Charlie or Nancy, so it had to be a stranger coming to the house. She wiped her hands on a towel and smoothed back the loose ends of hair that slipped from her braid before going to the door. Cold air shuddered through her as she stepped onto the porch, and she quickly closed the door behind her so the inside heat would not escape. She braced herself with her arms folded close as a tall, bearded man, well dressed but of undetermined age, dismounted from his horse and approached. He tipped his hat in a most genteel way when he saw her standing there. He was no lumberman or farmer. Maggie could see that right off.

"Mrs. Duncan?" The man had a rich voice, deep, educated-like.

"Yes, that's me."

"My name is Sheldon Earl, ma'am. Might I take a few moments of your time?"

"What about?"

"Nothing to worry you. I am here as a representative of Mr. Edward Wellington. I merely wish to talk to you about your lovely farm. I come with a proposition of sorts which I hope will interest you."

Maggie's nerves lit up, but so did her curiosity, and she was too cold to stand out there long and consider it. "I guess that'd be all right." She beckoned him to follow her into the kitchen. "Wipe your feet," she said as they went inside. "Like some coffee?"

"Please." The gentleman removed his hat and gloves.

"Have a seat." Maggie poured from the pot that had been sitting on the back of the cookstove since breakfast. "Sorry if it's getting a little bit thick." She brought him the cup.

Mr. Earl took a chair, setting his hat on the corner of the table. "Thank you. I'm sure it's fine." Most anyone could appreciate a hot cup of coffee on a day like today. "Mrs. Duncan, I won't take much of your time, but I wanted to let you know that I heard about Mr. Duncan, and I'm very sorry."

"That's kind. Did you know Bobby?"

He shook his head, looking grave. "No, I'm sorry to say, I didn't. But I travel these parts fairly often, and word of accidents like your husband's, well, it gets around." He took a long sip of his coffee and frowned.

Maggie crossed her arms and steadied herself against the dry sink, waiting for him to continue.

He set his cup aside and folded his hands on the tabletop. "Mrs. Duncan, as I said, I represent a gentleman from the east, Mr. Edward Wellington, and he has authorized me to approach you about the possibility of purchasing your property. He can offer you a very fair price."

Maggie's knees began to tremble. She looked away, out the

window. Long icicles had formed off the eaves of the barn, frozen hard after a sudden return of gray skies and a cold wind. "What's Mr. Wellington's interest in my farm?"

"Mr. Wellington is interested in building communities here in Wisconsin. He owns a number of other properties in this county, including the section adjacent to yours. His goals are farsighted and would be better accomplished with the addition of the vacant woodlot east of your pasture. He realizes that you would not wish to parcel your land, so given your situation, he is willing to help you ease the burden you now bear with an offer to purchase the entire farm."

She understood. Her trembling ceased as she looked him in the eye. "He's a speculator then." She didn't mean to sound harsh in her bluntness, but no one around here thought much of the eastern land speculators who came in and bought up good land to hang on to until values had been inflated. Then they made money hand over fist reselling or leasing it to regular folks at exorbitant rates of interest—folks who didn't understand or weren't prepared for what they had gotten into.

"I guess you might think of him that way. But he has the interests of the community at heart. I can assure you of that."

"Mm-hmm." Maggie was only twenty-two, but she squared her shoulders and braced herself confidently. She pictured this Mr. Wellington sitting behind a big desk, rubbing his greedy palms together. "I'm sure that's what he likes you to tell people when he's trying to cash in on their longings or misfortunes. But you can tell Mr. Wellington that I'm not interested in selling my farm."

"He'll be sorry to hear that." Earl was a tall man, and even though she stood above him, he seemed to look down his long, bent nose at her.

"You called my farm lovely, Mr. Earl. I think it is too. It's a good farm. Me and Bobby have a lot of sweat soaked into it to make it so. Just because I'm a widow doesn't mean I'm ready to forget that and hand the place over to some man I haven't ever met." Her thoughts immediately ridiculed her about the letter on its way up north, so she added, "Somebody who has no plans to put his own sweat into it."

"Mr. Wellington wouldn't expect you to 'hand it over.' He would pay you a very fair price, which I am prepared to negotiate. You could have money to do whatever you want, Mrs. Duncan. You could go anyplace you like and have a fresh start. Find a nice place in town, perhaps, where there is society."

"You don't know me, Mr. Earl, if you think that's what I'd like."

"You wouldn't like a short walk to church on Sunday morning and tea with other ladies in the afternoon? A nice house on a shady street?"

"You best not promise things you can't provide. And besides, my idea of society is right here on this farm with God and my family just down the road."

"It's a lonely life you describe."

"It'll do for me." She folded her arms, refusing to be cowed by his steely eyes. "I've heard you out, but I've got work to do, so if you don't mind. . ."

He pushed back from the table and stood, having hardly touched his overboiled coffee. "I see that at present you are determined to remain. However, I am happy to give you time to reconsider. All the time you need, in fact. So if you have a change of heart. . ." He reached into his coat and withdrew his card. "I'd be glad to hear from you. You know, it's hard work running a farm alone. And be aware, Mrs. Duncan, Wisconsin won't remain a wilderness forever. Small villages like yours will become thriving towns eventually, just the sort of place in which a pretty young widow can be comfortable settling down, but it'll take men with vision like Mr. Wellington's to develop these towns into all they can become. Even though you've suffered unfortunate circumstances, you could contribute to that and come out the better for selling your farm."

"Me and Bobby always figured it would take a lot of hard-working men and women to make it that way, Mr. Earl. I figure I'll contribute just by staying right where I am."

"You truly believe you can continue working the farm without your husband then, Mrs. Duncan?" he asked as she showed him to the door.

"Yes, I do. I've got things all figured out."

"I see," he said, but his voice belied a hawk-like curiosity and skepticism. Maggie was sure of it.

Chapter Three

The Reverend Del Branton could not put off reading Mrs. Duncan's letter at the next camp. He hadn't been able to bring himself to do it at the first one. He'd watched the motley crew of lumberjacks straggle in from the woods at day's end thinking of nothing but a hot meal and their warm bunks. After they'd filled their bellies and wandered to the bunkhouse, someone struck up a tune on a harmonica, and they'd gotten themselves a second wind before falling off to sleep with snores that could shake the chinking out of the logs. They'd all seemed temperate enough. Yet, as Del considered the contents of Maggie's letter while he watched them shovel their stew, slosh down their coffee, and strip to their long johns to flop on hard bunks, he knew what kinds of thoughts might travel through their minds when they heard her plea—thoughts they'd be ashamed to let their preachers or their mothers know.

The men seemed tame enough, but he'd known many lumberjacks who seemed so, yet they would ride into the nearest town on a Saturday night if given the chance and spend their pay drinking, carousing, and stirring up enough ruckuses to cause decent folk to shutter their houses until Sunday morning. Young Maggie Duncan was too fine a woman to be made part of such notions as might hatch in their fertile brains. Nevertheless, Del had made her a promise, and he'd even given it to prayer. Now all that remained was for him to follow through as best he could.

As he approached the new camp, he could smell the woodsmoke of the cookshack even before any shanty or bunkhouse came into view. Daylight lingered just a little bit longer in the evenings now. Still, that merely meant the men could add another half hour to their work in the woods each day. The season of ice breakup was just around the corner, and the winter's cut of logs would need to be piled on the banks and ready to let go when the river opened. The men raced against time. The single, compelling force of knowing they would be heading back to their farms and families once the spring drive was over pushed them on.

Generally speaking, when he didn't carry such a weight as Maggie's letter on his mind, Del liked arriving at the camps this time of day. The cookee would have a fine feed on, and the men would just be starting to ramble in, hungry as horses, but glad to see him.

He stomped the snow off his boots while men swarmed in around him. Ripping off their coats and hurrying over to the table piled with warm rolls, they filled their bowls sludging over the sides with hot venison stew. Coffee flowed by the gallon, and after that came the pies made from the winter supply of dried apples. Del joined in.

Afterward he walked over to the bunkhouse and chatted with the men for a while. This camp lay too far north for the men to find it easy to ride into town, so, tired though they were, a group of them gathered in a circle for some card playing. It was Saturday after all. Others, having stripped off their wet socks to steam by the fire, reclined to write a note to their families or simply to smoke a pipe and ponder. Del took note of those who didn't talk of having a wife at home and didn't seem inclined to play cards. He carefully selected five from among them whom he would approach with Mrs. Duncan's letter after his Sunday sermon tomorrow.

Del decided to preach about commitment to the Lord, about setting aside the sins of the flesh which entangled them in their Christian life, about being faithful and true in all aspects of their lives. While it was a sermon good for all of them at any time, he himself included, Del hoped a few of his words would stick well with the men he'd selected before he presented Maggie's letter to them. Shaking the hands of those who bothered to stay for the preaching after breakfast the next morning, he asked those five men to remain behind to have a word.

"Something you wanted to talk to us about, Preacher?" A barrel-chested man about thirty years old waited with the other four. Del didn't know much about him, but the fellow had listened to the preaching intently and respectfully, and he didn't nap through Del's sermon like some others did. A few brief questions of the cook earlier assured Del that this man, like these others, was unmarried.

Del sniffed. "Yes, if you don't mind me borrowing a few minutes of your time. I asked you men to join me because I have something to share with you, and it isn't the sort of thing I'd share with just anyone. Only men I consider trustworthy enough to receive it."

Another fellow sporting cropped, reddish blond hair and a face full of freckles grinned and pushed back his hat. "You gonna preach us another sermon?"

"Not at all. I have a letter here in my pocket." Del fished Maggie's missive out and carefully unfolded it, uncertainty keeping his movements slow. "It's from a lady named Mrs. Maggie Duncan. Perhaps you remember her husband, Bob Duncan, God rest his soul."

The first fellow hitched up his suspenders, and other shrugs and headshaking went round the group. Only one of the men gave a vague nod but made no comment as to whether he and Bob were friends or how well he remembered Maggie's husband.

"Well, let me begin. It's best explained simply by reading." Del cleared his throat and read Maggie's open request in its simple language. She was forthright and honest. She didn't beat around the bush and try to make herself sound like something she wasn't. She made it very clear what any future husband could expect—and what he couldn't.

Del glanced up from the reading. Boots shuffled. One fellow ribbed another, and the pair grinned with wildcat expressions when they heard her plea. One man simply shrugged the whole thing off. The two others looked speculative, but didn't say much about it. The result was not too different than he'd hoped for or expected.

"That's about it," he finished. "Just something for you men to think about, but most importantly, something to pray about." He looked them each in the eye to make his message clear. "Maggie Duncan is a fine woman, and by that, I mean she's a decent, good lady. I won't put up with anyone bothering her who doesn't have her best intentions at heart, so no shenanigans, if you take my meaning."

"Oh, we won't make any trouble." A gangly fellow with a sparse patch of whiskers winked at one of his compatriots.

"Ain't got no plans to think of marrying," said the man who'd shrugged it off. He turned and walked away, picking up his ax by the door.

Del sighed and nodded at the others as they dispersed. He'd made it through a first reading. Lord help him.

No. Lord, help *Maggie* as he took it to the other camps.

He used the same approach at the next two camps. That was all he could do. He couldn't keep reading the letter everywhere he went. He was too nervous about what the far-reaching results might be. It was time to conclude the matter.

Del rode off into the woods yet again, hunching his shoulders against a cold breeze. "It's in your hands now, Lord," he prayed as the ears of his horse twitched. "Unless you show me that there's someone else who needs to hear this, I'm letting it go. I trust that you'll keep a close watch on little Maggie. She's a good girl, and I'd hate to see anyone take advantage of her."

Chapter Four

Dear Gentlemen,

If any one of you listening to the reverend read my letter has ever met my husband Bobby, you know he was a good man who worked hard all winter long so he could come back home to me on our farm each spring. Together we'd do the tilling and the planting, and we'd castrate the new litter of pigs. Our farm's a pretty place over here near Cadotte. It's got good soil, and more than half of it is cleared for planting. Now, mind you, it is still a work in progress. Lord knows we have enough things to do around here to keep the place going, and the house always needs something fixed, but it's a good start Bobby gave it. Anyhow, if you knew Bobby, you might have heard he passed on a couple months back. Widow-maker took him home. Now it's up to me to work this farm.

Before you get to thinking any wrongful thoughts about why I'm writing this letter, you should know I got a brother and family that live close by. I'm not completely alone in the world. But I do love my farm, and I do want to stay put on it. That brings me to what I'm proposing.

My brother Charlie is busy with his own farm and his own wife and kids (me and Bobby never had time to start a family of our own) so Charlie doesn't have time to help me with the heavy work like hauling a plow and fixing things or fetching firewood. I'd like to hire a hand to help with those things, but the truth is I can't afford it. So I'm fixing to marry again, just as soon as I can. Here's what I'm asking. I'm looking for a man twenty-five to thirty-five (sorry, but I don't want to marry some feller whose joints are already starting to ache). I'm looking for a fellow who's got strength and years left in him and wants to put those attributes to good use.

You may be thinking right now that I'm out of my head or just some lonesome widow who misses having her man. Well, that isn't it. In fact, I'm not dreaming I'll marry for love, and I'm not looking for anybody to keep me warm at night, if you understand my meaning. I just want a fellow who'll agree to a sort of arrangement. In return for a home here on the farm, he'll be half owners with me. He can be my partner in running this place, long as he's willing to put his back into it and doesn't get the wrong notion about what I'm offering. It's a farm. A place to call home. That's it. And if that isn't enough, then don't bother knocking on my door. But if you think you might be the fellow I'm searching for, somebody who'll help me bring Bobby's dreams and mine to life (and you can grow your own dreams about the land too), well then, I'd like to talk to you. See if we can come to like minds. We can try it out for the summer. I'll offer room and board in my barn for the season's help, and we can decide whether we suit one another's company after that.

I guess that's all for now.

Sincerely,

Mrs. Maggie Duncan

Crazy thoughts plucked at Jack McAllister's brain, keeping him awake while the snores of a dozen men rumbled all around him. He tossed to his other side and pulled the scratchy wool blanket tighter around his shoulders. He'd never heard anything like it. While Jack stood among a small circle of selected men listening to the words read, he would've laughed outright if he hadn't recognized the seriousness with which the circuit preacher warned the fellows listening.

Someone could *have* Dunc's farm?

Two winters ago, he'd worked with Bob Duncan, the wiry lumberman everyone had simply called Dunc. The two of them had gotten on well together. Dunc was a good guy, fun to be around. He had a sense of humor that shone in his brown eyes and in the way he tossed his unruly shock of dark hair off his forehead when he laughed. Dunc never cut his hair that whole long winter.

"You'll get fleas," Jack told him. Fact was they all got fleas sleeping in such tight quarters that stunk of hard work and wet socks.

Dunc had waved off any concern. "I'll wait for Maggie to cut it in the spring. You single fellows don't understand what it's like to come home to a wife who wants to run her fingers through your hair." He closed his eyes with a sigh that made all the men in his shack fill up with longing. Now after hearing what the preacher read in that letter, Jack thought again of a woman running her fingers through his hair and nearly groaned.

Somebody to marry Dunc's wife? Jack's sleepless eyes narrowed to a stare at the cracks around the stove door in the center of the room where the red coals of the fire glowed. A good looking, even-tempered guy like Dunc wouldn't have been married to a work-hardened scold, would he? Jack tried to picture what sort of girl Bob Duncan would have married.

Maggie, the preacher said her name was. She'd be young and cute, sure. She'd like to laugh and maybe dance, because that's what Dunc did. Dunc had arrived at camp fit and healthy enough, so she must be able to cook passably well, and maybe Dunc even told him so once. Jack tried to remember if he imagined that. Then he realized he was imagining the whole business anyway and scolded himself. *What are you even thinking about this for? It's crazy and pointless. You aren't gonna go off and marry Dunc's wife and live on that farm.*

He turned over on his side and clenched his eyes shut, but he couldn't sleep. His brain jangled like the harnesses on a pair of oxen, and his thoughts kept rolling on the way logs bounced and churned on a river drive. He'd never planned to spend five years logging. It had just happened. Somewhere along the line his dreams to have a place of his own were simply forgotten. But now Dunc's farm kept leaping up between him and sleep, and his dream would not be quieted again.

When the call to rise sounded, daylight was merely a haze in the woods. Jack's head felt thick with weariness. The questions about Dunc's farm and his widow had piled into a log jam in his skull. Now Jack had to pry them loose and focus instead on breakfast and work with no time to pause and seek out the preacher. Right after sloshing down his coffee, he and the rest of the crew were headed off one direction into the forest while the preacher rode off in another. In a couple days, Del Branton would arrive at another camp, read the letter again, and give some other man ideas enough to keep him awake at night and dream.

Chapter Five

Maggie set a warm apple pie on Nancy's kitchen table and removed the clean cloth covering it.

"You didn't have to bring anything, Maggie." Nancy lifted a heavy Dutch oven and set it on the worktable, then closed the door to the cookstove. "We invited you to join us." She lifted the lid off the pot, sending the aroma of roast beef and potatoes wafting through the warm house, drowning out the spicy scent of apple pie.

"I needed to use up my dried apples. Without Bobby to bake for, they'd have gone to waste."

"It was mighty thoughtful. I didn't have time to make dessert. Charlie and the kids will certainly appreciate it. We'll have Pete bring in the cream from the springhouse, and I'll make some topping. It'll be a real treat."

She handed Maggie a stack of plates, and Maggie proceeded to set them around the table. "Looks like you gave me one too many."

Nancy turned her back. "Oh, didn't Charlie tell you? We have another gentleman joining us."

"No, he didn't." She'd not have thought anything of it except for the way Nancy seemed to brush the information aside. Her behavior only made Maggie curious. "Who is it?"

"Oh. . .I forget his name. He's a stranger to me."

Maggie paused with the silverware she'd started setting around the plates but kept her mouth shut. It didn't pay to ask Nancy about things Charlie might be up to. He didn't disclose much to his wife. The stranger was probably a buyer for one of last year's steers.

"Gracie, go outside and ring the bell for your daddy," Nancy said through the parlor doorway.

Charlie and Nancy's place was nice. It was only two bedrooms bigger than Maggie and Bobby's small house, but they'd been in it longer, and Nancy had done a lovely job of making the place homey with her tatted doilies scattered on the solid furniture and laced curtains pulled back on the windows. Nancy had gotten a pretty horsehair divan from her parents when she and Charlie married, and she treated it like a treasure, never letting the children scamper on it or even allowing Charlie to sit on it unless his trousers were freshly washed. She kept her kitchen floors polished to a shine and had real pretty glass dishware too. All the pieces matched and were painted with colorful spring flowers.

Maggie had always thought she might have such nice things herself someday, but now with Bobby gone there was no telling how long she'd have to get by on her old tin plates and hand-me-down curtains. It didn't matter all that much, to be truthful. She kept them clean and took good care of the things she did have. She had all her mama's pretty oil lamps and a nice braid rug by her bedside. Her own home was cozy enough.

Charlie came in a few minutes later, shagging off his coat and hanging it on a hook by the door. He took off his boots and left them there too.

He rubbed his palms together as the savory kitchen smells must've hit him. "No company yet?"

Nancy poured grounds into a boiling pot for fresh coffee. "You told him the correct time, I hope?"

Charlie glanced out the doorway. "Here he comes now."

Again, Nancy's glance flitted toward Maggie and away. They were up to something. This wasn't about any steer. Lord help her if they were matchmaking. After her and Charlie's argument a few weeks ago, she wouldn't put it past him trying to appoint the *right* man to marry her.

But it wasn't a suitor Charlie had in mind. She figured that out the moment Sheldon Earl's head ducked beneath the doorframe. She folded her arms, bracing herself as much on the inside as on the outside. Maybe it would be best to feign ignorance, pretend she didn't know or didn't care what Charlie was up to. Actually, she didn't. It didn't matter what Charlie said. He'd never convince her to sell her farm, and least of all to a lizard like Mr. Earl. She pictured him just like that, a giant lizard in a black hat, with big glassy eyes and a tongue darting out between his lips each time he spoke, his long nose flaring with each breath of interest.

"Well, hello, Mrs. Duncan. What an unexpected pleasure to meet you once again."

"Indeed. Unexpected," she countered, giving his lizard's claw the briefest handshake.

Mr. Earl carefully removed his hat and coat and handed them to Nancy as Charlie directed him to sit. Nancy returned to the table, waving the children to their places, then moving to her chair and encouraging Maggie to do the same.

Maggie took a seat next to young Pete and decided not to speak except to her eight-year-old nephew. She was not about to make this an easy evening for Charlie, if indeed he had brought Mr. Earl here with nefarious motives. Mr. Earl commented on how wonderful dinner smelled and how long it had been since he'd had a home-cooked meal. Maggie wished she'd not brought the pie. She leaned over to Pete and whispered that she'd save him the biggest piece.

She had looked forward to this evening with Charlie and Nancy. They rarely took the time to do family things together anymore. It wasn't as though she was jealous of her time with them, but to share the evening with Sheldon Earl went against the pale. She glanced at Nancy and quirked her brow as Charlie and Mr. Earl made small talk. Nancy busied herself serving Gracie.

"I suppose you're surprised to see Mr. Earl here, Maggie," Charlie said to her at last, beaming as though he'd given her a great treat.

"More than surprised."

"I met Mr. Earl last week at the town meeting. We talked for a while, and I thought it would be a nice idea to invite him out to the farm tonight. As he said, he doesn't get a home-cooked meal often."

"You thinking of selling your farm, Charlie?" Maggie couldn't help herself. Her resolve to mind her tongue and keep her lips closed fell short, thus the biting remark came out instead. She flashed him a wide-eyed gaze he couldn't possibly believe was amazement.

"No..." he answered, drawing out the word. "Funny you should take our visit that way." She could feel his irritation as if it were mud slung at her, which would have been a whole lot more welcome. She wasn't afraid to fight back.

Mr. Earl stretched his pale lips into a smile. "I understand your brother and his wife have lived here for some time. With such a fine family to raise, I wouldn't dream of letting him sell me his farm." He glanced at Nancy. "Wonderful roast, by the way, Mrs. Beckworth." He lifted a forkful of meat as if to toast Nancy before stuffing it into the cavern of his mouth.

"Thank you!" She sounded gushy to Maggie.

Charlie ignored the niceties passing between his wife and guest. "I was hoping you would hear Mr. Earl out, Maggie. He told me about the offer he wanted to make on your place, and it's more than fair. You should at least listen."

She hated it when Charlie pulled his big brother act of appearing to be wise and reasonable. It usually meant she would come out on the short end. "I've already listened to Mr. Earl's proposal, and I'm not interested, so unless you want to sell him your land, we should just enjoy our meal."

"There's no reason to be upset with your brother, Mrs. Duncan—"

She glared at Earl. "Isn't there? Didn't he invite you here to try and convince me to sell my place to you?"

Earl lifted his empty coffee cup, and Nancy pushed up from her place to retrieve the pot from the stove. He set the cup back on its saucer. "You might see it that way, but he merely wanted to make certain you weren't missing out on an opportunity that would serve you in the years to come." He picked up his cup again as Nancy backed away from filling it and leaned toward Maggie with the pot.

"No thank you." She jabbed at a potato. "The way I see it, Mr. Earl, is Bobby left me with opportunities. How I choose to use them is up to me. *Not* Charlie."

"Can't you see I'm trying to help?" Charlie growled. Nancy set the coffee on the stove and returned demurely to her seat, as if she'd prefer to melt away rather than be noticed by anyone and called upon to contribute to the argument.

"You want to help me? Then quit trying to convince me to sell my place! If you wanted to help, you'd be talking to me about spring planting." Maggie forced down a sip of coffee and burned her mouth. She reached for Pete's milk and poured a bit into her cup.

"Spring planting. . ." Charlie huffed.

"I don't expect you to help me, Charlie. Not really. But don't you worry. I have things under control."

Charlie slammed his fork onto the table. "If you're still nursing that cockamamie idea of yours—"

Maggie sprang from her chair. "It's no more cockamamie than you harassing me to sell my place to some speculator. I can't believe my own brother wants me to do such a thing."

"Sell it to me and Nancy then. I'll take care of your place and you can live here with us, just like I said before."

"You couldn't afford my place even if I did want to sell it to you, which I *don't*!" she shouted.

Sheldon Earl waved his hands, urging them to calm down. "Please, please, don't upset yourselves on my account. I'm not here to force anyone to do anything, Mrs. Duncan. I assure you I would never do that. I'm only here to offer you a promissory note." He reached into his vest pocket and pulled out a paper.

Maggie sucked down ragged breaths, forcing a calm she didn't feel as she watched him unfold the paper that resembled something poisonous. It was despised yet held her curiosity in suspense like a rattlesnake's vibrating tail. He slid it across the table so she could see what it said. A figure she'd never imagined was penned in ink. Her whole body grew weak and tingly, and her thoughts ran from one dark corner to the next. Mr. Earl tapped the paper. As her glance flitted, she noted Charlie's craned neck and even Nancy's curious gaze as they wished to see what Earl offered. It was their eagerness that finally brought her to bear. Even with such a tidy sum written down in black and white before her, she knew her farm's true value.

"I repeat, I'm not interested, Mr. Earl. My farm is worth much more. I fear you could never match the price I'd set." She pinched her lips together and sat back down, refusing to look at him again. She took a bite of pickled beets and then laid her fork down. "I think I'm ready for pie. How about you, Pete?"

Pete nodded vigorously. A coolness descended around the table, but Maggie ignored it. She cut and placed a full quarter of the pie onto Pete's dinner plate, and the boy's eyes rounded with thrill and admiration. Maggie set an invisible shield around them, one against which Nancy's protests wouldn't dare penetrate.

Chapter Six

By the time the ice finally gave way and the crews released the piles of logs into the river, Jack had run all the possible scenarios through his mind. Each one tumbled about with the same wild abandon as the trees that hit the water. The logs rolled over one another in a pounding cacophony and struck the pool with a thundering force, plunging down, then shooting up with a spray of power and foaming fury. Just like Jack's ideas about having a farm of his own.

Dreams he'd carried, dreams nearly abandoned, resurfaced and bounded along. He'd like to raise pigs and a few cows for milking. Maybe butcher a steer or two each year and market the meat. His wife—now there was a thought—his *wife*, Maggie Duncan, would market some butter and eggs and maybe even sell some of the things she grew in the garden. Only she wouldn't be Maggie Duncan. She'd be Maggie McAllister. That part of the dream was a bit harder to wrap his brain around. It was like a sharp bend in the river where the logs jammed up.

It didn't matter anyhow. She'd be like a sister to him. Wasn't that what the letter implied? But by agreement, the farm would be his as much as hers, as long as she meant what she'd said. Again, he wished he'd had the chance to talk to the preacher about it. He would've liked to know more about Dunc's wife before presenting himself on her doorstep. In the meantime, he kept his wild ideas to himself.

Jack worked the spring log drive like a fever raging. The same focus pushed the other lumberjacks, especially the family men. Jack never before realized how thoughts of home could spur them on. Maybe because the logging camp had been his only home since his ma died and he and his father set out for the camps. He'd stayed straight through the summers, working to bring in hay for the oxen and horses and laying corduroy roads through the swamps. A year after he and his father began, a tree kicked back during the felling, and his dad had gotten his leg badly busted up. He'd been laid up for months before taking a train back to Illinois to live with his spinster sister and find what odd jobs he could, his logging days over. Jack stayed behind to work in the woods. He usually sent a letter to his father at Thanksgiving time and received a reply written in his aunt's hand at Christmas. He thought now and then about his folks and the days before his ma passed away. Life had been good then. With the simplicity of childish thinking, he'd enjoyed being home on the farm his family tenanted, imagining that one day he too would become a farmer.

On the mild, sunny day Jack collected his final pay for the season and left the camp behind, a surge of excitement both calmed and tantalized him. He mounted his horse alongside another fellow who was pulling out too.

"Not staying on this year?" the man asked.

"Not for the summer anyway. Thought I'd take a break."

"Everyone needs a change now and again. Going to town with that check?" The man shot him a wry grin through a bushy, black beard. "If you are, why, I know a place you could spend some of it." He whistled, and Jack took his meaning.

"No thanks. I'm going to have a look at some property. Got a fair piece to travel today." Jack prodded his horse onto the wagon road.

The other fellow drew up beside him. "Thinking of settling down then?"

"Thinking on it."

"I guess I'll have to spend this money by myself then." He patted his coat pocket. "Trust me, I'm looking forward to it." He tipped the brim of his hat, gave his horse a kick, and trotted on ahead.

Jack moseyed along, letting the other lumberjack gain distance between them. He turned halfway in the saddle with only a brief glance back at the emptying camp. He would take his time heading south toward Cadotte. He had plenty to think about, such as how he'd introduce himself to Dunc's wife for one, and when he'd be able to start the planting for another. He'd put some of his pay toward that planting if she allowed him, just to show his good intentions.

Yep, there was plenty to think about.

Two days later Jack walked his horse slowly along the road close to Dunc's land. Gnarly oak trees and some scraggly jack pine flanked the way. He knew when he'd reached the farm, because a split rail fence marked the corner. His breath came a little shorter, and he had a sudden fear that maybe Maggie Duncan had already picked a husband. It had been nearly a month since Preacher Branton read her letter. She might have had a string of suitors seeking her out already. Some camps emptied out more than a week earlier. What if it was too late for Jack?

He shook off the thoughts as the Duncan barn came into view, then a farmyard beyond it, and finally a glimpse of the house. At the start of a short drive, he dismounted his horse and gazed at Dunc's place. His heart drummed. *It's just the way Dunc described it.* He remembered Dunc mentioning the new barn, modest but tight, and the white clapboard he'd laid up over the small log house and how it nestled against an oak grove. Casting his eyes to the east of the barn he saw a pair of does browsing on the other side of the field. His horse nickered. Taking the reins in hand, Jack led him up the drive.

All lay quiet; a pervasive serenity blanketed the scene. Jack took a deep breath of the spring farm smells, barnyard and wet earth, the hint of woodsmoke from a fire still necessary to shake off the coolness in the seasonal air. The only sound he could make out was the faint trickling of water running off beneath patches of crusty snow and the occasional call of a blue jay or robin claiming his territory.

A satisfied, proprietary sense filled Jack, and he expanded his lungs with a deep breath as he spied the pitcher pump just off the end of the porch. He dropped the horse's reins and walked over to it. Icy cold water spewed out after several vigorous pumps with one hand. With the other he slung splashes of water across his face. When he heard a dog barking inside the house he stopped, remembering that the place wasn't his yet. For the rest of his life he'd never forget how that fact was honed in on him in the next few moments.

The door burst open and a slight gal stepped out. With her head cocked so that a single braid hung over her shoulder and down to her hips, she fixed her gaze upon him, her eyes keenly sighting down the long barrel of a shotgun.

"What do *you* want?" Her voice was dangerous.

Jack shook water droplets off his hands and rubbed his palm across the two-day growth on his jaw. The girl tensed even more visibly, looking as though she would prod him with the gun before firing it.

"You Maggie Duncan?" Jack asked. He thought about taking

a step closer by way of introduction, but rejected the idea at the gleam hardening in her eye. Yet the spattering of light freckles across the bridge of her nose contradicted that fierce expression.

"What if I am? You thinking you got some sort of *comfort* to offer the poor widow Duncan?"

Comfort? A picture sprang into Jack's mind of the sort of trouble she'd asked for in writing to the logging camps. Real care would be needed to proceed.

"I was a friend of your husband's." He couldn't have picked a better way to start. The heavy-ended gun barrel drooped slightly. He pressed his advantage. "I worked with him back at Camp Six up in the northeast section a couple of winters back."

"What's your name?"

"Name's Jack McAllister." He waited, hoping maybe Dunc had mentioned his name at least once, and that favorably.

"So you came to talk about Bobby or what?" She rocked forward ever so slightly. It must have been getting hard for her to hold that gun steady. Jack turned his gaze away from her and took another look at the farm. For the first time, he noticed a scattering of chickens pecking along in the shadow of the barn. He got a mental image of Maggie Duncan calling, "Hey, chick, chick, chick," and tossing them handfuls of corn. He looked back at her.

"Look, ma'am, I'm not here to hurt you. I can see you must have had a fright lately or something. I just came to talk to you. I'll be upfront and honest. It's about a letter you wrote."

Mrs. Duncan lifted her chin at him. "I'm willing to talk to you, I guess. Can I put this scatter gun down?"

"I promise I won't come any closer if you don't want me to."

Slowly she lowered the gun, first to her waist, and then, seeing that he didn't move, she set the stock on the floor, tilting the barrel end clear of either of their heads.

"Can you really shoot that thing?" Jack asked with a smile.

"Would you like a demonstration?" The threat came back into her voice.

Jack laughed. "Nah, nah. I believe you."

A long quiet filtered between them, then Mrs. Duncan spoke up. "So, you listened to my letter?"

Jack nodded. Her eyes penetrated him as if waiting for him to say more. Jack wasn't quite sure how to proceed. He found himself looking back at her. *Really* looking. Now that Dunc's wife wasn't staring at him with an aim to kill, he could see that she was more than cute, more than pretty. He admired the spirit in her.

"Yeah, quite a letter," he said softly.

For a moment he thought she was going to blush, but maybe on second thought, it was pure emotion welling up in her.

"I just want to keep my farm, Mister. . .Mister. . . What did you say your name was?"

"McAllister. Jack."

"I just want to keep my farm, Mr. McAllister. If you say you knew Bobby then you know he loved this farm. I want to keep it for him but for me too. I don't want to lose it. If there was any other way for me to do the work alone or to hire someone, then I'd do it, but there's not. Now I got speculators knocking at my door, hounding me to drop my land in their laps, and a brother who thinks I'm crazy not to."

Jack nodded and allowed himself another appreciative glance about. "I can't say I blame you. It's a pretty place."

"Would you. . .like to look around?" The hesitancy in her question told Jack she hadn't settled yet that he could be trusted.

"Not just yet. Maybe I can take a walk later. I'd rather just sit here and rest for a little bit. My horse could use some water."

"Oh!"

The gal suddenly set the gun against the house and hurried down the steps. "I'm sorry. I didn't even think about your horse. Have you been riding long?"

"I left camp two days ago." He decided not to say anything else lest her attention be drawn back to the fact she'd just made herself defenseless.

She ran to the barn and disappeared inside, coming back out moments later with two pails, one empty and one holding some grain. Jack took long strides over to meet her and quickly relieved her of the empty pail, turning his steps back to the pitcher pump. With only a few deft thrusts of the pump handle the pail overflowed. He set it before his horse who'd buried his head in the grain bucket. Dunc's wife was stroking the horse's neck.

"This is a fine animal. Had him long?"

"Ten years. We're used to each other."

Used to each other. Jack looked again at Dunc's wife. Could it be possible that he would marry this woman and take over her farm so that she could nurture the dreams she shared with her dead husband? Would the two of them ever get used to each other?

Chapter Seven

Maggie stroked the horse's neck. Her whole mind was wrapped around this friend of Bobby's. Jack. Jack McAllister. There were so many fellows up there in the pineries Bobby talked about, but he didn't always tell her their names. Could this man be one of them? It was likely, but he might just as easily be making it up about knowing her husband.

Her nerves were finally starting to simmer down from seeing him standing out there looking like he already owned the place, like he already owned *her*. He'd called it right. She had had a fright. He wasn't the first to come down out of the woods to have a look at her and her place. The first she'd sent on his way after just a day. She could tell after only two short conversations they'd never be able to live together agreeably for long. Plus, she didn't like the way he treated her tools or his gruffness with the animals. He didn't seem threatening to her, but she also didn't think he would mind his manners for long.

The second man was more of a beast, really. He was the one who'd really put the fear in her, looking to comfort Mr. Duncan's poor widow, looking to take what she wouldn't give, and that without talk. He was dangerous. He'd cornered her in the barn before she knew anyone was there, talking smoothly at first then coming closer and with a purpose. He became demanding when she tried to extricate herself from the situation. She shuddered at the thought of what would have happened if Charlie hadn't come along when he did.

Shaken to the core and scolded heavily again by Charlie, she didn't know if she could stand another suitor coming to the farm as a result of that letter. Now one had. She tried to sort out her thoughts up to this point. She didn't like the way he gazed at the farm as though it were meant to be his, yet that's just the way Bobby had seen it. And didn't she want the right man to love the place? She also didn't like the way he kept saying the right things. Still, would she trust him more if he didn't? Was she confused because of the way that other devil had tried to smooth talk her? This one didn't seem to be dripping with deceit.

She looked at him candidly from beneath her lowered lashes. He was only a couple feet away unsaddling the horse, close enough for it to be hard to tell if it was the horse she smelled or him. It wasn't a bad smell. He had blue eyes. Bobby's eyes were brown. He had sandy-colored hair, cut sometime over the winter and smoothed back off his forehead. She'd never imagined touching hair that wasn't like Bobby's. Sunshine had given this man a leathered, outdoorsy look, but he couldn't have been more than two or three years older than Bobby—older than her.

He looked up at her suddenly and she scrambled for something to say. "You must be hungry after riding so far. I can fix you a cup of coffee and get you something to eat."

"Don't worry about that, ma'am. I ate some biscuits and dried beef a little while ago. I will take some coffee though, if you don't mind."

Maggie went into the house and lifted the pot off the back of the stove. She peered inside and raised it to her nose to sniff the bitter, black remains. She poured the last of it into a pair of cups and set them on the table. "Coffee's ready," she said, pushing the screen door open. "If you want to come into the kitchen." She didn't mean to glance down at the gun next to the door, but she couldn't stop herself in time. The man, Mr. McAllister, noticed.

"Why don't we just have some out on the porch," he said. "We can talk and you can tell me all about your place."

Relief washed over her and she brought their cups outside. There were no chairs on the porch, so she handed him his cup and sat down on the front step. Mr. McAllister took a sip and sat down beside her a couple feet away.

Maggie noticed now how tall he was. Taller than Bobby, and a little bit broader in the shoulders.

"Sorry if it's thick," she said. "Bobby always teased me about my thick coffee. My brother does too. I can't help it if I don't drink it fast enough and it cooks on the stove all day. Even the circuit preacher, Del Branton, is getting used to it."

"Then I'll get used to it too." He took a swallow and grimaced. "Whew! You aren't kidding!"

Maggie looked down in embarrassment.

"Oh, it's all right," he said. "I can make it for us tomorrow. I've got a few tricks."

Tomorrow? So, he planned on staying then, at least until tomorrow.

"I can cook," she murmured. "I'm best at breakfast."

"That'll be something to look forward to after I finish with the morning chores. After this coffee, maybe I can put my bedroll out in your barn and take a walk around. That is, if it's all right with you."

"It's all right."

"Look Mrs. Duncan, I don't wish to force myself onto

you—onto your place that is. If you don't think you like me or that you can trust me, just tell me so and I'll get packing. But if you're willing to give this whole thing a try, then I am too. What do you say?"

Maggie looked hard at Mr. McAllister. He wasn't like Bobby at all, but either she was going to do this thing, or she wasn't.

"If you stay, and if we. . .marry. . ." She could feel her cheeks flushing, so she looked all around him but not right at him. "You understand that I wouldn't ever expect. . . That it wouldn't be—you know—romantic or anything. We'll live like a—a brother and a sister or two old codgers or maybe even friends. It's the best I could do."

When she got the courage to look at him, she found he wasn't looking at her either. He was gazing off down the drive. A breeze had come up and lifted some of the fine strands of his hair. His eyes were creased in the corners, squinting into the brightness of the day. Finally, he looked at her.

"I have my own dreams. I've always wanted a farm like this one. I was jealous when Dunc, er, I mean Bob talked about his. I never would have imagined that he might be describing my own place someday."

Maggie soaked in his words, emotion rising in her throat.

He went on. "You seem like a nice gal, just the sort of gal Bob would be married to. I know the two of you had something priceless, and I don't expect you to be looking for anything else so soon. Truth is, I didn't come here to look for anything more than a contract either. You can hold me to that if you like."

Something like kinship moved through Maggie's spirit when he talked, and she made her decision. Jack McAllister could stay. For now. Del Branton wouldn't be coming this way again for a couple of months. They would have that much time to see if things could work out equitably between them. If they did, then the preacher could marry them. If they didn't, then Mr. McAllister could go his way at any time.

She raised her coffee cup to her chin and paused. "I think I will hold you to that, Mr. McAllister."

Chapter Eight

The sun sketched a line across the horizon as Maggie pulled herself out of bed. She wrapped herself in her thick but slightly tattered robe and moved on silent, stocking feet through the house to put wood in the stove. With a clank, she settled the cast-iron grid cover in place and went back to the bedroom to dress. She shivered into long wool stockings and her work dress and layered on a sweater over the top. Then she slipped into her shoes to begin her day.

The fire had worked into a blaze, so Maggie picked up the bucket by the door and went outside to pump it full of water as she gazed at the brightening dawn. Her glance swept past the barn. Then she remembered *he* was there. The stranger who was going to stay and maybe marry her. She carried the pail indoors while thoughts clung to the edges of her mind like mud on her hem. *You don't know him a whit. He talked fine yesterday. Seemed honest. Maybe he's only trying to catch you off your guard.* She remembered the incident with the last fellow in the barn and hoped she didn't have anything to worry about with Mr. McAllister.

She filled the coffeepot with water and set it to boil before going about preparations for breakfast. The sound of a whistled tune just off the porch startled her, but she quickly gained her composure, thankful for that simple warning that he was coming toward the house.

She opened the door to find him standing there with a fresh pail of milk in his hand. It gave her a moment's pleasure to glimpse his initiative. "Bring it inside." She turned her back, steeling herself with courage to have him inside her house and to face the day with a stranger.

"Thought you might want to get this strained right away. I grained your cow and thought I'd check with you on scraps before I slopped the hogs."

She gestured to the floor beside the sink. "I'll put the whey in there and you can give it to them later." She cracked eggs into a hot pan and wiped her hands nervously on her apron. "Have a seat. Coffee's set to boil."

"Mind if I fix it up?"

Should she mind? She remembered him saying he'd teach her how to do it his way. "Go right ahead." She moved aside and reached for a sack of coffee, already ground.

Mr. McAllister seemed at ease as he whistled softly and picked a spoon from a crock on the corner of her work space. He lifted the lid with a towel and looked into the pot. "She's just starting to boil." He scooped in four rounded spoons.

"That's all?"

"You said you made it too thick."

"I just pour it in."

"Nothing wrong with that. You might try measuring a couple times until you get a feel for the amount."

She harrumphed softly but wondered if it really would taste any better than hers.

"Now, we won't leave it boiling overlong."

"Like I said, it gets burned from sitting on the stove all day."

He grinned. "Won't have that problem if I'm around. I'll make sure it doesn't have time to burn."

What did he plan to do, sit at her kitchen table drinking coffee all day? "I'll see, I guess."

He nodded and put the cover on, moving the pot gently to the back edge so it wouldn't boil over.

She ladled eggs onto his plate and toasted him some bread. That's one thing he'd find he couldn't complain about. If Maggie could do one thing well it was bake up nice things, especially bread. Bobby always said hers was the softest bread with the nicest brown crust of any he'd ever had. He said she ought to come with him to the lumber camp and teach the cookee how to make bread like that. A sudden, fierce longing for Bobby seized her. She took a deep breath, pushing it away. "Tomorrow I'll bring up some bacon from the smokehouse so you can have something else besides eggs."

"I don't need any special treatment." His glance was friendly as he accepted the plate from her hand.

"Your work is cut out for you, Mr. McAllister," she said by way of reminder as to why he was there. "A man has got to eat."

"I thank you for it." He turned and picked up his fork, but first he bowed his head. She turned away.

When breakfast ended, Maggie washed the dishes while Mr. McAllister finished the morning chores. Then she donned her coat and exchanged her shoes for a pair of boots to join him outside. It was time to show him the lay of the land. They set out along the south fence line.

"Fence is in good shape. Bobby fixed it up tight before he left in the fall. Got to keep an eye on trees knocking it down in the wind or such like."

He nodded, and she thought maybe she was telling him things he already knew. Still, she didn't want to take any chances on his ignorance.

"Where did Dunc leave off clearing?"

She pointed. "Way up off the northeast pasture. We'll head that way next."

They trudged on. Now and again, Maggie glanced at him and saw that he wasn't just looking at the direction of his feet, but he seemed to be taking in the stands of wood and field with a measuring eye.

"Lots of dead wood over there," he said with a nod to his right. "I'll start collecting that soon as I can. Get a start on next winter's firewood."

Her shoulders relaxed. Firewood for each coming year was always a concern. Even if he didn't make good on any more clearing, if this McAllister fellow got her some wood up, that would be something.

She realized she was thinking again of winter alone. Would he stay or be long gone by then? Would they wind up marrying? The notion seemed even stranger to her, now that an actual man was here with that purpose in mind. He was no longer a figment of her imagination, an image dreamed up with the writing of her letter. She slid a glance at him. Even if they did marry, would he go off again to the lumber camps, or could they make it on farming alone? Likely, he'd go, just as Bobby did. In a way, the thought relieved her. He'd do his part, tend to the farm, get her set for next winter, then leave her be. After all, she couldn't expect him to live in the barn through a brutal Wisconsin winter. She hadn't thought of that before. How hadn't she?

She chided herself. *Don't be worrying about that now. He might not even want to marry you.* But when she glimpsed him again, she could see how he studied the land with real appreciation. He wanted it to be his.

He turned and caught her glance, startling her. "I'd be remiss if I didn't ask you something."

"What's that?" she asked, nervously.

"Well, ma'am, it's about your reputation. The preacher was clear about that, and I don't want to spoil it for you."

Her suspicion mounted. "How could you spoil it?"

"Just my being here might be cause enough. Do folks around know why you asked me here?"

She shrugged, looking at the dead grass beneath her feet. "I suppose they might come to wonder. Only the preacher and my brother know about the letter I wrote." She didn't think either of them would say a word, but then she remembered Sheldon Earl. Would Charlie say something to him about her trying to find a husband to keep her farm? Nancy wouldn't speak of it to any of the church ladies, would she?

"And all the men who heard him read it."

She hadn't figured that any of them would spread the word. But there were those two she'd run off. She shrugged again. "I doubt anything will come of it." She hoped not.

"Well, you can be sure I'll do my best to uphold your good name." He gave her a nod as though to emphasize the point.

"I appreciate that. Why don't you tell me more about yourself, Mr. McAllister?"

He held back a springy branch, allowing her to pass without getting struck by it. "I'd be happy to." They walked on, and he told her about his growing up years and about his ma passing, then on to his time in the woods up north and how the past few years had been different after his pa got hurt. Lastly, he told her how he always figured he'd like to settle down and farm someday if only he could figure out a way. "Maybe you can see why I wanted to take this chance."

Maggie stayed quiet for a long way, not sure he really expected an answer. It was a lot to take in, to try and mesh his dreams into her own future. But he at least deserved a response after his long explanation. When they reached the edge of the field nearest the house, she waited for him to draw up next to her. "I can see your reasoning. I suppose if I was in your place, I might do something drastic too."

He chuckled. "Doesn't seem like we're very different, if you think about it."

She studied him for a moment. "I suppose we're not." She moved on.

"You follow your dream, and I'll follow mine. We'll just see where it leads."

See where it leads. That's right. That's what they had to do. There was no one telling her she had to do this thing. Everything would be up to her. "That sounds good to me, Mr. McAllister, but for now, I'd best be starting some supper. All this walking has stirred me up an appetite."

Her stomach rumbled as if to emphasize her words, and Maggie couldn't remember the last time she'd felt so hungry.

Chapter Nine

The next day Jack hummed a tune as he harnessed the horses to Mrs. Duncans's wagon for their first trip into town. She'd fixed them up a fine breakfast, good as any the camp cookee had ever made, and now the sun warmed his neck, filling the day with promise. They'd discussed their plan over dinner the evening before. Jack had insisted on contributing the bulk of the funds for the seed. She'd not wanted to accept such generosity, but he insisted. He explained that if things didn't work out and she wanted to send him on his way, or if he chose to go of his own accord, he would feel better knowing that she would have a fall harvest. He'd have done everything he could to make his best go of their experiment. Brushing aside her arguments on the matter, he told her he didn't have anything better to spend a portion of his earnings on. In the end, she tired of arguing and graciously accepted.

"You sure about this, now you've had time to reconsider?" she asked, soon as they were on the buckboard, Jack holding the reins.

"Positive."

"All right then. Let's go face the music."

He understood. They'd talked about what it would look like, the two of them coming into town together to make their purchase. Heads would shake and tongues would wag. Mrs. Duncan insisted that she didn't care. Long as she had prayed about it and the preacher had been instrumental in directing them toward one another, what difference did it make what anybody else thought besides God? Jack gave a gentle slap of the reins and they rolled down the drive.

He kept his gaze straight ahead. "You said you have a brother."

Mrs. Duncan didn't answer right away, and he thought maybe she'd lied about that just to warn him to mind his manners, but no. He heard her slow intake of breath. "It'll be his place we pass up ahead about a mile from here. Can't miss it."

"Do you wish to stop and say hello?"

She shook her head at his quick glance. "He'll be sure and drop by soon as he hears. No need to go out of our way."

Jack scratched his chin. Her lack of eagerness to have him meet her brother said something, but what? Maybe she was ashamed to be seen with him. He'd washed and combed his hair. He even put on his clean shirt before they left home, so he figured he looked all right.

Dunc. That was it. Her brother was close to Bob Duncan, and here came Jack, trying to step in, take over his place, and even marry his woman. The man's *sister*. Maybe she feared her brother wouldn't take kindly to him right away.

"Your brother got a name?"

"Charlie." No preamble. No last name. Just *Charlie.*

"All right. I look forward to meeting him."

Her sidelong glance warned him that he'd probably change his tune. Hmm. . . Maybe he'd have to win Charlie over, treat him with a careful hand, just the same as her.

The wagon creaked beneath them as he pulled it to a stop in front of the feed and general store half an hour later. Across the street stood the bank and post office. On the corner was a smithy, and down the road a little farther from the other buildings stood the tannery. On the other end of the street, behind a picket fence, a town hall shared quarters with a barbershop. Mrs. Duncan nodded at a woman exiting the store. Jack didn't miss the way the woman's gaze narrowed with curiosity when she said, "Hello, Maggie," but Mrs. Duncan didn't waste conversation. Jack tipped his hat to be polite and jumped down off the wagon. Mrs. Duncan was already climbing down when he got to her side. She paused on the step and glanced at him holding his hand out for her, reluctantly accepting assistance as she stepped to the ground. She quickly withdrew her hand and brushed it on her skirt—or maybe she was only smoothing out a wrinkle. Jack couldn't be sure.

"Well then, shall we?" he asked.

She nodded and followed him into the store.

"Morning, Mr. Schumacher." Her voice carried over the counter to a balding man on a ladder who was placing cans on a high shelf.

He turned his head. "Ah! Good morning, Mrs. Duncan." Then he noticed Jack standing behind her. His smile wavered but he quickly reclaimed it as he climbed down the rungs. "What can I do for you today?"

"I've come to buy my seed and a few sundries. That is—" She glanced back at Jack. He moved around a floor display and came up beside her.

He extended his hand. "I'm Jack McAllister, Mr. Schumacher. I'm working for Mrs. Duncan, and I've come to help her with her purchase today."

"You don't say." He maintained his professional demeanor, yet it didn't hide his curiosity very well.

Jack forged ahead. "Mrs. Duncan, have you got your list?"

She reached into her coat and withdrew a slip of paper.

"Everything's on there. I got it from the journal Bobby kept of the things he planted last year and intended for this spring. Does it look all right to you?"

Mr. Schumacher peered over the brim of his glasses and ran his gaze down the list. "I think you've got everything." He turned and carried the list into the back room.

Jack turned his back on the departing Mr. Schumacher and faced Mrs. Duncan. "Anything else you need that you didn't put on that list?"

"I wrote down the flour and coffee and sugar too."

"Anything else?"

She looked at him like he was daft, but he pressed on.

"All the garden seeds you want?"

"I saved my seeds from last year."

"Nothing special then?"

She turned to finger a bolt of sturdy blue cotton cloth. "Nothing I can think of. Think I'll get me a few yards of this though. Long as I can afford it." She cast him the slightest of smiles, her way of offering thanks for the seed, no doubt.

"You go right ahead." He reached past her arm and picked up another bolt of sunny calico. "How do you like this one?"

She peeked at him with one brow raised. "It's pretty. Why?"

"You like it?"

She nodded.

He carried it over to the sales counter and set it down. Then he pulled out his own list and reached for a pencil on Mr. Schumacher's sales counter. After jotting down a note he returned the pencil and waited. His gaze roved after Mrs. Duncan now and then as she strolled about the store fingering bonnets and eyeing canning jars, studying homemaking supplies, soaps, and gewgaws. When Mr. Schumacher returned she came and stood beside Jack.

"I have everything you need in good supply. If you pull your wagon around the back, my nephew will help get you loaded."

Jack handed him his list. "Here are a few more things I'd like you to add if you have them. And give me some of this pretty cloth, as much as Mrs. Duncan tells you. Don't let her be stingy." He smiled at Mrs. Duncan, who watched him and waited. He hadn't mentioned buying anything extra, but he wanted to give her something special.

"The apple tree root stock I'll have to order," the storekeeper said.

"Yes, I know. But you have the rest?"

"Yes." He went in and out of the back and collected tins off the shelves.

Mrs. Duncan started to look alarmed. "What are you doing?" she hissed, close enough for only him to hear.

"I've been saving my money a long time, and I want you to have these things. It's my way of thanking you again for the opportunity, so I won't let you say no."

Her lips parted and closed. Seemingly she was aware he'd not back down.

He turned aside and gathered a pitchfork and a rake from a barrel in the corner. "Yours are old and bent. I can turn new handles and sharpen the tines so we have them as spares, but we'll need proper tools to work with if we want to get your garden turned in the meantime."

She reddened, and he hoped it wasn't from anger. It didn't matter. She needed the tools and that was that. She'd have them even if it meant him getting tossed out on his ear.

She bit her lip as Mr. Schumacher filled out the order for the two apple trees. Jack hoped he hadn't overstepped too far.

The storekeeper's glance covered little as he accepted Jack's cash. It held a mix of satisfaction and inquisitiveness. Jack waited for his change and thanked him.

"Thank *you*, Mr. McAllister." Mr. Schumacher smiled and bobbed his head while Jack picked a parcel with each hand off the counter. He turned with Mrs. Duncan toward the door just as it opened.

In stepped a wiry man with a lean face and keen eyes. Jack noted recognition in them when he spotted Mrs. Duncan. The man removed his hat and tipped his head in a dignified fashion. "Mrs. Duncan."

She gave a mere nod and strutted forward.

The man's gaze narrowed and followed Jack as he passed. "Good day to you."

"Good day," Jack said.

Mrs. Duncan held the door while Jack passed through. He went to the back of the wagon and loaded the parcels carefully inside. Mrs. Duncan gazed back at the door. Her face had lost its color from earlier, but she still seemed to be considering something.

"Friend of yours?" He followed her gaze. Through the front store window, past the stacks of merchandise, he could see the tall man leaning one elbow on the counter, deep in conversation with Mr. Schumacher.

"No. No friend of mine." Her voice called him back as she hoisted herself into the wagon.

Jack climbed aboard. "But he knows you."

"We're acquainted."

Jack pulled the wagon around the building to the loading dock where a young man about fifteen years old piled bags of seed. In a few minutes they had all their supplies and were on their way. Jack wanted to bring up the subject of the mysterious man again, but Mrs. Duncan spoke first.

"You bought a lot of things back there. I don't know why you did it."

"Because I want you to know I am in earnest. I fully intend to stay and help you keep your farm, Mrs. Duncan."

"You mean you want to keep it for yourself."

He turned his head to look at her and didn't look away until he'd caught her attention. "If you want to remind yourself of that, I don't mind. Yes, I'd be pleased as pudding to call it mine, but I'll not forget it's just as much yours. I thought you might like the trees. If you don't like apples—"

"Oh, I like apples well enough. It just seems like an extravagance."

"It's no extravagance. We need to eat."

She didn't respond too quickly, but after some thought said softly, "Bobby brought me apples last year. Got them from a peddler driving through who'd happened upon a few bushels to trade. It would give me pleasure to have my own."

He smiled and giddyapped the horses. "Then that's what you'll have." Town quickly fell away. Jack finally broached his other question. "How about you tell me about the man who came into the store when we were leaving."

She waved as though she were chasing away a fly. "Don't pay him any mind. That's Sheldon Earl. He's the speculator I wrote about in my letter."

Jack thought hard. "Yesterday you said something about speculators knocking at your door, but I don't recall you mentioning a speculator in your letter."

"Oh. Didn't I? I must've just been thinking about him when I was writing. Mr. Earl wants to buy my farm, and, truth be told, my brother would like me to sell it. He wants me to come live with him and his wife Nancy."

"Why don't you?"

"Didn't I tell you *that* in my letter?"

Jack worked up his recollections of what she'd said about her love for the farm and for continuing on with what she and Dunc had begun. "I guess you spoke of such."

"Selling would be bad enough. Selling to a man like Mr. Earl, well that'd be the worst. He'd probably tear the place down." She turned to him suddenly, a movement he felt as her arm brushed his side. "You can see now why I wrote that letter, can't you? Selling to him would be the worst thing I can imagine."

Worse than marrying a stranger? He considered her for a moment. There was a fire in her brown eyes he could appreciate. He nodded. "I can see why. Don't worry, Mrs. Duncan. I'll do my best not to let you down."

Her lashes fluttered and her eyes glassed. She turned her face forward. "Thank you, Mr. McAllister, for the apple trees and everything you did today."

"You're welcome." He glanced at her once more and formed his next question carefully. "Do you suppose you could try calling me Jack? I'd like to call you Maggie, if you don't mind."

She blinked. "I guess that would be all right." She nodded, seeming to reassure herself more than to assure him. "Thank you. Jack."

His shoulders relaxed and he turned off onto the road heading to the place he longed to think of as home. "You're welcome, Maggie."

Chapter Ten

By the time the snow had fully melted and the soft gray buds of the pussy willows had burst into yellow-green, Jack and Maggie's days had fallen into routine. Maggie rose early each morning to stoke the stove, put on the coffee, and fry up the eggs. She had to admit that boiling the coffee the way Jack liked it, it tasted better, and Jack, without lingering about and wasting daylight, would proceed to have the whole pot emptied long before the contents could simmer into syrup on the stove.

His whistle no longer startled her as he came up the porch steps each morning. After the first week passed, she found a sort of comfort in the sound. It felt good to know that someone was meant to help. He'd been as good as his word about the other things between them too. Only now and then did worries nag her, such as whether he'd change his mind and want her to pay for all the things he'd purchased, or whether the novelty of the farm would wear off him after a while.

She poured him his second cup of the morning, and he drank it while they discussed plans for castrating the new litter of piglets. He rose and carried his empty plate to the sink and rinsed it off. "Good breakfast."

"Thanks, Jack." It was the same breakfast as every day, but it was nice to have her efforts appreciated. Calling him by his Christian name had gotten easier too.

He lifted his jacket off the peg by the door and put on his hat. At the sound of the door closing behind him, Maggie turned to watch him through the window. He strode out to the barn with her dog skipping at his heels just like it used to do with Bobby.

Everything had gone smoothly so far. Even if he did leave, perhaps he would walk away as quietly as he'd come. And just maybe he'd stay.

Maggie pushed down her restless worries and turned to her own chores. It was a nice warm day with a good breeze, perfect for hanging out some washing. She would have to wash Jack's clothes. That was only fair. He'd been wearing the same two pairs of pants since he first arrived. Later she'd go out and ask him to turn at least one of them over to her.

She hadn't even been in the barn but once or twice since his arrival. As much as she loved going inside and smelling the hay or listening to the gentle sounds of the animals feeding, it felt awkward seeing Jack's sleeping quarters with the bed stand he'd built himself. She'd noticed he kept a notebook of some sort next to his oil lamp, and he had a Bible and one or two other books to read. His blankets were folded neatly, and the corner where he slept was swept clean and cleared of cobwebs.

She could be thankful he wasn't a slob.

Bobby hadn't been very neat, now that she thought about it. While he'd been meticulous with his tools and anything to do with his work, he was prone to tracking mud across her clean floor and to leaving his overalls lying in a heap beside their bed at night. She smiled thinking of him.

She kept smiling, thinking of Jack's other habits. As she went about her own room, making the bed and gathering her laundry, she considered his penchant for a bath. A couple of times a week he'd fill the tub in the morning and let it sit warming in the sun behind the barn. Then, after a day spent working on some project or another, he'd add just a little warm water from the reservoir in the kitchen before hopping in. She imagined that the water was barely tolerable to the touch. After all, it wasn't summer yet.

She jumped at the sound of the door bursting open. Charlie's voice echoed through the house, calling her.

"What is it, Charlie?" He sounded so urgent she dropped her laundry to the floor and hurried from her bedroom. Was someone hurt? Charlie looked past her. She glanced over her shoulder and back at him. "What's the matter?"

"Is he in here?"

"What? Who?"

"The new man."

Maggie glanced backward again to see where Charlie kept looking, and then the scope of his meaning hit her.

"Oh, for heaven's sake, Charlie! What are you going on about?" She turned him back to the kitchen and moved into the room ahead of him. She leaned back against the dry sink, folding her arms tightly across her chest.

"I heard you found some fellow to take you up on your crazy idea. That true?"

"We haven't talked in nigh on three weeks, and this is what you come to say?"

"Answer the question, Maggie."

She huffed. "I found someone who's interested in helping me run the farm."

Charlie grunted.

Maggie planted her hands on her hips. "Don't you grunt at me, Charlie Beckworth. I'm not your plow horse. I know perfectly well what I'm doing."

"Like you knew what you were doing that day in the barn the last time I came over?"

Fury rose in Maggie along with her words. Why she should be so angry was something she'd have to figure out later, but for now her only concern was that he had no business talking about Jack's intentions without ever having met the man.

"That's enough, Charlie. Jack's a decent man. I won't have you barging in my house and criticizing me or him."

"Oh, so he's caught your fancy then?"

Charlie's words hit her like ice water. "What?"

"You heard me! Where's he sleeping, in the barn?"

"As a matter of fact, he is, and I'm going to have to ask you to go on home if you're going to insist on implying otherwise."

"You're a confused woman, Maggie! Why don't you just sell the place? Then find a fellow if you want to, but make him want you for you and not for the farm you're going to hand over to him on a platter!"

"I'm not going to hand anybody anything!"

"I hope not, because frankly, Maggie, I don't think that by law you even have the right to make the decision about this property. I'm your older brother. I'm a man. That right should go to me!"

"Are you trying to tell me that you'd try to take my place right out from under me?"

"I'm not saying nothing, only that you should think real hard before—"

The way their voices were pitched, neither of them heard anything until the door flew open on its stretched-out spring and slammed against the side of the house, and Jack landed in the kitchen squarely in between them. He hauled Charlie out the door and sent him stumbling backwards down the steps.

"Jack!" Maggie tried to recover from the shock.

Charlie floundered for a moment before falling backward into the dirt, but he regained his feet as quickly as he could. Jack stood on the porch step in front of Maggie, waiting with his fists balled at his sides.

She reached out for the back of Jack's shirt. "Jack, it's my brother Charlie!"

Charlie took a step forward, and for an unsteady moment Maggie thought they might fall out. She put her hand on Jack's arm and he hesitated, but she could feel the tautness still in his muscles.

Her words seemed slow to sink in. "Your brother?" His tension finally gave way as he lowered his hand. She felt it was safe to let go of his arm.

The men stared at one another a moment longer, then Jack jumped down the steps and stretched out his hand to Charlie. Maggie admired the way he regained his composure. "Looks like I almost made a fool of myself." He offered Charlie an abashed smile.

Charlie brushed his hands on his overalls and peered at Jack's hand before slowly accepting it. His face was still stony. Maggie could see he wasn't ready to give an inch.

Jack continued. "Guess when I heard the two of you in the house, I thought Maggie might be having a little trouble. She told me about that other fellow."

Charlie cast a hard glance in Maggie's direction. "Is that right? And to think I came over to protect her from trouble, while all the time she had her own special hero to take care of her."

Maggie almost choked, but all the frustration bursting out of the seams of her was lost on Charlie.

Still, Jack seemed unperturbed. "No trouble here."

"Humph. We'll see. Maggie, I'm gonna ask you again. Will you come and stay with Nancy and me? I can help you settle everything with the farm later."

Charlie's shoulders were squared toward her and his eyes looked down a tunnel at her. His whole posture made it clear that Jack was not to be considered a part of their conversation, even though Maggie stood partially screened by Jack's broad shoulder. It made Maggie bristle. She stepped out around Jack.

"I told you, Charlie, no. I'm not coming over to your place unless it's for Sunday dinner. I'm perfectly comfortable here in my own home, and Jack's doing a fine job of helping me keep it up."

"For how long?"

Maggie felt a torrent like spring mud rise up inside her, but Charlie held up a hand as if to ward off the blow of words she wanted to spew. She backed down and he continued. "I've been talking to Sheldon Earl, Maggie. He's ready to up his offer. I don't think you've spent enough time thinking on it. You know, that offer's a sure thing. But this lumberman here, what's he? He might be gone tomorrow or next fall, or next year. Money in the bank is money in the bank, Mags."

"I don't need *money* in the *bank*." She gritted out each word. "I *need* this farm!"

"You need to think about your future."

"At last, you see my point!" She raised and dropped her arms to emphasize the validity of her argument. Charlie merely rolled his eyes.

She didn't expect that Jack would have anything further to say to her brother, but he spoke up, and he stood so close behind her that she felt the vibration of his voice. "I'm sure Maggie will think long and hard about your advice. She's a bright woman and will make up her own mind without influence from either of us."

Much later in her musings to herself, she would admit that it felt good to have someone standing up for her again and treating her like she had a good mind of her own, just the way Bobby would have. She never knew how much she missed that part of their life together, that part of having someone reaffirm her self-confidence. In fact, Jack sounded like he'd have complete trust in her decision when the time came.

"In the meantime, we'd be happy to come over for Sunday dinner sometime," Jack said, and Maggie suddenly found herself fighting a smile. She could feel his whole body humming with humor behind her, and a wonder flashed through her thoughts of what it might be like to turn around and see that humor so close up in his blue eyes. She crossed her arms over herself and narrowed her gaze at Charlie.

"See, Charlie, Jack's willing to be friendly. Maybe you could find it in your heart to give him a chance. You'd be giving me a chance if you did."

Like a thunderhead spoiling over river rapids, Charlie glowered at the two of them. "Have it your way, Maggie," he growled at last. "You always do!" He turned and marched to his horse. Once mounted, he cast them a final look, this time directed more at Jack. "You'd better take my warning, mister. You'd better watch your step with my sister!"

Maggie held her ground until he'd galloped down the drive and disappeared on down the road. Finally, she sighed. Weakness overtook her as her energy rushed out. She turned around to go inside. Jack hadn't moved and stood only inches in front of her. She looked up into his eyes. An apology rose to her lips, but she struggled to get it out.

His fingertips touched hers. "I want to stay, Maggie. I really do." He looked at her in a way that made her shiver just a little, and she found herself drawn into the deep blue of his eyes as she waited for his next words. "Are you willing to marry me when the preacher comes this way?"

Was she ready to make that decision so soon? Maybe she was. Maybe it was best not to wait till summer ended. She nodded. "I am, Jack, if you are."

"I think we can make it work out. I'm willing to do my part in trying."

Maggie had all kinds of crazy thoughts dance wild across her mind. It wouldn't be for love, not at all, and still she thought maybe there was something in it. Maybe God hadn't brought her a fool or anything less than a real good man.

Chapter Eleven

Summer heat hung in a sultry haze over the north country. Grasshoppers buzzed and sprang just ahead of the steps of man and beast during the day, while fireflies painted dots of light like falling stars against the velvet of the night. Smells of sweet grass and an impending warm rain filled the Reverend Del Branton's senses with calm. His days of travel were long, but he enjoyed the time spent worshipping under the canopy of God's creation as he plodded through the countryside. Maybe someday he'd settle down with a church of his own to shepherd, but for now he appreciated what youth he still had and the ability to travel and preach to those in the far reaches of the northern wilderness.

A familiar line of trees appeared as he turned the corner on the dusty lane he traveled, and for the next several minutes his thoughts turned from peaceful reverie to things more serious in nature. In the little town not far from Maggie Duncan's farm he'd heard the story. She'd hired a man, and word was that he was more than a farmhand to her. Del had wondered a thousand times how she'd fared after sending out that letter she wrote last winter, and many a time he'd berated himself for doing as she asked. He prayed for her daily, asking God to protect her if Del had made the worst mistake of his life in sending men her way. Maybe he'd been a fool.

The rumors may have merely confirmed it.

He topped a small rise where Charlie Beckworth's farm sat neatly carved out along the roadside. A weathered, split rail fence lined his drive. A whitewashed, two-story house nestled beneath a bower of oak trees fifty yards from the barnyard. All was tidy. Voices caught his attention, and soon he spotted two children running about the lawn. The older one's tone seemed to scold.

Del smiled. Best to stop at Charlie's place first and get a feel for things at Maggie's before heading over there. Who knew what he would confront? Surely Charlie had been keeping a close eye on her and this fellow whom she'd supposedly taken in. It encouraged Del to believe so.

But Maggie's got a mind of her own. He frowned. The rumors could be overstated. She certainly wouldn't have taken a man to her bosom out of wedlock, would she? He tried to pull back the thought. *Yes, Lord, she's definitely got a mind of her own.*

"Ma, it's the preacher!" young Pete shouted.

Nancy Beckworth appeared in the doorway, drying her hands on a towel. "Stop your yelling now, Pete. Go fetch your father." Pete raced off toward the barn. "Hello, Reverend. Won't you come inside out of the sun? When Pete gets back, I'll have him water your horse." She beckoned the little girl to come inside as well.

"Thank you, ma'am." Del swung himself down from his horse, giving his stiff joints a shake and taking his hat off before following Nancy and her daughter up the steps. She led him to her parlor and offered him a drink to quench his thirst.

Del gazed around the homey, well-appointed room. Nancy's womanly touch lay in everything. It was in homes like hers that he sometimes wondered whether the Lord would ever settle him down long enough to court a woman and marry. He didn't have long to ponder on it, however, as she appeared with a cool glass of water.

"It's straight from the pump, so it's good and cold," Nancy said as she took a seat across from him.

He emptied half the glass easily. "That's very refreshing. How's your family since I last saw you, Mrs. Beckworth?" He smiled at the little girl who stood next to her mother's chair.

"Well, as you can see, we're all fit as a fiddle. Gracie here is growing like a weed."

"And getting prettier all the time, I see."

Nancy beamed and Del coaxed a smile out of Gracie. "Everything is going good on the farm this year? Nice stretch o' weather we've had."

"So far so good. Crops are coming up. Got us a nice bunch of calves this year."

"How about over at your sister-in-law's place? Things going well there too, I suppose?"

Nancy glanced past Del's shoulder toward the front window, her demeanor growing mildly fidgety. "Well as it can be, I expect. Charlie's none too happy about her."

Del held himself in check. "Oh? Why not?"

"It's that man Jack McAllister. You should know who I mean, Reverend. You sent him to her." She gave Del a slight frown.

Del pulled to mind what he could remember of the men he'd met and spoken to late last winter. He wasn't sure he remembered a Jack McAllister. 'Course, some of them hadn't responded much or let on any interest when Del read Maggie's letter. Maybe this man Jack had kept his thoughts to himself. Now Del wished he'd gotten to spend more time with each prospect.

"Has there been trouble?"

"Trouble? Well. . .no, not that we're aware of. But he's just moved onto the farm like he owns it, and she's *letting* him." Nancy reached over and patted Gracie's hand. "Run get the reverend one of those molasses cookies, honey. You can fetch one for you and Pete too." Gracie scurried out of the room, and Nancy leaned forward. "She's created a scandal, Reverend Branton, and it's got Charlie madder than an old rooster. He's gone over there a couple of times and tried running the fellow off, but he hasn't been able to do it. And Maggie doesn't say a thing. She lets that McAllister fellow tell Charlie what for."

Del frowned. This wasn't good. Wasn't what he'd hoped to hear at all. "He's got a temper?"

Nancy lifted a shoulder. "I wouldn't say that."

Charlie came into the house then. Del was more confused than ever. "Hello, Reverend Branton." Charlie extended a hand.

"Charlie. I hope I didn't take you away from anything too important."

"I needed a break. I'm more than happy you've stopped by. You haven't been to Maggie's place yet?"

"I'm heading there after I leave here."

"That's what I was hoping you'd say. I want to warn you, Reverend. Maggie's had a time of it. She had to run off a couple of men this spring, and the one she has there now is no good."

Del forgot his cool water, more alarmed still. "Oh?"

"He thinks he owns the place. Been treating it like it's his since the day he arrived. He's got my sister bamboozled into— Well, into thinking so too, if you want to know the truth."

Del glanced to the window to be sure the children were still out of earshot. "Your sister and Mr. McAllister, they aren't. . .they aren't sharing a bed?"

Nancy blushed. A black look came over Charlie. "She says they aren't, but I don't know. I don't trust him."

"I see." Del didn't see. The whole business looked to him like a foggy mess. He brushed cookie crumbs into his palm and stood.

He'd best get over to Maggie's without delay. "I'll have a visit with her. Your wife tells me things are going good with you this year?"

Charlie's brow unfurled. "Fine. Things are just fine. We have room for Maggie here with us if she'd agree to sell her place. She's got a good offer, but she won't hear of it. She's just that stubborn and determined to bring herself to ruin."

Del said how sorry he was to hear that, and left them. What had Maggie gotten herself into? How in the world had it come down to this—that he might have helped bring her so low? There was no way to know for sure. Not until he had a talk with Maggie and Jack.

Chapter Twelve

Sweat ran down Jack's back, stained the underarms of his shirt and collar, and glued particles of hay to his arms and neck as he tossed forkful after forkful into the wagon. Maggie pitched along opposite him on the other side up the windrow. They both stalled, breathing deeply, at the hail of someone across the field.

"That Mr. Earl again?" Maggie peered around the wagon.

Jack turned and squinted. "Doesn't appear to be." He measured the man with a frown. Sheldon Earl had come by just two days ago, begging an audience in private with Maggie. Jack had departed only as far as the porch where he'd hear if Maggie called for him. She'd been gracious, though Jack could see Earl was stirred up some. He'd raised his offer. Maggie refused to talk about it, and Jack hoped the speculator hadn't begun to get to her. She was a widow, after all, and Jack didn't really hold any claim over her or the farm. She'd promised to marry him, but she could just as easily change her mind if Mr. Earl's offer was pretty enough.

The figure across the field came closer. *The preacher.* "Looks like it's Del Branton."

Maggie left her pitchfork and stepped around the wagon, smoothing the hair back from her brow. "I'm a sight to see," she muttered.

"He won't mind. He knows you're a hard worker, don't he?"

Jack didn't wait to see if she nodded. He walked forward to meet the preacher.

"Hello! Maggie, that you out there?" Branton called from his horse, a smile in his voice.

"It's me, Preacher!"

Branton slid off his horse and met Jack, reaching for his hand. Jack welcomed him. "Don't know if you remember me, but I remember you. I'm Jack McAllister. I met you back at Camp Six a few months back."

"You were one of the fellows I read Maggie's letter to."

The preacher got right to the point. Jack liked that. "One of 'em. I often wished I'd been able to catch up with you before you left and talk things over a little more. As it was, I came down here to meet Maggie and visit Dunc's farm—Bob Duncan's that is."

"You knew Bob?"

Jack nodded. "For a spell. Nice fellow."

The preacher's eyes left him and turned toward Maggie as if to test Jack's assertion.

"Only reason I let him stay on," Maggie said, as if she'd heard the unspoken questions too. "Didn't hit it off too well with a couple of them other fellows that came down after ice breakup. But I thank you for finding Jack. He's been a real help."

The preacher took his hat off and turned it in his hands. "Maggie. . ." His voice took on a heavy tone. "I spoke with Charlie and Nancy on my way over."

To her credit, she pushed her shoulders back. "I suppose they filled you full of falderal."

"I don't know. What do you say? They were. . .concerned." His gaze flashed at Jack.

She folded her arms. "They've become more busybody than anything else."

Time for Jack to step in. "It's no secret to me that they're worried about my intentions. I don't blame them any, but I'm being honest when I tell you that I mean good, Preacher."

Maggie gave a firm nod. "Jack's been a gentleman. He hasn't pressed any advantage on me. He—He sleeps in the barn." She stuttered, and Jack thought she might be blushing. "I can show you if you want. He's worked his back stiff on clearing and plowing. You see how he looks." She glanced at him, and though her skin was red from heat and pitching hay, her cheeks turned a deeper shade, and she turned her face with a sweep of her lashes. "You caught him out here working hard, just like he does every day," she quickly added.

Branton's mouth lifted at the corners. "I believe you, Maggie."

"How about we go on up to the house and sit down for a while to talk this out. Maggie and I could use a rest." Jack gave a nod toward the house and let Maggie step ahead of them.

Back on the porch, Jack brought out chairs, and Maggie and the preacher took seats while Jack splashed some water from the pump over his head and neck and pushed back his hair. He'd give them a minute to talk alone, figuring that's what the preacher needed. They both gave him a glance when he joined them, and he could see the preacher had gotten to the point.

"So that means you are still as opposed to the idea of selling as you were last winter?"

Maggie's chin lifted. "Nothing Charlie or Sheldon Earl say is going to change my mind."

Jack took a seat on the step and Branton turned to face him. "Maggie told me you've spoken openly about marriage. I trust her to know her own mind and heart. I would like it better if there were stronger feelings between you, but friendship has always been a good start."

Jack looked at Maggie. She sat there with her tanned hands pressed together in her lap. Bits of hay dust were stuck in her braid that was tattered from the wind and work. Freckles splashed her cheeks. She looked wild and somehow lovely. Had they become friends? They had fallen into a routine. They rose every morning and met for breakfast, spoke of their plans for the day, worked side by side or on different ends of the farm. They supped together in the evening and sometimes sat quietly and drank coffee on the porch. When it rained and Jack had done all he could do repairing harnesses or caring for other things in the shed or barn, he sometimes retired by his lamp and read. He wasn't sure what she did up here in the house, but it was always tidy. The floors were clean. Meals were fine and ready on time to meet the growl in his stomach. She washed his clothes, and he hadn't expected her to do that. They spoke of other things now and then, of their childhoods. He'd told her about his life growing up, and she'd shared her own story. He felt like he knew a lot about her brother and his family, and she knew something of his. They talked about Bobby and even laughed a time or two over some memory or other of him.

Yes, he supposed they'd become friends. He could think of a lot worse women to marry, and it wasn't like there was going to be anything else between them.

Jack nodded. Yes, friendship was a start. He glimpsed a nod from Maggie too. Their glances caught as though they were both thinking the same thing. They meant to settle this thing now.

"Preacher, Maggie and I have discussed all this, and we've come to an agreement. I've asked her to marry me. Right away."

Branton took a long breath and let it out slowly. "She told me. I know that's been her intention ever since I agreed to carry her letter up north. At the same time, as I just told her before you joined us, I don't want her to make a rash decision." He paused and studied Jack hard. "She assures me she hasn't."

Jack's insides relaxed. He gave Maggie a small smile and a breath of a laugh. "I'm glad to hear it."

"We should have witnesses," the preacher said. "I think I can straighten things out with Charlie. That would be best."

Maggie nodded thoughtfully. "I suppose you're right about that. I'd like it if Nancy were here. She stood with me when Bobby and I got married."

Jack cleared his throat. "How soon, Preacher?"

"Is Saturday suitable?" Saturday was three days off. Still time to change their minds.

Jack looked to Maggie. Everything depended on her. What would she say? Her gaze had gone to the road. Was she remembering the day she'd married Dunc? Would her memories of that love keep her from sticking to their arrangement in the end? She didn't look at them. Her gaze was wistful, but she said softly, "Saturday's fine."

Chapter Thirteen

Maggie sat on the edge of her bed, worrying the fabric of her dress. She jumped at the sound of a tap on the door.

"It's me." Her sister-in-law's muffled voice pressed against the wood.

Maggie wiped the heel of her hand over each eye as Nancy slipped inside. Maggie twisted around to face her.

"I came to see how you're doing. Charlie's outside with the children." Nancy's brow curled slightly and her glance darted over the worn, everyday work dress Maggie had on. "Is this what you're wearing?"

Maggie shook her head and sniffed. "I haven't started."

Nancy sat beside her and took her hands. "Are you all right?"

Tears sprang into her eyes again, and Maggie sucked hard but couldn't stop their trickle.

"Oh, darling, you can still change your mind. It's only Charlie and me out there. No one else ever need know a thing."

Maggie shook her head and pulled her hands away to stand. "I'm not going to change my mind. It isn't that." She brushed away the tears and pulled open a drawer to retrieve a hankie. She dabbed at her face and blew her nose before trying to explain. "I just keep thinking of Bobby and remembering. I'm missing him something fierce today." She smiled weakly, hoping Nancy understood.

Nancy nodded. "That's to be expected. He's been gone such a short time."

"He'd understand. I think he would. Don't you?" She didn't want to hurt Bobby's memory, but marrying Jack wouldn't do that, would it? She and Bobby had something special. It would never leave her heart.

Nancy stood too. She cast a glance over the bedroom. No one but Maggie had been in here since last fall before Bobby went away to the camps and later came back to her in a pine box. She waited for Nancy to speak, and finally Nancy nodded.

"He'd understand." Nancy's eyes were soft. "I understand too, even if Charlie doesn't. I don't know what I'd do if something happened to Charlie." Nancy shrugged and dropped her gaze. "The very thought of marrying somebody else. . ." She shook her head and looked up again. "But I know I wouldn't want to leave my home. Jack seems like a nice man."

Maggie sniffed again and tried to smile, but her cheeks felt stiff. Heavy. She shuffled with jerking movements to a dress hanging on one of the clothes pegs along the wall and lifted it off. Soft cotton felt like a balm against her hands and soothed her. "I made this. Jack bought me a bolt of cloth shortly after he arrived. I decided to use some of it for a new dress. Seems fitting I should wear it."

Nancy took the dress from her and held it up. "It's very pretty. The pattern will look so lovely on you. You slip it on, and I'll help you fix your hair."

Maggie breathed deep, allowing the air to expand her chest and push out her heavy thoughts. She released it with a sigh. She'd not thought about looking *lovely* for a very long time.

"That's right. Come on. Let's get you ready. You're getting married!"

This time her smile came. It must have been hard for Nancy to act happy for her when she could tell her sister-in-law had reservations and Charlie was still so upset. She'd accept her kindness now and be grateful for it. Maggie pulled the old dress off over her head and slipped into the new yellow calico, smoothing the pleats of the skirt over her hips. She'd taken special care when she sewed it, not wanting to ruin the gift of such fine material.

Nancy brightened. "I declare, Maggie! It's taken the years away. I hope that Jack McAllister is deserving."

Maggie flushed and turned away toward the mirror on her dresser. She stared. She'd tried the dress on a couple of times while she stitched it, examining the fit and the seams, but she'd not taken in the picture it made as a whole. Her blush deepened. "Is it too much?" Her voice was nearly a whisper.

"Too much for him, you mean?" Nancy stepped beside her and shared a look at her reflection in the glass. "Depends."

Maggie jerked around. "What do you mean?"

"Do you want him to know he's getting something more fetching than a roof over his head and some fields?"

"It isn't like that." Maggie frowned even as she bent to tug the dress back over her head.

Nancy stopped her. "Leave it be. There's no reason you shouldn't look pretty, even if it's not for him. It's still a big day, a day you've decided to make an important agreement, maybe an even bigger agreement than you made with Bobby. This one isn't based on how you feel but on what you need to do. That's just as important as anything. You wear that pretty dress."

Maggie slowly lowered her arms and let the dress fall back into place. She wanted to ask again if Nancy was certain, but it really didn't matter. It only mattered what Maggie felt. She'd figured on wearing the dress because, no matter how she reasoned against feelings, she was getting *married.* Today was an occasion she'd never forget. It was simple as that. She nodded. "You're right."

She sat in a chair in her parlor while Nancy brushed out her long braid and drew her hair up high on her head, letting the sides caress the sides of her face in soft loops. Maggie touched it self-consciously, saying not a word. She felt changed. Lovely, indeed. Whatever would Jack think? She had made it so clear their marriage subsisted only of a contract, a thing to exist solely on paper and nowhere else. Would he presume she had changed her mind? He'd agreed to everything they'd discussed. He only wanted the farm. He'd said so, hadn't he? As Nancy finished her work and stepped back to smile at Maggie, her hands pressed together in front of her chest in delight, Maggie's nervousness grew. She nearly jumped off the chair when the front door banged open and Gracie burst into the room.

"You're pretty!" she announced, her eyes large and round. "Your hair is so pretty and you have a pretty dress too!" she said, making Maggie wish she'd stopped Nancy before she'd gotten started.

"I don't know. It feels so strange. Maybe I should just braid it."

Nancy scowled and dropped her hands to her hips. "You'll do no such thing."

"I brought you flowers," Gracie said, pulling a hand from behind her back. She handed them to Maggie, a shower of wild daisies and buttercups that looked like they'd sprouted straight from her new gown.

Maggie couldn't refuse. "Thank you, Gracie. Did you get some for Jack too?"

Gracie's expression twisted into a puzzle. "Boys don't like flowers!"

"Sure they do." Maggie smiled, her worries lightening.

"Pete don't. He only likes to whack their heads off with the shovel."

The women laughed. Well, like it or not, Maggie was dressed for getting married. She only hoped Jack had changed out of his soiled work pants so that she wouldn't be completely embarrassed.

Chapter Fourteen

Jack tugged at his shirt collar, buttoned right up to the hollow below his Adam's apple. He could hardly swallow, but loosening it didn't seem to help. Branton had suggested they all move under the shade of the oak on the front lawn to wait for Maggie and Nancy to come out, and it was a good thing or he might have simmered in the heat. He'd gotten in a cold bathtub behind the barn this morning, and he didn't want the freshness to wear off before he stood beside her to speak the vows.

I'm getting married. I'm marrying Dunc's wife. I'm going to be part owner of my own place. Pa, you wouldn't believe it. Dear God, I'm marrying Dunc's wife...

Conversation rolled on in a steady stream in his head, reminding him he was going to be Maggie's husband, he'd have commitments, responsibility like he'd never had before, a family... At least there'd be the two of them. There'd not be children.

Would there?

Would they ever be more than the uncertain friends they were now?

A small commotion drew his gaze to the front porch of the house. Nancy held the door and first Gracie then Maggie stepped out.

Maggie. I'm marrying her?

She'd always looked cute and fresh in her long brown braid, even with her hands covered in dirt. But now. . . Why, she'd never looked so fine. *She's beautiful.* He swallowed hard against his collar again and blinked.

Charlie scowled and shoved his hands into his pockets. Del Branton beamed and rocked back and forth on his feet as he clutched his worn Bible. "Looks like we'll get started," he said.

Jack walked forward to meet her, ignoring Pete's giggle and his father's muttered warning to be quiet. He stopped in front of her, glad he'd taken care to bathe and shave and put on his best pair of pants. He'd even sneaked off to town and bought a new shirt for the occasion.

"You look. . ." He gazed over her face, forcing himself to stop at her shoulders. "You look real pretty, Maggie."

Her cheeks bloomed and it nearly lifted Jack off his heels. He cleared his throat and held out his arm. Nancy smiled and stepped away, tugging Gracie close. Maggie took his proffered arm and walked with him to the oak tree.

"I saw Gracie picking flowers. Now I know why."

"It was sweet of her," Maggie murmured. "Looks like we're ready, Preacher," she said as they reached the shade. "Glad you came, Charlie."

He didn't smile, but he nodded, a sort of acquiescent nod at best.

"I can't imagine a finer day for a wedding in God's great outdoors," Branton said, his smile having grown wider if anything. "So let's begin."

Jack looked down at Maggie, and she turned her head slightly to look back. A scent like soft sunshine and roses came from her, like she'd washed her hair with rose water.

"And I couldn't imagine two finer people to come together as man and wife. I've gotten to know you both a little better recently. Maggie, I've known you for a long time. I was honored to marry you and Bob when I was only a young preacher myself. You were a good wife to Bob, and now you've made the decision to keep his memory and his dream alive in the only way possible to you. But you've been wise about it. He'd understand."

She stirred beside him, and Jack looked down again, but she wasn't crying or anything.

"Jack, you were the answer to Maggie's prayer and to mine. Each time I read Maggie's letter I prayed with fear and trembling about what it might result in, who it might bring knocking at her door. We all know the devil tried to intrude." The preacher's glance flitted briefly past them to Maggie's family who'd feared the worst when those other woodsmen showed up. "But then you came along. A man fit, able, willing, and not wanting to harm her." Branton paused, allowing his words to find resonance, and for Jack they did. He knew it was the man's way of warning him yet again, to mind himself with Maggie, to bring her the best of himself.

Branton opened his Bible. "Today I see two determined people who are willing to look for something beyond starry-eyed romance. You both have a faith to build upon, and that's the most important thing. Yes, that's the best start anyone can have. But. . ." The word lingered, and Jack wondered what misgiving the preacher would remark upon. "But there will be many hurdles yet to come. Your friendship, your respect for one another, is being forged. But love?"

Maggie remained still as stone beside him. Jack wanted to look at her again, just to see how she was handling the words the preacher spoke, but he didn't dare. Branton studied them both, and it seemed that a sermon swam unspoken between their three heads. Finally, Branton sighed.

"Give me your hands."

Jack lifted his hand, and Maggie slowly raised hers. The preacher placed Jack's hand over Maggie's. It didn't feel work roughened at all. It was soft and warm. Jack cupped it gently and they lowered them. "That's better. Now, as I was saying. Love. That's another matter." He turned the pages of his Bible and read. " 'Charity suffereth long, and is kind; charity envieth not; charity vaunteth not itself, is not puffed up, doth not behave itself unseemly, seeketh not her own, is not easily provoked, thinketh no evil; rejoiceth not in iniquity, but rejoiceth in the truth; beareth all things, believeth all things, hopeth all things, endureth all things. Charity never faileth.' " Branton looked up and gazed at them. "I see promise in your lives. Life is a treacherous road, and friendship isn't always enough. People need each other. They need love, godly love, to thrive. Maybe the starry-eyed romance will come someday." He smiled, and Jack tried not to shift, to move his fingers over hers. "Let's bow our heads. Dear Father," he began.

Jack followed along, praying in his heart that they'd have a long, healthy union. That the dreams they created would hold up under the pressures of life's treacherous road. He held his breath as Branton closed.

"And give them love for one another, we pray. Help them to discover what it really means to be one. They'll need that too, to get them by. To make life rich and sweet. Each of us here today understands that their marriage is unusual, but it's only just beginning. If they just keep breathing in the good air around them and take one day at time, trusting in You and each other, they can make it a full and happy one. Maggie and Jack... Well, God, they're just the type to do it indeed. Amen."

Maggie stirred, and with the slightest squeeze, not one to intimidate, but meant only to reassure her, Jack released her hand

and turned to face her. He glimpsed Nancy dabbing a hankie at her eyes glistening with moisture.

Gracie tugged at her mother's skirt. "Is he going to kiss Aunt Maggie?"

"Hush."

"Is he?" the preacher asked Jack softly and with a steady gaze.

Jack looked to Maggie, who appeared about to shrink off.

"I think Maggie would rather you just let us speak the vows now."

The preacher's smile flattened. "Not yet, Gracie. All right. Jack McAllister, do you promise—"

Jack heard the words as he gazed at Maggie, and this time she didn't lower her eyelashes or turn away. Her expression lay open before him, her gaze clear and honest, her eyes a beautiful mixture of browns reflecting the sunlight. He concentrated on them as he spoke.

"In the name of God, I, Jack, take you, Maggie, to be my wife, to have and to hold—" He swallowed. "From this day forward, for better, for worse, for richer, for poorer, in sickness and in health." He took a breath and let the words come. "To love and to cherish, till death us do part. This is my solemn vow."

Branton turned to Maggie, and as she repeated the same words after him, Jack wondered how he'd ever fulfill them all. Especially the "holding" part. *How will she?*

Well, God had brought them together, and Jack would not go back on his earlier promises to Maggie. She trusted him to keep his place. Anything beyond that would have to be left to God. It would do him no good to entertain thoughts of them being more than they were.

"Now is he going to kiss her?" Gracie whispered loudly.

"Gracie!" Charlie growled.

"I now pronounce you husband and wife." Branton said the

words clearly but didn't add the final sentence.

"Thank you," Maggie mumbled. This time she did step away.

Jack shook the preacher's hand and turned around. "Maggie's got coffee and cake up at the house."

"I'll bring it to the porch," Nancy said. "No sense us being inside while it's so nice out." Her voice sounded forcefully bright.

"I think it's cooling down some," Charlie said to no one in particular as Nancy and Maggie walked off. He strode closer to Jack and held out his hand. "Guess it's time I got used to you sticking around then."

Jack accepted his handshake. "Guess so."

Charlie cleared his throat and looked off somewhere. "I'll tell Mr. Earl not to bother you folks anymore."

"I appreciate that. Maggie will too."

The women stepped out of the house onto the porch, their arms laden with items. The children rushed over for cake, and Branton stepped between Jack and Charlie. "Well, she did it, Charlie." He patted Charlie's back. "Your sister set off to find a husband with a letter, and she found just the man." Branton turned his head to smile at Jack.

"Yep... She did it," Charlie echoed, though he still didn't sound quite sure.

Chapter Fifteen

In the course of the week that followed, Jack stopped thinking about the place as Dunc's farm, and Maggie was just Maggie, not Dunc's wife. Now the land was his as much as hers. Even though he'd known it would belong to him once they signed their marriage contract, it hadn't really hit him as such until the next day. *My farm. Pa, I've got a farm.* He should write to his father the next chance he got. His aunt would be happy to hear he had a wife too. He wouldn't have to tell her about his and Maggie's arrangement. Let them believe the marriage wasn't mercenary. In the meantime, he'd finish clearing the back lot that Dunc had started on. Stumps had been standing for at least a season, maybe two, and once he got a solid quarter of the section pulled and free, he could figure on planting it with corn next year.

Maggie had come out to help him after he'd spent the entire morning grubbing around a patch of stumps. Now she positioned herself at the horse's head to lead him into pulling after Jack set the chains in place.

The particular stump they were working on was one of the biggest. Jack had to dig a little deeper to get the chain hooked on the fattest root. Then he dropped his grub ax and knelt in the dirt beside the unwieldy oak remnant. He worked the logging chain through the soil around the heavy root and fastened the hook onto one of the links. After tugging hard to make sure it was secure, he laid the chain back over the stump. "Go ahead." He waved Maggie forward.

Maggie gave the horse's bridle a gentle tug. "C'mon, Samuel. There you go."

The horse strained against the chain as Jack stepped back. The stump didn't budge. Samuel pawed the ground, giving pause, and Maggie encouraged him again. This time the log lurched a few inches. The chain was taut. "Keep going," Jack said. Maggie beckoned the horse forward, talking softly to him, not watching when Jack glanced up at her.

He turned his glance back to the chain, studying the length of it when the unthinkable happened. Instead of popping free from the ground, the root snapped in two. In the space of half a second, Jack's heart leapt. A cry of warning screamed through his mind with no time for the words to leave his mouth as the chain with its weighty hook cracked like a steel whip through the air, flying past Maggie's head within a breath.

The horse spooked with a forward lunge and Maggie held on, her eyes wide. "Easy, Samuel! Easy!" Samuel snorted and stomped before calming. She turned her head. Her voice lashed out. "What did you do?"

Her anger was palpable. Jack's shoulders dropped and he could feel his voice shake as the surge of his fear released. "I didn't do anything. The root broke and the chain came off. Are you all right?" He rubbed his face, scouring away the thought of what almost happened.

Maggie released the bridle. Her face was flushed. "Didn't you hook it close? Bobby always said to hook it close."

Jack frowned and walked past her to retrieve the chain end. "I hooked it close."

“Nothing like that ever happened before.”

“I’m sure it didn’t,” Jack snapped.

He didn’t appreciate her reprimand, and she must have understood because she turned away. She stroked the horse’s muzzle. “You all right, Samuel?”

Jack reconnected the chain around the stump. “You go on back up to the house. I’ll handle it.” He marched to the horse’s head and reached for the bridle.

“I’d rather stay and help. If you got hurt out here, no one would know.”

Her lack of faith in him churned his earlier fear into frustration. “I’ve been logging since I was fifteen. I know what I’m doing.”

She looked doubtful. Suddenly the place felt like Dunc’s farm again. Well, he wasn’t going to let the specter of his old friend hang around. *Even if Maggie wants to call him up from the grave.*

He softened his tone. “Go on. It’s all right.”

Maggie eyed the horse once more, then him, but at the last she turned away.

Jack dropped to his knees and hooked the chain around the stubborn remains of the tree, his heart slowing. He sat back on his heels and watched her walking slowly over the ruts and clumps of debris. All the while a voice in his head told him to apologize.

She’s the one accusing me, he argued as he rose to his feet. Nevertheless, the urging remained. “Maggie!” he hollered. She stopped and looked back. He took long strides, stopping in front of her. “I’m sorry for snapping at you. I was just scared you’d get hurt, that’s all. I’m glad you’re all right.”

She looked down to her toes and nodded. “I was a little shook, but I’m fine now. I’ll go fix your dinner.”

He let her go and went back to the task. Right about now she was probably wishing she’d sold the farm to Sheldon Earl.

Then she wouldn't have to deal with Jack stepping in her husband's shoes and walking roughshod over his memory.

On Sunday Jack came up to the house for breakfast and found Maggie setting his eggs and griddle cakes on the table as usual, but she was quiet. Jack hung his hat on the back of his chair and pulled it out to sit down. He watched her fetch the coffeepot and fill their cups, then sit down in the chair across from him. "Morning."

"Morning."

He reached for the little pitcher of cream she'd put in the center of the table and dropped a dollop in his cup. He looked forward to their morning ritual, and there was no mistaking that Maggie had learned how to make a fair pot of coffee. It was rich and black, but not thick like tree sap or tasting like bark the way it had when he first came to the farm. He'd be proud to let her serve her coffee to the camp cookee now. "You feeling all right today? You're awful quiet."

She finally glanced up at him for the first time since he stepped through the door. "I'm fine. Looks like another warm day coming."

He agreed. "I think I'll get the last of the hay crop off the field today. You want to help?" He hadn't asked for her help since the accident with the chain four days ago. In fact, they'd been a little stiff with each other since.

"If you want."

Jack started in on his breakfast.

"I tore apart some old things of Bobby's. Thought I could use the scraps to fix up that old pair of pants you've been wearing. I seen they haven't got much wear left in them, but maybe we can save 'em a while longer."

He felt uncomfortable hearing about Bobby's things, but he nodded as he whittled away on his pancake. "That would be welcome."

"By the way, I noticed you sharpening the scythe the other day.

Bobby sharpened it up real good before he went away last fall."

His eyes rose to meet hers. "It was sharp before I finished the first cutting, but it needed a fresh going over, so I gave it one."

She half-nodded and forked a piece of egg.

He wiped his fingers on a napkin and reached for his cup again. "Maggie, today's Sunday. I was thinking that after chores, before we get on with these other things, maybe you'd like to sit outside and read a passage from the Bible together. I'd kind of feel like we were remembering the Lord's Day proper if we did that. I could read alone, but I thought maybe you wouldn't mind joining me."

Her chin lifted and her eyes lit as though some of the discomfort between them had been cleared away. "Yes, Jack. I'd like that."

"Fine. I'll get my Bible after breakfast."

She laid aside her fork and pushed back her chair. "Would you like more coffee?"

"Don't mind if I do." He offered her a smile as he lifted his cup to the pot. "Thank you, Maggie. It's a real good pot this morning."

Chapter Sixteen

Maggie stabbed clothespins into place on the clean laundry, trying unsuccessfully to halt the direction of her thoughts. She'd not had any trouble whatsoever thinking of Jack merely as "extra help" at the beginning, but since their vows a little over a week ago, reality had settled in. The full impact of their changed arrangement hit her just days ago when the logging chain gave way off the stump they'd been pulling. Its recoil had nearly slammed into her head. She might have been killed or seriously hurt. Jack had been as shaken as she, maybe even more so. She'd been wrong to accuse him of not connecting it rightly, or more importantly, not doing it like she imagined Bobby would. Dangers lurked in farming. Anyone could suffer injury in a bizarre accident. Everyone knew that. Her brother had often stressed the fact. So had Bobby.

Yet, she hadn't been able to apologize to Jack. Her own stubbornness had widened the gulf between them, and it hurt more than she ever thought it could. She'd heard tell that Sheldon Earl was still in town, and that William and Bertie Amundson had decided to sell some of their property to him. For a moment, when she'd fought angry tears over the cookstove while fixing Jack's dinner that day, she almost wished she'd sold the farm and run off to start over. But yesterday, when Jack offered her the olive branch by inviting her to read scripture with him, the ice had finally broken. She swore to herself she'd not let Bobby's ghost rise up between them again. Not if she could help it.

She reached for Jack's clean and newly mended britches and gave them a shake before hanging them on the line. He was taller than Bobby. When he sat on the porch step reading his Bible, she was able to study him without him paying any mind. He was taller, but broad shouldered and trim at the middle, so he didn't look too skinny. He had a nice voice when he read about Jacob wrestling with the angel, and she could follow along real easy. Bobby hardly ever read the Bible to her like that. After Jack finished reading, he didn't get up right away. He leaned back against the stair rail, and they talked for a spell. He told her a story of his own about the time a fellow at their logging camp got to dreaming and wrestling in his sleep with one of his bunkmates and earned himself a black eye. Jack was a good storyteller. He had a sense of humor and a nice laugh that made his eyes crinkle at the corners.

Maggie brushed her hands on her apron and caught herself smiling. Her thoughts turned to him on those days before the preacher arrived. That early episode on the day he'd stood up to Charlie had left her thinking about what a fine man Jack was, and how steady and smart he'd made her feel. Right after that Maggie began to recognize the peace she felt about their agreement. In fact, if she dared admit it now, she wondered if it wasn't even more than peace. She'd surely begun to think about him in more . . .personal ways.

On their wedding day, when she thought Jack might have looked at her in a more personal way too, something startling and not altogether unwelcome soared through her. When Preacher Branton had him repeat those words, "to love and to cherish, till death us do part," the look on Jack's face set her heart thudding so that she thought her face might catch fire. She hoped the others presumed it was the day's heat, but she tried to avoid looking at him until the ceremony was over, just in case.

And he was considerate. Take yesterday morning, for example. After breakfast, he'd stayed and helped her with the dishes before they stepped outside to read together. Bobby had never done that in all the days she'd known him. And Jack always complimented her cooking and thanked her for the smallest things she did. She'd never expected that when she'd sent that letter. A man like Jack, why, he was more than she'd ever hoped for.

Shaking out one of Jack's socks and pinning it to the line with its mate, she realized there were a lot of ways Jack differed from Bobby. She frowned, feeling disloyal. It made her want to bring Bobby back to the surface of her memories even though she'd just sworn not to let his ghost rise between them again. *Maybe I should be spending more time remembering the man who really loved me than the one who's taken his place in name only. After all, Jack hasn't asked me to forget Bobby. He was Bobby's friend.*

What would Bobby think of her being married to Jack? Would he be pleased about her choice or disappointed? She sighed. There was no sense in wondering. She'd done what she had to, and there was no turning back time. She should just be glad that things had worked out amicably between them, and Jack was the sort of man who could be her friend too.

Maggie peeked between the damp linens swaying on the clothesline and stole a look at Jack out there now splitting shingles by the woodshed. Warmth swept over her even with the cold, wet sheets flapping against her legs. "But how can I think of just being friends with a man like that?" she whispered to the breeze.

Chapter Seventeen

Jack didn't expect Maggie to simply forget Dunc's life and impact on their farm. How could she? She still loved the man—her *Bobby*. It wasn't difficult for Jack to remember that Dunc was the man she'd married for love, not him. Sometimes Jack noticed the faraway look in her eye when she didn't know he was looking, when she must have been thinking about the man she loved and then lost. Jack didn't expect her to forget him, and he didn't want to intrude on her memories. Still, he walked a precarious line—respecting things that reminded her of Dunc while wanting to make the farm his own and do things his way. It seemed they'd finally reestablished their tenuous alliance, and he hoped things would eventually settle into something finer between them.

He mulled the situation again as he strode in from the field, intending to apprise Maggie of his progress on the back clearing, and spied her bent over a row of green beans in her garden, a pot next to her nearly full.

Jack dropped his hat by the pump and filled a pail. Carrying it near the garden, he offered her a dipper of water. She stood to drink and thanked him.

He tipped his head toward the north. "I'm going to start turning over the soil in the new field tomorrow. It'll take some real breaking up to make it workable, but I'll plow it again in the spring before I plant it. Oats it'll be, I think."

Maggie lowered the dipper. "What about alfalfa?"

"We have enough pasture."

"But I thought you meant to make it into a hayfield."

"Where did you get that notion?"

Her brow twitched. "Bobby always planned on putting it into hay and pasture."

Bobby again. Jack took the dipper. "Oats is what we need." He wanted to give her all the reasons why he thought oats would suit better, but he didn't want to say that Bobby was wrong, so he determined not to debate her on the subject. He plopped the dipper into the pail with a splash and turned away.

Maggie's voice took on a sharp edge. "I'm not saying that you have to do it that way, Jack. I'm only saying that Bobby always thought that north field would make better pasture than cropland."

He flung the water into the herb bed beneath the window and hung the pail on the pump. "There isn't anything wrong with that field a little fertilizer won't set right."

"I'm not arguing with you. I'm just saying, that's all."

Resigned, Jack turned around and saw her standing there, waiting for more discussion on the subject. He took a deep breath and his cheeks puffed when he expelled it. Maybe it was better to face their trouble head-on and stop beating around the bush. He squinted at her. "Why don't you trust my judgment, Maggie?"

Maggie flushed. "I do trust you."

"No, you don't. I thought you did, but lately everything's been Bobby this or Bobby that."

"That's not true."

Jack hardly heard her. She started to turn, to go back to her beans, but he walked closer. "Maggie, wait." She looked back and he went on. He had to say it all. "You're so afraid I'm going to hurt *Bobby's* farm. Well, look, I'm not Bobby. I'm Jack, and my staying and marrying you means this is Maggie and Jack's farm, not Maggie and Bobby's. Not anymore. All right?"

She stared at him, wide-eyed with shock, or confusion, or just plain hurt maybe. Just plain anger, more likely.

He sighed again, his own good sense telling him he'd probably made matters worse. No sense waiting around for her rebuttal. Jack turned and retrieved his hat he'd left lying on the ground. He crammed it on his head. "Don't wait supper on me."

He stalked to the barn and then to the field, growing angrier at her lack of response. Did she really not see the truth? She'd married him and made him owner with her of their farm, but only on paper. In her heart, the farm was still, and always would be, Bob Duncan's. Nothing would change that as long as she loved him.

"Haw!" Jack jerked the reins of his horse as he followed behind the staggering plow tearing through the rough sod. His arms and shoulders ached but he was glad. The sweat and pain burned away the agony of his frustration as the day wore on, and eventually he started thinking clearly.

It wasn't really true that she'd been talking more about Bobby than usual. Maggie had made reference now and again to her first husband's vision for the farm since the day she first penned that letter. What really galled Jack, he finally admitted as the sun began to sink in the sky, was that it had started to matter to him. It wasn't that Dunc's ideas were wrong or that Jack's plan was best. "Woah." Jack dropped the reins and wiped his brow as he accepted the simple truth. Maggie herself mattered to him a whole lot more than he would have considered possible two or three months ago.

He unhitched the horse as he considered their relationship. August was upon them. They'd been married for almost a month.

Del Branton had listened to them say their vows in the middle of July's hot haying season. It had been such a busy time with the demands of the farm that they had both been able to turn back to their work without giving much personal significance to the step they'd taken. Yet, during that time, they had reached many small understandings. They'd come to know one another as partners and friends. And Maggie had pulled at something deeper inside him.

Jack led the horse toward the barn, where he removed its bridle and offered a bucket of grain. Jack had given Maggie his word that their arrangement would remain purely contractual. He'd continued to keep residence in the barn at night, and they'd not spoken anymore about it. Lately however, Jack had been having a hard time keeping his mind on anything but Maggie McAllister—his wife.

While the horse bent his nose into the grain bucket, Jack rubbed him down with clean straw, the motion scrubbing away at his thoughts. He hated that he'd stalked off this afternoon without finishing their conversation. . .without finding out what the wide look in her eyes meant. He owed her the courtesy of listening to her ideas no matter where she'd gotten them, even if they came straight from his dead rival. Jack curried his horse while Maggie's sweetness filled his thoughts like the aroma of clover. Doggone if he hadn't gone and fallen in love with her.

Wouldn't she be surprised if she knew the way of things? But I've got no right to spoil her dreams.

Jack turned that fact over in his mind. Yes, all his frustration about Dunc was only his sensibilities stirred up because Maggie wasn't ready to move on. It didn't matter that she had swept him off his jack boots with her brown eyes and a smile that could melt butter fresh out of the churn. There were times Jack wanted to reach out and touch her cheek, stroke it once or twice just to see if those freckles would rub off. When she bent over to pick up the milk pail or the laundry tub, he wanted to touch her braid and run his hand the length of it. He wanted to. . .

He rubbed a hand down his face and turned his thoughts toward cleaning up from the day's work. It was nearly dark and he was exhausted. He'd purposely kept at it late to avoid seeing her, sure now that she'd probably gone to bed or was doing some quiet evening needle work. Once he'd freshened up, he could slip into the house and grab a hunk of bread for his supper, then he'd slip on out to the barn and do some reading to get her off his mind.

Jack shuffled to the pump, stilling the chirp of crickets in the darkness. He took more time than necessary to scrub his arms, face, and body. After dousing his head with water, he finally made his way up the porch steps. His glance turned for a moment onto the moonlit shadows falling across Maggie's rocking chair beside him. He'd ordered it from a craftsman over in Chippewa Falls as a gift for her when they agreed to marry. She seemed to love sitting outside with coffee in the morning or for a short spell after supper. Lately she sat there of an evening when they read together with him perched on the step near her feet. The rocker had been a sort of thank-you to her for giving him this chance. He liked to watch her sitting there, rocking and knitting when she didn't know he was nearby. It gave him pleasure she'd never realize.

He drew his gaze away and reached for the door handle, but a hint of movement passing by the living room window caught his attention. Slowly, he stepped across the porch and looked in at her. She moved about the room, tidying things carefully. She wore a modest white nightgown, and her long brown hair was unbraided and hung down in glimmering ribbons all around her, clean past her waist. Mesmerized, Jack's heart thumped against his chest. *Maggie.* He wanted to call out to her, to have her lift her face to him, but he didn't dare.

He stepped back and took a breath to pull himself together then stepped back toward the door. With a stomp of his feet on the landing to warn her, he pushed the latch and stepped inside. A kerosene lamp burned low on the kitchen table. He turned up the wick just a bit and looked around to find bread wrapped in a towel on the sideboard.

"I kept you a plate anyway, even though you said not to. It's on the warming shelf above the stove."

Her voice, soft as dusk, startled him and set his heart to pounding again. He was almost afraid to look at her, afraid she'd see everything he felt written on his face. She stood in the doorway, a wrapper over her nightgown. When she glanced toward the stove, he noticed she must have hastily tied her hair back loose in a silk ribbon, but it still shone like he'd never seen it before.

His mouth was dry. "Thanks." The single word came out hoarse and every movement awkward as he reached for his meal off the warming shelf. A sudden flash of lightning outside made him jump, and the rumble of thunder that followed felt like it came from his inside his own body.

"Looks like we're going to get some rain." She stood in front of the window and another flash of lightning made her appear almost ethereal. He sat down at the table with his plate and took a bite, hardly tasting his food.

Seconds later the patter of rain hit the roof and windows. Jack looked up, glimpsing her watching the rain streak the glass. It quickly built into a roar of water slashing against the house. Neither spoke, and Jack felt cocooned inside with Maggie and the glow of the lamp.

After only a few bites, he pushed his plate away. Not that he wasn't hungry, but he couldn't force himself to go through the process and he couldn't taste it anyway, not with these feelings raging through him, and not with her standing there like that watching the storm, unaware of the one stirred up inside him. For just a moment, he allowed his gaze to linger on her. Suddenly she turned and looked at him, purposeful.

He pushed his chair away from the table and stood up. "I'd better get on out to the barn."

"Jack." Her eyes were fixed on him and he stood looking back, wondering over the expression on her face, not sure what to make of it. "It's raining pretty hard."

Clumsily he reached for his hat, taking a step closer to the door.

"Jack?" He raised his eyes to look at her, and she took a step toward him. "Why don't you just stay in the house tonight."

"What?"

"I want you to stay in the house tonight—if you want to."

Her eyes fell away from his, and even in the dim light he could see she was blushing. She'd never been more beautiful to him.

"What are you asking me, Maggie? Are you scared of the storm?"

"You know I'm not."

"Then what?"

"I'm asking you. . ." He knew she was having trouble, but he couldn't help her. He had to know for sure. "I'm asking if you'll stay with me. If you'll think differently about what I promised, about you and me—I mean—about our agreement."

His throat felt like sand, but he had to be sure. "Do you want me to be your husband, Maggie? Is that what you're saying?"

Maggie barely whispered, but she was looking straight at him. "I am."

Compelled toward her, not even knowing or caring how he found himself with his arms wrapped around her, he kissed her, lightly at first. Then deeper as she melded to him and her own matching passion unfurled. Her smallness felt right against him in the soft folds of her gown, her hair a skein of silk wrapping around his fingers.

Slowly he drew away and looked down into her eyes. They were soft, like a doe's. Her throat's pulse matched the rhythm of his heartbeat. He reached for the knob on the lamp and turned down the wick until they were engulfed in darkness. Carefully Jack lifted her into his arms and walked through the house, led by the light in the other room. Her eyes never left his face, even when he stepped through the bedroom door and set her gently on the bed.

"Maggie, there's something I've got to say." He got down on his knees and took both her hands in his. He steadied himself, hoping that she wouldn't change her mind once he told her, or worse, that she wouldn't change her mind tomorrow. "In my heart, I broke my agreement with you a long time ago. It's been a while now, and I just want you to know that if it wasn't for love before, it is now. I love you, Maggie."

A smile crept into the corners of her eyes and lifted his heart. "Really, Jack? Really?"

He nodded as her hands clung to his and the wave of her relief washed over him.

"I love you too."

For only a moment longer, they studied one another, believing one another, then Jack raised his hand and slipped the ribbon from her hair.

Chapter Eighteen

Maggie woke early the next morning, her eyes fluttering open to fix upon Jack. Joy unleashed inside her. Who could have thought he'd love her? How had it happened that she loved him so easily? Because she did. With everything in her she loved this man God had sent. He'd heard her prayer, He'd seen her tears, and He'd answered her need—even the one she didn't know she had. Maggie would always remember Bobby and the brief years they'd had together, but she was young. There would be many years to come. Now she no longer expected them to be lonely and bittersweet. Jack's love had changed all that.

She didn't want to wake him. She only wanted to study him—to trace the planes of his unshaved jaw and the thick curve of his neck, and with loving eyes to stroke the lock of blond hair falling across his forehead. One bare arm was tucked beneath his head, and the other lay atop the coverlet. Those two arms had held her oh-so-close last night. She closed her eyes, remembering, and bent her head so that her cheek feathered his shoulder. Sometime during the night, after the storm had stopped and she slept, he had risen from beside her and lifted the window sash to let in the warm night air. Now fresh, clean-washed smells swept over them on a soft breeze. The hour was later than they usually rose to start their day. Normally, their chores would have been finished by now, and he'd be coming into the house for his breakfast. The cow must be getting impatient to be milked, and the chickens would be scratching in the dirt for their feed, but Maggie didn't care. She was too busy soaking in the wonder of what had happened between them. She tilted her head back and swept her gaze to his face to find his eyes were open, blue and clear as the cloudless sky, watching her.

His lips bowed gently. "How long have you been awake?"

She shrugged. "Only a little while."

He pulled his arm from under his head and tucked back a tendril of her hair. "What are you thinking about?"

His fingertips tingled along her jaw making her eyelids dip. She shrugged. "Just you and me."

"You're not sorry?"

She shook her head. "How could I be sorry? I never thought... I didn't believe—"

"Me either."

His hand rested on her shoulder, and she looked at him a moment longer just to be sure, but he didn't look sorry either. His fingers stroked her throat, lifted her chin, and he kissed her. The joy swept over her again, the fact that she and Jack were truly married. That they were in love.

Maggie McAllister. That's who I am. I'm Jack's wife. He's my husband. It meant so much more this morning. She melted into longing, kissing him back, until responsibilities came pressing in. She broke the kiss and flushed. "I'll get your breakfast."

She turned to rise, but Jack reached for her. "No, Maggie. Just stay."

There were times, she remembered, that she and Bobby stayed abed for joy. Yet, the recollection now was not like others she'd had in the past few months. It wasn't a memory of comparison or regret or longing. It just was. And looking at Jack, all those old thoughts dissolved. The farm could wait a while longer. No one would come knocking at their door. It was a fine morning, and she was married to a wonderfully good man. They had married for the sake of the farm, and they had married for a dream they each carried inside. But as everything else ceased to matter and she lay within the circle of his arms, one thing would carry them on. From this day forward, no matter what came, they were married for love.

Naomi Musch is an award-winning author who writes from a deer farm in the pristine north woods of Wisconsin, where she and husband Jeff live as epically as God allows near the families of their five adult children. When not in the physical act of writing or spending time loving on her passel of grandchildren, she can be found plotting stories as she roams around the farm, snacks out of the garden, and relaxes in her vintage camper. Naomi is a member of the American Christian Fiction Writers; Faith, Hope and Love Christian Writers; and the Lake Superior Writers. She loves engaging with others and can be found all around social media or at her website where she encourages readers to sign up for her newsletter at www.naomimusch.com.

Undercover Logger

BY JENNIFER LAMONT LEO

To Thomas,
who cares lovingly for the forest
and for me.

Chapter One

CHICAGO, ILLINOIS
FEBRUARY, 1890

The morning edition of the *Chicago Tribune* landed on the mahogany breakfast table with a resounding thud, jarring Michael Tate from his sleepy stupor.

"What is the meaning of this?"

Towering over him, a tall, silver-haired gentleman dressed in a sharply creased custom-made suit stabbed one long finger at the front page.

Michael winced at his father's roar. He'd had too little sleep, after too many steins of beer, to tolerate the furnace blast of the old man's ire. He didn't need to look at the headline to know what it said. But he glanced anyway.

Bank President's Son Tossed Out of Saloon.

He tugged at the stiff collar of his dress shirt where it pressed against his neck. Running his bleary eyes over the story, he caught the gist. *Michael Tate, son of Gordon Tate, president of blah blah blah. Brawl. Punch thrown. Tooth knocked out. Charges pending.*

At least it had been the other fellow who'd lost the tooth. But Michael presumed that such a detail wouldn't do much to impress his father in his present mood.

The older man crossed his arms. "Do you care to explain yourself?"

Michael cared to do nothing of the sort. Bits and pieces of the night before popped into his mind in imprecise yet excruciating detail. A sumptuous, boozy dinner with friends, the exquisite Maude Ryder among them. Her glorious mane caught up in ornate jeweled combs. Slumming through the Levee bars after the theater. Some oily West Side fellow taking liberties with Maude. The tinkle of Maude's responding laughter. Hurt and confusion mixed with red-hot anger roiling in Michael's chest. The crack of fist on jaw. The cold roughness of the sidewalk under his fast-swelling cheek.

"I'm sorry, Father," he said. And he meant it. His knuckles still ached from where they'd made contact with the fiend's front teeth. Fortunately, his mother hadn't come downstairs yet, so the only witness to this humiliating conversation was the butler standing by the sideboard, his discreet gaze fixed on the silk-draped windows across the room.

"I don't know what to do with you, Michael," his father said, suddenly sounding deflated. "Kicked out of two prep schools, tossed out of Princeton for bad behavior. . ." He sighed, pulled out the chair at the head of the table, and sat heavily. "I thought giving you a job at the bank would settle you down. You're a valued employee, and you're bright, especially when it comes to working with complicated financial statements. When it suits you. But *only* when it suits you. I thought working with me would help you find some direction, some purpose in life. Clearly I was wrong."

"No, you weren't, Father," Michael said, truly contrite. "I just had too much to drink. The fellow made me angry, and I—"

"A gentleman knows how to hold his liquor." Father unfolded a white linen napkin and laid it neatly across his lap. "A gentleman doesn't settle his disagreements with his fists."

"But—"

Father held up a silencing hand. "I don't want to hear it."

"But you asked—"

"Enough! Let me think." The elder Tate picked up a slice of toast, took a bite, and chewed it slowly.

His father's icy tone sent a chill down Michael's spine. The thought of food made his stomach lurch, but he signaled to the butler for more coffee.

"Please, Father, can't we just go to the bank as usual and forget this ever happened?"

"And have the entire staff witness your hungover state? How much respect do you think they'll have for you then? Especially after reading this morning's enlightening headline?" His glare held a mixture of anger and disappointment that filled his son with shame. "You've embarrassed this family for the last time, Michael."

Michael fought down a rising sense of panic. "What does that mean?"

Gordon Tate set down the toast and rubbed his fingers on the snowy napkin. "What it means, son, is that you will not be going to the bank with me today." The words landed between them, cold, precise. "Instead, you will spend the morning packing your bags."

"My bags? Where am I going?"

"If all goes as planned, you'll soon be on your way to Idaho."

Michael slammed down his cup. "Idaho! That no-man's-land?"

Father smiled grimly. "Hardly a no-man's-land, son. The territory achieved statehood seven months ago."

"But it's in the middle of nowhere," Michael sputtered.

"Precisely," his father said without sympathy. He tugged at the cuffs of his Brooks Brothers suit. "The bank has a small branch in the northern, mountainous part of the state, in a town called

Timber Coulee. Your uncle Sebastian took charge there some years ago. I'll send him a telegram this morning, telling him you're on your way to undergo a stint of field training on behalf of the bank. According to his letters, the region is remote and sparsely populated. It won't be so easy for you to get into mischief there." He dabbed at his mouth with the napkin. "Strangely enough, Sebastian seems to enjoy small-town living. He always was a bit of a maverick."

"Field training? In Timber Coulee, Idaho? You must be joking. Surely I can learn nothing of value in that godforsaken wilderness."

"On the contrary," Father continued. "The Idaho branch serves the mining and logging interests there. It's a small branch, but a thriving one. It will give you good ground-level experience. And it's hardly a 'godforsaken wilderness.' The city of Spokane, Washington, is just a short distance farther on the train line."

"Is the bank ruining small businesses there too?" Michael asked with a hint of a sneer.

His father's gaze was steady. "If you're still upset about that business with the Italian grocer, I suggest you let it go. Bleeding hearts don't lead to sound financial decisions." He picked up a biscuit. "Your uncle is perhaps not as firm with the bank's clients as I might be. Nonetheless, he is a man of sterling character and sound business sense. You'd do well to emulate his ways and carry out whatever he asks of you. Then maybe you can come back here to the headquarters and make something of yourself."

"But what about my job here?"

"The bank has plenty of eager young men capable of taking over for you." His father lifted an eyebrow. "Young men who don't take three-hour lunches or spend their spare time brawling in bars."

Michael reached for the last resort of the powerless. "But it's not fair!" Even as he said it, he heard his own whiny, adolescent tone, and hated himself for it.

His father leaned over the table, his voice tinged with ice. “What’s not fair is your taking advantage of your family’s name and position to try to skate through life.” Then his tone softened slightly. “I’ve gone too easy on you, son. I blame myself for stepping in whenever you’ve gotten into trouble. But it’s got to stop.” He straightened. “Maybe Idaho will toughen you up. In any case, you will not return to Chicago until such time as I’m satisfied that you’ve mended your ways. When I hear a good report from your uncle, I will reconsider.”

“But if you’d only give me another chance,” Michael said, miserable.

Father’s gaze was steely. “You’ve had plenty of chances to prove yourself, son. This is your last one. I trust you will make the most of it.”

“Or else. . .?”

“Or else Easy Street comes to a dead end, here and now. There will be no position for you at the bank, nor free room and board in this house. You will need to earn your living by whatever means your sketchy education has prepared you for.”

Desperate, Michael grasped at one last straw. “But—but didn’t the newspaper article say ‘charges pending’? I don’t think the authorities will allow me to leave the state.”

“I’ll take care of that,” his father said. Michael knew that he would too. Gordon Tate had friends in high places and enough money to persuade them to do his bidding. “You just pack your bags and say goodbye to your mother,” he continued crisply. He set his napkin beside his plate and stood. “By tonight you’ll be headed westbound on the Northern Pacific. I’ll pay your train fare, but you needn’t expect another dime from me until you turn your life around. Best of luck to you.” He turned on the heels of his polished wing tips and left the room.

"More coffee, sir?" the butler said serenely, as if nothing out of the ordinary had taken place. Gloomily Michael thrust forth his cup and saucer. Idaho! Might as well be exiled to Siberia. There'd be no time to go to Maude's house and say goodbye. But under the circumstances, perhaps that was for the best.

Chapter Two

From his stiff seat in the day coach, feeling grimy and travel-worn, Michael reflected darkly on his predicament. His father had refused him even the comforts of a first-class Pullman, arranging only for second-class, which meant cramped, stuffy quarters for three days and two nights. Was there no end to the humiliation?

Inside Chicago's bustling Union Station, he'd scanned the crowd in vain, hoping to spot a certain fashionable hat perched atop abundant red hair. He'd hastily sent word to Maude's house, telling her he was leaving and pleading with her to come to the station to see him off. Clearly she was ignoring his pleas. He couldn't exactly blame her after the way he'd acted in the barroom. While the lovely heiress might have enjoyed the novelty of "slumming" at a Levee bar with their circle of fancy friends, her breeding would not permit her to accept such bad behavior from a suitor, especially now that his mishap had been made public in the newspaper. Well, he'd mail her a gushing letter from Idaho, begging her forgiveness. Several letters, if that's what it took. And with any luck, he'd be back home by spring, in plenty of time to pin a magnolia blossom into that luxurious red mane of hers.

With a loud squealing of brakes, the train suddenly lurched to a stop, yanking him from his daydream. A split second later, a jumble of blue serge and feathers landed heavily on his lap, practically knocking the wind out of him.

A feather landed on his tongue and he spat it away.

"Oh, dear. I beg your pardon. I'm terribly sorry." As the young woman struggled to regain her footing, Michael helped as best he could by giving her an ungentlemanly shove from behind. Gripping the seat-back for support as the train slowly began to move, she turned to face him, mortification radiating from her flushed skin and wide eyes.

Her wide, blue eyes. Blue as the morning glories that entwined the white latticed gazebo at home every summer. Something akin to an electrical current jolted him—a peculiar sensation he hadn't experienced since that moment the previous summer when he'd first spotted Maude Ryder across a crowded ballroom.

"It's all right. No harm done," he assured her. Then, with a sudden rush of optimism, he gestured to the empty space beside him. "Care to sit?"

"No, I'm—I'm over there." She gestured to a seat across the aisle.

"You've been there this whole time?" he blurted. How had such an exquisite creature escaped his notice?

She adjusted her hat. "Since Missoula."

"Ah." That explained it. He'd been so caught up in his own thoughts that he'd barely noticed the train stopping at Missoula, much less who'd gotten on or off.

"I was just on my way back from the rear car." She gestured toward the back of the train. "I wanted to catch a breath of fresh air, you know. It's so stuffy in here. But it's awfully cold outside." Her rush of words made her seem flustered. Had the sparkle in her eyes been caused by the cold air outside, or the sudden warmth that seemed to surge between them? He'd felt it. Had she?

"Yes, well. It is February, after all," he concluded unhelpfully.

"Yes." She looked at Michael for a long moment. "Anyway, I'm sorry, and thank you again." She crossed the aisle and daintily took her seat, her dignity apparently restored. As she moved away, he caught a delightful whiff of rose water. He hated to think what she might have caught a whiff of.

As the train resumed its course, Michael stole surreptitious glances at the woman across the way. The mass of auburn hair swept up under the feather-trimmed hat reminded him of Maude.

Maude.

He dropped his gaze. A small pang stabbed his heart at the callous way his so-called sweetheart had neglected to see him off at the station. He buried his disappointment in a desire to forget about her completely, to pretend she'd never existed. But deep down he sensed that erasing the memories of their starlit evenings together would prove tougher than he thought. *Women. Who needs 'em?*

Nonetheless, as the train rolled through western Montana, he stole an occasional glance at the stranger's comely profile. He briefly considered moving to a seat near hers, striking up a conversation—just to pass the time, of course—then decided against it. After two days and nights of second-class travel, he felt worn, wrinkled, and decidedly ripe. Nights spent in an ordinary sleeping berth amid other snoring men meant Michael hadn't gotten a good night's rest, and he was certain his face showed it. Best not to draw attention to himself. He forced his gaze away from Miss Missoula and fixed it on the passing scenery instead. The flat, snow-covered plains of the upper Midwest had gradually given way to tall mountains and icicle-covered evergreen forests, like something out of a fairy tale, providing a much more interesting view. Not quite as interesting a view as the young woman seated across the aisle, but almost.

Chapter Three

Carrie Coker settled in her seat and smoothed her skirt in an attempt to settle her jangled nerves. What a clumsy ox she was! Fortunately, it appeared that those passengers who'd witnessed her graceless maneuver quickly lost interest and resumed their reading or woolgathering, or whatever they'd been doing to pass the long hours on the train. Everyone, that was, except the good-looking man into whose lap she'd fallen.

Of course he'd have to be good-looking, with his high cheekbones and strong jawline. She couldn't have lost her footing around, say, the stout woman with the stuffed bluebird on her hat. Or the monocled professor-type with his nose buried in a book.

To be sure, the man had been a perfect gentleman about her mishap. But now she could feel his gaze resting on her. And to her great consternation, the sensation wasn't entirely unpleasant. She would have liked to glance at him too but to do so she'd have to turn her head in an obvious manner. So she fixed her gaze out the window as the train crossed the mountains into Idaho and tried her best to think of something else.

That something else turned out to be the ugly words "sixty days."

She didn't need to reread the letter burning in her reticule to know what it said. Every word was embroidered onto her brain with unbreakable thread. The bank had given her sixty days to bring her loan current.

A loan she hadn't, until two days ago, even known existed.

Mentally she began practicing what she'd say to the bank manager once she reached Timber Coulee. A week or so prior—feeling stronger and more optimistic about life than she had in months—she'd written him a letter, requesting information about how to obtain financing to build a music camp. The camp had been the great dream of her late husband, George: to dedicate a large portion of the Coker property to a summer camp where talented but impoverished young people could escape the sweltering cities, enjoy wholesome recreation in the pure mountain air and beauty of God's creation, and study music. Especially young people like Carrie's sister, Maggie, who adored music and whose natural talent in piano went unnurtured due to the inability to pay for lessons and music scores and even a decent piano. He'd planned to name it "Camp Harmony," a choice Carrie heartily supported. She had every intention of making George's dream come true.

But instead of the positive response Carrie had expected, she received in reply a stern letter from the bank, informing her of the outstanding loan and giving her sixty days to pay it off.

Technically, of course, it wasn't *her* loan. It belonged to the Coker Lumber Company. But now that Carrie owned the company, according to the terms of George's will, it amounted to the same thing. She was the one ultimately responsible for the company's debts. She needed to figure out a way to come up with a lot of money, and she needed to do so quickly, lest she lose the company and the thickly wooded acreage it stood on. Losing the land that had been in her husband's family for generations would be an unmitigated disaster. She wouldn't just lose the potential camp; she'd lose everything George and his father and grandfather before him had worked for.

The other thing she needed to do quickly was to learn how to manage a lumber company. She could hardly make smart decisions concerning loans and such when she knew nothing of the business. The whole situation was completely overwhelming to a woman who'd spent her twenty-three years of life preparing to be a wife, mother, and homemaker, not the owner of a logging company. She didn't know the first thing about logging. Nor about running a company.

She'd spent nearly the entire train journey from Missoula considering and then discarding every idea she could think of to come up with the money to pay off the loan, each one more impractical than the last. She could sell her wedding ring—a thought that made her heartsick. Besides, the amount of cash she could get for it wouldn't be nearly enough to pay off the debt. She could ask someone to lend her the money, but who? Her widowed mother certainly wasn't in a position to help her. She could ask Reed Coker, George's cousin, who'd been so helpful to her over the past year. But she doubted he had the money either. Moreover, if she borrowed money from Reed, then she'd be obligated to him to an extent she didn't want to be. His most recent letter had contained hints of a deeper affection toward her, which she had no intention of returning. Not right away, anyway. While Reed was a kind man and a protector in her time of need, her grief was still too fresh to consider any new romantic entanglements.

Which made her fleeting, unbidden attraction to the dark-haired man seated across the aisle that much more disconcerting.

"You *could* marry, you know, if you wanted to," Maggie had pronounced with all the authority of her fifteen years. "Widows are allowed to remarry after a year."

"Thank you, Professor Hill," Carrie had responded dryly, citing the etiquette expert whose weighty tome of approved behavior stood on their mother's bookshelf. "I'll keep that in mind."

Undeterred, Maggie had pressed her case. "Why don't you want to marry Reed? He's been so nice."

"Because he hasn't asked me, for one thing."

"But he will," Maggie said with certainty.

Carrie had looked her sister straight in the eye. "Listen, Mags. When Reed stepped in to manage the company during George's illness and then agreed to stay on for a while after his death, I was deeply grateful to him. I still am. I didn't—*don't*—know the first thing about running a lumber company, and I don't know what I would have done without his help. I'm sure he feels a sense of responsibility toward me, but that's not the same as love."

The conversation, together with the ominous letter from the bank, had cemented her resolve concerning something that had been buzzing around the edges of her mind for weeks. She needed to return to Idaho, pick up the reins of her company, and release Reed to go back to his own life. He'd been juggling both her business and his own hardware store for the past year or more, and it was time to relieve him from the burden of taking care of her.

At long last the train pulled into Timber Coulee. Standing on the station platform awaiting her baggage, Carrie's chest swelled with a bittersweet anguish as the sights and smells of Timber Coulee released a torrent of memories. She breathed deeply of the crisp, frost-tinged air, of the pine-scented mountains that ringed the town, and the woody aroma of fresh-cut lumber wafting from the sawmills and lumberyards. From her vantage point she could see the tents of ice fishermen dotting the frozen expanse of the gray-blue lake. She remembered with a pang how George had loved to ice fish.

So much beauty. So much pain.

Carrie's throat felt thick with longing. She and George had been so happy here in tall timber country, until he'd gotten sick. In some ways she felt comforted by the mountains, the lake, the familiar buildings—the things she loved about the place she'd called home during the two blissful years of her marriage. On the other hand, these same things caused her to miss George even more deeply. Had she made a mistake by coming back?

As Carrie handed the porter some coins in return for delivering her suitcase, she spotted Reed's tall form crossing the platform toward her, looking every inch the successful small-town businessman in a suit, tie, and bowler hat. He greeted her with a discreet peck on the cheek and a grunt as he hoisted her suitcase.

"Welcome back to Timber Coulee, my dear."

"Thank you, Reed. It's good to be back."

He gave her a look that spoke plainly of his admiration. "I must say, I'm glad to see you out of those widow's weeds. Blue suits you much better than black."

Carrie didn't reply. Outwardly she'd completed her time of mourning, but inwardly her heart was taking longer to catch up. She couldn't imagine ever being interested in any man other than dear George. . .her brief and thoroughly inappropriate reaction toward the good-looking man on the train notwithstanding.

Speak of the devil. As Reed propelled her toward his horse-drawn carriage parked at the curb, she spotted the man from the train. Their eyes met, and he touched the brim of his black top hat. She gave a brief nod in return. He was quite tall—much taller than she'd realized when she'd hurtled heave-ho onto his lap. She would have liked to have spoken to him, to apologize again for her clumsy misstep. He seemed kind, more concerned about her well-being than his own even after she'd fairly squashed him, and she wished she could have thought of something more clever to say to him than rattling on about the weather. But it was too late now to charm him with her sparkling wit, and impossible in any case, with Reed grasping her elbow with a possessive air.

Besides, she'd likely never see him again. Better to focus on her purpose for returning to Timber Coulee and the daunting task that lay before her.

"You must be exhausted," Reed remarked. "And famished. Shall I take you to supper? Or would you prefer to go straight to your lodgings to rest?"

"Both," Carrie admitted, "but what I'd really like to do before anything else is to call the bank and speak to Mr. Tate."

A look of surprise flitted across Reed's square-jawed face. "The bank? What about?"

"This." Carrie produced the bank's letter from her reticule. "Apparently Coker Lumber owes quite a large debt. Do you know what it's all about?"

Reed looked at the letter. His face colored. "I'm surprised Tate wrote to you."

"Why? I am the owner of the company, after all."

Reed hoisted her suitcase into his carriage. "Yes, you are. Technically. But since I've been managing things in your absence, I'd directed the bank to send all business correspondence to me, so as not to burden you with such things during your time of mourning."

Carrie lifted the corners of her mouth in what she hoped was a smile. "That was thoughtful of you. But now that I know about it, I'd like to get to the bottom of it, starting with a conversation with Mr. Tate."

"Of course. But maybe supper first."

She steeled her spine. "Bank first. It's nearing five o'clock. They'll be closing soon."

"As you wish."

Leaving the carriage parked, they walked across the brick-paved street to the bank only to be told by a clerk that Mr. Tate had left early due to a family matter. Discussing the loan would have to wait. As Carrie set up an appointment for the following day, she thought Reed looked relieved and realized that, at some level, so was she. Much as she wanted the matter resolved as quickly as possible, she'd have a clearer head for such a discussion after a nourishing meal and a good night's sleep.

They continued up the street to the restaurant of the brand-new Timber Coulee Hotel. Carrie was impressed by the handsome four-story edifice, which Reed told her had opened just three months earlier.

"I thought you might have enjoyed staying here instead of bunking with the camp cook," he remarked with a look of distaste.

"It looks nice, but a fancy hotel room is not in my budget," she replied. "Frenchie—I mean, Mrs. Duval—and I taught Sunday school together when I lived here, and she was kind to offer me her extra bedroom. Besides, I prefer being up at the camp rather than in town."

The hostess seated them at a table near a window. After she'd gone, Reed looked earnestly at Carrie and said tenderly, "I hope the bank loan isn't the only reason you've returned. When I got your telegram, I must admit, I hoped at least part of the reason for your coming here was to see me." He reached across the table and laid his hand over hers. "Have you given any thought to the feelings I expressed to you in my last letter?"

She avoided his gaze, unsure how to answer. Apparently

mistaking her hesitation for shyness, he continued.

"You needn't feel bashful, Carrie-Girl. Over the months of our correspondence I've come to see in you the qualities that I would most value in a wife."

Carrie withdrew her hand and picked up her water glass. She hadn't anticipated him bringing up the subject of romance, much less marriage, so quickly, and she took a slow sip of water to buy herself time to think of a response. Reed had been so kind to her, so considerate of her recent widowhood. He'd essentially put his life on hold for a year to help her out of a bad situation. Did such a sacrifice win him the right to her heart?

Chapter Four

As Uncle Sebastian drove the carriage up Timber Coulee's main road, he pointed out various wooden structures, most of which looked haphazard and ramshackle to Michael's city-bred eye.

"There's the new hotel," his uncle said, nodding toward a four-story building. "And next door to it is the men's clothing shop." He glanced quickly at Michael. "Remember that one. You'll be headed there shortly."

Michael felt his hackles rise. Was Uncle Sebastian implying his appearance wasn't up to snuff? Naturally, he was rumpled after the long train ride. Who wouldn't be? But surely his finely tailored suit from one of Chicago's most prestigious men's shops was far superior to anything to be found in this measly backwater—

"And there's the bank." The older man's hearty declaration interrupted Michael's unspoken tirade.

"Where?"

"There, on the corner."

Michael peered at the stone edifice. Just then, he caught a glimpse of a familiar feathered hat and blue skirt as the young woman from the train and her escort swished past on the sidewalk and disappeared through the bank's entrance.

"Let's stop and go in!" he practically shouted.

Uncle Sebastian gave a rueful smile. "I appreciate your enthusiasm, my boy, and I wish we had time to pop in for a moment so you could have a look around. But we'd best head straight home or the soup will be cold, and the only thing steaming will be your Aunt Becky."

Michael could scarcely admit to his uncle that it was the intriguing woman in blue who'd caught his attention, not his breathless enthusiasm over touring the bank. Minutes later the carriage halted in front of a gabled white Victorian, one of Timber Coulee's statelier homes, though modest by Chicago standards. Michael leaped from the carriage and grabbed his bags. The prospect of a home-cooked meal quickened his steps.

"Hold on there, lad," his uncle protested, chuckling. "These bones aren't as spry as they used to be."

In place of the expected housemaid or butler, Aunt Becky herself greeted them warmly at the door. Michael immediately took a liking to the short, plump, smiling woman whose grayish-brown curls were escaping from her bun. After an exchange of pleasantries, she gave Michael a quick tour of the main floor, then led him upstairs to the guest bedroom.

"Are you sure it's no trouble, my staying here?" Michael asked as they climbed the stairs. "I fully expected to stay at the hotel."

"Nonsense," his aunt huffed. "We wouldn't hear of it. Just drop your bags here and wash up. Supper's nearly on the table, so come on down as soon as you're ready. Later we'll get you unpacked and sort out what needs washing and pressing." She paused, then added, "I hope you won't mind eating in the kitchen. We seldom use the dining room except for company. And you're not company. You're family."

Family. Something about the way she said the word glowed deep inside Michael's chest. After a quick wash with the warm water, soap, and soft towel he found next to the porcelain basin, he dressed in fresh clothing, then hurried downstairs.

As Aunt Becky set a platter of pork chops and dumplings on the table, Michael suppressed a grin, watching Uncle Sebastian tuck a napkin into the front of his shirt. His father wouldn't be caught dead wearing a napkin over his chest like a baby's bib, but in Aunt Becky's kitchen the gesture seemed normal and fitting. With a faint sense of rebellion, Michael removed his own napkin from his lap and tucked it into his shirtfront.

Uncle Sebastian speared a pork chop. "I hope you're ready to put in some hard work, son."

"Oh, Seb," Aunt Becky chided. "Do you have to talk business now? The boy just traveled halfway across the country. Let him eat in peace."

"My dear, I'm afraid this can't wait," he responded.

Michael straightened his spine. "Yes, sir. I'm ready to start at the bank first thing in the morning."

"That's just it," his uncle said. "You won't be going to the bank."

"I won't?" Michael frowned. Wasn't that his whole purpose for being here?

"Instead," Uncle Sebastian continued, "I have a very special project in mind for you."

"What sort of project?" Aunt Becky voiced Michael's question before he did. She took her own seat and reached for the basket of rolls.

"It has to do with the Coker widow," Uncle Sebastian said. "I'm being pressured to call her loan, but I dread doing it."

Aunt Becky's brow puckered. "Pressured by whom?"

"The head office is insisting on it."

"You mean *Gordon* is insisting on it." Michael caught the note of disdain in her tone as she spoke of his father. "Can't you talk him into making an exception? Extend the loan a bit longer? Carrie is such a dear."

"I've tried, but I'm afraid dearness doesn't count for much in Gordon's world. I couldn't make a strong enough case for leniency. We've already granted one extension. The bald fact is, she can't make her payments. If the timber harvest doesn't come in strong this spring, I see no other alternative."

"The poor thing," Aunt Becky said with a mournful look in her eyes.

Michael seethed with silent rage. His father was a man of zero patience, notoriously ruthless about calling unpaid loans no matter what the reason. He thought of his good friends, the Lanza family, who had lost their little Italian grocery due to his father's lack of compassion concerning an overdue loan, reducing Mr. Lanza to peddling sandwiches on street corners to support his large family. And now it sounded like some sweet little old widow's livelihood was in similar jeopardy.

Uncle Sebastian shook his head. "I truly don't understand it. The Cokers used to have one of the healthiest tree loads in the county. I don't think there's a better stretch of timber in the whole state." He set down his fork and turned to Michael, his expression grave. "Here's the situation. The Cokers are a logging family, going back generations. The old man moved out here after the Civil War and they've done all their banking with us since the day we opened our doors. Loyal customers, real decent folk. Unfortunately, they've fallen on hard times. The most recent owner, Mr. George Coker, God rest his soul, wasn't the businessman his father and grandfather were."

"So George Coker is—was—the widow's husband," Michael said, fitting the pieces together.

Uncle Sebastian nodded. "And since his death just over a year ago, the company has failed to turn a profit. The harvest came in short at last spring's run—thousands of board feet shorter than in previous years—and nobody at the company can account for it."

"That's too bad," Michael said, for lack of a more incisive comment. What did any of this have to do with the special project his uncle mentioned?

Uncle Sebastian sliced into his pork chop. "Coker Lumber owns a good-sized tract of timber surrounded on three sides by land belonging to the Goldwood Corporation."

"Goldwood," Michael repeated. "The big lumber corporation out of Minnesota? Aren't they a major customer of the bank's Minneapolis branch?"

"The same. They have operations all over the Northwest, clear over to the coast. Moved into this area a couple of years ago and bought up several of the small-time operators."

"But not the Cokers."

"No, siree, not the Cokers." Uncle Sebastian took a sip of coffee. "Goldwood's been trying to get hold of their tract, but they've always refused to sell. George's father swore he'd die before he'd let them put an ax to a single tree, and he did. George refused to sell as well, in honor of his late father's wishes. But, frankly, his heart wasn't in logging. Went off to some music conservatory, planned to become a concert pianist, but when his father died, his plans changed."

"He chose logging over the life of a musician?"

Uncle Sebastian nodded. "Funny thing about those Cokers. They have a strong sense of honor and duty. Trouble is, shortly before he took sick, George needed some new equipment and ran low on capital, so he took out a good-sized loan from the bank to keep logging. Now that he's gone, his widow is also refusing to sell to Goldwood. But unless she can cough up the money to repay the loan, she'll lose the land anyway."

"I don't understand it," Aunt Becky said, stabbing a pork chop for emphasis. "How could the Coker land go that quickly from being profitable to unprofitable? Didn't George's cousin come out from Spokane to help Carrie run the place?"

"He did." Uncle Sebastian lifted a forkful of mashed potatoes. "Since George's death, Carrie's been at her mother's place for a rest. Reed Coker came out to run the company until such time as she'd be able to take it over. His involvement was the reason we were willing to extend the loan the first time it came up for repayment. We had high hopes that under his management things would turn around, but they haven't."

Aunt Becky's forehead puckered in disapproval. "Poor Carrie. Will she have to sell out?"

"Goldwood would snap up the land in an instant were she to put it on the market. At a handsome price too. But from what I gather, she hates the thought of the land passing out of the Coker family on her watch, especially to a big conglomerate like Goldwood." He shook his head. "Can't say I blame her. If I could figure out a way to avoid foreclosure, I would. All the bank's going to do is turn right around and sell the property to Goldwood anyway. Either way, she loses." He burped quietly. "I can't help but think there's something not quite right going on over there, but I haven't been able to put my finger on it."

"That timber is hers, and she has a right to profit from it," Aunt Becky said firmly. "Sounds to me like someone needs to march right over there and do some investigating." She pointed to Michael's plate. "Eat up, dear. A boy needs a good meal in his belly."

"Yes, ma'am." Michael speared a second pork chop from the platter at the center of the table. He liked Aunt Becky and didn't bother to point out that he was no longer a boy, as he would have had his own parents dared say such a thing. He especially admired the way she took a genuine interest in her husband's business, asking intelligent questions and offering suggestions. Michael couldn't think of a time when his mother had shown interest in any details of his father's work.

"Becky, you're brilliant. That's exactly what I have in mind." Uncle Sebastian's booming voice startled Michael. He struggled to remember what his aunt had said right before distracting him with pork chops.

"The bank, of course, has done a thorough audit. We've gone over every page of their ledgers and haven't found anything amiss," his uncle continued. "But I just have a gut feeling something's not right over there."

"Do you think the owner's up to something shady?" Michael asked.

Uncle Sebastian stopped in midchew. "Carrie?" His blue eyes widened, giving him an owlish appearance. "Oh, I can't imagine that. Sweetest woman west of the Mississippi. Present company excepted." He winked at Aunt Becky, who playfully swatted his arm as she set down a plateful of apple pie. "All the Cokers I've known have been square as dice. But there might be some error, some mistake in operations, that's causing her to lose money. Or, somebody might deliberately be trying to cheat her. So our next step is to put a fly on the wall, a man on the inside, to see how the operation is really being run. That's where you come in, my boy. I'm sending you in to Coker Lumber to investigate."

"You mean do another audit of their books?" Michael felt a puff of pride. His father hadn't yet trusted him to do outside audits on his own, on behalf of the bank. Such a responsibility would be a promotion of sorts. Make him look good to his father and earn him a return ticket to Chicago.

"Well, sort of," Uncle Sebastian replied cagily. "The only way to handle this case is from the bottom up, from inside the company. I don't know any of the current work crew well enough to know if they have the necessary skill for such a task, much less the ability to be trustworthy and discreet about it." He served himself a wedge of pie, then grinned at Michael. "So I'm sending you. Tomorrow you'll hire yourself on as a laborer."

"I'm—what?" Michael nearly dropped his fork. "You mean, go to work as a logger? Not as a representative of the bank?"

"That's exactly what I mean." Uncle Sebastian settled back in his chair, looking pleased. "You're new in town. Nobody's met you yet or knows you're my nephew. You can hire on over there and find out what's really going on. And maybe soon we'll have some answers."

Michael sat in stunned silence, his mind swirling. This was not what he'd anticipated at all. On the other hand, the thought of working outdoors in the fresh air, using his muscles, instead of being cooped up inside a stuffy office appealed to him. So did the prospect of doing a heroic deed, of helping a beleaguered widow save her land from the grasping clutches of his father.

"I'll do it," he blurted before thinking the matter through. Then reality seeped in. "But, to be honest," he admitted, "I don't know the first thing about logging."

"Ah, but you *do* know what to look for in a struggling business, what the signs of trouble are," the older man said, his eyes bright. "Your business training will have taught you that much. Maybe you can catch some irregularity that I've missed. Tell them. . ." He thought for a moment, then snapped his fingers. "Tell them you're a college student from back East, taking a year off to earn tuition money. They won't expect you to know what you're doing right out of the gate but will appreciate your youthful energy and strength to handle the work."

"I don't know, Sebastian." A crease formed on Aunt Becky's forehead. "I don't like the idea of sending the boy out to the woods, so far from anywhere. Suppose something should happen? We promised his parents we'd take good care of him. If he got injured, I don't think I'd ever get over blaming myself for letting him go."

Michael leaned forward eagerly. "I can take care of myself," he assured her. "I'm sure I can handle anything I might run up against."

Uncle Sebastian gave his wife a reassuring smile. "Indeed, Becky. The young man is perfectly capable of making his way in the woods." He lifted a forkful of pie to his lips.

"I suppose so," she hesitantly conceded. "But will they be hiring? I mean, the season's already well underway."

Uncle Sebastian swallowed, then patted his lips with his napkin. "I've heard the crew is bulking up in anticipation of the spring run. The foreman is taking applications in the hotel lobby this very week." He looked at Michael. "And I know for a fact they've been lacking a clerk for the office. The last fellow quit right before Christmas. It's worth a try anyway, don't you think?"

They lingered at the table, discussing the details of their scheme, as Aunt Becky washed the dishes, tossing in her opinion now and then. The longer they talked, the more appealing the enterprise sounded to Michael. Work away from the stuffy bank! Help solve a mystery! Best of all, Uncle Sebastian and Aunt Becky seemed to really care about this Widow Coker person, whom Michael pictured as frail, elderly, and bewildered by the details of business. If Michael could help save her land, it would feel awfully good. Maybe even somehow, in a small and indirect way, make up for what his father had done to good people like the Lanzas. In any case, Uncle

Sebastian would surely put in a good report to Michael's father. And if he received a favorable report, perhaps Gordon Tate would cut short his son's exile and allow him to return to Chicago sooner rather than later. All things considered, Michael could hardly wait to get started.

Chapter Five

Reed's gaze bore into Carrie's as she struggled to formulate a firm yet gracious response to his proposal. She'd thought she'd have a little more time before the topic came up. *Oh, well. No time like the present.* She took a sip of water and shot up a quick prayer that God would give her the right words.

"Oh, Reed," she began. "I'm—I'm most grateful and flattered by your attention." She paused.

His face tightened. "But. . ."

"But I'm afraid it's too soon for me to make such a momentous decision. I'm not ready for another. . .involvement, with you or anyone else. I implore you to understand."

He straightened his back. "Of course, you must take all the time you need. I'm a patient man. But you and I, together, would make a good match. Our correspondence over the past year has shown me the kind of decent, honorable woman you are. A woman I have grown to love."

"Thank you," she said, as though he'd just complimented her hat. She couldn't return the word *love*. Affection, yes. Gratitude, yes. But love?

"Would I have upended my entire life for you if I didn't?"

A wave of guilt washed over Carrie. "You've been a good friend when I needed one. It's just that. . .I don't know that I'll ever marry again. You could be waiting an awfully long time."

He smiled and snapped open his menu. "I'm in no rush."

Carrie sensed she should have been firmer in her refusal but lacked the words. Eager to change the subject, she gazed out through the velvet-draped window at the busy main thoroughfare. "It looks like Timber Coulee has grown quite a bit since I was last here."

Reed nodded. "The trains bring in more people every day. Lots of new houses and buildings going up."

Carrie picked up her menu. "Resulting in lots of lumber orders, one hopes."

"We're keeping busy."

She looked at him squarely over the top of the menu. "Then tell me honestly. If there's so much demand, why isn't Coker Lumber thriving? Why is the company in debt?"

Reed shrugged. "There's plenty of competition. Goldwood in particular is bearing down hard."

"Tell me more about this loan."

Reed's eyes shifted away from hers and onto the menu. "There's not much to tell. Apparently, George took it out some months before his death to invest in some needed equipment. He intended to pay it back with the proceeds from last spring's timber harvest, but by then he was gone. And then the harvest came in much poorer than expected and we lacked sufficient proceeds to cover the loan."

"But why?" she pressed. "Are we running out of trees or something?"

He made an odd noise, half chuckle, half cough. "No, nothing like that." He shrugged. "My guess is that George made some mistakes in his calculations, that's all. Perhaps his mind was clouded by his illness. In any case, the bank granted an extension. It's nothing we can't make up with the proceeds from this spring's harvest." His gaze penetrated hers. "And it's nothing you need to worry your pretty head about. You can trust me. I would have even written to you about it myself, only I wanted to spare you unnecessary worry. I never dreamed Tate would write to you, or that the news would cause you to leave your mother's home and hightail it back here."

Carrie tilted her head. Something in his tone sounded. . .off, somehow. "Are you sorry I came back?"

"Oh, no. Not at all," he quickly reassured her. "I'm delighted to see you. Delighted." He paused while a waitress took their orders, then turned back to Carrie. "I'm pleased you've come for a visit. What are you planning to do while you're here?"

"Oh, I'm not here for a visit," she said firmly. "I've come to stay."

He blinked. "And do what?"

"And work beside you at the company. You'll teach me all about how to run it. And then, depending on what the future holds, you'll be free to return to your hardware store. Or, if you choose to stay, we'll be true partners." Her face heated. "I mean, in the business. Business partners."

"Of course I'll stay, if you want me to." Reed said warmly, gazing at her across the table. "I daresay, your response gives me hope."

Carrie immediately regretted her words. She hadn't meant to give him hope.

"But as far as your working for the company," Reed continued, his tone turning businesslike. "Well, I never thought—" He seemed uncharacteristically at a loss for words. "That is, I thought you'd likely want to sell the business to Goldwood. Be relieved of the burden of it. Not take it over yourself."

Carrie inhaled deeply as the waitress set a savory bowl of beef noodle soup before her. "I realize it's unusual for a woman to run a logging company."

"Highly unusual," Reed agreed. "Unheard of, actually."

"But selling out is not what George would have wanted. If it were, he would have made provision for it in his will. As it is, he left the company to me, with the intention that I carry out his greatest wish."

"Which was?"

"The music camp, of course." Carrie tilted her head. Why was Reed acting so obtuse? "You remember. I'm sure I've mentioned it in my letters."

A small crease formed in his forehead. "Remind me."

"George dreamed of eventually turning the property—or a good portion of it—into a summer music camp for young people."

"Ah. Yes. The camp idea." His jaw tightened.

Carrie didn't care for his dismissive tone but chose to ignore it for the time being. "Anyway, Mr. Tate wrote to me in response to a letter I'd written him about borrowing funds to build the camp facilities. He explained such financing would be impossible until the current loan is repaid. And of course we can forget the whole idea if we lose the land entirely."

"We aren't going to lose the land," Reed reassured her. "I'm sure the money we'll earn in the spring harvest will more than cover the repayment." He picked up his spoon. "But really, Carrie, is building a camp such a good idea? I strongly think you should give serious consideration to Goldwood's offer to buy up the property. You'd be a rich woman."

"It's what George wanted, and I want to honor his wishes," she said firmly. "Now, shall we pray before the soup gets cold?"

"Uh, sure." Reed set down the spoon he'd raised, bowed his

head, and uttered a perfunctory prayer for the meal. Carrie added a silent petition. *Lord, help me do the right thing in this situation, whatever it may be.*

Chapter Six

The next morning, Michael awakened to the sound of sleet pattering against the window. He pulled his arms out from under the downy comforter and lazily stretched them overhead. Then, remembering where he was, and that his valet was some twelve hundred miles back East, he mulled over the necessity of getting himself up, shaved, and dressed. *But not quite yet.* Lying between pristine sheets, relishing the warm, soft bed after the torturous berth on the train, he let his mind wander back over the events of the previous evening.

After supper, he and Uncle Sebastian had taken a sleigh down to the frozen river, where acres of wooden booms stood empty, awaiting the torrent of logs that would fill them once the ice thawed. His uncle pointed out the huge sawmill standing downstream where, come spring, logs would be measured, weighed, and accounted for.

"How can they tell whose logs are whose?" Michael had asked as they gazed out over the acres of booms. "How do they sort them all out?"

"They're sorted right there in the river," his uncle said. "Each log carries the brand of the company that cut it. So Coker's logs would be marked with Coker's symbol—a bright red C inside of a star. And the sawmill gives them credit for it. That's what's supposed to happen, anyway." Uncle Sebastian paused to pack tobacco into the bowl of his black pipe.

"Seems pretty straightforward," Michael reasoned. "As long as the sawmill's doing a good job of sorting the logs according to brand."

"That's part of what you'll need to figure out. Is everybody on the up-and-up, doing their jobs the way they're supposed to? Keep your eyes open and your mouth shut. Not only must you watch what happens around you, but keep an eye on the scaler, and check up on the time book and the supplies. Of course you can only do those last two if they put you to clerking. I'm thinking that's what they'll do, with your college education. In any case, once you're on the inside, you can take a look around and figure out what's going on."

Last night in the moonlit darkness, with the snow crunching under their boots, the notion of going undercover as a logger to snoop around had seemed exciting. Now, in the pale light of morning, Michael wondered what he'd gotten himself into. But justice must be served. The widow's husband was hardly even cold in the ground. Greedy bankers like his father didn't need to be circling like vultures overhead, just waiting for a chance to shred her to pieces. They could at least give the poor woman a chance to get her feet underneath her. The latter seemed to be Uncle Sebastian's approach, which made Michael admire him all the more.

Soon the enticing aroma of bacon wafted into his thoughts, propelling him out of his comfortable nest to wash, shave, dress, and hurry down to the kitchen.

"Sebastian's already gone off to the bank, but he left you this." Aunt Becky pointed to an envelope lying on the table next to Michael's plate. In it were some bills, along with instructions concerning the clothes and gear to buy in town. *So that's what he meant about visiting the haberdashery*, Michael said to himself. He didn't need sprucing up for his new job; he needed sprucing down.

"He also requested that you *not* stop in at the bank today," she said. "He thinks the fewer people who know you're related, the easier it will be to pass yourself off as a stranger in town."

Michael agreed.

"After breakfast, bring down your soiled garments. Gretchen will be here today to help with the laundry, while you're off getting whatever Sebastian put on that list."

As he ate, he watched his aunt bustle around the kitchen, amazed that she did most of her own cooking and housework, with only part-time help from a neighbor woman with the laundry and heavy cleaning. Back in Chicago, Michael's mother relied on a full retinue of servants to run her lavish household. Yet Aunt Becky seemed to enjoy the myriad humble tasks of homemaking. Last night she'd beamed with pleasure at Uncle Sebastian's praise of her cooking. Their affectionate ways with each other seemed strange to Michael, though he found himself oddly drawn to them too.

After finishing breakfast and relinquishing his dirty clothes to Aunt Becky, he walked downtown. He invested in a few red flannel shirts, canvas trousers, and tools that his uncle had advised him to buy. Next, following instructions, he entered the hotel lobby, where a representative of Coker Lumber sat behind a table, taking applications for skilled loggers to help with the spring log run. It was easier than he'd thought to convince the heavyset man doing the hiring that he was a college student from back East taking time off to earn tuition, looking for seasonal work in the great outdoors.

The man peered up at him from behind a table. He seemed to be examining Michael's fine woolen overcoat with a skeptical eye.

"You one of them young bucks studying forestry science at one of them land-grant colleges?" The sneering way he pronounced *forestry science* seemed to indicate he didn't think much of such academic programs.

"No, sir. Business and finance," Michael said with honesty.

The man removed his hat and scratched his balding head. "Don't know as how book learnin' will help you much in this trade. Unless yer lookin' to become the boss one day." He chuckled as if the idea struck him as ludicrous. "Well, yer in luck. We're short a man, and you might do." He squinted at Michael. "We'll try you out. If you can handle the work, you've got yerself a job What's yer name?"

"Michael Ta–Taylor," he stammered, remembering at the last second that he wasn't to identify himself as a Tate. Not yet.

"All righty, Mike Taylor. Be at the depot Monday morning, crack of dawn."

Coming out of the hotel, Michael caught a glimpse of the young woman from the train entering the mercantile next door with a basket over her arm. He was seized by an almost irresistible impulse to follow her and introduce himself properly. But why? Was it her passing resemblance to Maude that made her intriguing? Or something else?

Before he could act on his impulse, he remembered Uncle Sebastian's warning about the need for discretion, that the fewer people who knew Michael's true identity, the better. Getting acquainted with the young woman would have to wait, if indeed he could still find her when the need for secrecy was over. He bit back his disappointment and turned in the direction of Aunt Becky's house. Hopefully Miss Missoula would still be in Timber Coulee when he got back from his adventure in the mountains.

The next morning, a Sunday, Michael came downstairs to find

his aunt and uncle getting ready to go to church.

"I think it's best you don't come with us this time, my boy," Uncle Sebastian said. "For the time being, we want as few people as possible connecting you to me or to the bank."

So Michael stayed home and stayed indoors, reading first the newspaper and then a book chosen from his uncle's sizeable library. He didn't bother telling his aunt and uncle he wasn't in the habit of attending church. While the Tate name did appear on the membership roster of a prominent Chicago church, his family seldom made the effort to attend. But based on the prayers before meals and the titles on the shelves, Michael sensed his aunt and uncle took church attendance seriously, and he found himself oddly reluctant to disappoint them.

To his surprise, he found himself getting thoroughly absorbed in the autobiography of a man named George Müller, who'd had a reputation as a liar and a thief until his Christian conversion. But after that event, he devoted his life to the care of orphans. Michael had known many families, his own included, who gave generous endowments to orphanages and other charities. But no one he knew became as personally invested in the work as this Müller fellow. Time passed quickly as he sank into the story. Before he knew it, his aunt and uncle had returned, and soon dinner was on the table.

Early the next morning, with about twenty other men, Michael waited to board the small freight train that would haul the workers, plus supplies and horses, up to the Coker property on Long Mountain. He wore the same caulked boots and the same canvas trousers, cut off at the top of the boots, as the other loggers, although his looked conspicuously new.

A long whistle sounded, and Michael followed the others as they climbed onto the top of a boxcar. In sharp contrast to the elegant leather valise he'd carried from Chicago, his bundle consisted of a grain sack tied at either end with a rope worn slung over his shoulder. It contained one change of clothing, a toothbrush, a comb, the George Müller autobiography which Uncle Sebastian had encouraged him to borrow, and a sack of sandwiches courtesy of Aunt Becky. Similar bundles were scattered across the tops of the cars, with their owners using them as cushions or pillows. Mindful of the sandwiches, Michael deposited his bundle on the running board beside him. As he glanced at the bewhiskered faces all around, he was glad he'd chosen to leave his shaving kit behind.

The cars jerked and swayed as the train chugged upward through the snowy forest. A thrill of excitement and adventure seized Michael as he breathed deeply of the pine-scented air. This was miles better than being stuck in a stuffy office all day.

When they reached the camp, he joined the others in settling in at the bunkhouse. Then the foreman, Sully, summoned him.

"Hey, College Boy. You said you know how to do figurin', right?"

Michael nodded. "Right."

The foreman jerked his thumb. "Come with me. Boss wants to talk to you."

Michael followed Sully to the staging area, where a tall, blond-bearded man stood talking to the fellow operating the measuring scale.

"Reed Coker. Mike Taylor," Sully said by way of introductions.

The blond man studied Michael for a moment, then said, "Ever work in the woods?"

"No, sir."

"Sully tells me you've been to college."

"Yes, some."

"I need someone to figure up time books, keep track of supplies, and set down the log figures when they're given to you. Think you can handle that?"

"I think so."

"I'm going to put you to clerking. Your job will be to make yourself handy around camp and keep the books. Follow me."

An enormous, black-bearded fellow named McTavish sneered as Michael passed. "Off to push a pencil, eh? Shuffling papers around is for weaklings," he said, eliciting chortles from the other men. "It's for them who can't hack it out with the real men. Chopping down trees and hauling logs, now that's a job well done."

But Michael ignored them. He could hardly believe his good fortune. Or in God's providence, as the biography he'd been reading called it. Apparently, after his conversion, this George Müller fellow had trusted God for everything, and God had been faithful in His provision. This was a radical new idea to Michael, and an intriguing one, that God would take any interest in people's day-to-day affairs. He'd been turning the idea over in his head ever since, wondering if he had what it took to have that kind of faith.

In any case, working in the office would give him access to all the company's records, including any possible under-the-table ones. He'd be able to discover the ruse, if there was one, and solve the mystery of the widow's plight that much sooner.

Chapter Seven

Carrie stood on a precipice, overlooking snow-covered acres of towering pine, larch, birch, and fir trees stretching in all directions. A stiff winter breeze caressed her cheek and lifted a few unruly strands of hair that had escaped from her bun. She clutched her coat more tightly around her slender frame and drew a deep breath, savoring the fresh, cold air in her lungs. She could swear the wind carried the promise of spring, even though the thaw was still several weeks away.

How she loved this land! She always had, from the first moment she'd laid eyes on it when she and George were newlyweds. Such a shame it still had to be logged, when it would make such a peaceful, restful place for young people to gather and appreciate God's creation.

She tried to imagine how the area would appear to a city-weary child arriving at Camp Harmony. They'd need to erect a big sign at the front entrance, of course: WELCOME TO CAMP HARMONY. And they could convert the current buildings to house the camp office, kitchen, and dining room, and build a large, tented platform for the concerts, and several cabins scattered about for guests.

Of course, she reminded herself, in reality, she could do as she pleased. The property was hers now, willed to her by her late husband. If only she could figure out a way to—

Suddenly a pair of leather-gloved hands clamped over her eyes from behind and a deep voice said, "Guess who?" Roughly she shoved the hands away and whirled around to face Reed's laughing face.

"Don't do that," she snapped.

"Don't do what?" His eyes widened. He reached for her but she backed away, just out of his grasp.

"Startle me like that. You know I don't like it." She placed a hand over her heart to quell the pounding.

"I'm sorry," Reed said, not sounding sorry at all. He ducked his head, but his eyes still crinkled with amusement. "You should know by now that I'd never do anything to harm you."

"So you've said." She turned away from him and went back to surveying the acreage, but the moment of wonder had passed. Sighing, she turned back to Reed. "Come on, let's go inside and have our lunch. I've made us a fireside picnic in Frenchie's cabin."

"A picnic in the middle of winter? Sounds intriguing," Reed said.

Carrie smiled. The truth was, she didn't feel ready to eat in the dining hall with all the men staring at her. Eventually she'd get used to it, but until then, she preferred to take her meals alone in Frenchie's cabin. In fact, she'd offered to help Frenchie in the kitchen starting that evening, just to avoid having to sit out in the dining hall among the men. But Reed didn't need to know all that. She didn't want him to think she was easily intimidated.

As they passed the cookhouse, they had to weave their way through a crowd of loggers heading toward the dining hall. "The camp seems so busy," she remarked.

"We're swinging into full operation now that the higher elevation snow's been melting and the days are getting longer."

"Can we afford to employ so many men?"

"We can't afford not to," Reed responded. "Not if we want to pull in a good run this spring. In fact, Sully was down in Timber Coulee this week, hiring on more men."

"I see." Carrie realized that staffing was just one of the company matters with which she was completely unfamiliar. George had always handled things like that, while Carrie had stayed in town to take care of their home and cook their meals. Thank goodness Reed had stepped in when she needed help. She owed him a great debt of gratitude.

She sighed. A very great debt, indeed.

She opened the door to a small three-room cabin, where earlier she'd spread a plaid blanket on the floor in front of a cheerfully crackling fire. Kneeling beside a picnic basket, she pulled out two plates, two sandwiches wrapped in waxed paper, and a small paper sack of carrot sticks. Frenchie had generously invited her to raid the camp food stores and had even contributed a cherry pie to the occasion, made from preserves from the previous summer.

Reed sat beside her on the blanket and stretched out his long, denim-clad legs. She handed him a plate with a sandwich on it. "Looks mighty tasty, Carrie-Girl," he said before taking a bite. "Mmm. That's what I call good cookin'."

"I'd hardly call it cooking. It's just ham and cheese," she said, feeling unaccountably irritated by his praise. Immediately she chided herself for her sour disposition. He was only trying to be nice. Goodness, what was wrong with her this afternoon? A bright winter day, a blazing fire, a feast spread before her. . .what was there to be sour about?

All at once she remembered. *Of course.* Anxiety over yesterday's meeting with Mr. Tate at the bank was dampening her mood. The banker had kindly but firmly restated the terms of the loan, unwilling to budge. He was sorry, he'd said, but his hands were tied. Reed had told her not to worry, but the specter of that blasted overdue loan was never far from her thoughts. She sensed Sebastian Tate was a reasonable sort of man, but she hadn't wanted to push her objections too far. He held all the power in the situation. If he wanted to, he could demand immediate repayment at any time, and then what would happen to them all?

She moved closer to the fire, letting its seeping warmth relax her taut muscles.

"When we're done here, we should go into the office so you can start showing me the ropes," she said.

Reed sighed. "Can't we just enjoy each other's company for a while, not talk shop? There'll be time enough to discuss business later."

"But I'm here now. No time like the present."

"All right. If you insist," Reed grumped. "But let's enjoy our meal first."

She turned her attention to her sandwich, stealing surreptitious glances at Reed while he ate. He may have been a cousin to her late husband, but she could see little resemblance between the two, other than their height. Where George had been trim and dark-haired, Reed was husky and blond. Where George had had a serious and quiet nature, the gregarious Reed was forever laughing and making jokes. Not that being affable was a crime, Carrie reminded herself. She just needed to get used to it. And she would, eventually—especially if they ended up becoming man and wife, as Reed insisted he wanted.

He glanced over and caught her staring at him. He grinned. "Penny for your thoughts."

Her face burned. Quickly she swept her arm across the vista that lay outside the gingham-curtained window. "I was just thinking. I don't understand how there can be so many trees, and yet still the land fails to turn a profit." So much for avoiding shop talk.

"I've told you, honey. It has to do with the markets." He repositioned himself to face her. "Demand is down, and so are prices. The logs just aren't bringing in the same amount they used to."

"But why? It seems like all the other local operations are thriving, and you yourself said that lots of new construction is going on."

"It's a bit complicated to understand."

"It can't be *that* complicated." A shiver of irritation swept up the back of her neck.

"Are you saying you don't trust me to manage the company's affairs?" He was no longer smiling as he uncapped a thermos of coffee and poured himself a cup.

"Of course I do. I just can't stand the thought of having to sell out to Goldwood—or anyone else."

"Just give it a little more time," Reed soothed. "Haven't I promised you that things will turn around soon?"

"But maybe not soon enough."

She wanted to believe him. She trusted Reed. After all, he'd charged in like the cavalry to run the company after George's death. Who could foresee he'd take a shine to Carrie on a personal level? Now he wanted to marry her. Would that be such a terrible thing, to marry a kind, good-hearted, protective man? He'd promised to be patient, but she knew he was waiting for a definite decision on her part.

"Let's have a look at that pie," Reed said, his good humor apparently restored. Carrie dragged her mind back from disquieting thoughts of marriage, picked up a knife, and cut them each a wedge.

Well, at least one thing's clear, she told herself. *If I do marry Reed, the key to winning an argument will be to ply him with treats.*

Chapter Eight

Michael stared around the cluttered office of the Coker Lumber Company, wondering how in the world things had gotten this bad. He'd seen some messy offices during his tenure with the bank, helping the senior bankers with audits, but none quite as crazy as this jumbled heap.

Earlier that morning Reed Coker had given Michael a perfunctory tour of the office, shown him the rickety chair and patch of desk he was to use, and then left him alone, citing a pressing lunch engagement.

"I suggest you start by cleaning up in here," he'd said. "Since the former clerk quit, things have gotten a bit out of hand."

A bit, Michael thought with a tinge of sarcasm. Silently he questioned Reed's ability to run a company at all, by the look of things.

"As you can see, we've been sorely in need of a clerk," Reed continued, "so I hope you're up to the challenge. My time and attention are necessarily divided, of course, between this business and my hardware concern in Spokane."

Michael made a mental note that Reed was trying to run two companies at once. He hadn't known that fact, and doubted that his uncle knew it either. *No wonder Coker Lumber is in a financial tangle,* he thought. No man, no matter how skilled, could competently run two companies at once.

As if reading Michael's thoughts, Reed added, "Of course, my partner handles things at the hardware store when I can't be there. Still, it will be a great help not to have to worry about all the day-to-day details here. Now, I suggest you start by getting acquainted with the filing system. Later I'll be back to go over the ledgers and show you how we do things around here."

System? was Michael's skeptical thought as he scanned the chaos. If there was a system, it was well hidden under all the flotsam and jetsam.

It occurred to him that if Reed was willing to readily entrust the company records to his care, Michael was unlikely to find any intentional irregularities or subterfuge. But he'd have to make sure anyway. It could be that another employee was taking advantage of Reed's distraction and frequent absences to do some shady business. But it was more likely any financial problems were caused by sheer neglect and ineptitude. These were the sorts of problems Michael could help correct—as soon as he could figure out what they were.

He didn't even know where to start. Sighing heavily, he picked up a stack of papers and riffled through them. Then he dropped the pile on the desk. The whole situation was ridiculous. But he supposed he should have expected it, with only a half-time, temporary manager who lacked lumber experience, and a doddering old widow at the helm. Perhaps the woman was even *non compos mentis* at this point, which would explain her complete neglect of the paperwork, not to mention the loan fiasco. People who stayed on top of the paperwork, filing, and bills didn't usually risk having their business repossessed.

Desperate to make some sort of progress, he returned to the

desk and slumped in his chair, picked up the first paper from the stack, and stared at it, forcing himself to focus. Soon he found himself making headway, creating orderly stacks of receipts over here, correspondence over there, bills next to that. He'd made it through about an inch of paper when the sound of boots stamping off snow came from the porch. He glanced up as the front door opened and in strolled Reed Coker, accompanied by a blast of frigid air.

And a woman.

Michael stared at her. She stared back. Time stood still as his mind scrambled to make sense of this latest development.

No doubt about it. Those incredible blue eyes. That rose water scent. It was definitely the young woman from the train standing before him. Scarcely believing his eyes, Michael shot to his feet. A vague memory tumbled through his brain, an image of a tall blond man greeting her at the station. That man must have been Reed, and so the woman must be his— They must be—

Reed's smile indicated strained patience. "At ease, boy. This is Mrs. Carrie Coker, owner of the company. We're just here to have a look around."

Michael nearly choked. "*You're* Carrie Coker? But I thought you'd be old," he blurted as his mind rapidly recalculated his initial assumption concerning her age.

She drew herself up—all five-feet-nothing of her. "I beg your pardon?"

"Mind your manners, boy," Reed snapped.

Heat rushed to Michael's face. "Sorry, no, I mean— " He struggled for words, feeling immensely foolish.

Carrie peered up at him. Even in heeled boots, she barely reached his shoulder. "Hello again."

Reed looked from one to the other. "You two know each other?"

Michael recovered his aplomb. "We met on the train the other day. We had a. . .a brief encounter."

Her cheeks turned a delicate shade of pink. "How kind of you to remember," she said coolly. Then she added, in a friendlier tone, "Why, I had no idea you worked here. But then, I've been living in Missoula this past year."

"I didn't. I mean, I wasn't. Working here. Not at the time we met, anyway." Hearing himself rambling, he extended his hand. "It's good to see you again, Miss Coker. I—I mean Mrs. Coker. Michael. . .Mike Taylor, at your service." He grasped her small, cool hand in his.

"Nice to meet you, Michael-Mike," she said with a mischievous smile.

Heat rose in his face. *Gotta be more careful.*

Reed interrupted. "And now that you two have met, there's work to be done. Speaking of which. . ." He turned to Carrie. "I'm terribly sorry, my dear, but I just remembered I have some pressing business back at the store. Perhaps we can pick this up at another time." The way he looked at Carrie spoke of an affection that went beyond a business partnership.

Of course, Michael realized as the pieces suddenly fell into place. The "Widow Coker" may have been the widow of one Coker, but now belonged to another one.

"I thought we were supposed to spend the afternoon together." Disappointment tinged her voice. Then she brightened. "Well, then, perhaps I could stay here and assist Mr. Taylor. He can start showing me around."

Show her around? Wasn't this her company? Shouldn't she be the one showing Michael around?

Besides, while he could have used some help sorting through the mess, the presence of a second person in the office would only get in the way of his secret investigation. She'd be a distraction—an attractive distraction, to be sure, but a distraction nonetheless, not to mention out of bounds—while he needed to work quickly and not lose focus. And he certainly didn't need her reporting all his movements back to Reed.

But before he could respond, Reed quickly squelched the idea. "I hardly think so," he scoffed. "Waste of time. It's his first day as our new clerk. He knows even less than you do. Besides, I don't think the office is really the place for a woman. It's all likely to go straight over your head."

For a moment Carrie looked stung, then she said coldly, "I see. Well then, perhaps Frenchie can use my help in the cookhouse." She nodded to Michael. "Good day to you, Mr. Taylor."

"Good day." Michael reached up to touch his hat, then realized he wasn't wearing one. He awkwardly covered the gesture by smoothing his cowlick instead.

As the pair turned away, Michael observed the possessive way Reed placed his hand on Carrie's waist. Clearly, they were a couple, even if Reed hadn't introduced her that way. When the door closed behind them, he slumped down in the chair, stared at the piles of paper, and considered the situation.

A company owner who'd been absent from the business for a year. A part-time, distracted manager who'd let things slide in her absence. And the clock ticking on a loan that could cause the woman to lose her company and the land it stood on.

Michael had his work cut out for him.

Chapter Nine

Stomping through the packed snow on the well-traveled path between buildings, Carrie was halfway to the cookhouse when she stopped in her tracks, whirled around, and headed back toward the office. Who was Reed to discourage her from working in the office, learning the ins and outs of running the business? *Her* business, after all, at least on paper. Reed's effrontery in telling her what she could and couldn't do, or what she was and was not capable of understanding, thoroughly irritated her.

Not to mention, the thought of speaking alone with this Mike Taylor, out from under Reed's watchful gaze, made her blood pump a little faster. A fleeting shaft of guilt pierced her conscience, but she bit it back. *Carrie Coker, you are a ninny,* she silently scolded herself. *This is strictly business.* After all, she had only met Mike Taylor briefly, when she'd literally stumbled into him on the train. It was only fitting that they ought to get better acquainted. She ought to know the people who were working for her company. That's what any good manager would do.

Bursting through the door, she walked over to where Michael was standing and looked up at him. Waaay up. This fellow was tall as a Douglas fir. If she spent much time around him, she was going to get a kink in her neck.

A risk she was willing to take.

Clearly, he was surprised to see her. A lopsided grin, like a little boy's, lighted his face. "Back so soon? What can I do for you?"

She smiled back at him, aware of a peculiar little fluttering in the general vicinity of her heart.

"I was just thinking," she said with a conspiratorial grin. "Since neither of us knows what we're doing yet when it comes to running the company, why don't we figure it out together?"

His brow creased. "Together?"

"Yes. I mean, look at this mess." She gestured to the chaotic tables and shelves. "Let's work together to clean things up and get organized. Two heads are better than one. Then we'll both be relatively up to speed when Reed comes back to show us the details of how to run things."

He hesitated, then said slowly, "I suppose that would work."

She deflated slightly, having expected him to show a little more enthusiasm for her idea.

"Reed's just humoring me," she continued. "He doesn't really think I'm capable of understanding business matters. I intend to prove him wrong."

His brown eyes looked down at her, full of friendly reassurance. "I'm pretty sure you can do anything you set your mind to."

A warm wash of pleasure flooded through Carrie.

"So show me what to do."

"All right." He picked up a piece of paper from the desk and held it toward her. "This is a bill that apparently hasn't been paid yet. It goes in this stack."

She examined it. "I see." Placing the paper where he pointed, she felt her anxiety build. She'd grown up in a home where every nickel was accounted for, and it bothered her on a visceral level to see bills go unpaid.

He picked up another paper. "This one's a letter from a supplier. We'll put it over here until we can determine whether or not it's been answered."

On and on he went, picking up papers, explaining what each one was, and placing it on the appropriate stack. She thrilled to the nearness of him, to the enticing scents of woodsmoke and soap that clung to his shirt. Now and then his hand brushed against hers as he handed her a piece of paper, causing a pleasurable current to shoot up her arm.

He handed her a document without comment. She scanned it, then set it on the "receipts" pile.

"See? I knew you'd catch on in no time," Michael said approvingly. "You're a natural at this."

Her face warmed. "I'm glad you think so. Reed doesn't agree. He doesn't seem to think I'd make a very good businesswoman, and perhaps he's right. I've never had a reason to learn about things like profit-and-loss statements. Nothing more taxing than a household budget, I'm afraid."

"Malarkey. If you can run a household, you're capable of running a business," Michael said firmly. "Sure, there are some additional angles to it, but you can pick those up, if you've got the basic skills. And I'm right here if you need help."

She gazed out the window at the acres of trees. "Reed keeps urging me to sell the land to Goldwood. He says I'd make a tidy profit and be freed of the responsibility of trying to run the company. And he'd be free to go back to his hardware store."

"But you don't want to sell."

"No. I don't particularly want to be freed of it. In fact, I'd like to see it prosper, for George's sake."

"George was your late husband," Michael said quietly.

"Yes." As they continued to sort papers, she gave him an

abbreviated explanation of George's illness and death and how she'd spent the past year at her mother's house in Missoula, recovering from her grief.

"I don't know what I would have done if Reed hadn't stepped in to run the company for me," she concluded. "He kept it afloat when I wasn't able to put two coherent thoughts together."

"I see. And are you two partners in life, as well as in business?" The words exited his mouth before he could stop them.

She stared at him. "Who? Reed?" A bit of hysteria burst from her lips. "Heavens, no. I mean, he's helped me out tremendously. I owe him a great debt of gratitude. But that's all."

"Oh. But I thought—well, it looked as though you two might have some sort of an understanding." He began to feel very foolish, and the look on her face confirmed that suspicion. "Anyway, now you're back."

"Yes, I am. And I *so* want to make good on George's dream of turning part of the land into a music camp. But come to find out, there's a debt against the property that makes it impossible." She paused. "I'm sorry, I must be boring you, going on and on. You don't want to hear all this."

"Yes, I do," Michael blurted. Suddenly his face turned red. "I mean, I don't mind listening," he added in a calmer tone. "As the clerk here, I should probably know about these things."

This reasoning made sense to her. And, frankly, she enjoyed the close attention he paid to her words.

"The trouble is, after George died, the company became unprofitable, and nobody's been able to tell me why," she continued. "Not even Reed. Not even Mr. Tate down at the bank." She huffed. "I'm not blaming Mr. Tate. He seems like a true gentleman. But I tell you, that bank of his gives me nightmares. If I never heard the words 'Tate National Bank' again, I'd die a happy woman."

Michael made no response, except to slam a file drawer somewhat harder than necessary.

"It's all quite overwhelming," she admitted. "But I feel it's important that I pick up the reins and take charge, as George wanted. My first priority is to pay off the loan. Only then can I proceed with building Camp Harmony."

She half expected him to smirk at the idea, as Reed would have, but he only nodded.

The conversation turned to lighter topics as together they worked their way through the piles on the desk, then moved over to a filing cabinet. All at once, the loud clang of a gong resounded across the camp.

"Goodness! That's the supper gong," Carrie exclaimed. "I hadn't realized how much time had passed. I hope Frenchie wasn't counting on my help to get supper ready."

"Frenchie?" Michael set down the papers he was holding.

"Mrs. Duval. She's the camp cook, and I promised to help her in the kitchen in exchange for her hospitality, letting me stay in her cabin."

"Hmm. So apparently cooking is a job Reed does find acceptable for women," Michael said, his expression deadpan.

Taken aback by the remark, Carrie giggled, followed immediately by a sharp sense she was being disloyal to Reed. "He means well. He's just very traditional in his views," she said in his defense. "He's fallen prey to the fallacy that women's brains aren't well suited to business."

"Nonsense." Michael exhaled sharply. "Sounds like the sort of thing my father would say."

"Does it?" she asked, intrigued. "What does your father do? Is he a logger too?"

A shadow passed over his face, as if he'd put on a mask. "Guess you'd better hurry if you're going to get supper." By the way he quickly changed the subject, she sensed he didn't appreciate her asking personal questions. At least not questions about his father. She'd have to be careful not to be so nosy next time. If there was a next time.

She slipped on her coat and scarf, then paused at the door. "Are you coming?"

"I'll be along in a minute." Then, as if as an afterthought, he added, "Thanks for your help this afternoon, Mrs. Coker."

"My pleasure." She felt her cheeks light up. "And please, call me Carrie."

Although she felt drawn to the man as if by a centrifugal force, she made herself open the door and step outside. A cold gust buffeted her as she turned toward the cookhouse and quickened her pace. She burst into the kitchen, full of apologies. The cook muttered something in disgruntled-sounding French and immediately put her to work ladling stew into bowls.

The next hours were hectic with serving hungry loggers, cleaning up after them, and eating her own supper. But no matter how busy she was, she couldn't get a certain disarming little-boy grin out of her mind.

Michael watched her go and kicked himself for bringing up the topic of his father. How was he ever going to successfully complete his mission if he kept slipping up about his undercover identity as "Mike Taylor," dropping hints left and right about his true identity? And good grief, why did he promise he'd be around to help her, when he had no intention of sticking around one minute longer than necessary to get the job done?

Oh, yeah. The job. He looked around the office. A lot of papers still remained to be sorted, but he and Carrie had made some headway. They were a good team. If they kept up this pace, they were sure to uncover the source of the problem soon. And then he'd turn the matter over to Uncle Sebastian and be on his way back home.

But against the brilliance of a certain smile, the bright lights of the city suddenly dimmed by comparison. One cheerful bit of news was the fact she wasn't married to Reed, after all. Yet another assumption Michael needed to adjust.

On the other hand, she hadn't exactly clarified the nature of her feelings for Reed, or his for her, and Michael hadn't wanted to pry. Or rather he *had* wanted to pry, just a little, but found himself oddly reluctant to hear the answer.

Chapter Ten

Over the next several weeks, Michael and Carrie continued to work side by side in the little office every day. As they sat close together, heads bent over paperwork and ledgers, Michael loved inhaling the rose water scent of her hair. Every so often her fingers touched his, or his hand brushed hers, and he rejoiced silently that she didn't move away.

He also rejoiced that Reed made only occasional appearances at the lumber camp, citing a busy season at the hardware store and bookending his departure announcements with profuse apologies for his absences.

Little by little, not only did Michael and Carrie eventually clear up most of the random stacks, but along the way he taught her what each paper meant, each receipt and bill and letter. As he took care of daily business, he showed her step-by-step what he was doing and why. He was impressed by her bright mind; she caught on quickly. By the end of the second week they'd started on the ledgers. Together they deciphered the specialized vocabulary of the logging industry, from board feet to blister rust.

As they worked their way through every drawer and cabinet, Michael kept hoping he'd unearth the answer to the company's lack of profitability—a second set of books, say, or some other indication of shady dealings. Carrie talked about Reed as if he were her knight in shining armor, riding in to save the day. Well, Michael sure would like to usurp him in that role by finding the perfect solution to all her financial difficulties. To his frustration, he found nothing of the kind.

But his frustration was tempered by the delight of spending every day in Carrie's presence. If it weren't for Reed—but no. Clearly Reed and Carrie had feelings for one other, with all that "my-dearing" and whatnot, and Michael wasn't about to interfere. Besides, he'd be going home to Chicago soon. To Maude. Maude, whose face grew less distinct in his mind every day. Maude, who hadn't bothered to answer any of his letters.

He'd been pretty vigilant lately and hadn't dropped any careless hints about his identity. He steered clear of conversations about his family and his background, and mercifully Carrie didn't pry. So his "cover story," as the Pinkerton agents called it, remained intact.

On the other hand, he found the ruse exhausting, especially as his friendship with Carrie grew. How was she ever going to get to know him, the *real* him, if he couldn't be honest with her about who he really was?

And who was he, after all? He didn't feel like the same Michael Tate who'd left Chicago wearing a black silk hat and a bad attitude. He rather enjoyed being Mike Taylor. Lying on his bunk at night, listening to the old-timers' tall tales while McTavish scratched out tunes on his fiddle, gave him more pleasure than the most lavish theater production. Even playing cards with his coarse-mannered bunkmates proved more entertaining than gambling at his exclusive club. He didn't think he was quite ready to trade in city life for logging, but the thought did cross his mind a time or two.

Things came to a head one morning in the office, a week or so later, when Reed once again did his disappearing act.

"I'm sorry, my dear," Reed explained to Carrie, ignoring Michael completely. "Spring is nearly here, and that brings out customers wanting to stock up on paintbrushes and gardening tools and such. I'm afraid my presence is required at the store more than I'd like."

"You needn't worry about us," Carrie replied sweetly. "Michael and I have everything under control."

Reed looked at Michael with a sour expression but said only, "I'll be back as soon as I can." He gave Carrie a gentle peck on the cheek, a sight that made Michael's blood boil in his veins. "Don't overwork yourself, my darling." The door clicked behind him.

For a long moment, anger sparked white-hot in Michael's chest. He tried to speak but his mouth wouldn't form words. He stomped over to a filing cabinet and slammed the drawer shut. He knew he was being unreasonable, but he couldn't seem to get a grip on his emotions. It was one thing for Reed to call Carrie "my dear." It was quite another to kiss her in broad daylight, right in front of God and everybody—somehow that seemed so much worse.

After several minutes of his ill humor, Carrie snapped, "What's the matter with you?"

Michael turned and glared at her. "Well, are you?"

She touched her throat. "Am I what?"

"His 'darling.'" He spat the word.

He expected her to laugh it off, to tell him he was being ridiculous, to say, *Why, that's just a silly expression*, but to his dismay, she gazed out the window instead of at him.

"You *are* his darling?" he sputtered, incredulous.

She pulled at a ribbon on the cuff of her sleeve. "It's not that simple."

Michael threw his hands in the air. "What's not simple about it? Are you his 'darling,' yes or no?"

"Don't yell at me."

"I'm not yel—" He paused and worked to soften his tone. "I'm not yelling."

She sighed. "If you must know, Reed has asked me to marry him."

Michael felt something crackling behind his eye sockets. "And you told him. . .?"

"I haven't given him an answer yet."

"You don't love him." It was a statement, not a question.

"Sometimes marriage is about more than love. It's about. . . security. Protection. Loyalty."

He snorted. "For security, protection, and loyalty, you can get yourself a Saint Bernard." Seeing the wounded look on her face, he immediately regretted his words, but couldn't think of any way to take them back.

He took a step toward her and said as gently as he could, "If I may be so bold, is it at all possible that the reason Reed wants to marry you is to gain possession of the company and the land? Maybe he resents the fact that George left Coker Lumber to you and not to him."

He knew he was walking on a thin edge, that she might take offense at the suggestion. But to his surprise, she said, "I've thought of that. By marrying me, Reed could assure the land would always remain in the Coker family." She shook her head. "But no, he's never shown any interest in owning the land, nor in buying me out. In fact, as I've told you, he keeps urging me to sell the whole thing to Goldwood, lock, stock, and barrel." She looked up at Michael with a mischievous twinkle in her eye. "So he must have some other reason for wanting to marry me. Hard as that may be to imagine."

"Not hard at all," Michael assured her. "Any man would consider himself lucky to marry a powerful lumber baroness such as yourself."

She smiled at that. He loved making her smile.

Then she turned and looked out the window, as if searching for a reasonable explanation among the pines. "It's just that Reed has been so good to me," she said quietly after a moment. "He's been such a great help."

"And you deserve to be helped," he said earnestly. "That doesn't mean you have to marry the fellow."

Her lips curved in a sad little smile. "Funny. I remember saying something similar to my sister not too long ago."

He sensed a tiny crack in her resolve. "Then don't rush into anything. Don't feel you have to give him an answer yet, even if he presses you for one."

She nodded. "Don't worry. I'm not the type to rush into things."

He felt a small *whoosh* of relief. As long as she was not yet promised to Reed, there was still a chance. A chance for *what*, exactly, he hadn't quite thought through yet. But a chance, nonetheless.

One Friday morning not long after that conversation, as Michael and Carrie worked together on a ledger, she suddenly straightened her back and set down her pen. She looked at him, eyes sparkling with mischief.

"I'm tired of all these numbers. Why don't we knock off work early and do something fun?"

Michael grinned. "If you say so, boss. Like what?"

"I don't know." She was silent for a moment, watching the snow swirl outside the window. "Ever been ice skating?"

He laughed. "Not since I was in school." Although he'd played ice hockey at his prep school, he hadn't been on skates in years. But who could resist getting out of the stuffy office and getting some fresh, clean air into their lungs?

She clapped and stood. "Let's try it, then. Come on."

A visit to the equipment shed yielded two worn pairs of skates: a larger pair for him and a smaller, boy-sized pair for her. Even so, when she tried them on, they were still too large for her tiny feet.

"Let's try stuffing the toes with rags," he suggested, which turned out to be an imperfect solution, but reasonably effective.

After tying the laces together, they slung the skates over their shoulders and headed outside, where they paused to strap on the snowshoes they'd also found in the shed. Then Michael led the way to a pretty stretch of creek nearby that he'd found on one of his Sunday hikes.

"So you're a hiker," she commented. "I wondered where you disappeared to during your free hours."

"Now you know." A burning sensation squeezed his chest as he realized she'd been curious enough about his comings and goings to wonder where he went.

The day was bright and frosty. The trees sparkled under their thick mantle of snow. He scanned the length of the creek for a wide, clear area free of branches and other debris.

"This looks like a good spot," he said finally. She seated herself on a log on the creek bank while he helped her swap her snowshoes for skates. Then he laced up his own skates, extended his arm to her, and together they headed out onto the frozen creek. When her oversized skates slipped and she began to stumble, he caught her in a close embrace.

"I'm not so sure about this," she said, but she laughed as she said it. She put her tiny, black-gloved hand in his.

"Now relax," he told her encouragingly. "That's right."

Soon enough they got their bearings and fell into a smooth rhythm, right, left, right, left, arms linked. Like dancing, only better. No stuffy cotillion or debutante ball had ever made him feel this exhilarated.

The more suave and sophisticated he tried to act, the more breathless he found himself. Carrie's cheeks blushed a delightful rosy pink and her blue eyes sparkled, possibly from the cold, but Michael hoped something else made them sparkle, and he hoped that something else was him. He was falling for this girl. Falling hard—and almost literally, as he suddenly hit a rough patch and nearly lost his balance. He regained his footing, and they resumed skating. *Careful, old chum*, he chided himself. *Watch what you're doing. In more ways than one.*

"You're a beautiful skater," he said, looking down at her. Then, slowly, he lifted his arm and touched her cheek with his gloved hand. "Beautiful."

Before he thought about what he was doing, he drew her into the tight circle of his arms. His lips sought hers, holding them in a demanding kiss, feeling the frantic pounding of his heart as she began to respond.

Then, suddenly, she broke away. "Mike, I—I can't do this."

He immediately dropped his arms. "Of course. I understand." What had he been thinking?

She looked up at him with a pleading expression. *Those eyes.* "It's not that I don't like you. I do, very much. It's just that—"

She seemed to be groping for words. He decided to help her out.

"It's just that your heart is previously engaged."

"Well. . .yes. Something like that."

"You don't need to explain." He skated backward, putting distance between them. The last thing he needed to hear was how she was committed to someone else. Being George's cousin and all, Reed obviously reminded Carrie of her late husband. Probably a family resemblance, similar mannerisms, same sort of personality, whatever. It was only natural that she'd prefer him to anything

Michael could offer her.

Besides, there was no way he could get close to her when he couldn't even tell her who he was.

"Come back, Mike," she pleaded as he skated away. He pretended not to hear her. Instead he picked up speed, trying to burn off the frustration of longing for what he couldn't have. The snow-banked landscape, the shimmering trees, the silvery frozen creek, all blended into a whirl as he sped in circles, round and round. He launched into some fancy maneuvers he'd learned playing ice hockey in school. Maybe he couldn't give Carrie what she needed, but he could leave her with some impressive memories of his skating skill. He hoped for a chance to challenge that stuffy Reed Coker to do *this!*—he leaped into the air and landed blithely on one skate—or *this!*—he leaped again and executed a masterful airborne spin—or *thi*—

Suddenly his flying skate collided with something immobile. He landed hard on the ice and felt it crackle beneath him, felt himself sucked down into the frigid wetness.

What just happened? was his final thought before everything went black.

Chapter Eleven

Carrie stopped her pacing long enough to approach the nurse's desk in the waiting room of the tiny rural hospital.

"Any news yet?" she demanded.

The white-capped nurse peered at Carrie over her spectacles. "Not in the five minutes that have elapsed since the last time you asked."

Carrie grimaced. "Sorry. I'm just so worried."

The nurse softened her tone. "I promise I will let you know just as soon as the doctor has completed his examination."

Reluctantly, Carrie took a seat. At one time the hospital had been a private home, and the waiting room was situated in the former sunroom. Although the many windows filled the room with hazy rose-gold light from the setting sun, and a woodburning stove provided further warmth, Carrie felt anything but comforted. In fact, she was chilled to the core.

She'd begun praying the moment Mike had started leaping around on his skates like a crazy fool. *Please, God, don't let him kill himself.* In horror she'd seen him skate too near the bank, watched him stumble over the stray branch sticking up through the ice, and heard the sickening crack of ice shattering beneath him.

Mercifully, God had answered her prayer. As Mike fell, his

jacket snagged on a thick tree limb, a divine intervention which kept his head out of the water. He'd hung there unconscious, partially suspended above the waterline, for as long as it took for Carrie to rip off her skates and rush for help. She'd found Sully and together they hoisted Mike out of the water. She never could have done that under her own strength. It wasn't until they were flying down the mountain in Sully's wagon, with Michael lying wrapped in blankets and shivering uncontrollably, that she realized her own clothes were sodden. But there was nothing she could do about it now, except sit as close to the woodstove as possible as she waited to learn about Mike's condition.

Suddenly the front door blew open and an older woman in a beaver coat hurried up to the desk.

"I was told my nephew is here," the woman said to the nurse in a worried voice.

"What is your nephew's name, please?" the nurse said, opening a ledger.

"Michael Tate." A look of confusion passed over her face. "Or—or maybe something else. He was told to change it."

The nurse adjusted her spectacles. If she wondered why the woman was unsure of her own nephew's name, she didn't say so. Instead she scanned the ledger. "Hmm. I don't see a Michael Tate. We do have a Mike Taylor." She glanced up at the woman. "Could that be your nephew?"

"That must be him. May I see him, please?"

"I am sorry. The doctor is examining him at the moment."

When she heard Mike's name, Carrie stood and walked to the desk.

"Here is the young woman who brought him in," said the nurse by way of introduction. She pointed an accusing finger at Carrie. "You told me his name was Taylor."

Carrie nodded. "Yes, that's right. Mike Taylor."

The nurse turned back to the older woman. "You see?"

But now the woman had fastened her attention on Carrie. "Carrie? Carrie Coker?"

"Yes?"

The woman pressed a hand to her fur-clad chest. "Do you remember me? I'm Mrs. Tate. We served coffee together at Timber Coulee Church when you were. . .when you used to live here."

"You do look familiar," Carrie said politely. But in fact Carrie had met a great number of women of Mrs. Tate's generation when she and George had attended Timber Coulee Church, and all their faces sort of blended together in her memory. Gently she touched the woman's hand. "Why don't you take a moment, catch your breath, and tell us again who you're looking for?" she said soothingly.

The distraught matron wrung her hands. "I was playing whist at my next-door neighbor's house. Her son works up at your family's lumber camp, same as my nephew. He stopped by the house and told his mother he'd come to town to deliver an injured man to the hospital, someone called Michael. That's my nephew's name, so naturally I became concerned."

"Naturally." Confusion fogged Carrie's mind as she tried to make sense of the woman's words. "I'm sorry," she said finally. "I know Mike Taylor quite well. He came here from back East, and he's never mentioned having any relatives in the area."

"Oh, he was *told* to say that," Mrs. Tate said. "I *told* Sebastian it was a terrible idea."

Carrie's mind whirled. "Told to do what? What idea?"

Mrs. Tate made a sweeping motion with her kid-gloved hands. "According to the fellow who brought him down the mountain, he had some sort of accident on the creek."

"Yes, but—wait." Carrie felt a strange knotting sensation in the pit of her stomach. "You said your nephew's name is Tate? As in Sebastian Tate? As in Tate National Bank?" The room tilted slightly.

Mrs. Tate cocked her head. "That's right. Mr. Tate is my husband." She clucked her tongue. "I warned him he oughtn't to send young Michael up into the woods. The boy's from the city, you see, not at all used to the rough ways of a logging camp. . ."

The woman's words faded away as Carrie sat down heavily. She thought she might be ill.

"Are you quite all right, Mrs. Coker?" Mrs. Tate asked, shutting off the torrent of words and peering at Carrie. "You've turned quite pale, dear."

Behind the desk, the nurse rose from her chair, ready to spring into action. Just then, a white-coated doctor entered the room.

"Which one of you ladies brought in Mike Taylor?"

Carrie stood. "I—I did." Mrs. Tate looked uncertainly from Carrie to the doctor and back again.

"He's awake now. He suffered a concussion, along with a broken arm and a cracked rib. He's in a good deal of pain, but I'm happy to say he's out of danger and will make a full recovery. You may see him if you like."

Both women followed the doctor down the hall, each jockeying to get ahead of the other, and turned into a small room where Michael lay on a bed, his head bandaged and his face as white as the starched pillow beneath his head.

"Michael! You poor thing!" Mrs. Tate rushed toward the bed. Carrie's feet were rooted to the floor.

Michael groggily turned his head toward his visitors. "Aunt Becky," he croaked. "Why are you—?"

And then he looked past his aunt and saw his other visitor.

"Carrie." His eyes widened like those of a fugitive facing the wrong end of a gun. He glanced at Aunt Becky, then back at Carrie. Then he closed his eyes and let his head flop back onto the pillow. She heard him say, "Oh, no," as she headed for the door. His voice followed her. "Carrie, come back! I can explain."

But she was already halfway down the hall.

Chapter Twelve

A week later, Carrie sat at her desk in the Coker Lumber Company office, staring out the window at the trees as if they held the answer to what she should do next. Listlessly she lifted a piece of paper from the desk, the latest letter from her mother, telling her that her sister's asthma was acting up.

The doctor says she must get away from the city, to breathe good clean air. It would be good for all of us to get out of the city, to get a fresh start.

Good clean air. Carrie sighed as she stared at the words. Northern Idaho had good clean air in spades. It was the perfect place for Maggie, right here on Long Mountain. But if something didn't change soon, Carrie would lose the property.

Please, Lord. Tell me what to do.

The door opened and Reed entered the office, carrying a sheaf of papers. "Bad news, I'm afraid," he said with a dour expression. "This preliminary report from the scaler is not looking promising. I don't think the spring timber harvest will yield as much as we'd hoped, after all."

"How so?" She held out her hand. "Show me the report."

"Never mind, Carrie-Girl. It's quite complicated. I just wanted to brace you for the disappointment, that's all, if we don't make enough profit to cover the loan."

"Show it to me, Reed," she said firmly. "I understand the business now. At least as well as you do. Mike taught me all about it." Her heart cracked at the mention of his name. She'd vowed to forget all about him, but he kept popping back into her thoughts. It was high time to put Mike Taylor—or Michael Tate, or whoever he was—out of her mind.

Reluctantly Reed handed her the report. She read it over carefully, then leaned back in her chair, her head beginning to pound.

"As I keep telling you, the only reasonable course of action is to sell the land to Goldwood," Reed insisted. "They've made you a very generous offer. You're not likely to get a better one. And then you—we—can live in style. We'll buy you some fine dresses, maybe invest in one of those new horseless carriages."

"I'm quite happy with the horseful kind, thank you very much," Carrie muttered. She shook the paper in his direction. "I don't want fine dresses. I want my profits. And my music camp."

Reed huffed in exasperation. "Carrie, will you please stop talking about that blasted music camp? You need to accept that it's never going to happen, and that's final."

She glared at him. "Is it?"

He glared back. "I'm sorry to have to be so blunt, darling, but you know it is. The camp was a fanciful notion, and a thoroughly impractical one. You need to face facts. The only sensible thing to do is—"

"—to sell to Goldwood," she repeated in unison with him.

She looked at him steadily for a moment. Whatever it was she had once felt for Reed was gone. There wasn't so much as a trace of it left.

She pushed back her chair and stood.

"I've made a decision," she said firmly. "I will sell the land to

Goldwood. But not because I'm afraid of them, or of you. I will sell because doing so is a sound business decision." She swallowed hard, choking back the emotion that suddenly swelled in her throat. "Maybe it's true that Camp Harmony was a pipe dream. Maybe I won't be able to fulfill George's wish to create a camp for talented young musicians like Maggie. But I can at least use the money from the sale to support her and my mother, to get my sister a proper musical education, and keep a roof over all our heads."

Reed's features composed themselves into a look of caring. *He's quite good at this,* Carrie thought. *Quite convincing, this pretending to care for me, when all he really wants is to possess me. Just another piece of property.*

He took a step forward and clasped her hand in his. "You're making a very wise decision my dear. Now I hope you will make another one and consent to become my wife."

She withdrew her hand. "I appreciate all that you've done for me, Reed Coker. I really do. But I will never marry you. Never. Not if you were the last man on earth."

Chapter Thirteen

Squinting as the morning sun poured in through the guest room window at Uncle Sebastian and Aunt Becky's house, Michael folded a shirt—well, folded it as much as a fellow could with his right arm in a cast—and stuffed it into his suitcase, feeling utterly morose. Not only had he failed in his mission to save the Coker Lumber Company from financial ruin, but he'd failed even to discover a cause for it. One of the hardest things he'd ever done was to face Uncle Sebastian, admit that he'd failed to find any reason or remedy for the company's keen losses, and recommend that the Coker Lumber Company be repossessed in satisfaction of the Tate Bank loan.

He felt like a complete and utter failure.

To make matters worse, the revelation of the fact that he was not a humble logger, as he'd claimed to be, but a banker—and worse yet, the heir to the very bank that would soon foreclose on Carrie's company—had ruined any chance he had of sharing any kind of future with that remarkable lady. Rocked to her core by his deceit, she wanted nothing to do with him, and he understood why. She'd be better off without him. So, while it was unlikely that his father would welcome him back, he had no choice now but to return to Chicago and try to pick up the shards of his shattered life.

And what kind of life would that be, after all? The things he used to find amusing in Chicago no longer held any attraction for him. Even Maude held little appeal anymore beyond her striking good looks. Striking and yet superficial. Carrie was a much stronger and braver woman, much more the type he'd want to stand by his side for always, to be the mother of his children. But that was not meant to be, and there was nothing he could do to change that.

One thing had changed though. One major thing. Just as George Müller had faithfully put his trust in God to provide, for the first time in his life, Michael did too. Putting his trust in his father, in the Tate family's fortune and social standing, had not turned out well. But putting his trust in his heavenly Father. . . now that had changed everything. He didn't know how he'd explain this change of perspective to his parents and former friends, but he had a long train journey ahead of him to figure it out.

A gentle knock sounded at the bedroom door. "Come in," he muttered.

Uncle Sebastian entered. "Just wanted to see how you're coming along, son," he said. "Your aunt and I are very sorry to see you go. Are you sure we can't convince you to change your mind?"

Michael shook his head. "You've both been very kind, but I don't belong here," he said sadly. "My place is in Chicago."

Uncle Sebastian settled himself on the edge of the bed. "Well, I've written your father that I've been very satisfied with your work, that you've conducted yourself admirably, and that I'd welcome you back wholeheartedly anytime you wished." From his vest pocket he pulled a white linen envelope bearing the seal of Tate National Bank. "I've made this copy for you too. It will serve as a glowing letter of reference should you decide to seek a position elsewhere."

Michael accepted the envelope and swallowed past the lump in his throat. "Thank you." He could scarcely look his uncle in the eye.

"I've set up a deal whereby the Cokers will sell their company to Goldwood outright, without the bank taking possession. Goldwood will in turn repay the loan to the bank. The arrangement will both benefit the widow financially and allow her to avoid the stigma of a bankruptcy on her record."

This information made Michael admire his uncle even more. In spite of being a banker, he was a much kinder man than his father had ever been and had his clients' best interests at heart.

"When will the sale take place?" he asked.

"This evening, after the bank closes for the day. I want to give the matter my full attention." The older man paused and caught Michael's eye. "You mustn't blame yourself, son," he said, his expression grave. "You gave it your best shot. Sometimes this is the way things go in business."

Michael nodded mutely and picked up another shirt to fold.

"Your aunt would be happy to do that for you, you know," Uncle Sebastian said, nodding toward the shirt. "You needn't struggle."

"I know. I just feel better doing it for myself." In some strange way, the challenge felt good to Michael. He'd struggled so little in his life. Now he welcomed the confirmation that he could do things, could take care of himself, injured or not.

Uncle Sebastian nodded as if he understood. "The rumor mill says that Mrs. Coker is planning to marry Reed Coker and move with him to Spokane, where he'll resume his hardware business." He paused. Then a sly little smile made his mustache twitch. "I suppose that will make her Mrs. Coker Coker."

A cross between a cough and a chortle escaped Michael's throat. He felt that if he didn't laugh, he'd cry. His uncle had no way of knowing the deep feelings he'd developed for Carrie while working on the mountain. The thought of her marrying Reed, of giving up her dream of building the music camp, made him feel ill. But, after all, why shouldn't she marry Reed, or anyone else she wished? Michael was returning to Chicago. They'd never see each other again. He was moving on with his life, and she needed to move on as well.

"The important thing," his uncle continued, "is that she'll be all right, in the end. She'll be well taken care of."

Yes, Michael agreed miserably. Yes, that was the important thing.

"Well, I'll leave you to it." His uncle stood. "One last thing before you leave. May I prevail upon you to accompany your aunt to Spokane today? She has an appointment with the eye doctor there and also wants to do some shopping. I'd go myself, but I need to prepare for the Coker sale, and I'd rather she not go alone."

"Of course," Michael agreed. "My train doesn't leave until tomorrow." He looked forward to the diversion from brooding about Carrie's pending meeting with Goldwood as well as his own heartbreak.

"Good, good. I'll see you at supper then." Uncle Sebastian left the room, closing the door softly behind him.

On the ninety-minute train ride to Spokane, Michael listened with one ear to Aunt Becky's chatter, his mind occupied elsewhere. Most of his thoughts rested on the auburn-haired woman now forced to say goodbye forever to her dream of running a summer camp on what had been her rightful land. Which would still be her land, if Michael hadn't messed things up so badly.

Wandering Riverside Avenue while waiting for his aunt to finish her appointment, Michael spotted a sign indicating the Donovan and Coker hardware store. Curious as to whether this was Reed's store, he started to cross the street, then hesitated. Did he really want to see Reed's business, to have the image of his rival's success and prosperity stuck in his head?

After several minutes' hesitation, curiosity won out. He decided the best thing to do, under the circumstances, was to pop in and have a look around. If Reed happened to be there, Michael would wish him well on his forthcoming marriage to Carrie, to show there were no hard feelings, even though his heart felt smashed to bits. It was the gentlemanly thing to do.

He pushed open the thick glass door, jangling the overhead bell. A rotund man working behind the counter glanced up.

"G'day."

"Good afternoon." Michael removed his hat and approached the counter. "Are you Mr. Donovan?"

"I am." The man thrust forth his hand to shake Michael's. "Tim Donovan, at yer service. What can I do for ya?"

"I'm here to see your partner, Reed Coker."

"Ah. Sorry," Donovan said. "Afraid yer out of luck. Mr. Coker no longer works at this establishment. You a friend of his?"

"Acquaintance," Michael said quickly, relieved not to have to face Reed after all, but confused nonetheless. "I thought he might be coming back here full-time, now that his commitments in Idaho have ended." Some of them, anyway. "I hadn't heard he'd given up the business."

Donovan looked puzzled. "Fellow hasn't worked here in over a year. Not since he sold his share of the business to me."

"A *year*?" Then where had Reed been going, what had he been doing, all those times he'd said he was "checking on the store"? Michael pointed toward the front door. "But the sign outside still says Donovan and Coker."

Donovan shrugged. "Ain't gotten around to changin' it yet. But Coker hightailed it out of here a year ago, soon as he got that swanky job with the Goldwood Corporation."

Michael frowned. "Goldwood?"

"That's what I said. Left me high and dry, he did, after all his promises about stickin' together through good times an' bad. We was friends since way back in kiddygarden, you know, and—"

Michael swept a hand over his face in frustration. "You must be mistaken. Are you sure it wasn't the Coker Lumber Company he went to work for?"

Donovan shook his head. "No, I'm sure it was Goldwood. Now I rarely see the man 'cept when he comes in now and then to mix up batches of that special paint of his."

"Special paint?"

Donovan stared at Michael, disgusted. "What are you, a parrot? Now if there ain't nothin' I can do for you. . ." He gestured toward the door.

A cold prickle ran up the back of Michael's neck. "Please. What sort of paint?"

"Beats me. Some kind of special disappearin' paint. He's all hush-hush about the formula, won't even share it with me, even though we been friends since way back in—"

"Since kindergarten. I know." Michael exhaled sharply, his thoughts clicking rapidly. What would Reed want with vanishing paint?

"Fine by me if he don't want to tell me," Donovan continued. "Most folks got no use for disappearin' paint. They want paint that sticks around a long time and come a-squawkin' to me when it don't. This stuff of Coker's looks all right at first. But just wait until the first hard rain. The thing you painted gets wet, and pretty soon it's like it ain't never seen a lick o'paint. Now, you tell me, what's the point of that?" He crossed his arms and glared at Michael, as if waiting for an answer.

Michael felt a sudden chill. He played a hunch. "This—this paint you speak of. It wouldn't happen to be *red* paint, would it?"

Donovan's bushy eyebrows lifted. "As a matter of fact, it is. Bright crimson red. Looks for all the world like blood runnin' fresh from the vein, it does."

Michael could hardly contain his agitation. "Do you have a sample of it?"

"Nope. T'ain't somethin' I got call to. . . Now, wait a minute." The proprietor's expression turned thoughtful. "Hold on. As I recall, last time he mixed a batch, he left a can behind by mistake."

"How long ago was that?"

"Not more'n a week or so ago. I been holdin' it aside to give him the next time he comes in, but who knows when that'll be? If you wanna buy it, I can give you a good price, seein' as how nobody else's got any use for it."

Donovan shuffled off to a back room at an unreasonably leisurely pace. When he returned, Michael slapped some bills on the counter, grabbed the unmarked can with his good arm, and raced back to the optometrist's office to collect his aunt. Breathless, he arrived just as she was emerging onto the sidewalk in the company of another woman of similar dotage. Spotting Michael, she smiled broadly.

"There you are! Here's someone I'd like you to meet. Annabel, may I present my nephew, Michael Tate. Michael, this is my dear friend, Annabel Cartwright. Annabel is my neighbor in Timber Coulee. We just ran into each other by chance, and—"

Michael dipped his head in a semblance of a bow. "How do you do," he said curtly to Mrs. Cartwright, who blinked like a startled robin. Then, "I'm sorry, Aunt Becky, but we've got to hurry. There's something very important I have to do back in Timber Coulee."

Aunt Becky's blue eyes widened in confusion. "But I haven't

done my shopping yet. And Annabel and I were just talking about going to the Crescent for tea. We haven't had a good visit in ever so long." Her eyes took on a mischievous twinkle. "And the Cartwrights happen to have a very attractive daughter named Maisie, who—"

"I'm sorry," he said again. "Truly. I don't mean to be rude." He faced Annabel and turned on his most charming smile. "Mrs. Cartwright, will you be returning to Timber Coulee this evening?"

"Yes, of course," the woman said.

"Would you mind if my aunt accompanies you on your journey home? That way you two can enjoy your visit and I can get back to the—the urgent business I must take care of."

"Why, certainly," Mrs. Cartwright replied. "That is, if it's all right with you, Becky."

"Of course it is," Aunt Becky agreed. "But Michael, what on earth—"

He gave his aunt a hurried peck on the cheek. "I'll explain later. I haven't time. I must rush back to Timber Coulee to head off a disaster."

If he wasn't already too late.

Chapter Fourteen

Carrie sat at Sebastian Tate's large oak desk in his private office at the bank, feeling very small and insignificant in his oversized leather chair. Her feet barely touched the ground.

A shaft of late afternoon sunlight shone through the window, illuminating the sheaf of papers stacked before her. She stared at the pile with a sense of dread mixed with resignation. Once she signed these papers, the Coker Lumber Company and all its acreage would no longer be hers.

"You're making the right decision," Reed assured her from his post near the window, looking far more cheerful about the situation than he had any right to look. At least Mr. Tate, standing next to Reed, had the decency to wear a suitably somber expression. On the other side of the room stood a well-dressed representative of the Goldwood Corporation, practically twirling his mustache in true villain fashion. At least that's what she imagined him doing.

Suddenly all heads swiveled toward the closed door as sounds of an apparent commotion reached them from the outer lobby. Seconds later Michael burst through the door of Mr. Tate's office, chased by a stammering clerk.

"Stop!" Michael shouted, lunging at the desk and slamming the can of paint down on the stack of papers. "Don't sign anything!"

Carrie stared at him open-mouthed, fountain pen frozen in her hand. Sebastian Tate's face grew crimson.

"Michael?" his uncle sputtered. "What are you doing here?"

Michael leaned across the desk toward Carrie, obviously struggling to catch his breath. His words came out in a rush between gulps of air. "Reed's on the payroll of Goldwood." He pointed at the startled Goldwood representative. "Isn't that true, Mr.—Mr. Whoever-you-are?"

The man blinked, his expression owlish behind his round spectacles.

"Goldwood!" Carrie sputtered. "Michael, have you gone crazy? Reed works for Coker."

Michael came around the desk and bent down to Carrie's eye level. "Listen to me carefully. Reed's trying to cheat you out of your logs so you'll go bankrupt and be forced to sell to Goldwood. He did it during last year's spring run, and he's aiming to do it again."

"It's a lie," Reed sputtered, making a move toward Michael as if he were going to hit him. Michael drew himself up to his full height. Mr. Tate quickly stepped between the two men. Then he put his hand on Michael's shoulder.

"Slow down, son. You're not making any sense."

Michael faced his uncle and slowed his torrent of words. "Reed worked out a scheme last winter that turned a twenty-thousand-dollar profit into a fourteen-thousand-dollar loss."

"How so?" the older man demanded.

Michael's good fist clenched and unclenched. "Reed instructed the river crew to use a paint that looks just like the regular red branding paint, except it's water-soluble."

"That's crazy. *You're* crazy," Reed shouted. Michael ignored him.

"When the logs have been in the water awhile during the trip downstream, this water-soluble paint washes off. Then, when the logs reach the sorting gap near the Goldwood camp, those that are no longer branded get rebranded with Goldwood's mark."

Carrie gasped. "But. . .but that's *stealing*." She felt dizzy. She didn't know where to turn. She looked up to Reed for reassurance, but he seemed to be avoiding her gaze, his face now ashen. She then turned to Mr. Tate, who was staring at Michael in open-mouthed incredulity.

Michael placed a gentle hand on her shoulder. "Sure it is. Last year, with Reed bossing the river drive, by the time they got to the mill, all the logs Goldwood felt like stealing were wearing Goldwood's yellow triple-X instead of Coker's red star. There's no way to know for sure, but I'm estimating they rebranded at least three million board feet before they left the sorting gap. Maybe more."

"So Goldwood got the credit for all those logs instead of us." Carrie breathed. "That's where all our profits went last year. Goldwood stole them."

"*Reed* stole them," Michael clarified. "Working in cahoots with Goldwood. And apparently they intend to do the same this year. Reed's former partner at the hardware store told me he stocked up on water-soluble paint just a week ago. He gave me this sample." He gestured toward the can of paint on the desk.

"*Former* partner?" Carrie stared at the can, trying to make sense of it all.

Michael nodded. "Reed's been on the payroll of Goldwood for more than a year."

A headache formed at Carrie's temples. She sighed and laid down the pen. "Goldwood's put more honest companies out of business than they can count. But they aren't going to get mine."

Suddenly the door burst open and the county sheriff, followed closely by Sully, entered the office.

"Reed Coker, you're under arrest," the sheriff said, "Hands behind your back."

Reed stared in mock innocence. "Me? What for?"

"For stealing logs from the Coker Lumber Company."

Seconds later, Reed wore a pair of handcuffs. He glared in sullen defiance while the sheriff read the warrant.

"You'll never make this stick," he snarled when the sheriff had finished. "You have no proof."

Michael pointed. "I have that can of paint. And I'm sure Tim Donovan will be more than willing to testify to where it came from."

Sully spoke up. "I'll testify too." He'd removed his shabby brown hat and gripped it with both hands. "I come down here today to put a stop to these shenanigans when I heard Mrs. Coker was fixin' to sell out." He glared at Reed. "You've been talkin' to my crew behind my back, intimidatin' 'em and givin' 'em that there lousy paint and makin' us all look bad."

"So you see," the sheriff concluded dryly, "the State of Idaho is mighty interested in you, Reed Coker. In fact, I'll wager they'll offer to pay your room and board for some time to come. And as for you, Mr. Smith—"

The bespectacled Goldwood representative, who'd been quietly sneaking toward the door during this whole conversation, stopped dead in his tracks.

"We'll need you to stick around, sir," the sheriff continued. "The State wants to have a word with you too."

After they'd gone, Carrie slumped in the chair. She couldn't believe how close she'd come to signing away her company.

"How did the sheriff know to show up here?" she asked in a quivering voice.

"I sent the livery driver to fetch both him and Sully," Michael said. He briefly recounted how, in his rush to return to Timber Coulee, he'd hired a coach and driver rather than wait for the train.

While the driver had sped the team toward Timber Coulee, Michael had sat in the coach and worked out the details of Reed's scheme.

"And you needn't worry about Aunt Becky," he assured his uncle. "She and Annabel Cartwright are traveling back together this evening."

"I wasn't worried, son," his uncle said, clapping him on the shoulder. "Not for a moment. I'm just glad you solved the case when you did." He picked up the stack of papers and ripped them into pieces.

"So what do we do now?" Carrie asked, trying to quell the tremor in her voice. Michael pulled a chair close to hers and reached for her cold hand, which he held securely in his warm one.

"All we've got to do now," he said soothingly, "is put a crew to work and brand the logs with regular paint and get them into the water. But there's no time to waste. When the river lets go, the logs will start rolling. Could happen as early as next week. So the crew better get busy with paint buckets and brushes repainting all the logs."

Carrie felt a surge of hot anger rise within her. "I can't believe I trusted Reed all this time. Believed he had my best interests at heart. Why, I'll bet he only wanted to marry me so he could take ownership of my land and hand it over to Goldwood. If I were a man, why, I'd— I'd—"

Michael squeezed her hand. "Let the sheriff handle him. It's best to let the law deal with crooks like that."

Carrie stared at him for a moment, wide-eyed. "Just so I'm sure I understand. . . Your real name is Michael Tate."

"Yes."

"You work for Tate National Bank."

"Yes."

"Your family *owns* Tate National Bank."

"Yes."

"And yet you went to great lengths just to find out what the trouble was. To help me save my company."

"Yes."

"And now you're going back to Chicago."

"No." He gazed at her with those liquid brown eyes of his. "And now will you believe me when I tell you I love you?"

Her heart melted in her chest.

"Yes."

The Coker crew, with Michael's help despite his injured arm, worked furiously around the clock to get the logs repainted. Just about a week later, the powerful river burst forth with a rush and grind of broken ice. When the great moment came, Michael stood beside the cook's raft, called a wanigan, with Frenchie and Carrie. They listened as Sully shouted the order to break out the first rollway. A few preliminary blows of axes rang out, followed by a loud snapping of restraints and a collective holding of breath. Then, with a mighty, earth-shaking roar, the gigantic pile of logs shot down the steep bank and landed in the river with a splash that sent a tower of water shooting into the air.

Michael watched in amazement as the logs formed a platform that spanned the river from bank to bank. The most highly skilled men on the river crew stood erect on huge logs or leaped nimbly from log to log, working them with peaveys and cant hooks to keep them moving in the right direction. It was an extremely dangerous job. Even the most experienced log driver risked falling into the water and being crushed to death if he lost focus even for a moment. Some of the less experienced men stayed near the banks, using pike poles to keep straggler logs from getting hung up on rocks and trees. To Michael, following from behind in the wanigan, it was like watching an intricate machine at work. Or like a ballet, although he didn't suppose the tough loggers would appreciate that analogy very much. He prayed earnestly for the safety of them all.

The crew worked steadily all day and into the night. From the wanigan, Michael helped Frenchie and Carrie supply the men with hot coffee and sandwiches around the clock. And when, at last, the logs cruised into the waiting booms at the sawmill, the silvery-pink light of dawn revealed that every one of them clearly bore the red star of the Coker Lumber Company.

Chapter Fifteen

The July sun beat through the window on Michael's back as he sat at his desk, staring at the final report from the sawmill. Mopping his forehead with a bandana, he read the report two, three times in disbelief before unexpected moisture in his eyes blurred the numbers. Abruptly he scraped back his wooden office chair and stood.

"Back in a minute," he said to Carrie, who sat at the neighboring desk, frowning over a ledger. "Just need a breath of fresh air." She nodded distractedly, as if only half listening, and he walked out the door with the report in his hand. He stood on the porch and drew a deep breath of the pine-scented air, grappling with a sudden rush of emotion. He didn't know whether to yell, shout, laugh, or burst into tears. So he simply stood staring out at the trees, trying to quell the hammering in his chest. The Lord had come through. More than come through. *Thank You*, he whispered.

Carrie walked out of the office and stood beside him in the warm breeze. Sensing her presence, he reached out, put an arm around her waist, and drew her close to his side. She looked up at his face, concern etched on her delicate features.

"Everything all right?" she asked. "You look a little pale."

Wordlessly he handed her the report. She took a moment to

read it over. Then, her voice thick with emotion, she whispered, "Fourteen million board feet." She pressed the paper to her chest and bowed her head. "Fourteen million. Praise God."

"Indeed."

As they stood together silently, Michael bowed his head and thanked God for His provision, just as George Müller would have done. And he sensed Carrie was doing the same.

Lifting his head, he marveled at how peaceful the woods had become without the constant thud of axes and shouts of men. Following the successful log drive to the mill, most of the workers had gone home for the summer. Only Sully and Frenchie remained. But very soon—any minute, in fact—that peace would be shattered by noise of quite a different sort. Michael could hardly wait.

He gave Carrie's waist a squeeze, then released her. She handed the report back to him. He folded the paper and slid it into the breast pocket of his linen shirt.

"And now our new adventure begins."

Carrie looked up at him with anxious eyes. "Do you really think our plan will work? To log the land during the fall, winter, and spring, then open it up as a music camp in the summer?"

Michael shrugged. "We'll never know until we try. As we've said, this summer will be an experiment. But I think it's a sound plan, and Uncle Sebastian agrees. If all goes as planned, maybe by next year we'll be able to enlarge the dining hall and replace the bunkhouses with cabins."

She gave an involuntary shudder. "And to think that, under other circumstances, I might be married to Reed by now, and all this"—she swept her arm to indicate the forest around them—"would be in the clutches of the Goldwood Corporation."

Michael slipped a protective arm around her slender shoulders. "Reed will be in jail for a good long time," he said. "He won't be tampering with your logs—or your life—ever again. And with the proceeds from the sawmill, we can not only pay off the bank, but make improvements as well. You own all this land, free and clear."

"I still can't believe it." She turned and regarded him steadily. "You're sure you won't come work for Coker Lumber full-time? I could really use your help."

Michael shook his head. "I said I'll be here whenever you need me. And I will. But you're more than capable of running Coker Lumber," he assured her. "You're smart as a whip and have a good head for business."

She smiled modestly. "Who knew?"

"God knew." He grinned. "You've also got Sully and Frenchie and the rest of the team to help you. And I'll always be nearby. When you need me, I can be here, lickety-split." He smiled. "If there's one thing Uncle Sebastian has taught me, it's that bankers don't have to be ruthless men like my father. Banks can serve a vital role in a community, helping small businesses get the capital they need to buy equipment, hire workers, and keep things running. Working together at the bank, he and I can really make a difference, helping Coker Lumber and the rest of Timber Coulee prosper."

She smirked. "But you won't do it in disguise anymore."

"No, not in disguise." He laughed. "Besides, Uncle Sebastian's generously giving me summers off to work with you at Camp Harmony. Where else could I find a better working arrangement than that?"

"No place else. So you'd better stick around." Carrie lifted her face for a kiss. He could have remained forever in that kiss, basking in the glowing certainty of her love. But moments later she gently broke way, then cocked her head. A look of mild panic crossed her face. "Are those wagon wheels I hear, turning off the main road?"

Hearing the unmistakable squeak of wagon springs, he gave

her shoulders a squeeze. "Ready?"

"Ready as I'll ever be," she said with a nervous laugh.

They watched with eager anticipation as a wagon filled with young people approached up the long drive, driven by Uncle Sebastian, who'd volunteered to collect the first batch of campers from the Timber Coulee train station. At the very front of the wagon bed sat Maggie, wildly waving her handkerchief. Seated beside Maggie was her mother, who'd be spending the summer helping Frenchie cook and serve the meals. Carrie squealed and ran toward the wagon to welcome her family, along with the other campers. Sully emerged from one of the bunkhouses, ready to help the campers manage their luggage and get settled in.

Uncle Sebastian pulled the wagon to a halt, dismounted, walked up to Michael, and pulled him aside.

"A letter has come from your father," he said quietly. He pulled a piece of paper from his coat pocket. Michael unfolded it and swallowed hard. He hadn't heard from his father since writing him a letter that announced his intention to not return to Chicago, but to stay here in Idaho and work with Uncle Sebastian. He'd told him about Coker Lumber and Camp Harmony. And now he dreaded his father's response, fully expecting it to be filled with critical words like *shirker* and *dreamer*.

Instead, to his great shock, in the envelope was a generous donation check to help fund Camp Harmony.

"In addition," his father wrote, "we will be shipping you the Steinway from the music room. No one plays it anymore, and I'm sure the camp will make good use of it."

Michael's eyes misted. It took him a moment to regain his composure and read the rest of the letter.

"Your mother and I are looking forward to visiting Idaho later this summer," his father wrote. "I am long overdue for a vacation and could use the rest. I would love to see the work you're doing there—and to meet your intended bride, of course."

With a wide grin of satisfaction, Michael folded the letter and put it in his breast pocket just as Carrie approached, holding the hand of a beaming young woman with long brown braids.

"Michael, this is my baby sister, Maggie," she said. Then, looking at Maggie, "Well, not such a baby anymore. Maggie, this is Mr. Michael Tate."

"I'm honored to meet you, Maggie." Michael gave a formal bow, then reached out and surprised the laughing girl with a hug. Then he squared his shoulders and extended a respectful hand to the older woman with hair the color of Carrie's who'd come up behind Maggie. "You must be Carrie's mother. I'm very pleased to meet you, Mrs. Jackson."

"Pshaw!" The woman brushed aside his hand and grasped him around the shoulders. "I intend to hug my future son-in-law," she boomed.

Michael enthusiastically returned the hug. Then, with one arm around Maggie and the other around Carrie, he turned and greeted the wagonload of campers.

"Welcome, all of you," he exclaimed past the sudden tightness in his throat. "Welcome to Camp Harmony!"

AUTHOR'S NOTE

The town of Timber Coulee, while a product of my imagination, is loosely based on Sandpoint, Idaho, a historically significant logging and railroad town situated on the shores of Lake Pend Oreille in Idaho's heavily forested northern panhandle. Surrounded by the Selkirk, Cabinet, and Bitterroot mountain ranges, the region has received numerous accolades for its stunning natural beauty. To my knowledge, no one in real life has ever actually committed the type of shenanigans described in the story. But in the mind of a fiction author, anything is possible.

With deepest thanks to: my husband, Thomas, for his unwavering support and encouragement; my writing partners: Anita Aurit, Melissa Bilyeu, Cassandra Cridland, Terese Luikens, and Grace Robinson; the Bonner County, Idaho, Historical Society and Museum; and to my friends at Odenwald Forestry and Inland Forest Management, who patiently answered my questions about working in the woods.

JENNIFER LAMONT LEO captures readers' hearts through stories set in times gone by. Her novels include *The Rose Keeper*, *Moondrop Miracle*, *Ain't Misbehavin'*, and *You're the Cream in My Coffee* (winner of an ACFW Carol Award for debut novel). She also hosts the podcast *A Sparkling Vintage Life*. A Chicago-area native who has set many of her stories in the Windy City, today she writes from her home in the northern Idaho mountains, which she shares with her husband, two spoiled cats, and abundant wildlife. Visit her at https://JenniferLamontLeo.com and on Facebook and Goodreads.

You May Also Enjoy These Books!

Available Now:

The Librarian's Journey

By Patty Smith Hall, Cynthia Hickey,
Marilyn Turk, Kathleen Y'Barbo

Part of FDR's New Deal was the Works Progress Administration, which funded the Pack Horse Library Initiative. Four book-loving women bravely fight for literacy in remote communities during the Great Depression by carrying library books via horseback. Grace doesn't anticipate the hard work or meeting a handsome one-room schoolhouse teacher. Loss of her dream job takes Ruth back to her roots and face to face with her lost love. Lily's own shyness connects with a reclusive father and daughter. Lottie connects with a backwoods bully's wife by secretly carrying messages for her in exchange for books. Will the women's efforts be rewarded by finding love in the process?

Paperback / 978-1-63609-025-2 / $14.99